SENTENCED TO TROLL 6

S.L. ROWLAND

ALSO BY S.L. ROWLAND

Tales of Aedrea

Cursed Cocktails

Sword & Thistle

The Halfling's Harvest

Pangea Online

Pangea Online: Death and Axes

Pangea Online 2: Magic and Mayhem

Pangea Online 3: Vials and Tribulations

Sentenced to Troll

Sentenced to Troll

Sentenced to Troll 2

Sentenced to Troll 3

Sentenced to Troll 4

Sentenced to Troll 5

Sentenced to Troll 6

Path to Villainy: An NPC Kobold's Tale

Collected Editions

Pangea Online: The Complete Trilogy

Sentenced to Troll Compendium: Books 1-3

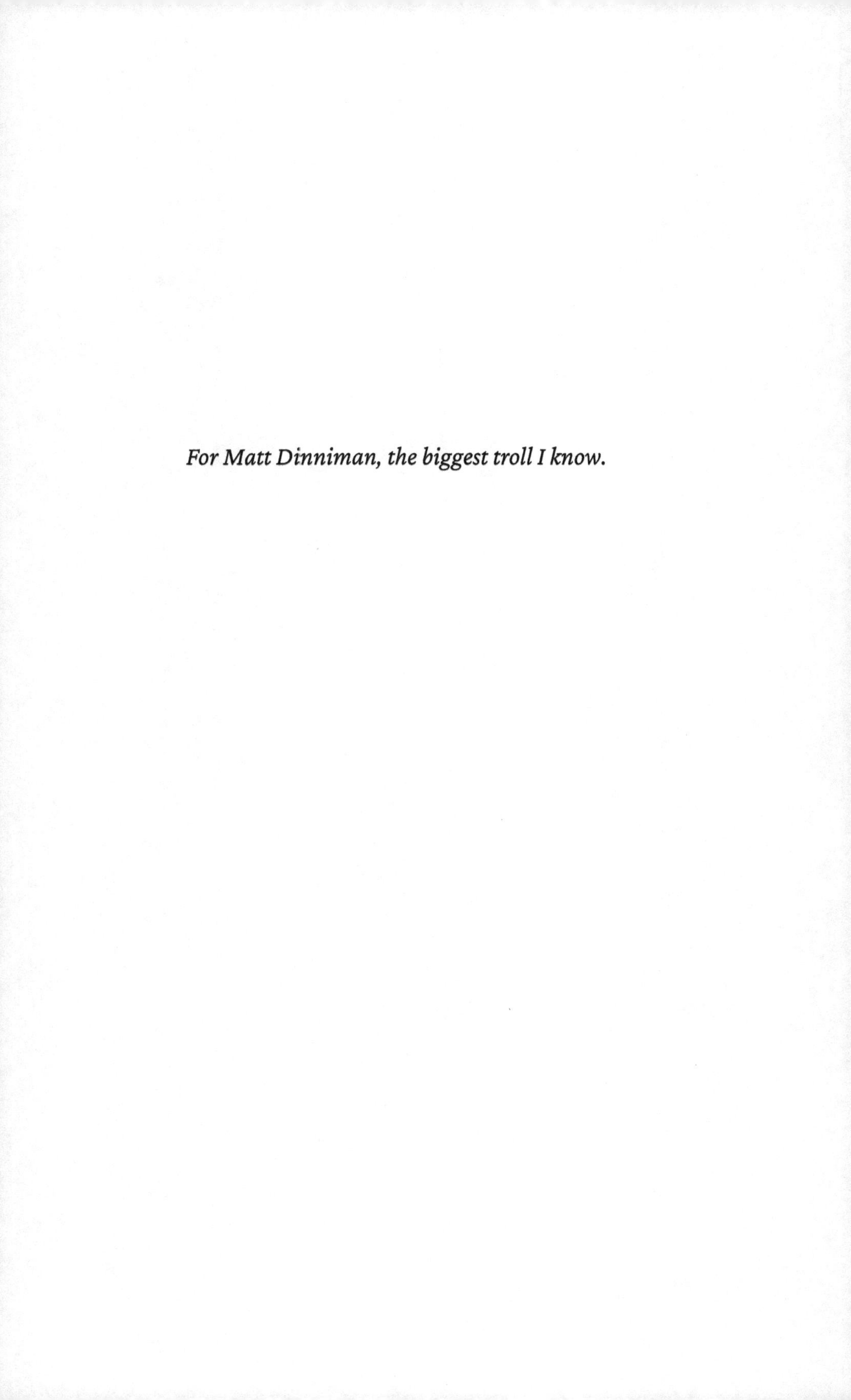

For Matt Dinniman, the biggest troll I know.

PREVIOUSLY IN SENTENCED TO TROLL 5

AFTER LEAVING the frozen lands of Frostmoor, Chod and company ventured into Wandermere, one of the few regions with the life aura necessary to hatch a dragon egg. Upon arrival, they discovered that the forest was sparsely populated and that creatures from the shadowlands had begun to spread through the sprawling woods.

Within the forest's depths, Chod was welcomed into the ancestral home of the centaurs, the Hidden Village, where he met Swift Thundercrest, the leader of the herd. With mesmer wisps overtaking the forest, the centaurs were forced to remain in the safety of the village's protective barrier. Chod and Swift struck a bargain—in exchange for eliminating the threat of the wisps, Swift would help Chod hatch the green dragon egg.

Through clever tactics utilizing the radiant energy of Pharos, Chod's spirit guide, along with Limery's fire and a generous helping of fairy dust, Chod, Taryn, and Limery were able to defeat the intruding monsters. They also ran into an emissary of King Orso, who had been tracking them across Mythos, with news that

Chod had been given the deed to Tawdrybluff Castle for his help opening the portal in Seascape long ago. Chod elected to offer the castle to the trolls as a temporary base so they would be closer to Seascape.

Once back in the Hidden Village, Taryn honored the memory of Stompy with a tattoo of a carrot upon his chest. During the process, he experienced a vision where he was finally able to say good-bye to his devoted pet. After enough life aura had been channeled into the egg, Chod took it into the forest to hatch.

With little Caustic in tow, they set off for the gnomish kingdom of Pruxford and were greeted with an announcement for the Quincentennial Tournament of Champions upon arrival. For the five-hundredth tournament, forty competitors would fight against one another in the Crystal Arena. The winner would be granted an audience with the gnomish council, where they could request their boon.

After discovering that Pruxford's councilmembers did not consider the return of Valmar Worren a threat, Chod decided that his only recourse was to enter the tournament and attempt to win as many allies to the cause as possible. Of the forty competitors announced, fifteen were heroes from the Isle of Mythos, including Ethan French the warlock, Otis Wiggins the barbarian, and Kevin Harris the sorcerer—the same trio that had ambushed Chod and Taryn outside of Lynchton many moons ago.

While there were enemies about, Chod and company also found allies. Arty, a cyclops adventurer, helped them clear a local dungeon in preparation for the tournament, while Michael Didato, once an enemy, swore a paladin's oath to offer Chod aid whenever he may need it.

As the tournament progressed, Chod found common ground with Don Othello the void mage, Randy Billson the rogue, and a lizardfolk assassin by the name of Drizz'rt.

Taryn, Chod, and Limery fought their way through the tournament, with Chod making it to the final round, where he squared off against Ethan the warlock. During the battle, Ethan opened a portal to Blacktide, home of the seafaring orcs, and two ships attacked the arena, killing numerous gnomes and wreaking havoc across the city. While some of the competitors fled, many fought alongside Chod to turn back the orcs.

During the chaos, Caustic and Chod formed a Draconic Convergence, linking the two with an unbreakable bond destined to grow stronger over time. Unfortunately, Ethan and his cronies escaped during the battle, but the devastation was enough to convince the gnomish council that the threat from the shadowlands was real. They agreed to hold a council of Mythos's greatest leaders, with the fate of the free world hanging in the balance.

If that wasn't enough, Chod received a message from Dorothy Jordan, the streamer he'd harassed on national television. His actions toward her were the reason he'd been assigned to the Mythos Rehabilitation Project, and she promised revenge.

NOTABLE CHARACTERS AND LOCATIONS

MAIN PARTY:

Chad Johnson (AKA Chod)- Forest Troll. Barbarian/Summoner. Hero of the forest, mountain, and arctic trolls.

Limery- Imp. Everyone's favorite character. Talks like he lived in a cave for hundreds of years guarding his "Precious."

Caustic- Juvenile green dragon. Bonded with Chod via Draconic Convergence.

Pharos- Chod's Spirit Guide (frost goat).

Taryn Jones- Ebony dwarf. Shadow druid. Chod's best friend.

Berry (pet)- Umber bear.

Ruby (pet)- Jackal.

Jordy (pet)- Frost goat.

Flubs (pet)- Forest slime. Sometimes absorbs a cat skeleton and takes on the appearance of a spooky gelatinous feline.

Notable Heroes:

Pressley Allen- Death knight

Randy Billson- Rogue
Michael Didato- Paladin
Don Othello- Void mage
Scotty Heyden- Sniper
Sam Taylor- Monk
Jon Bailey- Enchanter
Richard Hummel- Cleric
Otis Wiggins- Barbarian
Ethan French- Warlock
Kevin Harris- Sorcerer
Jude Duggan- Warrior
Glenn Orickson- Warrior
Dorothy Jordan- ???

Isle of Mythos:

King Orso Brightgaze- Blood dwarf. King of Seascape.

King Favian- Human. King of Vanaria

Kurzol- Blood dwarf. Cleric. King Orso's advisor.

Warwick- Human. Captain of King Favian's kingsguard.

Lord Kassidy- Human. Teleportation mage.

Lady Brollen- Ebony dwarf. Ice mage. Leader of Sandholde.

Hawkin- Human. Bard. Ringmaster of the Underground Circus.

Lillith- Imp. Limery's mother.

Bazel- Imp. Limery's father.

Leo- Imp. Limery's brother.

Forest Trolls:

Chief Rizza- Chieftain of the forest trolls. Wyrm rider.

Yashi- Potions master/archer. Wyrm rider. Smallest of the forest trolls.

Ismora- Weapons master.

Tormara- Councilmember. Wyrm rider.

Gord- Councilmember. Guardian troll.

Jira- Shaman. (Phoenix totem)

Malak- Guardian troll.

Jojin- Guardian troll.

Watu- Guardian troll.

Mountain Trolls:

Kronan- Former chieftain of the mountain trolls.

Brutus- Kronan's second-in-command.

Cheevus- Goblin. Leader of the goblins that formerly served the mountain trolls. They now follow Chief Rizza and the wyrms. Rides a mangy wolf.

Seaside Trolls:

Chief Lida- Chieftain of the Seaside trolls.

Imoko- Seaside troll who captured Chod when they stumbled upon the seaside troll village.

Arctic Trolls:

Chief Laojin- Chieftain of the arctic trolls.

Senzala- Shaman. (White dragon totem)

Nesira- White dragon that roams the mountains of Frost-moor. Senzala's totem.

Goldspire:
Jegaar- Wolfkin. Battle scholar.
Portia Swiftwill- Foxkin.
Dakota- Minotaur. Gladiator.
Festa Forgetooth- Tiger beastkin. Emperor of Goldspire.

Wandermere:
Swift Thundercrest- Centaur. Leader of the Wandermere Herd.
Daimun Stonewhisper- Centaur. Wandermere scout.
Sylvie Redmane- Centaur. Wandermere scout.
Thannis Smokehoof- Centaur. Wandermere scout.

Pruxford:
Dezmin Dreamwader- Gnome. Head of the Pruxford Council.
Felston Boonspan- Gnome. Pruxford Councilmember.
Breebis- Gnome. Owner of the Rusty Bucket Stable.

Tournament Challengers:
Arty- Cyclops. Warrior.
Roddick- Human. Arty's adopted brother.
Reddick- Human. Arty's adopted brother.
Drizz'rt- Lizardfolk. Assassin.
Tozzet Girok- Merfolk. Tidal mage.
Kazzandre Strongback- Giant. Warrior.
Lanxkuri- Catfolk. Blood mage.

Shadowlands:

Valmar Worren- Elf. Wizard/necromancer. Ruler of Mosstar. BBEG (Big Bad Evil Guy).

Kingdoms:
Seascape- Home of the Dwarves
Vanaria- Home of the Humans
Goldspire- Home of Beastkin
Frostmoor- Home of the Mountain Tribes
Wandermere- Home of the Centaurs, known for its ancient forest
Pruxford- Home of the Gnomes, known as the City of Glass
Antadale- Home of the Catfolk
Mistville- Home of the Merfolk
Ellynmylly- Home of Elves, Halflings, Giants, and many others. Known as the Melting Pot of Mythos
Shadowlands- An area shrouded in perpetual darkness. Home to creatures of shadow. Over the ages, its darkness has spread to surrounding lands, enveloping Mosstar, Blacktide, and others.
Mosstar- Home of the Elves
Blacktide- Home of the Seafaring Orcs

Characters from Outside Mythos:
Valery Barrett- Head of the Mythos Rehabilitation Project.
John Barrett- Valery's Father. Head of Mythos Games.

CURRENT STATS

Cʜᴏᴅ, Level 29 Barbarian/Summoner Forest Troll
HP: 7755/7755
Mana: 5000/5000
Rage: 0/1000
XP: 1,031,344/1,095,000

Strength: 46
Dexterity: 32
Constitution: 47
Intelligence: 10
Wisdom: 15
Charisma: 6

+1 Strength and Constitution racial bonus per level.
+1 Ability point per odd level.

2 stat points available.

1 ability points available.

Abilities:

Bite. *Using your massive tusks and powerful jaw, you take a bite out of an opponent, dealing immense damage. Cost: 10 rage. Level 2.*

Claw. *You attack with sharp claws, swiping at an opponent and dealing extra damage. Cost: 5 rage. Level 2.*

Intimidation. *You stare down your opponent, confusing them so that they are unable to attack for two seconds. Cost: 10 rage.*

Berserker Rage. *(Ultimate) Attacks and physical damage build your rage meter. 5 rage per attack. Rage meter deteriorates over time when out of combat at a rate of 5 rage per second. Activating Berserker Rage fills rage meter. For 30 seconds, rage meter does not decrease, deal increased damage, health regenerates at 5x the normal rate, cannot be stunned, slowed, or otherwise affected. Cooldown: 10 minutes.*

Increased Regeneration. *(Passive) Regenerate health at a faster rate. Level 2.*

Rapid Regeneration. *(Passive) When below 10% health, regeneration is doubled.*

Nightvision. *(Passive) Increased vision in darkness and low light.*

Thick Skin. *(Passive) Take 10% less damage from physical attacks.*

Savage. *(Passive) Ability to eat uncooked meat without consequences.*

Camouflage. *(Passive) When out of combat and not moving for 20 seconds, trolls blend in with their surroundings.*

Sweeping Slash. *Form a sweeping arc in front of you, dealing damage and knocking your opponent off balance. Cost: 5 rage.*

Conceal (Passive). *Hides level from anyone who is not a guard on city grounds.*

Summon Horror (Passive). *Ability to summon a horror. Each horror grants a unique ability. For every horror active, gain 1% increased damage and health points. Horrors decay 10% for every minute outside of combat.*

Horror of Power. *Summon a horror with 20% of your Strength. Cost: 100 mana. Cooldown: 30 seconds. Bonus: Your next attack deals double damage.*

Horror of Vitality. *Summon a horror with 20% of your health points. Cost: 100 mana. Cooldown: 30 seconds. Bonus: Opponents near Horror of Vitality are slowed by 20%.*

Horror of Finesse. *Summon a horror with 20% of your attack speed. Cost: 100 mana. Cooldown: 30 seconds. Bonus: Your next attack heals you for damage dealt.*

Sacrifice. *Sacrifice X amount of horrors to receive a temporary buff. Horror of Power: +1 Strength. Horror of Vitality: +1 Constitution. Horror of Finesse: +1 Dexterity*

Kamikaze. *Sacrifice a horror to deal a burst of damage.*

Champion. *Summon a copy of the most recent enemy you have defeated. Decays 10% every minute out of combat. Cost: 50% of mana pool. Cooldown: 6 hours.*

Spirit of the Beast. *The Spirit of the Beast path is composed of five phases.*

Phase 1: Spirit Inquiry. *A spirit animal is a guide from the spirit world, possessing traits similar to those of the individual. Unlocking one's spirit animal leads to a better understanding of the self and one's place within the world.*

Spirit Animal: *Frost Goat*

Phase 2: Spirit Embodiment. *Bonding with a spirit beast is only the beginning of the Spirit of the Beast path. By finding an amulet that connects you to your beast, the bond between the two will grow stronger, unlocking further advancements.*

Spirit Embodiment: *Ram Horns*

Phase 3: Spirit Enhancement. *Just as your body has undergone a change reflective of your spirit beast, your spirit may be enhanced in the same manner. Gain a new passive ability based on your spirit beast.*

Spirit Enhancement: *Ram Rage: Barbarian rage now lasts twice as long. Physical attacks deal splash damage.*

Phase 4: Spirit Guide. *Your body and spirit have undergone great changes, but your bond with the spirit world is only beginning. Summon a spirit guide of your spirit beast.*

Spirit Guide: *Summon a frost goat spirit guide. The spirit guides may lead you through darkness and guide you to locations you have previously visited, even if you do not know the way. Spirit guides may be consumed for a 50% increase to Wisdom for 10 minutes. Cooldown: 24 hours.*

Phase 5: Spirit Power. The path of the beast is not for the faint of heart, and those who complete all five stages are blessed with a mighty power from their spirit beast.

Spirit Power: Concussive Force: Physical attacks can be imbued with concussive force, knocking opponents back with a chance to stun them. Cost: 100 mana.

Spirit of the Beast path complete.

Draconic Convergence: The convergence fuses an unbreakable bond that grows stronger over time. No two convergences are the same, each one evolves based on the relationship between the dragon and their chosen counterpart.

Name: Caustic

Species: Green Dragon

Level: 15

Convergence Level:

1. Draconic Bond- You have made an unbreakable bond with a dragon and forged a telepathic link that may expand in the future. In its current state, intense spikes in emotion may blend between psyches.

Available Abilities (1 ability point to unlock):

Massive Bite. Deals double damage. Cost: 20 rage.

Claws. *Swipe at opponent with both hands, dealing extra damage. Cost: 10 rage.*

Multi Attack. *Bite and Claw at the same time. Cost: 20 rage.*

Iron Will. *Immune to slows and stuns for 30 seconds. Cost: 50 rage. 180 second cooldown.*

I'm Always Angry *(Passive. Available at level 10). Once rage meter is at 50%, it will not deteriorate below 50% when out of combat.*

Perception. *For 10 minutes, gain increased awareness of your surroundings. Spot hidden objects, as well as unusual sounds, odors, and tastes. Cooldown: 6 hours.*

Cleave. *Your next attack causes bleed damage, dealing 1% of opponent's health per second for 5 seconds. Cost: 10 rage.*

Battle Cry. *You let out a ferocious roar, increasing rage by 20. No cost. 60 second cooldown.*

Class Advancements. *Upon reaching level 25, you have unlocked a class advancement. You may only advance one class at a time. A second class may not be advanced until completion of primary advancement.*

Summoner Advancement.
Dreadbeasts. Unlock for further details.
Dual Subclass. Unlock for further details.

Current Items:

Item. Phoenix Feather. 10% resistance to fire-based attacks. *A very rare item, phoenix feathers can only be gathered if they are will-*

ingly given by the host. Feathers plucked from unwilling birds turn to ash.

__Item. Tiger's Eye Pendant. Removes one debuff. Cooldown: 10 minutes.__ A rare stone believed to ward off evil and bring balance to life.

__Item. Aquatic Boots.__ Allows user to walk on water.

__Item. Petrified Staff. An enchanted staff capable of taking on the properties of up to 3 attached stones. +3 Intelligence. +3 Wisdom. Bonus:__ While holding Petrified Staff, the user can cast ranged physical attacks once every 10 seconds.

__Item. Forlorn Scepter. +5 Intelligence.__ Increases the range of summoned creatures by 50%.

__Item. Glouwseeker Venom.__ When injected into the bloodstream, glouwseeker venom immobilizes target. Length of stun dependent on size of target, resistances, and amount injected.

__Item. Sea Scorpion. +3 Strength.__ An enchanted trident capable of taking on the property of 1 enchanted stone. Bonus: deals splash damage.

__Legendary Item. Angel of Death Brandy.__ When drinker falls below 1HP, a metaphysical event will occur, rewinding time for the user to two seconds prior to death.

__Item. Brimming Tankard.__ A magical tankard that, once filled, will never go empty. Warning: Once filled, contents cannot be changed. Only works on beverages.

__Item. Expandable Satchel.__ A bag capable of holding enormous content and only burdening the wearer with ten percent of its weight. Simply focus on the item inside and it will appear in your hand.

__Item. Destroyer. An enchanted warhammer capable of taking on the properties of up to three stones. +2 Strength, +3 Constitution.__ This ancient warhammer was forged in the heart of a volcano. __Bonus Ability: Inferno.__ With each consecutive hit, Destroyer grows hotter, allowing it to warp or pierce through even the hardest metals. *Multiplier works when hits are less than five seconds apart. Cost: 10 mana per attack. Cooldown: 10 sec.*

Item. Spaulder of Swiftness. +1 Constitution, +1 Dexterity. *Lightweight, durable leather mail designed to protect the off-hand shoulder during battle.*

Item. Halite Shield. *A lightweight translucent shield capable of taking damage without reducing visibility.*

Item. Frosted Buckler. +2 Constitution. *A lightweight and small shield capable of deflecting blows as well as being used offensively.* **Bonus Ability:** *Physical attacks blocked with Frosted Buckler cut attacker's Dexterity in half for ten seconds.*

Item. Dream Dust. *A powerful and potent substance capable of unlocking hidden realms of the mind. Effects are dependent upon amount ingested.*

Item. Sleep Dust. *Often mixed with liquid and drank as a tonic, sleep dust offers effects ranging from drowsiness to instant deep slumber.*

Item. Renewal Spear. *Capable of holding life aura equivalent to 500 HP. The Renewal Spear gathers aura passively while equipped and can steal health from enemies during battle. Life aura may be absorbed by the wielder at any time.* **Bonus:** *When paired with Regeneration Stone and Shield of Vigor, user will be granted a ten-foot aura that provides 20% increased regeneration for companions within its radius.*

Item. Shield of Vigor. *Increases HP by 30%.* **Bonus:** *When paired with Regeneration Stone and Renewal Spear, user will be granted a ten-foot aura that provides 20% increased regeneration for companions within its radius.*

Item. Regeneration Stone. *Increases health regeneration by 20%.* **Bonus:** *When paired with Shield of Vigor and Renewal Spear, user will be granted a ten-foot aura that provides 20% increased regeneration for companions within its radius.*

Notice! Complete Set: Regeneration Triad. *While wearing all* three pieces of the Regeneration Triad, user will be granted a ten-foot aura that provides 20% increased regeneration for companions within its radius.

Item. Nullification Bomb. Disable magical abilities of those within the blast radius for 30 minutes.

Item. Effect Stone. Effect: Return to Sender. When activated, the item equipped with this effect stone will automatically return to user. Cooldown: 1 hour.

Active Buffs:

Oath of Protection: The goddess Onera's champion (Michael/Paladin) has sworn to offer you aid against the forces of darkness.

Revive Potion: Upon receiving fatal damage, user will portal to a preset location with 1HP while simultaneously activating a full-heal and returning the body to its natural condition. A corporeal doppelgänger remains behind at the death site.

PROLOGUE

Valery stood overlooking the two newest pods at the far end of the laboratory. Several technicians worked behind her, taking readings and analyzing data for the other twenty-five pods.

Things had finally been running smoothly. At least until her father had started his meddling.

She crossed her arms and sighed, wondering just what he was playing at. Taryn Jones's participation, she could explain. The program had been on the verge of collapse and introducing him to the game was enough to keep Chad content while they searched for a solution. But Dorothy Jordan... She was a wrinkle no one had expected.

The young woman had a history with Chad, and it seemed the months since the trial had done nothing more than stoke her anger.

Chad was widely known as a rager in online games. His outbursts had landed him here in the first place. But looking at Dorothy's avatar as she wreaked havoc across Mythos, Valery couldn't help but wonder if all gamers were a dormant volcano just waiting to erupt. Dorothy had only been in the game a few days, but she'd left a trail of destruction in her wake.

Valery rubbed her temples, pushing back the inevitable headache. Her father loved to stir the pot, introducing chaotic factors just to see what would happen. It was part of the reason her mother had left him. It was also the mindset that had made him one of the greatest innovators in gaming. Valery respected her father as a businessman and visionary, but this wasn't his pet project. It wasn't a test for an expansion or new mechanics for one of his games. This was Valery's passion. This world, the AI, it had all become something more, something special. Not only was rehabilitation happening before her eyes, but they'd only begun to scratch the surface of how the AI and nanites could work together. If Chad's situation could be replicated...

She'd started this program with a desire to help people. She'd wanted to help those that society said were irredeemable through methods no one else had attempted. She'd given them a chance to become heroes.

Some had taken it. For others, time would tell. She'd always known it would take time to see progress. If half of the test subjects showed improvement, she'd count that as a success.

Her father was risking everything she'd built when they were already balanced on a razor's edge.

Valery straightened her back. The next time she saw him, she'd tell him to stop meddling.

The elevator beeped just before the door whooshed open and a man wearing a black suit stepped into the laboratory. His face was set in a straight line as he tapped at his tablet. The technicians froze at the appearance of an interloper, and the man's shoes clicked as he walked across the pristine floor.

Valery forced a smile. "Can I help you?"

"Jim Cradle, Federal Bureau of Prisons. I'm here for an inspection." He swiped through his tablet without meeting her eyes.

"Inspection?" She frowned, stepping away from the pods.

"Yes." He looked up, taking in her appearance before finally meeting her eyes. "I assume you're Valery Barrett. I've been looking through your files. It seems you're overdue."

A knot twisted in her stomach. "Is that so?"

He nodded.

She regained her composure and turned on the allure that had opened countless doors for her. "Would you like the tour?" She smiled. "I'd be happy to show you around."

"He'll do fine." Jim pointed at Thompson, and the technician gulped, his eyes darting between Valery and the inspector. "Now, if you please. Give us some privacy, and I'll find you when the inspection is complete."

Valery's heart pulsed, and she fought to steady her trembling hands. "Certainly. I'll be in my office."

The minutes ticked by while Valery paced next to her desk, unable to quiet her nerves. The psychologists and doctors responsible for inmate safety were all appointed by the Bureau of Prisons, but this was the first time an inspector had returned to the lab since the project began. Her mind raced. Had someone filed a complaint or was this merely a coincidence?

The knock on the door startled her.

Valery took a deep breath before opening the door. She gestured for Jim to enter, but he stood there, face as stoic as ever.

"I've seen enough." The man's tone was so sharp it cut through the air like a knife. "There's no point in beating around the bush. I will be recommending that the Mythos Rehabilitative Project be shut down immediately."

"Shut down?" Valery stepped toward Jim as he tapped his tablet. "Inspector, you can't be serious."

He met her eyes. "Do I look like a man who plays games, Miss Barrett?"

"But, sir, we're only scratching the surface of what this technology is capable of. Look what we've accomplished already. This could change the way we look at rehabilitative therapy going forward."

"Accomplished?" The man looked over his shoulder at the laboratory, shaking his head. "The only thing you've accomplished is a blatant disrespect for operating procedure. Not only are you allowing those under your care to run through this world unchecked, you've allowed civilians into the game. Not one but two now. You breach protocol at every corner. Honestly, I'm surprised you've stayed in operation this long."

"It's a process. We've seen improvement in a majority of the inmates, and the AI has made great strides in—"

"You had a strict set of guidelines, Miss Barrett, and you didn't follow them, regardless of what you may think you have accomplished." He shook his head. "This may be hard for you to comprehend, but this isn't corporate America where you can do as you wish and ask for forgiveness later. You signed a contract with the Federal Bureau of Prisons and the State of New York. I mean, really, you bring civilians into this? What did you think would happen? I suggest you begin making arrangements because we *will* be shutting this project down."

Valery blinked rapidly, fighting back tears that threatened to pour out like a waterfall. She'd spent years laying the groundwork for this project, and it was on the verge of collapse after only a few months.

She took a shaky breath. "How long do I have?"

I. KILLING TIME

Dust covers my feet as I descend deeper into the cavernous dungeon alongside Caustic, my bonded dragon, and Limery. The area has been overtaken by tunnel drakes, and their claws scrape against stone as they scurry about, agitated by our appearance. The monsters are great at burrowing, constructing dozens of tunnels through the various levels of the dungeon.

Caustic sniffs at one of the empty tunnels and huffs while Limery sits on my shoulder playing with a shiny pebble he found in the last room.

The dragon has been growing at a rapid rate, and he's nearly twice my height now. His green coloring has darkened, and the golden scales of his beard grow denser by the day. The little branch-like horns atop his head resemble full-blow antlers.

Breebis has warned me that she won't be able to feed a creature of his size for much longer, and he'll need to start hunting exclusively for himself soon. Dragons grow up quickly, but they require a massive amount of sustenance to do so.

Compared to some of the other dungeons we've cleared, this

one is pretty monotonous work. Pruxford has enough dungeons that adventuring is a full-blown industry, but ancient dungeons are in short supply. Adventurers like Arty and his brothers make a living clearing mob dungeons like this one to keep the local monster population in check.

With so many heroes still in Pruxford in the wake of the tournament, we've agreed to take turns with the ancient dungeons since there are so few of them. While we might not have any epic loot in store for us today, it still beats sitting around and twiddling our thumbs. For the past three days, there's been little else to do until the leaders of Mythos all convene, so we've been grinding.

This particular dungeon is home to a hive of tunnel drakes. They're a subspecies of dragon, kind of like wyrms with legs, and the thick-scaled, armored bastards are pretty pissed we've encroached on their nest. They were living here happily, filling the caverns with thousands of eggs. I don't blame them for being upset, but it's our job to put a dent in their numbers before the eggs hatch and they start invading neighboring towns and villages.

While Limery, Caustic, and I work our way through the dungeon, Taryn is enjoying a night away from the grind. We had tickets to revisit the Underground Circus, but I gave him mine so that he could take Breebis. He's grown rather attached to the gnomish stablemaster, and the circus will be a lot more fun than hanging around the stables all evening. Not that Taryn would complain. Between Breebis and the animals, he'd be happy to be there.

He deserves some time to unwind, though, and I know I've been a pain to be around. Between the attack at the tournament and the letter from Dorothy, there's a lot on my mind.

The dungeon offers me an outlet for my frustrations, and I

unleash them with every hit of Destroyer. Drakes scurry across the muddy floor, hissing and biting, each one the size of a crocodile but with longer legs and a hooked snout for burrowing. I lose myself in the primal power of Berserker Rage, and it flows through the warhammer as I cave in the armored hides of the countless tunnel drakes as they crawl down the cavern in a steady stream. As the cooldowns allow, I summon horrors, casting Sacrifice and buffing my stats until I'm a hulking brute of a troll.

Steam wafts from my shoulders as I rage. The end of Destroyer sizzles as it gains stacks of Inferno, and with each consecutive hit, the tip glows like molten lava.

I try to focus on the fight, on the monotony of ruthless smashing, but thoughts cloud my mind. Things were finally looking up when I made it to the final match of the tournament. We had allies and new friends.

And then it all went to shit. Anger surges as I recall the attack on the arena, where countless gnomes died.

That's what it took for the council to finally understand the severity of the situation—a warlock opening a portal to Blacktide and killing hundreds of innocents. War is brewing, and Valmar is testing us. I'm certain of it. His tendrils snake out from the shadows with an attack here, a roaming monster from the shadowlands there. and a growing list of heroes under his command.

Ethan, Otis, and Kevin have admitted to joining the dark wizard. At the Challenger's Ball, they were awfully friendly with some of the other heroes, and no one has seen Richard the cleric since the tournament.

Jude and Glenn will take any chance they can to gain the upper hand over me. It's only a matter of time before they join as well.

All the more reason to act before it's too late. But the wheels of politics move slowly.

With each swing, sludge flies in an arc, painting the walls and ceiling with the viscous goop secreted beneath the drake's armored scales.

And then there's Dorothy. She warned me to watch my back, but I haven't heard from her since. I think it's best to ignore her. At least until I have more information on what she's doing here.

I'm more concerned by what Valery meant when she said things were out of her control. I've sent her countless messages, but she still hasn't responded.

More tunnel drakes crawl into the cavern, and I redirect my frustration. I smash as many of the monsters as I can, but there's enough that they swarm past me toward Limery and Caustic. Each one is nearly six feet long with a flat tail meant for swiping. Their sharp claws are dangerous, but it's their hardened snouts that are capable of tearing through flesh and bone. One rears onto its back legs and roars, flashing dangerous teeth before it charges.

Destroyer smashes into the side of its head, sending the drake spinning into the wall. Behind me, Caustic unleashes a roar of his own as he and Limery take on the drakes that get by me. Their synergy of toxic gas and fire has become extremely effective, and when Berserker Rage finally times out, I fall back and let the duo mop up the rest.

Steam fades from my body, leaving mud and gore caked upon my shoulders like hardened clay.

I watch Caustic unleash his fury on the poor creatures, and when the last drake falls, notifications flash in the corner of my vision.

Congratulations! You have reached level 30. +1 stat point to distribute. +1 Strength and Constitution racial bonus.

I stare at the notification. Level thirty! It's about damn time.

This means I can finally track down Jegaar about unlocking

the legendary Warforged class in Goldspire. If we didn't have the council waiting, I'd already be on my way.

I dismiss the notification and move on to the next one.

Congratulations! Draconic Convergence has reached level 2.

Draconic Convergence: *The convergence fuses an unbreakable bond that grows stronger over time. No two convergences are the same. Each one evolves based on the relationship between the dragon and their chosen counterpart.*

Name: *Caustic*

    Species: *Green Dragon*

    Level: *15*

Convergence Level:

1. *Draconic Bond- You have made an unbreakable bond with a dragon and forged a telepathic link that may expand in the future. In its current state, intense spikes in emotion may blend between psyches.*

2. *Spatial Bond- You are now able to mark the location of the dragon no matter how far apart you are.*

Caustic's approval radiates through me as he gnaws on the remains of one of the drakes. With each passing day, our telepathic bond has grown stronger, allowing me to better understand the dragon's emotions. It's been weird, having another's feelings intrude into my mind at times, especially the overwhelming hunger that envelops me each morning before Caustic has eaten. But I believe that with practice, our bond will be another valuable skill in our arsenal. Now that we have Spatial Bond, it'll be easier to keep tabs on him as he hunts.

"Limmy is hungries." The imp lands on my muck-covered shoulder and rubs his belly. "We's been in the dungeonses all days. Limmy wants to eat and sees Taryns."

I can't blame him. It's almost nightfall, and this is the third mob dungeon we've cleared today. At least we got what we came for.

"Alright." I close out my notifications and gently poke his belly. "I guess that's enough for one day. Let's head back to the city."

Enchanted signs and lampposts cast the streets in a neon glow by the time we arrive at the Puzzling Peacock. The tail feathers on the sign flick back and forth above the rowdy inn. The tavern downstairs has somehow become the watering hole for many of the heroes and contenders from the tournament. Even though the inn has been at full capacity since we first arrived in Pruxford, it doesn't stop others from swinging by for an evening of drinks before stumbling back to their rooms down the street.

At the far wall, several tables are pushed together and littered with empty plates and mugs. Arty lets out a boisterous laugh that carries across the room. The muscled cyclops sits between two of his adopted human brothers. Next to them, Randy the rogue and Drizz'rt the golden-scaled assassin huddle over the table, pointing at a map and talking in hushed voices. Randy laughs and squeezes the lizardfolk's arm excitedly. Those two have become fast friends, tackling dungeons with their speed and deceptive tactics. Michael the paladin has an arm draped around Don the void mage, the two deep in conversation. Don strokes his long gray beard as galaxies of the void swirl within the mage's eyes.

I spot a few others I recognize as I search the room for Taryn, but he's nowhere to be found. He must still be at the circus.

"There he is!" Arty yells across the room as he points at me, his large eye bloodshot from drinking.

Limery flies over, stealing a piece of sausage from Arty's plate before perching on the cyclops's shoulder.

"Here I am." I smile, walking over. As shitty as things might seem, there's still hope. Looking at the eclectic group before me, there's a small comfort in knowing my attempt to find allies hasn't been in vain.

The barmaid brings Limery and me each a drink, and I take a seat across from the cyclops.

Arty leans forward, both elbows shaking the table with his weight. "I thought I was a hard worker, but you've put me to shame. First one out the door and last one in." He raises his mug. "Cheers."

"It keeps me grounded." I clink my mug to his and take a big gulp of the malty ale. After a long day in the dungeons, it hits the spot. "I'm trying to make the most of our time here."

"You're c-certainly doing that," Drizz'rt hisses his words.

"Someone has to keep up with you two scoundrels." I grin.

"Hey now." Randy wags a finger and flashes me a smile. "All rogues aren't scoundrels. Drizz'rt here is halfway decent."

The lizardfolk cackles in a way that's part screech, part growl, and completely unsettling.

"Any word on the council?" I ask.

Michael the paladin answers. Even in the dimly lit tavern, divine radiance casts him in a soft glow. "The centaurs arrived this afternoon. Those from the Isle of Mythos should be here tomorrow. Apparently, there was another attack on Seascape."

My hair stands on end. "What happened?"

"More monsters from the shadowlands. The kingsguard dealt with them swiftly enough, but King Orso has chosen to wait until the last moment to leave the city."

"He's a good leader."

There are several nods of agreement. Without the support and initiative of the dwarven king, I doubt we would have made any progress in uniting the other kingdoms.

We share a few more drinks, detailing the day's exploits from the many dungeons around the city. Taryn must be enjoying his day off because he's still not back by the time Limery and I head up for the night.

"Good nights, Chods." Limery plops in the bed and begins snoring before I have a chance to respond.

I lay down beside him, and the imp nestles instinctively in the crook of my arm. His naturally warm body is like a heating pack against my ribs.

Even with a buzz from the many ales, my mind still comes back to the situation at hand. There are only two more days until the council meeting, where leaders from across Mythos will once again gather to discuss Valmar Worren.

Last time, King Orso's goal was to warn them of the dark wizard's return. Now, his resurgence is all but certain. This will be a council for war.

I push the thoughts aside and pull up my stats. With nothing to do but grind dungeons, I've managed to level twice in the past week. Fighting sea orcs during the attack put me on the edge of leveling. I hit level twenty-eight on the first day back in the dungeons. Three days of constant grinding and now I'm level thirty.

Just as I have for the past two nights, I pull up my available abilities and consider what I should use the ability point on.

Available Abilities *(1 ability point to unlock):*

Massive Bite. *Deals double damage. Cost: 20 rage.*

    Claws. *Swipe at opponent with both hands, dealing extra damage. Cost: 10 rage.*

    Multi Attack. *Bite and Claw at the same time. Cost: 20 rage.*

    Iron Will. *Immune to slows and stuns for 30 seconds. Cost: 50 rage. 180 second cooldown.*

    I'm Always Angry *(Passive. Available at level 10). Once rage meter is at 50%, it will not deteriorate below 50% when out of combat.*

    Perception. *For 10 minutes, gain increased awareness of your surroundings. Spot hidden objects, as well as unusual sounds, odors, and tastes. Cooldown: 6 hours.*

    Cleave. *Your next attack causes bleed damage, dealing 1% of opponent's health per second for 5 seconds. Cost: 10 rage.*

    Battle Cry. *You let out a ferocious roar, increasing rage by 20. No cost. 60 second cooldown.*

Class Advancements. *Upon reaching level 25, you have unlocked a class advancement. You may only advance one class at a time. A second class may not be advanced until completion of primary advancement.*

Summoner Advancement.

    Dreadbeasts. Unlock for further details.

    Dual Subclass. Unlock for further details.

If I were strictly a barbarian, the Massive Bite, Claws, or Multi Attack would be fine. They would imbue each attack with bonus damage powered by my rage. Between my horrors, weapons, and other abilities, my barbarian attacks are severely lacking compared to what I'm capable of with my summoner class. Every time I cast a Horror of Power, my next attack hits for double. While new barbarian abilities might stack, making the attacks even more powerful, I know it's not the right choice for now.

There's really only one ability I'm interested in. Dreadbeasts. It's an advancement of my horror summoning, and I'd unlock it right now if I wasn't worried that I might need an ability point for the Warforged class.

As it is, I don't know if the class requires an ability point or if it's something that unlocks automatically upon completion. Until I meet with Jegaar, I can't risk using this point.

According to the battle scholar, the Warforged were a subclass of barbarians, and the most dangerous fighters in Goldspire long ago. The process of becoming a Warforged was said to kill more than half of those who attempted it. Those who survived were granted abilities that turned their skin to fluid steel when they raged. On the battlefield, they were unmatched, and when we face down Valmar, that's the exact kind of advantage we're going to need.

No one has attained the class in many generations, but Jegaar said that once I hit level thirty, I should return to Goldspire and find him. That's exactly what I intend to do once the council is over.

Unlocking the dreadbeast path would help me survive whatever challenges may be waiting, but until I know more, I'm not ready to risk it.

Even though Taryn's not here, I already know what he would say. He'd tell me to go to the library and do some research. Maybe he's right. Tomorrow, I'll stop by the Pruxford Library and see what they know.

2. PRECIOUS KNOWLEDGE

Taryn is already downstairs when we arrive for breakfast. Platters of sausage, bacon, and biscuits fill the table. Flubs sits on the windowsill in the form of a cat. Morning light shines through the window, giving a glow to the slime's gelatinous body and setting its jeweled eyes ablaze. The skeleton that floats inside the creature only adds to the hypnotic effect. I don't even want to imagine what kind of shady back-alley establishment Taryn purchased that from.

The barmaid places a bowl of brown gravy in the center of the table. "I hope you're hungry, big fella."

My stomach rumbles as I inhale the savory aroma. "That's my secret. I'm always hungry."

She taps me playfully on the arm. "You and the little one both, enjoy."

"Morning!" Taryn says with a full mouth. Biscuit crumbs speckle his beard and tunic.

"Mornings, Taryns!" Limery flies over, taking a sausage in one hand and several pieces of bacon in the other.

Ruby places her paws on Taryn's leg, begging until he gives her a piece of meat. She takes it and prances toward the corner with her prize.

"You were out late." I raise a brow suggestively. "Must have been a good night."

"It was a great night." Taryn grins. "The circus was amazing as always, and then afterward, Breebis and I went out drinking with Hawkin and some of the other performers. Let me tell you, those guys know how to party. They said to give you their best." He picks up a sausage and bites it in half. "How were the dungeons?"

I fill a plate of my own until it's overflowing. Caustic must sense my hunger because I'm suddenly overcome with a ravenous desire to eat even stronger than my own. I'm not sure if I'll ever get used to having another's emotions inside my head.

"Not as fun as a night at the circus, but we managed to clear three mob dungeons. And I finally hit level thirty." I stuff more bacon in my mouth and savor the smokey flavor. "Saving an ability point for this long seems wrong, but it'll take at least a couple of days of constant grinding to gain another. I wish I had Jegaar on speed dial right about now."

"Well—"

I hold up a finger, and he pauses. "You'll be proud of me. I've decided to stop by the library and see if they have any information about the Warforged."

"Warforged?" a deep voice calls as heavy boots thunk down the stairs. "I thought that was the stuff of legend. Goldspire propaganda used to make them seem even more fearsome than they already are." Arty takes a seat at the table. "Is there actually truth to it?"

"You know it's rude to eavesdrop." I narrow my eyes at the cyclops until his cheeks flush, then I grin. "There's truth to it, alright. I saw one with my own two eyes. He was a watered-down version from where the trait had passed through generations, but even so, he was a force to be reckoned with. If there's a chance to unlock that kind of power, I have to take it."

Arty sits back and crosses his arms. "Dark wizards. Warforged. This world grows more ludicrous by the day."

Limery lets out a loud belch that carries across the tavern. Several guests glance at him, but he rubs his belly. A look of contentment spreads across his demonic features as he fills his plate with more food.

"What are the lot of you up to today?" I ask Arty.

"Michael and Don have asked me and my brothers to join them with clearing one of the ancient dungeons. Roddick wasn't interested at first, but Michael promised a blessing from Onera if we helped. It's not often one has the opportunity to receive a divine blessing."

I recall the Oath of Protection that the paladin swore to me at the Challenger's Ball. The description was kind of nebulous, but I get the feeling it prevents him from stabbing me in the back. I still don't know much about deities and their role in this world, but being in one's good graces can't be a bad thing.

We finish the rest of our meal with small talk before heading to the library.

***

Compared to the hustle and bustle during the Quincentennial Tournament, the streets are a vestige of the excitement and grandeur that waited on every corner a week ago. Gnomes come and go with their business, but the street performers and mirth are gone. It's as if a cloud has descended over Pruxford.

Limery perches on my shoulder as we pass through various neighborhoods on our way to the library. Taryn walks to my right,

Ruby darting between his legs with every step while Flubs leads the way. The slime's skill for mimicry is unmatched, and if not for its slimy appearance, I'd never be able to tell it wasn't a real cat. Flubs has the feline movements and mannerisms perfected, complete with flippant attitude as it struts through the city. The gelatinous cat garners more attention than the rest of us combined.

The last time we attempted to visit the library, it was closed in celebration of the tournament. With the festivities canceled in the wake of the attack, I'm hopeful we'll have better luck this time.

While we walk, I focus on my bond with Caustic. The young dragon is much too big for casual walks through the city now, so I use our time apart to strengthen the link that tethers us. The description for Draconic Bond says that it should grow stronger over time, and I've found that I can always sense his presence if I try hard enough. It's similar to my horrors, but where my connection to them is more of a generalized feeling of their location, with Caustic, it's almost like I'm sensing his mood.

Right now, he feels unfettered and free. He must be exploring somewhere across the countryside for his morning hunt. Now that he's capable of flying, Breebis says he should spend as much time in the air as possible to build his endurance.

The Pruxford Library towers over the surrounding buildings. Much like the arena and Crystal Palace, it's a work of art. The beautiful, cylindrical building is several stories tall with an exterior of sea-green glass. Its many shelves are visible through the translucent windows, each one filled with books and scrolls.

A ravenous and primal hunger overtakes me, and I relax my connection to Caustic while he hunts. It wouldn't be a bad idea to also research our bond while we're here.

Taryn stops to admire the building. "You know, the color reminds me of this antique glassware my mom keeps in the dining cabinet. The glass is supposedly mixed with uranium and somewhat radioactive. It looks cool, but we never got to eat off it. Sometimes, I would see its faint green glow when I was sneaking into the kitchen for a late-night snack."

"So, every night?" I grin.

Taryn shoves me in the side. "How do you think I got so big and strong?"

I look him up and down. "Big, you say?"

He rolls his eyes, and we enter the library. Inside, the scent of parchment welcomes us, along with a gnomish clerk wearing a seafoam green robe. He stands behind the desk, organizing a cart of books. His half-moon spectacles with amber-colored lenses nearly fall from the tip of his nose.

The gnome has a light blue tint to his skin and thick curly, sapphire hair that's cropped close at the sides. "Welcome to the Pruxford Library, the crown jewel of our fair city."

Taryn tilts his head. "I thought that was the Crystal Palace?"

The gnome scoffs. "So they would have you believe, but tell me, master dwarf, what is more precious than knowledge?"

"You've got me there."

The gnome clasps his hands behind his back. "Calfin Dazzle-dust, at your service. How may I assist you today?"

I step forward, and his eyes widen slightly. "We're here to do a little research."

"Most excellent! Just let me send this on its way and I'll be right with you." Calfin picks a book from the cart, and it flies from his hand, floating through the air toward the shelves. That's when I notice several more books flying of their own accord throughout the library.

Limery grows warm against my shoulder. "Spooky bookses."

"Levitation magic?" I ask, watching the book as it soars across the library before finding its place among the shelves.

"Gods, wouldn't that be something." Calfin chuckles. "No, I wasn't blessed in such a way. The book fairies are the ones that keep the shelves in working order."

"Book fairies?" I look around, but I don't see any signs of fairies. Is this what counts as a joke among librarians?

"Well, technically, they're called bibliophilic fairies, but that's a mouthful. We call them book fairies around here." He removes the glasses and hands them to me. "Here, take a look."

The frames are much too small to fit my head, so I hold them in front of my eyes, looking through the crescent-shaped lenses.

"Shit..." I move the lenses up and down several times, amazed at what I'm seeing. There are at least a dozen fairies flying about the library.

Each fairy is about the size of Limery, with small gray bodies and wings so dark that they scream of nothingness. Short, pearlescent horns jut upward from just above their brow line. Unlike the celestial fairies in Wandermere that leave a sparkling trail of glitter in their wake, these leave a trail of shadow that dissipates as they fly.

I focus on one as it returns to the desk to retrieve another book.

Bibliophilic Fairy. *Level 22. Book fairies, as they are commonly known among scholars and academics, are a rare breed of fairy only found within the halls of the Pruxford Library. The first book fairy was bred by happenstance ages ago when two scholars found themselves trapped among the snowy peaks of Frostmoor during a research mission. Their fae companions—a void fairy and a light fairy—mated, producing offspring with the more temperate demeanor of the light fairies and the ability to vanish without need of the void. Since then, book fairies have been the primary assistants to the librarians at the Pruxford Library.*

I hand the glasses to Taryn and return my attention to the gnome. "So they just work here?"

He nods. "Indeed. Before they were discovered, we used a variety of fairies. Celestial fairies are great workers, but they leave a dust trail everywhere they go. Void fairies would occasionally lose a book while traveling through the void. Don't even get me started on the various elemental fairies. Book fairies have the best qualities for our particular field. They can stay within our realm while still hiding from sight so as to avoid disrupting our patrons. We have these special lenses for tracking them down if we need to."

"That's wild." Taryn makes to hand the glasses back, but Limery flies from my shoulder and grabs them.

"Limmy wants to sees." He uses both hands to hold the frames to his head so they don't fall off. When he sees the fairy, Limery gasps in delight before zooming away.

"He'll bring them back." I apologize before he gets us kicked out.

"Do not worry. I always bring an extra pair." Calfin winks as he pulls another pair of spectacles from his robe. "Now, what is it that I can help you with today?"

I close another ancient tome and slide it across the table next to a dozen other books and scrolls.

"Nothing?" Taryn lifts his gaze from a massive book bound in green leather.

"More of the same." I press my knuckles to my eyes and take a deep breath. "They have the entire lineage of Goldspire's emperors, tables of various sub-races of beastkin, lists of gladiators and their victories, but when it comes to the Warforged, it's like they never existed. Do you think Jegaar was messing with us?"

Taryn shakes his head. "No, I don't."

"Then what gives?" I gesture at the stack of books we've already pored through.

Taryn strokes his beard, and the chime of the metal clasps carries across the empty library. "Jegaar is a member of the Scholars Guild. He said their job is to maintain the histories of Goldspire and to search out rare items and artifacts. He also said they do foreign reconnaissance. So maybe the reason you can't find information on the Warforged is because they don't want you to."

"You might be right." I sigh. "I guess I won't be spending that ability point any time soon then."

"Maybe not, but there's still plenty we can learn while we're here." Taryn taps the book he's holding. "There's a wealth of information on the various druid classes. I bet you can at least learn something about dreadbeasts and your bond with Caustic."

"You're right. I'll go see if the clerk can help point me in the right direction." I look around, suddenly aware that Limery has disappeared again. "Where is the little guy, anyhow?"

Taryn grins. "He saw a book floating by and went to investigate."

I laugh. Of course he did.

In the center of the library, there's a resource desk located next to a spiral staircase that goes all the way to the top floor. I find Limery zipping through the air and waving his arms as he talks to Calfin.

The gnome smiles when he sees me. "Were the materials helpful in your research?"

I push the cart loaded with books on Goldspire to the desk.

"Unfortunately not. Do you have anything on dreadbeasts or dragon bonding, specifically, a Draconic Convergence?"

He taps his chin and flips through a massive book that I assume is an index. "Hmm, let me see what I can find. I'll bring them to you when I'm done." He turns to Limery and grins. "Would you like to see how we request books from the fairies?"

"Oh yes! Limmy would loves to sees." The imp clasps his hands together excitedly. "And then we's can sends thems back to the shelveses."

I meander through the library while Calfin and Limery work with the fairies to locate more books. As frustrating as it is to come up emptyhanded regarding the Warforged, I can't help but be impressed by the depth of this world once again. We're in a library filled with thousands of books that detail the history and lore of Mythos long before anyone logged in. Each piece of info has been created by the AI in vivid detail, existing whether we discover it or not. No wonder Valery would try anything not to lose this place. If a reset means starting from scratch, there's no promise that they could recreate any of this.

Taryn has his face buried in a book when I return.

"Find anything good?" I ask.

"Tons." He taps the page. "I'm reading about Rane Darkbrow. She was a shadow druid who tamed some of the most dangerous creatures from the shadowlands. Pretty fascinating stuff."

I sit in silence while Taryn reads, ruminating and brooding until Limery flies over carrying a stack of books nearly as tall as he is.

"Calfins saids these should helps." He drops the books to the table with a thud. "Limmy has to goes now."

He disappears down the aisle of books before I have a chance to respond.

"Maybe he's making a career change." Taryn grins, but he doesn't look up from his book.

I sort through the material Limery brought and a few of the titles catch my eye. These might be exactly what I'm looking for.

Beasts of Shadow
   Dragons: A History
   The Untamable
   Summoners Through the Ages

Over the next few hours, I manage to gain some useful information. *Summoners Through the Ages* has detailed accounts of various summoners and sheds light on some of the paths I could have taken. If I had a higher Intelligence, the elemental class would have been pretty destructive. The brood summoner also has some pretty nasty abilities. There's only one mention of horrors, though.

Elwin Iceheart. *Horror Summoner. Known in her time as the Wayward Summoner, Elwin toed the line between decency and devilry. While she fought for the forces of good, she would use any tactic at her disposal to achieve victory.*

Her summons were dark and foreboding, some referred to them as nightmare beings, capable of casting fear into the hearts of her opponents before the battle started. Where most summons are formed from the world around them, horrors come from another plane altogether and are considered a true rarity among summoners. Little is known about the origin of horrors, save that they reside somewhere between the mortal and shadow realms. Some believe that they thrive in the darkness of the shadowlands, but there is little evidence to support this theory.

She sounds like a badass to me.

Beasts of Shadow mostly focuses on monsters found in haunted forests and dungeons, but there are a few references to the shadowlands and dreadbeasts.

This tome would not be complete if I did not at least touch on the beasts of the shadowlands. Those unforgiving lands remain a large mystery to academics and scholars, for far too many who have ventured into the darkness in search of enlightenment have become victims of its gloom. I have no understanding of why a portal was erected into those lands in the first place. If I had the authority to close it, I would.

The Scholars Guild no longer sanctions research missions into the shadowlands. For those who would seek out its secrets, know that its reputation has been paid for in blood. The horrors, demons, dreadbeasts, behemoths, terrors, and monstrosities within these lands were born in suffering. If they do not kill you, they will lure you to join their ranks, for the call of darkness is sickly sweet while on shadowed ground. The search for knowledge is a noble pursuit, but some secrets should remain hidden.

A chill passes through me as I recall the mesmer wisps in Wandermere. Their whispers were all-consuming, drawing me toward them. Valmar was born in the elven lands of Mosstar but according to King Orso, the dark wizard's journey into the shadowlands is what gave him the strength to invade the other portals.

I close the book when I realize my claws are starting to dig into the binding. Reading about dreadbeasts and the shadowlands is only adding to my already high anxiety, so I decide to focus on one of the bright spots from the past few weeks—my bond with Caustic.

Dragons: A History is so fascinating that I could read it all day. Its pages are filled with tales of the dragons of Mythos. From the legend of the first dragon all the way to Verdaria's appearance in Wandermere. There's even a section on Senzala's totem, Nesira.

I wonder if the powerful white dragon joined the arctic trolls when they traveled to Seascape, or if like Jirra, Senzala can still tap into her totemic bond when they are far apart. Now that I think of it, I wonder if something as large as a dragon can enter a portal, and what I'll do with Caustic once he's full-grown if he can't fit.

The pages are full of illustrations as well. There are at least a dozen species of dragons across Mythos, each one as interesting as the last. The black dragon looks like a terror to behold with its obsidian scales and wings made of darkness. While the gold dragons are one of the smallest species, they are said to hoard the biggest treasures.

According to the book, most prefer to stay far away from civilization, and anyone who would disturb their peace must be prepared to face judgment. It makes me feel even luckier to have bonded with Caustic.

While *Dragons: A History* focuses on dragons as a species, *The Untamable* is exactly what I'm looking for, a plethora of information on dragons and their interactions with people.

A dragon does not heel like a pet, nor does it follow orders like a work animal. A dragon cannot be tamed. They are proud creatures and bond with those they choose. A dragon would rather die than bond with someone it believes unworthy.

Throughout history, several types of bonds have been recorded. Totemic bonds are the most common, where a dragon bestows favor upon someone, granting a sliver of their power to mages or shamans. The bond remains until it is severed by the dragon.

Some dragons have been known to grant pacts, where there is no tether between the two, but a commitment to work together until a goal is achieved. The most famous is the case of Lady Stonearm of Pruxford, when the gnomish princess partnered with a blue dragon to force her father from the throne. Lady Stonearm never revealed the details of her agreement with the dragon, but mining in the Sapphire Mountains was abandoned soon after she took the throne.

The most prized and rarest bond is that of the Draconic Convergence. A convergence only happens when a dragon has determined someone worthy of binding their spirits. The two spirits converge, granting a familiar link between a dragon and its partner. Senses and emotional pathways become one in this unbreakable bond, and as it develops, both are able to see through the other's eyes. This has granted tactical advantages to mages as their dragons survey the battlefield from above, but none more so than the illustrious dragon riders.

The book goes on to detail examples of the various bonds throughout history, but all of the accounts are several hundred years old. There is one part that I find particularly interesting.

Dragons are solitary creatures by nature, though they do convene with one another on occasion. Once a century, dragons from around Mythos gather in secret for a draconic conclave. Even those who have bonded with a dragon are forbidden from attending the assemblage.

I wonder when the last conclave was, and if there are enough dragons across Mythos to hold one again.

"Chod. Earth to Chod" Taryn waves a hand in my face, pulling my attention from the book.

"Sorry, I got sucked into this one."

"No kidding. I've never seen you so enthralled." Taryn laughs. "Are you ready to head out? It's almost nightfall, and I'm sure Calfin could use a break from Limery. Plus, I want to stop by the stable to check on Berry."

"Check on Breebis, you mean?" I pucker my lips and mimic a kiss several times. Too bad Limery isn't here to chant a chorus of 'Taryns has a girlfriends.'

Taryn narrows his eyes. "You're just jealous."

We gather Limery, and I give my thanks to Calfin as we depart. Once we're outside, I realize just how dangerous the green-tinted windows are for losing track of time. Across the city, enchanted lights flicker to life in the twilight.

I didn't learn as much as I would have liked, but it was far from a wasted day. While I have no better understanding of the Warforged class, I deepened my knowledge of dragons. When it comes down to it, my bond with Caustic might be the greatest advantage I'll have going forward.

3. REUNIONS

"LIMMY LOVES THE LIBRARIES!" The imp zooms through the air, telling us all about his adventures with the book fairies. "Calfins says Limmy can comes back anytimes."

As we make our way down the sparsely populated streets toward the Rusty Bucket stable, I lean into my bond with Caustic to let him know we're coming. I get nothing, so he must be taking an evening nap after a long day of hunting. Either that or he's ignoring me.

There's a faint crackle as an enchanted streetlamp flickers to life, giving the cobblestones a warm glow.

Up ahead, there's a crowd gathered around the square of the Pruxford portal. It's strange considering how empty most of the streets are. My heart races as I recall the attack on the square, and my hands buzz with mana. The moment passes as I realize there's no fighting and no terrified gnomes trying to escape. Whatever it is, though, it has them intrigued.

"What's going on up there?" I squint to try and get a better view.

"Oh, nice! They're finally here." Taryn points. His causal tone confirms that there's not a threat.

"Who's here? I can't see that far away." He must have better eyesight than me because I can't make out much more than a mass of people from so far away.

"Limmy sees! It's Daddies!" He darts toward the portal faster than I've ever seen him move.

My chest flutters, and the blue sheen of a mana-infused wyrm shimmers in the glow of enchanted lights as it rises like a cobra. Chief Rizza sits upon the wyrm's back, waving to the crowd while they gawk and point.

Now, that's badass.

I take off running, and my excitement stirs Caustic, piquing his curiosity. Behind me, Taryn curses as he tries to keep up. I catch several puzzled looks as I sprint down the street, but I don't care. After the past week, it'll be nice to see some familiar faces.

Guards have been stationed around the portal since the attack, and they clear a path as the large group exits. Several dozen people spill into the square. In the center, Limery hugs his father. Tears well in Bazel's bulbous yellow eyes as he has a long overdue reunion with his son.

This is the first time I've seen the two together, and Limery is the spitting image of his father, though about half the size. Both have the same shade of reddish skin, spindly limbs, and forked tails.

Limery's mother, Lillith, and brother, Leo, hover next to them. Leo looks like a little punk rock imp with his black mohawk but once Limery releases his father, the brothers embrace as well.

I wave to Lillith and return my attention to the rest of the group.

To the left, there's a mixture of ivory, ebony, and blood dwarfs that make up King Orso's personal guard. The dwarven king stands out among his kingsguard, nearly a foot taller than the rest. His bushy black hair falls to his shoulders and his dark beard is braided and oiled, a shadow against skin the color of cooling magma. Silver clasps catch the light and glimmer. Power radiates from his crimson armor and glowing red crown. The king's senior advisor, Kurzol, stands by his side.

To the right, a group of humans wear the silver-and-blue armor of Vanaria's kingsguard, led by Warwick. The man's youthful eyes scan the crowd for threats. Next to him, Lord Kassidy the teleportation mage, holds a pastry in one hand as he whispers something into King Favian's ear.

Closest to the portal, Chief Rizza towers above them all upon her massive wyrm. It's nearly full-grown now, and almost the size of the one I fought in the forest so long ago. I search for Gord's massive frame among the crowd, but the only other troll I see is Jira. The wizened shaman stays close to Chief Rizza's wyrm as it slithers across the square.

"Chod, is that you?" King Favian raises a hand, and the escort stops. "By the gods, what have you done to your head?" He pushes his way through and extends a hand, gripping me around the forearm.

Warwick stays at Favian's side, his dark eyes always alert. His state of alarm makes me wonder what all I've missed on the Isle while we've been traveling. Kassidy gives me a nod as he stuffs the last remnants of the pastry into his mouth.

The King of Vanaria is the picture of royalty as he stands before me. He's put aside his boiled leather armor and riding gear in favor of polished plate mail. Adorning his breastplate is detailed metalwork in the shape of a griffin with a sapphire for the eye. A flowing blue cape hangs from the king's shoulders, and a sword with a jewel-encrusted pommel rests at his side. King Favian's brown hair is as windswept as ever, but it only adds to his aesthetic. He knows just how important this meeting is.

I squeeze his arm. "A lot has changed since we last saw one another."

"Too much, I fear." His tone is somber.

Leathery wings flap over my shoulder, and Favian's eyes go wide as Caustic descends, landing beside me with a huff. The dragon sniffs at the air, like a dog picking up a scent. The king takes a step back, and both kingsguards draw their weapons.

King Orso calls them off. "Lower your weapons." His deep voice booms as he joins King Favian, patting him on the back. Orso raises a brow as his gaze shifts between me and Caustic. "So this is where my dragon egg went."

Caustic sniffs at the air as if sizing up the group before him. He clicks his snout, and Chief Rizza's wyrm responds in kind.

I rest a hand on the dragon. "I hope you aren't angry. You said we had full access to your troves."

"That I did." King Orso laughs and casts a glance at Kurzol. The cleric was with us when I snuck the egg into my satchel. "When I was a young dwarf, I won the egg in a game of gloomkeeper with my father's advisor, Durkis. He was a renowned tactician and said to be the best in the kingdom. It was that day that I won not only the respect of my father but his council as well. Alas, there's nowhere on Isle of Mythos with the life aura needed to hatch a dragon, so the egg has sat among the treasures of Seascape ever since. Truth be told, I hadn't thought about it in years. But if you've found yourself worthy of a dragon's companionship, then who am I to argue? We will undoubtedly need you both in the days to come."

Taryn finally catches up with Ruby and Flubs in tow. He bends over, bowing as he gasps for breath. "Your Highness."

"Master Taryn." King Orso grins. "A shadow druid? You make our kingdom proud."

I lean in and whisper to Taryn, "Why didn't you just fly?"

He rolls his eyes. "And leave my pets to walk by themselves? Now, that's just cruel."

I chuckle at his theatrics. "Whatever you say, T."

Chief Rizza's wyrm lowers its body, and she slides from its back. Her golden eyes lock onto mine, and she rushes forward, embracing me with her lithe but powerful arms. "It is good to see you, Chod."

I return the embrace. So much has happened since the days when my biggest challenge was restoring the ley lines to the troll forest. "Where are the others?"

She releases me, smiling as she touches the tip of my horn with her finger. "We all have our parts to play. Gord, Laojin, and Kronan are attempting to unite the seaside and desert trolls."

"Wow. Do you think they can do it?" Chief Lida had made it very clear that the seaside trolls would take no sides in the issues outside of their village, but perhaps a visit from the chiefs of the arctic and mountain trolls might be a little more convincing.

"I believe that they must." She holds out a hand to Caustic, and he nuzzles against it. "Who do we have here?"

"This is Caustic. He's a juvenile green dragon."

She caresses the dragon's jawline. "A worthy member of our tribe."

Caustic's chest rumbles like the purr of a monstrous cat. He must sense my attachment to Rizza and the rest of the tribe.

"How is everything on the Isle? We heard there have been more attacks in Seascape."

Before she can answer, a horn blares just before wheels clatter down the street behind us. A crystal carriage, pulled by the whitest ponies I've ever seen, comes to a stop at the edge of the square. Guards from the Crystal Palace march beside the carriage, their rainbow armor gleaming like the iridescent shell of a beetle.

The carriage door opens and Dezmin, the head of the gnomish council, steps down. His matching yellow robes and pointed hat remind me of a garden gnome, but there is nothing humorous about his grave expression.

He nods slightly. "Your graces, chieftain, we are glad for your safe arrival. Normally, we would welcome you to settle in first, but time is not on our side of late. We have elected to convene a midnight council."

4. MIDNIGHT COUNCIL

By the time we arrive at the Crystal Palace, night has fully descended upon the city. Somehow, it makes Pruxford even more beautiful. The glass palace shimmers in the light of the moon with streaks of emerald and amethyst that remind me of the Northern Lights.

Chief Rizza and Jira are amazed by the enchanted lights and signs that give the city a life unlike any other I've traveled to.

Taryn converses with Kassidy and Kurzol, and Limery has been talking nonstop, giving Leo and Bazel an account of our adventures together since we first set out to clear the obstruction of the ley line so long ago.

Lillith sits on my shoulder while her boys talk. "You know, Chod, before you came into our life, Limery and Leo bickered all the time. I was hesitant to let them out into the world, but it seems they've finally found a common interest."

"It's our experiences that make us who we are." I smile at Limery and Leo laughing together. "The more we have, the more we become."

Once Limery and I left their little burrow, Leo set out on his own adventure, and he's been busy exploring dungeons on the Isle with some of his friends ever since. He's managed to reach level nineteen during the past few months. If he's anything like Limery, then his level is only a glimpse into the imp's true power.

Chief Rizza walks beside me, her wyrm lying low to the ground as it slithers beside us. She stops for a moment, letting several guards pass us as she admires the palace. "I never left the confines of the forest before you showed up, Chod. Not in all my years. Now, in a matter of months, I've traded with the humans in Lynchton. I've traveled to Seascape and Vanaria, where they have buildings that stretch taller than our mightiest trees. I've held council with kings, and now here I am about to sit among the great leaders and discuss the future of Mythos." She intertwines her arm with mine. "When you left us to continue your adventures, you said it was time for the trolls to find our place in this world once again. Thanks to you, we've unlocked a world beyond even our wildest dreams."

My cheeks burn under her intense gaze. "It wasn't all me. I had a lot of help along the way."

We stop to let King Favian and King Orso pass before continuing. They are more subtle in their admiration of the illustrious city than the trolls, but I catch them gawking as we arrive at the palace. There's a moment where everyone just stands at the foot of the magnificent structure, taking in the spectacle before climbing the hundreds of stairs.

It's easy to lose focus as we climb. Every third stair is transparent, granting a view of a stream that runs down from the palace. Colorful fish dart through the water beneath our feet.

King Orso leans toward Favian, but his deep voice still carries. "I can admire gnomish craftsmanship. Their ability to bend glass and gemstones to their will would impress even our foremost jewelers. But to me, there is nothing greater than stone. It has a presence that is powerful and unforgiving. When you touch it, you can feel a connection to the earth from which we sprang."

Dezmin turns around from the front of the procession. "I assure you, Your Highness, that these walls could withstand the attack of a dragon and neither melt nor shatter. We don't just craft, we enchant."

King Favian coughs to cover his laughter.

At the top of the stairs, guards stand sentry. Their iridescent armor fits perfectly among the palace's exterior. Since the attack, the palace has been closed to tourists and only open to those there on official business.

The palace has its own stables, but Chief Rizza and I elect to have Caustic and her wyrm wait outside the entrance to avoid the detour. One guard shifts uncomfortably when the dragon and wyrm begin clicking their snouts at one another. Maybe Caustic has finally found a playmate he doesn't have to hold back with.

I give Chief Rizza a reassuring smile as we enter. As great as it is to have found a place in the world, there may come a time when the trolls wish they were still forgotten within the forest. The stakes of this council are far greater than the last.

Valmar's presence is no longer just a worry.

Limery rejoins us, taking a seat on my shoulder opposite his mother.

He wraps his small arms around my neck and squeezes. "Limmy wants to thank Chods for bringing Daddy backs."

"You're welcome, buddy." I reach up, caressing him gently on the back. "I'm sure he's glad to see you."

"Oh, yes." He clasps his hands together and grins devilishly. "And one days, Limmy and Leos is going to goes into the dungeonses."

Footsteps echo through the cavernous building as we ascend

the stairwell toward the council chambers. At the top of the stairs, we return to a familiar landing with its elaborate mosaic mirrored on the floor and ceiling. Guards and escorts of various kingdoms fill the landing. There are several merfolk, lizardfolk, and catfolk mixed with a spattering of humans, halflings, and gnomes that obscure the council room entrance. Some talk in hushed voices, but more stand silently.

The clack of hooves against the marble floor draws my attention to two centaurs from Wandermere. I acknowledge Daimun Stonewhisper and Sylvie Redmane with a nod. That must mean that their leader, Swift Thundercrest, is already inside.

"Make way," Dezmin orders. The crowd parts, revealing an arched door carved with intricate designs of birds and flowers and fitted with hundreds of colorful gemstones. It wasn't that long ago that Taryn used his Nimble Key to pick the lock.

Back then, Councilgnome Felston Boonspan said there was nothing he could do for us. Aside from him, the rest of the council refused to believe the threat was real.

This time, we are welcomed inside. Massive pillars run along both sides of the room, and a set of rainbow-colored stairs lead to a platform where a throne once stood. Now, there's a massive sculpture of a cornucopia and giant gemstone fruits spill out from the crystal horn. There are lemons carved from topaz, emerald limes, sapphire and ruby berries, amethyst grapes, and more I couldn't begin to identify. According to Felston, it is a reminder to the council that the citizens are the bounty of Pruxford.

The smaller hexagonal table where the council meets has been replaced with a circular table that fills the majority of the room. More chairs have been placed around the perimeter. Even with the guards waiting outside, the room doesn't feel quite as big as it did on our first visit.

The doors shut behind us, and there are a few minutes of

chaos as old friends and acquaintances reconnect. I recognize many of them from the Challenger's Ball, and several more from the original council in Seascape. King Orso greets Councilgnome Felston, and I make my way over to the centaurs Swift Thundercrest and Thannis Smokehoof, his most trusted advisor. Swift is as stout as ever with his silver lower half and matching gray beard trimmed to a point. His beard ends just above a large chest tattoo that depicts a dragon curled around the base of a towering tree.

"It is good to see you again, Chod." Swift squeezes my shoulder. "Though I wish it were under better circumstances."

"Better than pretending there's no need for this meeting." King Orso joins us, grasping Swift firmly around the forearm.

"Don't hold it against them." Swift looks around the room. "Better late than never."

At the last council, most of the attendants were advisors from other kingdoms. This time, everyone with a position of power is here.

"You'd have better luck uprooting a mountain than softening the edge of a dwarven grudge." King Favian grins. "Dwarven anger cuts deeper than enchanted steel."

"Too true." Swift laughs and turns to me. "How are you faring with the young dragon?"

Before I can answer, Dezmin clears his throat and it carries above the chatter, magically amplified. "As much as I wish this were a festive occasion, there are grave matters to discuss. Please, take a seat so that we may begin with the business at hand."

Everyone takes their seats, with kings, queens, councilors, and heads of state sitting at the main table and advisors and other attendants sitting in the chairs around the room. I sit between Jira and Taryn. Limery and his family claim the top step near the cornucopia.

"I didn't realize there would be so many people here," Taryn whispers.

He means it as a compliment, but as I look around, I realize that this is it—the totality of kingdoms not allied with Valmar. Somehow, it doesn't feel like enough. How many of these leaders will rally to the cause? Or will some be content to hide away until the darkness inevitably swallows them?

Dezmin stands and bangs a crystal gavel until the room falls silent. If not for the severity of the situation, I would laugh at how he and the council look like a set of garden gnomes dipped in watercolor with their matching clothing in an array of pastel shades.

Instead, I hang onto every word the gnome says, sunshine yellow outfit and all.

"Several days ago, Pruxford fell victim to a senseless attack. Many of you were here that day. When we should have been celebrating the quincentennial and the achievements of hard-fought battles in the arena, we were instead forced to bury hundreds of innocents who lost their lives. A warlock sworn to Valmar Worren opened a portal inside the Crystal Arena, allowing two ships filled with sea orcs from Blacktide to lay siege to one of our most timeless traditions. At the same time, there was a secondary attack outside of our primary portal, where hundreds of innocent civilians were killed in cold blood. The arena can be repaired, but those lives will forever be a grim reminder of the evils of this world."

Dezmin pauses, taking the time to make eye contact with many of the leaders. "The worst part is that it could have been prevented. We should have listened when King Orso first called a council in Seascape. We should have listened when rumors began to swell of monsters appearing from the shadowlands. I chose to ignore it because it was far easier than admitting what might actually be happening—that Valmar Worren is still out there. Still plotting. This is the reason why the Pruxford Council has called you all here today." Dezmin leans forward, resting his hands on the table and sighing. "There are those of you who still doubt if the threat is real. You believe King Orso too cautious or too worried because of Seascape portal's recent awakening. Pruxford and Seascape are not the only ones to face attacks, and I encourage others to share their accounts now."

The first to speak is Swift. He tells the room of the mesmer wisp invasion of Wandermere and how if not for Taryn, Limery, and myself, the herd would have eventually been cut off from the portal and the other kingdoms.

Next, a member of the Mistville Court stands. I recognize the merfolk from the Challenger's Ball. He has slick green skin and a set of gills along each side of his neck. Sunset-colored fins streak from his head to neck, fading from orange to yellow. He clenches his webbed hand into a fist when he speaks, slow and deliberate.

"After the attack on Pruxford, we returned home with our challengers while we waited for the council to gather. No more than a day passed before a dark fog began to encroach upon Mistville from the south. Shrieks howled through the night, and tumultuous waves crashed into our cove. The next morning, bodies of our sea guardians washed upon the shores. We gathered all of our fighters and searched the waters until we found a kraken lurking within its depths. We lost two of our own in the battle, but we forced the beast to retreat with grievous injuries. It had already laid dozens of eggs, but we dispatched those easily enough. Had we not acted swiftly, we would have found ourselves in a similar state to Wandermere."

I'm surprised it's King Favian who stands to speak next. His armor gleams beneath the enchanted chandelier, and the griffin on his breastplate seems almost alive as its eye catches the light.

"Many of you are familiar with the hesitancy of my forbearers, and how hiding behind the safety of our ivory tower almost ensured the defeat of those who stood against Valmar in ages past. That is precisely why I am here today. To make sure those mistakes are not repeated."

I'm always amazed when Favian puts on his kingly persona. It's so different from the carefree spirit who would prefer to spend his days flying among the clouds on the back of a griffin. When it's time to rally the troops, I don't know if there is anyone better.

"For those of you who might not recall, Vanaria is home to perhaps the greatest threat to the undead in all of Mythos. Our tower was constructed during the Age of Heroes and consecrated by the most powerful cleric this world has ever known. The tower still blesses the lands that fall beneath its shadow. Recently, Valmar has chosen to test the tower's constitution. For a full day, undead poured from the portal." He pauses, letting the words build in the silence. "Their bodies vaporized as they entered. The stench of sulfur swelled within the city walls, but the blessing held. There is no doubt of what we are up against. Valmar tests us one at a time. He is searching for weakness. To what end, I'm not sure, but now is the time for us to present a united front and to finally admit that the threat is real."

"How are you so certain?" A silver-haired catfolk stands at the opposite side of the table. She's from Antadale, but she wasn't at the last council. "How are you so certain that this wasn't the result of a hero gone rogue, the work of someone without the fear of true death meddling with powers beyond their control? I have heard the stories. Tales of heroes appearing upon the Isle of Mythos, and somehow, only the Isle. Tales of humans, and dwarves, and..." The catfolk looks at me and her whiskers twitch. "Trolls. Why is it that they appear and now we find ourselves in danger? Why is it that none of this began happening until Seascape and Vanaria opened their portals?"

Swift huffs before Favian can respond, and his tail flicks in agitation. "You've always been a sourpuss, Ofelia. Many owe their lives to these heroes. If not for this troll, then those from the Isle of Mythos would not be here today. If not for this dwarf—" Swift gestures to Taryn. "—then the centaurs of Wandermere would not be here. If not for the many human heroes from Vanaria, then who knows where the death count of Pruxford would have ended. They fought among your challengers hand-in-hand. Forget your grievances with the heroes, or the lack of them, in Antadale, and look at the evidence before you. There have been attacks all over Mythos. If we stand idly by, there will be more."

"Call me names if you wish, Swift, but I will not spread panic and fear among my people when there is nothing to be done." She crosses her arms. "Even if there is a threat out there, the portals to Mosstar and the shadowlands are still closed. Yet you call us here as if an attack is on our doorsteps. To hear my kin tell it, the warlock was engaged in battle with another hero when he summoned the orcs. Many died, yes. A tragedy, certainly. But squabbles among heroes are hardly a call for war."

I know it's not my place to speak, but I can't help myself. "A war is coming whether you choose to acknowledge it or not." Several heads turn in my direction, but I continue. "You have the luxury to dismiss it now, while Antadale and Ellynmylly remain untouched, but eventually, you won't."

There's a murmur around the room, and Taryn pokes me in the side. "Chod, what the hell are you doing?" he whispers.

Ofelia's claws emerge from her paws as she presses them to the table. "Is that a threat, troll?"

"That's enough." Dezmin's voice booms as he tries to regain order.

I stand, staring down the elder catfolk. "I have no grievance with you or your people. Since coming to Mythos, I've found a tribe, I've found friends, and more than that, I've found a purpose. Death might not mean the same thing to heroes as it does to you, but I will die a thousand times if that is what it takes to protect this place."

Every part of me wants to scream and yell and pound the table until I can make everyone here understand. Not that long ago, I might have done just that. It's taken me a while to realize it, but I know that's not the way. At least not every time.

I rest my hands on the table, feeling the cool marble against my palm before continuing. "I know that I can't do this alone. I don't know how we can defeat Valmar. I don't know how we can open the portals. There's so much that I don't know, but I do know that we have to try. There has to be a way. Where I come from, there's a saying, and I've never paid it much attention until now. United we stand. Divided we fall."

Ofelia and I lock eyes for a long moment, neither one of us wanting to be the first to break eye contact.

Eventually, her claws retract. "I admire your commitment. If you and the other heroes fight for Antadale with the same fervor, then perhaps there is hope."

Dezmin lets out a sigh of relief. "So we are all in agreement then."

Ofelia nods. "We will listen to your proposals, but I don't see how this changes anything. Valmar has the advantage because he has the ability to open and close his portals at will. We have all found ways to open our own portals, but there is no way to open those still closed from the other side."

"Actually, I might be able to help with that." A hooded figure wearing a dark gray robe emerges from between two lizardfolk on the far side of the room. I recognize the black chain around his neck immediately.

Taryn grips my forearm. "Stay calm."

"And who are you?" asks Dezmin.

"Me? I'm just the messenger." He removes the hood, revealing the blonde hair and chiseled jawline of Richard Hummel, the cleric who serves the god of chaos. "But I'm here to help."

5. Mark of the Damned

Some time ago.

Dorothy crept silently through the forest. On the outside, she was calm and collected, a hunter on the prowl, but inside, a maelstrom of emotions swirled. A child-like wonder fought against the grudge that weighed heavily on her slender shoulders. High above the obsidian trees, lightning cracked, igniting their skeletal branches, and strands of Dorothy's silver hair fluttered in the electric air as the thunder rumbled.

Not far ahead, the blaze of a low fire flickered where several hobgoblins sat around the camp muttering to one another.

Dorothy stalked her prey, a shadow among the darkness. She was on top of the group before the first hob noticed her, its orange, cat-like eyes wide as she plunged her dagger into the skull of the hobgoblin across from it. Bone shattered beneath the ancient blade as the hob collapsed to the ground. With the finesse of her elven body, she spun, stabbing the next hob in the throat and pulling the blade until a streak of crimson arced through the air. She moved like a huntress, sharpening her skills with each kill until only one remained.

The lone hobgoblin ran through the woods in an attempt to escape. Dorothy activated True Strike and threw the dagger. When the weapon released, it flew like an arrow, lodging in the back of the creature with a thunk.

Over a dozen hobgoblins lay scattered throughout their primitive outpost, the unfortunate victims of her destruction. This was the third camp she had destroyed this evening, and it wouldn't be the last. Notifications flashed in her vision, but she pushed them away.

Dorothy should be having fun. On some level, she was. She was experiencing the best gameplay of her life, and full-immersion was better than she could have ever dreamed. The sights. The smells. The feel of the leather-wrapped hilt of a dagger against her skin, and the tactile feedback of bone crunching beneath the blade. It was amazing, and yet all she could think about was how Chad Johnson had gotten to enjoy this at her expense. In a land of darkness, he still managed to cast a shadow.

They could call it punishment all they wanted, but the truth was that he'd been rewarded for making her a laughingstock.

Dorothy pressed her foot on the hobgoblin and pulled out the dagger lodged in its ribs, imagining the creature as a monstrous blue troll. She wiped the blood from the blade on her pant leg and sheathed the weapon. When she focused on her map, it appeared across her vision. The location of her mark pulsed slowly.

That brought a smile to her face.

He was still in Pruxford, and the word *Mark of the Damned* hovered over Chad Johnson's icon. No, not Chad Johnson. Here, he was Chod, and he had the nerve to call himself a hero.

The guy was anything but. He was a bully, a rager, an asshole, and he was a middling gamer at best; otherwise, he would have gone pro. Instead, he hurled insults at teammates who were trying their best and belittled people for comedy.

Thanks to John Barrett, Dorothy would have the last laugh.

The man had been right. His daughter was on to something special with this game. Valery wanted to use it to help people. To try and rewire neural pathways and reform criminals. John believed it could be more than that.

Judging by the few days Dorothy had spent in Isle of Mythos, Valery had her father's knack for innovative gameplay.

John had hand-picked Dorothy, pulling the one card he had over his daughter. Finance.

He was fascinated by his daughter's work. Not just the technology of the pods, but the AI and how it allowed for world-building that constantly evolved.

Dorothy had encountered more depth during her first day in this world than she had in years playing other games. Part of her wondered if John was jealous of his daughter's creation. Not that it mattered. Dorothy had her own reasons for agreeing.

As the head of Mythos Games, John Barrett was a gamer to his core. He studied lore like some studied business and finance. It was the reason he ran the best gaming company on the planet. Profit was a byproduct of his success, not the reason for it.

Thanks to him, Dorothy had entered Valery's trial with knowledge the other testers didn't have. She picked her race and class with one goal in mind—revenge. Soon enough, she was going to destroy everything Chod loved about this world. But first, she might as well enjoy herself a little.

Playing as an elf was the only way for her to choose a class that would spawn her in Mosstar. The kingdom's portal was closed to the rest of Mythos, but John assured her that wouldn't matter for much longer. If she allied herself with Valmar, it would put her on a collision course with Chod.

For her class, she'd chosen revenant. It allowed her to keep some of the traits of her original race but altered her appearance, giving her elven body ashen gray skin and eyes that burnt like embers. As an undead, she wouldn't need to sleep or eat, and poison had no effect. But that wasn't the best part.

The biggest advantage of being a revenant was that, unlike the other heroes of Mythos, she had no reason to fear death. When a revenant died, they didn't lose a level. She'd used this to her advantage several times already and was already at level fourteen.

Dorothy took a final look at Chod's icon before dismissing the map. Finding an item to use to bind him as her mark had been difficult, but Valmar had his ways. In exchange for her loyalty, the dark wizard had had one of his minions secure what she'd needed. She had a long way to go before she would be ready to fight the troll, but unlike him, she had plenty of time to prepare.

She glanced at the bar filling the corner of her vision. *Rage of the Damned* was nearly replenished.

The scouting outposts were all gone, leaving the hobgoblin encampment free for the taking. Clearing it out would be a nice chunk of experience. Once Dorothy hit level twenty, she'd return to the necropolis for her next mission. Until then, she could hone her skills.

6. No More Heroes

Valery's eyes burned, and she fought the urge to cry. Her father had instilled in her early on that in a world where the strong survived, crying was a sign of weakness. Those words had hurt, and yet controlling her emotions in the corporate world had been a blessing to a young woman climbing the ladder.

For the first time in a long time, she felt helpless, like everything she'd worked for was collapsing all around her. What did it matter if she shed a tear? The inmate rehabilitation program was going to be shut down soon. There was no getting around that. Not even her father could stop that train now that it was moving. His little stunt with Dorothy Jordan was going to ensure there were no pieces left to pick up.

Valery never should have allowed him to get anywhere near this project. When the game first started crashing and the only option to stabilize the AI was to keep Chad Johnson immersed, she'd asked for her father's advice. A one-time favor to see if he could find the problem. If there was a way to exploit a game, John

Barrett could find it. In the end, asking for his help had been her undoing.

She stood over Dorothy's pod as the woman massacred another encampment. It was unsettling how often she chose violence.

A revenant? Valery cursed her lack of foresight. She'd unlocked the advanced races for Taryn when he'd logged in, but she'd never turned them back off. Why would she? There weren't supposed to be any more testers, much less someone who would want to spawn in Mosstar while Mythos was on the brink of war.

Now, Dorothy was advancing her character at a rapid rate. Not even Chad had leveled up this quickly. It was only a matter of time before the two met, and their personal rivalry would leave a lasting change on the course of Mythos.

The AI wouldn't favor the heroes, especially when a handful of them had already joined forces with Valmar. It would let the chaos play out, and if the forces of darkness won, the game would continue to evolve. In a few months, the entire world could shift.

Part of Valery wanted to force Dorothy to log out, but that would only make things worse. Her father had financed this venture, and he hated when he didn't get his way, especially now that she'd given him a peek behind the curtain. Crossing him would mean a freeze on her funding and the certain demise of this project instead of what she was facing now.

She should have known better than to trust him when he said this was her show and he wouldn't get involved.

He'd never believed she would be able to succeed in using artificial intelligence to mimic therapy in a fantasy video game. Now that she had, of course, he was interested.

Removing his little pet from the game might be worse than what was coming from the Bureau of Prisons. He'd destroyed upstart companies for less.

Valery turned to one of the bright spots of this whole endeavor—Chad Johnson. His bravado and interaction with the ley lines had provided hope for advancements beyond mental rehabilitation. Like some of the greatest inventions, the connection had been discovered by accident. If she had more time to study the effects on his body, they could be in store for something truly groundbreaking.

She had more of her father in her than she'd like to admit. She'd grown attached to this world. It evolved by the day. Every choice the players made reverberated across the continents. Starting from scratch would be like losing a child. It would be the end of the AI as she knew it. There was no telling what the next iteration would be like. They'd gone through half a dozen before this one.

If the inmates were all going to be pulled, then they needed to leave Mythos in a state where it could survive with no heroes.

Valery wiped her eyes. The clock hadn't run out yet. She still had work to do.

7. BEYOND THE VEIL

My claws dig into the chair as Richard weasels his way toward the table. He stands next to Councilgnome Dezmin, so close that he practically hovers over the gnome. The cleric's blue eyes scan the room, and when he finds me, a wry smile spreads across his stupid face. It takes everything I have not to explode a horror on top of him.

Taryn has told me countless times that I'm overreacting when it comes to Richard, but the man is responsible for turning Pressley into a death knight. Who knows what other calamities he's caused in the name of chaos.

Whatever he has planned, it can't be good. There's too much on the line to trust the word of someone who causes chaos for fun. Or his god.

Richard runs his fingers over the black chain around his neck and it jingles softly. The full attention of the room is on the cleric.

"You say you can help us." Dezmin shifts uncomfortably at the cleric's proximity before taking a step to the side. "What exactly is it you're offering?"

"I can get you to Mosstar." He says it so nonchalantly, like it's the easiest task in the world and not something that has plagued Mythos for hundreds of years.

"Impossible." Ofelia laughs and sits back against her chair. The silver-haired catfolk crosses her arms. "Everyone knows it's impossible to open a portal from a foreign side. Otherwise, it would not have taken our kingdoms so long to regain contact."

Richard's grin grows more mischievous. "Impossible for you, maybe."

"Tell me, who are you?" The merfolk with the sunset-colored fins glares at the interloper.

"Like I said, I am but the messenger. My god has taken an exceptional interest in the predicament you find yourselves in. They have asked me to lend my services to the cause."

"And what cause might that be?" King Orso's voice booms. "Don't think I have forgotten your actions in Seascape."

I turn to Taryn, giving him a knowing look. I'm glad to see I'm not the only one who distrusts this guy.

Richard throws up both hands. "Once again, Your Grace, I am only the messenger. Would you punish your guard for following orders?"

"Carry on with it, then," Orso growls. "What is it that your god can help us with?"

Richard grabs his chain and squeezes, almost like a priest clutching a rosary. "When the time comes, I will be granted the authority to open portals for your forces. When this happens, you must be prepared to enter immediately. The gateway will be open to both sides, putting all of Mythos at risk the longer it remains open. The most prudent course would be to route the portals outside of the city to allow you time to mobilize your forces before storming the city."

"Is this possible?" someone asks, followed by a roar of chatter around the room.

Dezmin bangs his crystal gavel to gather everyone's attention. While he's regaining order, a message notification flashes in the corner of my vision. My chest tightens at the thought of another message from Dorothy. What else could she possibly have to say? More threats, perhaps. There's too much going on right now for me to deal with her revenge quest, but I am curious. I pull up the message while Dezmin attempts to quiet the room.

I frown when I notice the message is from Valery. That's some relief, but she's picked a terrible time if this is about scheduling the next logout.

__Incoming Message (Admin):__ Chod, I realize this is not the best timing, but what I'm about to share with you cannot wait. There may not be another opportunity for you to be in a room with this much influence, and time is of the essence. For both of us.

I'm not sure where to begin or how much to say, but the short of it is that the rehabilitation program is being forced to shut down. That means all of the inmates and testers will be pulled from the program, and the lab will be shuttered while the bureau conducts an investigation. I don't know how much time we have before that happens. Maybe a few days. A few weeks if we are lucky. The wheels of government turn slowly, so I'm praying for the latter.

You're probably wondering why I am telling you this. That's one of the few answers I do have. You've grown attached to this game and this world as much as I have. It's easy to see. Like me, you view Mythos as more than lines of code. That's not the case for most of the inmates. I trust that you will only divulge the state of the program to those you can trust with such information.

Even with the program's impending demise, not all hope is lost. The system will still run, and the AI will allow the world to propel down whatever path it is taking. I never imagined the scope of these quests would move beyond the Isle of Mythos during the first phase of trials. Thanks to you, all of Mythos has been unlocked. With the portals opened, we have seen the true breadth of this world, but that has also left it in a precarious position at the most inopportune time.

Which is why I'm reaching out to you directly. We've worked so hard to build this world, and I don't want to see it crumble. So, I have a quest for you, Chod. With however much time we have left, I need you to leave Mythos in a state so that it can survive without heroes.

If you can do that, I'll do everything within my power to make sure there's something to come back to. -Valery

My ears ring, blocking out all sound aside from my thunderous heartbeat. For the longest time, I just stare at the message. Why would they just shut down the program? How could they do that?

I close the message, and the conversation with Richard continues around me. I can't hear anything over the ringing in my ears.

My gaze lands at the top of the stairs where Limery sits next to his brother, an arm wrapped around Leo's shoulders. His bulbous yellow eyes lock with mine, and he grins his devilish smile.

The pit in my stomach widens to the point that I think it may swallow me from the inside. What would happen to Limery if the program ends? What would happen to all of this? As absurd as it is, my mind goes back to grade school on the day that Ms. Harris asked us what we'd do if we knew the world was ending. How would we want to spend our final days? Kind of morbid when you think about it, especially for children, but it was supposed to remind us of our priorities in life. Some kids said they would spend time with their families. Others wanted to go on a trip or play their favorite games. I don't remember what my answer was, but here I am, presented with the same question all these years later.

Whether it's three days or three weeks, this world is ending. My friends. My tribe. Everything I've grown to care about. All gone.

My world is ending.

Unless I save it.

I read the message again, trying to parse out any information I can from Valery's words. She wants to save this world as much as I do, and we don't have a lot of time. She's right, though. There may not be another chance where I'm in a position with this much influence.

The phrase cycles on repeat in my mind—what would I do if the world was ending?

I'd save it. I have to save it. For Limery and Chief Rizza, for the trolls, and for everyone who lives a life as real as my own even when I'm not around.

The ringing fades and chaos resumes as leaders argue over whether or not Richard's offer is real.

I move toward the table. Taryn reaches for my arm, but I shrug him off. I make my way between King Orso and King Favian and slam my fist down with enough force that the table splinters.

Several people jump at the sound, and one of the halflings squeaks with surprise.

My chest heaves with each breath as I fight the panic rising inside. I meet Richard's eyes. "Tell us, after all you've done, why should we trust you?"

Richard meets my gaze, and the smile he's been wearing all night finally fades. "There it is."

I'm not sure what he means, but something changes in his

demeanor. He closes his eyes and clenches both hands around the obsidian chain. Power radiates from the man. The air in front of him crackles, and dark energy sparks above the table.

Chairs screech against the marble floor as people move back. I don't flinch an inch even as my braid rises from my shoulder from the electricity in the air.

The darkness flares until it is about the size of a doorframe. There's a ripping sound as a gash forms in the void, as if the fabric of reality is tearing in front of us. The rift widens, giving us a bird's-eye view of a city at night. The buildings are outlined in an eerie green glow. The view shifts, as if we're flying over the city. We pass a castle, where four massive green flames burn on the tops of towers surrounding an obsidian keep. A spire sprouts from the center of the castle, even taller than the flames, and the walls gleam with their reflection. The perspective shifts again and we're soaring over the city. Far below, the buildings are speckled with the dull light from thousands of windows. We move higher until clouds conceal our view. For a long moment, all we see is gray mist. The silence of the room is palpable as we pass through the clouds until suddenly, they are gone.

An expanse of darkness stretches forever across the horizon. Then, the view shifts again. Patchy snow covers the ground outside the city walls. We zoom closer, and my blood runs cold when I realize it's not snow.

An army of skeletons stands outside the city, unmoving. The view zooms in on the bone-white warriors with their rusted weapons and shields. They stand, lifeless, like a group of mannequins. There's no telling how long they've been stationed there. The view widens, revealing more and more skeletons that stretch around the perimeter of the city. Thousands of them. Tens of thousands.

The portal closes, and the entire room sits in shocked silence.

Richard clears his throat. "Why should you trust me?" His gaze is still fixed where the portal was moments before. "Because I'm your only hope."

8. PARTS TO PLAY

THE AIR above the table crackles one final time as the portal vanishes. We all stand in shocked silence. Any doubts about Valmar's resurgence have been demolished. Not only is he out there, he has an army.

A fucking big one.

My hands twitch with nervous energy. I knew Valmar was the big baddie ever since I saw the paintings and tapestries in Vanaria that depicted the battle against his forces I knew, but I wasn't prepared for this. Thousands of undead warriors wait outside the gates to Mosstar, and that's not even counting whatever monsters and other kingdoms he's rallied to his cause. Inside the city, there are elves that haven't had contact with the outside world for hundreds of years.

According to Valery's message, we have weeks, maybe days, to deal with this threat. Without heroes, what chance does the rest of Mythos have against an undead army?

It almost feels hopeless, but I refuse to wallow in self-pity. In a world where anything is possible, there has to be a way out of this. There aren't that many heroes, but together, we have the power to turn battles. We don't die like everyone else. And when we do die, we only lose a fraction of our power each time we return. If I have to, I'll charge the gates of Mosstar until there's nothing left of me.

Somehow, I'll need to convince the rest of the heroes to do the same.

"Can any of our clericss confirm that what we ssaw is real?" one of the lizardfolk hisses.

"It is," Kurzol answers, his face grim. "I could sense a divine radiance surrounding the portal. Ithus may be a trickster, but the portal was true."

Ithus. That's the first time I've heard the God of Chaos's name said aloud.

"What now?" Ofelia's gaze darts around the room, the hair on her neck more bristled than usual. "Much to my dismay, the threat is real. Valmar has an army in waiting. How do you propose we prepare?"

"I take no pleasure in this confirmation." King Orso's face is set in stone. "But we must mobilize our forces, empty our troves, and end this threat once and for all." He speaks with authority, but not everyone is convinced.

"We must not rush into battle." A shaggy-haired halfling shakes his head. "We don't know the full extent of Valmar's resources. It would be more prudent to take our time and prepare."

"Take our time?" King Favian scoffs. "That must be easy for Ellynmylly to say when the dead are not spilling into your streets. Every minute we delay is another moment for the dark wizard to grow stronger."

"Now, now." Dezmin raises his hands in an attempt to calm the room. "We are all on the same side here. We must fight, but

Milbun is right. We cannot be quick to dismiss caution out of fear. We must be prudent, and we must choose our course of action wisely."

"How long would it take?" I speak calmly despite the worry that continues to build inside of me. Monsters, the undead, and even Valmar himself don't scare me, but the possibility of losing all of this does. "How long would it take to mobilize your forces if you had to?"

There's a moment of chatter as the leaders speak with their advisors.

"Fighting with only what we have at the ready, a week," Dezmin answers. "But we have precious few Revive Potions. Not enough for even a quarter of our greatest warriors. Too many were used during the tournament."

I recall the description of the Revive Potion I was given before the tournament started. The one that still buffs me and Ethan the warlock even now with an extra life since neither of us died in the final match. Each potion takes a year to brew. Forty years' worth of work was wasted during a single day of entertainment. If only they'd listened...

Richard taps his fingers on the table. He's the only one still standing close to it. "As thrilling as it would be to watch these negotiations play out, I do have other matters to attend to. If you decide to partake in the service my god has to offer, you can find me at the Dragon's Rest Inn." He looks in my direction. "Chod, would you do me the honor of escorting me out of the palace?"

I'd like to give him the honor of a swift kick in the nuts, but he may have a part to play in all of this.

"Give me a moment." I sigh before turning to King Orso and whispering in his ear. "I don't know what he's up to, but we must convince the council to attack Mosstar within a week. There's not enough time for me to explain right now, but I will."

Orso's eyes widen slightly and I wonder what must be going through his mind. He nods solemnly, and I'm grateful to have earned his trust.

Next, I move to King Favian and then to Chief Rizza, telling them the same thing. I've earned their trust through my actions. Convincing everyone here to go against the greatest threat this world has ever seen on a week's notice will take a skillset that I don't have—diplomacy. The three of them will have more influence over the other leaders than I possibly could.

Finally, I kneel next to Taryn. "When this is over, there's something I need to tell you. Don't let them leave this council unless they are ready to fight."

His brow arches. "Should I be worried?"

I nod grimly. "We all should."

"We'll handle them." He pats me on the arm. "Just keep your claws to yourself."

That may be easier said than done.

Richard and I pass the guards and envoys outside the council chambers and descend the stairwell into the vacant palace. Without the throngs of crowds waiting for tours, it seems even larger. Our footsteps carry across the emptiness.

"What is it you want?" I ask once we are out of earshot.

"If only it were that simple." He gestures down an empty hallway, and we walk. "You know, when I was a child, my mother took me to mass every Sunday. I was always enthralled by the priests. They wore these vibrant vestments, each piece with its own special meaning. Fragile clothing, but somehow, it was the armor of God. They looked divine, almost magical, standing on the pulpit with the crucifix behind them and the statues, tapestries, and morning light shining through the stained glass. I always thought it must be pretty special to hear the voice of God." He chuckles. "Turns out it is."

For a long moment, he doesn't speak. I stare at him, unwilling to play whatever game he has planned.

"I know you don't like me." He turns, tilting his head until he's looking up at me. "Trying to take a meaningful item from you when we'd just met. I'll admit my first impression was a bit heavy-handed. But as I've explained before, the rules are different when you don't have the brute strength to clear a dungeon by yourself."

I scowl at the man. "What are you getting at, Richard?"

"Fair enough. I suppose time is of the essence. There's a difference between causing pain and causing chaos. Despite what you may think, Jude, Glenn, and I are not the same." He resumes his stroll down the corridor, not waiting for me to catch up. "For what it's worth, I hope you're able to figure this out. Everyone loves a good underdog story."

Richard disappears around the corner, and when I arrive, he's nowhere to be found.

There might be some truth to his words. They aren't the same. Glenn is a legit psychopath, and Jude has anger issues that trump my worst days. Richard, I'm not sure. There's something about him that doesn't sit right with me, but maybe Taryn is right. It could be that I've never given him a real chance because of our first meeting. Or maybe this is just another thread of chaos. Either way, while the council decides the fate of Mythos, I have work to do.

Outside the palace, Caustic and Rizza's wyrm peck at one another with their hardened snouts, almost like birds grooming one another. I give them both a firm pat, but they pay me no mind. The palace guards on each side keep a safe distance from the two young dragons.

I elect to leave Caustic at the palace while I handle business. Once the council is over, he'll fly back to the stables, but for now, it'll be good for him to spend some time bonding with a similar beast.

Knowing how stubborn some of the leaders are, I wouldn't be surprised if they are arguing about the best course of action through the night. There's no point waiting around for the council to finish their discussion, so I head back to the Puzzling Peacock.

As I walk through the barren streets, I send a message to Michael the paladin. One of the benefits of his Oath of Protection is that we have access to message one another without being in a party.

Message (Chod): *Are you at the inn by chance? The leaders are having a council right now and things are about to hit the fan. If you're able, I need you to gather as many heroes as you can. I'll be there shortly to explain.*

After a few minutes, he responds.

Incoming Message (Michael): *You're going to make me regret this oath, aren't you? There's a few of us here already. I'll see who else I can track down.*

I run through various scenarios while I walk, trying to decide the best way to deliver the information. If I tell the other heroes that they're soon going to be pulled from the game permanently, I doubt any of them would agree to go to battle. They'd likely party away their final days in inns and taverns across Mythos.

I'll need to be creative, and I'll need to convince them to grind harder than ever over the next week.

By the time I arrive at the inn, the ground level is filled. There are the usual heroes and champions from the tournament that have made the Puzzling Peacock a bustling tavern the past few days, but there are some new faces.

"A few of you." I laugh as I join Michael by the bar. "Right."

Michael grabs a half-dozen mugs from the barkeep. The paladin's hair shimmers with divine radiance even in the dull light of the tavern. "Lucky for you, it was two-for-one night at the Brown Boar Tavern a few blocks over. It only took a promise of a round on me and some news from you to get them over here." He nods toward the barkeep as he fills more mugs. "Help me pass these out."

I grab as many drinks as I can carry and begin disseminating them among the crowd. Arty and his brothers are here, and the cyclops chats with a half-dozen others who I can only assume are adventurers. Randy the rogue and his newfound friend, the golden-scaled assassin Drizz'rt, claim a table in the center. Don the void mage sits with them, galaxies swirling within the depths of his eyes. Next to them, Sam the barefoot monk, and Scotty the sniper accept their mugs with a smile. I'd never spoken to them before the attack on the arena, but they both joined the fight just the same.

Lanxkuri, the catfolk blood mage, and a couple of her companions sit together at the far wall with the giant Kazzandre Strongback. She's by far the largest person in the room, making the halfling next to her look comically small. Across from them, another halfling and a lizardfolk I don't recognize sit with a pair of gnomes.

This isn't everyone, but it's a damn good start.

Once we've passed out the drinks, Michael clears his throat, and the beam of light that falls upon him intensifies. "Thank you all for gathering tonight, even if I had to bribe some of you. Leaders from across Mythos are currently holding council at the Crystal Palace, and Chod assures me he has some big news."

The tavern is quiet aside from the slurping of drinks and the noises of people shifting in their seats. Even the bartender leans against the counter in rapt attention.

For a moment, I just stand there, stomach in knots and unsure of the best way to proceed. I have to persuade them to fight, convince them that the possibility of dying on a battlefield is a better cause than what they're doing right now.

My mind wanders to the Christmas parties and business functions I was forced to attend with my parents as a child. There were always speeches. I never really thought about it, but it takes a special skill to convince those with everything that you have something they want. Or if you're real good, something they need.

My father was always great at that part of the job. Mom said he could sell water to a drowning man and leave him thirsty for more. Right now, I wish I had some of that confidence.

How can I possibly convey the gravity of the situation to people who weren't there to witness the portal? I don't know, but I have to try.

"What Michael says is true. Right now, leaders from all over are currently meeting to discuss the fate of Mythos. Ithus granted one of his clerics the power to open a portal above Mosstar, allowing us to view the city for the first time in centuries." Michael frowns at the mention of the trickster god, but I continue.

"It's worse than we feared. Valmar has an undead army surrounding the city. Thousands of skeleton warriors that are waiting for his command. Not to mention the other kingdoms and alliances he has under his thumb."

"What's that have to do with us?" asks Randy.

My grip clenches around the mug. This is the reaction I was worried about.

"By the end of the night, I expect the council to give the order to prepare for war. We've found a way to bypass the locked portals, and if we can rally together in time, there may be a chance to attack Valmar before he suspects anything."

Randy takes a long swig of his ale. "Let me guess, you want us to come fight the undead army?"

"That's the gist of it."

Now comes the part where they argue that this isn't their fight and that none of this really matters.

Randy drains the rest of his mug and slams it to the table. "Alright, tell me when and where."

I cross my arms, staring at the troublesome, dark-haired rogue and wondering what I actually heard him say. Because there is no way he agreed that easily.

"What?" Randy frowns.

"You'll fight?" I can't keep the incredulous tone from my voice.

"That's what we're here for, right? To be heroes?" He grins.

"I'll be honest, I thought you would take more convincing."

"What? You think we were all just hanging out in Pruxford after the attack for our health?" He laughs. "We made our choice when we decided to fight back in the arena. We could have tucked tail then. For me at least, competing in the tournament made me realize something. That I can actually leave my mark on this place. And how better than cutting my way through the biggest bad this world has ever seen." He stands up and looks around the room. "Who's with me?"

Heavy mugs thud against the tables in response.

I turn to the bartender and raise my glass. "Keep 'em coming. We've got a lot to discuss."

We stay downstairs until the wee hours of the morning discussing the best ways to level and grind over the coming week. There's still no word from Taryn on the council's decision, but we're moving forward with our plans all the same.

As stressful as it may be, my heart is full by the time we say good night. Tomorrow, we'll go our separate ways and reconvene in a week.

Michael the paladin is the last one to leave. He puts a firm hand on my shoulder, and his deep blue eyes stare into my own. "The goddess approves of our work here today, though she is wary of the promises of Ithus. They are a trickster by nature, but chaos itself is not inherently bad, just unexpected."

I take a deep breath and pat him on the back. "I hope you're right."

I'm walking upstairs when several notifications flash in the corner of my vision. I hurry to my room and open them.

Regional Alert! *The Pruxford Council has declared war upon Mosstar. Able-bodied citizens must report to the Crystal Arena at first light for conscription.*

> **Regional Alert!** *Mistville has declared war upon Mosstar.*
> **Regional Alert!** *Antadale has declared war upon Mosstar.*
> **Regional Alert!** *Ellynmylly has declared war upon Mosstar.*

Regional Alert! *Vanaria has declared war upon Mosstar.*
Regional Alert! *Wandermere has declared war upon Mosstar.*
Regional Alert! *Seascape has declared war upon Mosstar.*

Holy shit! They did it! I can feel the knots in my shoulders release as I read through the alerts from each kingdom.

Below the regional alerts, there is one more.

Alert! *The Forest Troll Tribe has declared war upon Mosstar. Gather at the troll castle in Tawdrybluff for further instructions from Chief Rizza.*

I imagine every citizen from each kingdom received a similar alert with instructions on what to do next. My plans lie far from Tawdrybluff, but I'll convene with Chief Rizza in the morning before leaving.

We've crossed the first hurdle, but we are far from the finish line. Now, we're in a race against the clock.

9. SOMETHING WORTH FIGHTING FOR

The next morning, Taryn and I sit down for a final breakfast at the Puzzling Peacock before heading to the palace to meet with Chief Rizza and pick up Limery. After that, we'll be off to our next adventure.

We grab a table in the far corner, out of earshot of the other patrons. None of the other heroes are here, so they're either already on the road or still sleeping. Considering I was the final person to turn in last night, my money is on the former.

I still need to tell Taryn about the message from Valery, but I haven't found the right opening. Flubs perches on the windowsill, pawing at the glass as the streets come to life. Ruby curls between Taryn's feet underneath the table. It's strange not having Limery here, but he's long overdue for some family time.

The barmaid quickly brings a steaming platter of food, and we fill our plates. The smell of savory sausage and bacon has my mouth watering.

"Remind me to never go into politics." Taryn talks with a full mouth as he holds a piece of buttered bread as if deciding whether or not to stuff it in as well. "What did Richard want with you, anyway?"

"More of the same." I roll my eyes. "But he says we can trust him. Not that we have much of a choice." I take a bite of warm sausage, letting the sweet and spicy juices explode in my mouth before changing the subject. "Was the rest of the council that bad?"

Taryn leans his head back, and his dreadlocks fall down the back of the chair. He stares at the ceiling a moment before answering. "Worse."

"For what it's worth, I never doubted you for a second."

He chuckles. "It wasn't me. It was all Orso, Favian, and Rizza. Between the three of them, they weren't letting anyone leave that council room without getting what they wanted. Some of the others though, ugh. They were so stubborn."

I take a bite of egg and let my fork rest on the plate. "They're scared. Worried for their people, too."

"Yeah, I know. But we're here to help." Taryn sighs. "We won't be here forever."

My posture stiffens, and he immediately notices.

"What?" His brow arches as he gives me a questioning look.

"There's something I need to tell you." I nervously run a claw through the tip of my braid. "I received a message from Valery while we were at the council."

I do my best to keep my voice down as I read him the message in full.

Taryn's eyes go wide, and he forgets all about the plate of food in front of him. "Why do you think they're shutting it down? You think it's unsafe?"

"I don't know. She didn't make it seem like we were in danger. Maybe it has something to do with letting me stay in here after my sentence. Or you and Dorothy joining. Somehow, I get the feeling that mixing a program designed for prisoners with the general public might be frowned upon." I shrug. "Whatever it is, she thinks there's hope to keep the program running even if we're forced out. You're the only one I've told, and I think we should keep it that way. The other heroes are going to help us fight. But we need to level up as much as we can between now and then, starting with Goldspire."

Ruby places her paws on Taryn's leg and nuzzles against his arm, begging for food.

Taryn scratches her behind the ears. "I know, girl. I won't let anything happen to you."

We finish our meal in silence, each of us left to our own thoughts. Taryn cares for his pets just as much as I care for Limery and the trolls. I know he'd do anything to save them.

Our first stop before heading to the palace is the Rusty Bucket so we can gather Jordy, Berry, and Caustic. Berry stands on his hind legs, looking over the enclosure, and nearly tackles Taryn to the ground when Breebis opens the gate. Jordy is more reserved, lowering his head and gently ramming Taryn in the leg until he gets his attention.

Caustic's wingspan is now wide enough that he's forced to tuck his wings and waddle down the corridor as he exits. He's almost unrecognizable from the dragon that was smaller than Jordy when we first arrived in Pruxford. He huffs and lowers his head until it's inches from mine.

I lean forward and touch my horns to the top of his head. "I hope you had fun last night, because we've got some tough times ahead of us."

His chest purrs in affirmation, and I stroke the firm, cool scales of his jaw.

After we pay for the pets's stay, there's an awkward moment where Taryn and Breebis are staring at each other. I get the sense that they're wanting a chance for a more intimate good-bye.

A grin tugs at my mouth, and I clear my throat to try and conceal it. "Thanks for taking such good care of Caustic. I'll be outside whenever you all are done."

Breebis offers me a warm smile. "Stay safe out there. Caustic is powerful, but he's still young."

I raise my brows suggestively at Taryn, as I leave and his cheeks flush with color. I'm glad he's found someone he enjoys spending time with. It's just one of the many reasons why we have to leave this world better than we found it.

A few minutes later, he rejoins us outside the entrance.

"Not a word." He narrows his eyes at me.

Luckily for him, Limery isn't around to sing "Taryns has a girl-friends" on repeat.

<hr>

We make our way through crowded streets toward the palace. This is the busiest the city has been since the tournament as all of the able-bodied citizens in Pruxford report to the Crystal Arena to begin the war effort. Taryn rides atop Berry with Ruby curled in his lap and Flubs tucked somewhere within his cloak. Jordy brings up the rear, following close behind the umber bear and occasionally ramming Berry in the backside when traffic slows. We tower over the diminutive gnomes all around us, surrounded by a sea of jeweled-toned skin and hair.

I can sense the tension in the air as gnomes talk in hushed voices about the threat beyond—and within—their borders.

There's mention of the sea orcs from Blacktide and the elves of Mosstar, but no one speaks of the undead army lying in wait. They have no idea what's coming. Everyone knows of the attack on the arena, but the regional alert didn't explain what we are up against. Most of them don't even know that Valmar still exists, let alone what he's been up to.

They will soon enough.

The flow of traffic shifts when we pass the arena and continue toward the palace. We push our way through the steady current of gnomes, and a gnawing thought tugs at me as we pass by. How many of them won't return from Mosstar? How many families will be forever changed by what happens in the next week?

I wish there was another way, but there isn't. There's a time for diplomacy and there's a time for action. After seeing the undead army, I know we're going to need every able body we can find to put an end to it.

Caustic roars overhead, pulling me from my morose thoughts. There's no doubt that he senses my unease.

Up ahead, carriages are parked outside the steps to the palace as the leaders depart. I catch a glimpse of sunset-colored fins through a carriage window as the Mistville Court passes by. At the bottom of the stairs, the gleam of the mana-infused wyrm's scales shimmers in the morning light. Caustic dives from the sky, landing with a thud beside the wyrm.

The two dragons click their snouts and peck at one another in greeting, and the guards surrounding the palace entryway take a couple of steps back.

Chief Rizza, King Favian, and King Orso stand together, their conversation interrupted by the raucous dragons. Jira and the other advisors are nearby. Lord Kassidy waves his hand, and a fruit tart teleports in front of him. Limery and Leo sit on the stairs, watching the bright-colored fish as they dart beneath the translucent glass while Lillith and Bazel sit a few steps higher, holding hands and watching their children.

"Chods!" Limery flies over once he notices me, wrapping his warm, spindly arms around my neck. "We dids it! Now we's can fights the bad mans."

"You did good." I pat him on the back. "We're going to have to leave soon to go train. Spend some more time with Leo and I'll come get you when it's time to go."

"Okies." He squeezes me one more time before returning to his brother.

"There's the troll of the hour." King Favian offers me his arm, and we shake. His smile is friendly, but his gaze is penetrating as he squeezes my forearm. "We held up our end of the bargain, but we'd all like to know what is so urgent that we're rushing the attack?"

I look around at the crowd of soldiers, advisors, and leaders. "Is there somewhere we can talk in private?"

Between the crowded streets and departing council, there's not a lot to choose from. We cross the street and enter an alley between two shops that are currently closed. Taryn and Berry guard the entrance to make sure no one overhears.

The three leaders of the Isle of Mythos watch me expectantly.

I meet each of their eyes before speaking. "I need your word that what I'm about to share with you will remain between us. Not even the other heroes can know."

They each share a questioning glance before voicing their agreement.

"There's no easy way to put this." I rub the back of my neck as I try to find the best way to deliver the news. "The reason we need to rush the attack is because the heroes won't be here for much longer. Taryn and I are the only ones who know this, but we'll be returning to the world from which we came soon. There are powers beyond our control. I'm not sure how much time we have, but I believe it's at least a week. Possibly longer, but there's a chance we have even less time. That's why we must act now, while we have the opportunity." I pause to let the words sink in, and though each of the leaders holds their stoic expressions, I'm certain this is alarming news for them.

"I'm not sure if or when we'll be coming back to Mythos, but I want to end this threat before we're forced to leave. The good news is that most of the heroes have agreed to fight Valmar. They'll be training and preparing as much as possible between now and then. As much as I'm grateful for their participation, I don't know if they would have the same fervor if they knew their days here were numbered."

"I see." Chief Rizza nods solemnly. "Mythos will be forever grateful that a troll such as yourself showed up in the forest when you did, Chod. If this is the time we are given, then the trolls will be ready."

"Vanaria as well." King Favian echoes. "We face the challenge of our lifetime. It's a chance to leave the world better for our sons and daughters, and for those who come after."

King Orso strokes his beard. "You were wise to press the matter as you did. Seascape will be ready when the time comes. What are your plans in the meantime?"

"We'll be returning to Goldspire. There's a final task I must complete."

King Orso glances at Taryn before extending a hand. "If you require anything of us, you need only ask."

"Thank you."

We say our farewells, and then Taryn guides Berry into the street so that we can exit the alley.

I stop beside him as the leaders return to the carriages. "What was that all about?"

"What?" He shifts uncomfortably in the saddle.

"That look between you and Orso."

"I'm..." His brow furrows, and he wears a pained expression. "I'm not going with you to Goldspire."

I take a step back, surprised at his words. "What do you mean you're not going?"

"I mean I'm not going." He sets his jaw with determination. "I love you, Chod. And I love the adventures we've experienced together in this world, but right now, we need to do what is right for all of Mythos. Your path is in Goldspire. You need your warforged class for what's coming. Limery and Caustic will be there to help you but for me, I feel like I need to be in Seascape with my people. I can help the dwarves. Maybe Chief Laojin can guide me further down my druid path. There's a lot I can do that doesn't involve waiting around while you get your ass kicked." He offers me a weak smile. "I hope you understand."

As much as I don't want to see him go, I do.

"You're right. Now is the time to push ourselves, and you should do that in the way that's best for you. Once I become Warforged, we'll find you. And then we can kick some undead ass together."

Taryn laughs. "Try not to die too much without me watching your back."

I give him a hug. "I'll do my best."

We return to the others as they are saying their final good-byes. Lillith and Bazel's bulging eyes glisten with tears as they embrace Limery.

"Don't cries, Mommy and Daddies. Limmy will be back soons."

Lillith locks her bulbous yellow eyes with mine. "You take care of my boy, Chod."

"Most of the time, he's the one taking care of me." I wink. "We'll see you soon enough."

Once his parents release him, Limery turns to his brother. "When we's gets back, maybe Limmy and Leos can goes on adventures together?"

Leo runs his spindly red fingers through his mohawk and grins. "Sounds good, little brother."

Limery extends his hand like I taught him, forming a fist, and the two brothers fist-bump, mimicking an explosion as they pull apart.

The imps join Chief Rizza atop her wyrm, and Taryn follows behind King Orso and King Favian's carriage on Berry as they clatter down the road. My best friend gives me a salute and turns away.

Limery perches on my shoulder, and Caustic grunts his displeasure as his new friend slithers toward the portal. For a moment, I stand there, watching them go. These are the people I'm fighting to protect. They might not be living, but they're real, and they've changed my life for the better because I met them.

If some dark wizard thinks he can take that away from me, then I'll raze his entire kingdom to the ground.

10. GOLDSPIRE

Limery, Caustic, and I arrive at the Pruxford portal ready for our next adventure. While there are more guards stationed around the square than when we first arrived in the city, it feels strangely empty with most of the citizens at the arena.

White energy swirls within the portal as I search the gateway for the rune to Goldspire. I find the one resembling a house with two vertical lines and a caret symbol over the top. The land of beastkin is the only portal I know of that has two separate entrances —one for newcomers that exits into a gladiatorial arena and a second one for those who have already proven themselves worthy.

Despite having open borders, Goldspire is a tough place to enter. Anyone who wishes to visit the kingdom must defeat one of the gladiators in combat. The first time we tried to enter, I got my head stomped in by a minotaur, losing all of my items in the process. According to Portia Swiftwill, the foxkin bartender, those who have passed the test enter through a separate portal on subsequent visits. This will be the first time I put it to the test. Just in case, I summon horrors and equip the Renewal Spear before we enter.

While I wait for the cooldowns on my horrors to reset, I talk to Limery. "I'm not sure where the portal will send us since Caustic has never been to Goldspire. We'll need to be prepared for a fight either way."

If we're forced to fight again, we're going in guns blazing.

We go over a few tactics as my horrors slowly build up. Aside from the dungeon with the tunnel drakes, this will be the first time the three of us have fought together without Taryn, so we need to be on the same page. We'll have less support than usual, but I'm confident in the synergy of our abilities.

Once I have sixty horrors summoned, I turn to Limery, who still sits perched on my shoulder. "You ready?"

He flashes me a demonic grin. "Limmy is readies."

Caustic growls his affirmation. We're ready.

The rune for Goldspire flares red when I focus on it, and white energy surrounds us as we enter the portal enveloped by a sound-less vacuum. A weight settles on my shoulders in that brief moment. I might have the benefit of the Revive Potion but failure is not an option. Not anymore. Bright light greets us as we enter an arena, along with the chaos of battle.

Of course. I should have known this wouldn't come easy.

We're surrounded by a rustic stone coliseum with high walls that block the view of the city beyond. The air is hot and dry from the morning sun that beams across a clear blue sky, casting much of the arena in shadow and showcasing the gladiators as violent silhouettes across the sandy expanse. Several battles rage around us, and the clink of clashing metal sings a harmony with roars, screams, and blaring trumpets that echo across the pit. In the center, Mordrir—the spear-wielding satyr—fights a lion beastkin.

They trade blows in a flurry until the spear pierces the lion's chest to the delight of the crowd.

Caustic's chest rumbles in challenge.

As I take in the gladiators, I notice something that I missed during my first two times here. Most of the fights are actually gladiators fighting one another to entertain the crowd. Since the arena is enchanted, whenever a gladiator dies, they respawn a little while later.

Challengers are not so lucky.

My grip tightens on the Renewal Spear, and mana surges to my fingertips, tingling with the excitement of battle. "I guess we're going to have to do this again."

When we first entered Goldspire, I was only level twenty-one. With Taryn and Limery, it had proven too much of a challenge. On our second attempt, I was level twenty-four and aided by Pressley, Limery, and Taryn.

This time, I'm level thirty with a dragon.

"Nice horns." Dakota's deep voice carries over the other fights. The level-thirty-three minotaur cracks his knuckles as he approaches, every bit as intimidating as I remember. "Seems you've been busy." His mouth curls into a smile.

I return his smile with a grin of my own. "I'm just getting started."

The minotaur is as tall as I am and a bit wider, with broad shoulders covered in radiant golden fur. His muscles ripple and sand stirs with each step, leaving a plume of dust in his wake. Two massive obsidian horns stretch the width of his body, and a silver nose-ring gleams in the morning sun. He wears a black leather loincloth, and two vambraces cover his powerful fore-arms. His weapon is unique, a thick chain weighted on one end with a metal ball and tipped on the other with a sickle. When out of combat, he wears the weapon wrapped around his waist like a belt.

He stops a few dozen paces from the portal and steam shoots from his nostrils. "You know the rules. If you wish to enter the lands of Goldspire with your new companion, step forward. Otherwise, be gone."

Limery grows warm against my shoulder before taking to the air, and Caustic huffs as he moves to my side.

I step into the arena, and my hands tingle with excitement. "Unfortunately for you, we're in a bit of a hurry, and you're standing between me and something I desperately want." I grin again, showcasing my tusks in all their glory. "Limery, use Whispers."

Limery pulls the stopper from the Whispers of the Damned pendant around his neck, and the screams of sea orcs flow out in silver wisps. The dying breaths of the last three enemies he killed charge toward Dakota, penetrating his fur and confusing him for the next five seconds.

The giant minotaur sways back and forth as the sounds of anguish surround him. I almost feel bad for the guy as we go on the attack.

Almost.

Caustic's wings flap like sails as he flies, and he unleashes a stream of toxic gas that shrouds the gladiator in a green cloud. As soon as the torrent of gas halts, there's a crackle as Limery summons a fireball, tossing it at the gas and setting off a thunderous explosion.

Warm air whooshes past, stirring up sand as the smell of toxic gas and singed fur fills the area. I cast Sacrifice on all of my horrors and wait for the smoke to clear. My muscles bulge from the influx of stats to Strength, Dexterity, and Constitution. As soon as I see the tips of Dakota's horns appear, I take a step and throw the Renewal Spear like a javelin with every bit of power I can muster. The bonus Dexterity keeps my aim true. There's a half-second where the minotaur regains his senses and his eyes go wide in surprise before the tip of the spear plunges into his skull.

Dakota collapses to the ground, a pile of smoking meat, and the crowd erupts. I wave to them, savoring the moment because I know things will only get tougher from here.

Congratulations! *You have defeated a gladiator in the Goldspire Arena. You now have access to the continent.*

Caustic lands next to the downed gladiator and sniffs at the burned corpse. I activate Return to Sender, and the spear dislodges from Dakota's skull with a sickening crunch before flying back to my palm. In a few minutes, he'll respawn to battle once again.

"Easies peezies." Limery returns to his perch on my shoulder, his body still warm from the fight.

I chuckle at another of the phrases Taryn has taught him. "Good job, both of you. Now, let's get the hell out of here."

Once outside the arena, Goldspire is just as I remember it. The city moves around us without a care in the world. Beastkin of all shapes and sizes stroll leisurely down the stone streets, as if time doesn't exist. There are temples with colorful mosaics, and olive trees sway gently in the breeze on every corner. Many of the businesses are open-air, with beautiful arches and elaborate columns, and verandas with expansive views line the top floors of buildings along the streets.

Caustic catches the eye of many beastkin as we make our way to the Wilty Rose Inn. Even in a land of beasts, dragons are still revered. And unlike the last time I was here, I can finally hold my own against the threats of this continent.

We pass several gardens with lush vegetation, and Caustic stops for a drink by a gurgling canal that carries water to the many bathhouses. In the forum, there are musicians and poetry readings around the towering golden spire for which the city is named.

From the open courtyard, we can see the far side of the city where the royal palace looms from the hilltop. As much as I disagree with Emperor Festa Forgetooth's decision to keep her lands free from foreign conflicts, I do understand it. They have a thriving, peaceful way of life here.

Compared to the tension in Pruxford, this is like a different world. But even if Goldspire doesn't join the fight, this is what we are fighting for, to ensure that every kingdom has the opportunity for this kind of peace.

First, we must find Jegaar. Portia will be our best hope of tracking down the battle scholar since I don't have the faintest idea of where the Scholars Guild is located or where her childhood friend may be. Luckily, I still have the Wilty Rose Inn marked on my map.

When we arrive, I order Caustic to wait outside now that he's much too big to enter most buildings. The days of him snuggling on my chest as I fall asleep are long gone. Now, I'm the one to rest against his massive body.

Inside the inn, a black-feathered falcon beastkin works the bar. The downstairs tavern is empty except for a minotauress and a panther beastkin sharing a bottle of rose-colored wine.

They play a game with different colored stones on a checkered board.

"How may I help you today?" the falcon asks.

"We're looking for Portia. Any idea where she is?"

He shakes his head. "Currently, no, but she should be in for her shift in a couple of hours. You're welcome to have a drink and wait."

Limery's eyes bulge as he leans against the counter. "Oh, yes. Limmy would loves a drinks."

"Excellent. It's a warm day out. Might I suggest an ice wine? The rosé we just got in is especially nice."

"Limmy loves the ice wines!" The imp clasps his hands together and grins. "Its makes hims feels tinglies."

I hold up two fingers. "Make it two."

The bartender pours us both a glass and slides them across the bar. The wine has a faint pink color and the bubbles that rise from the bottom of the glass have a calming effect.

Item. Ice Wine. _-2 Intelligence for one hour. Bonus Effect: Grants a cooling chill all over the body._

I take a sip, and it's like I've stepped into a freezer on a hot day as chills erupt along my body. The sweat on the back of my neck crystalizes, a welcome feeling, and next to me, Limery sighs contentedly. The feeling must be euphoric to his naturally hot body.

I raise my glass to the bartender. "Good choice."

He raises an eyebrow as he examines me. "You know, you look familiar. Unless I'm mistaken, you were here with a dwarf some time ago." He leans in closer, squinting. "Something's different about you, though."

I laugh, tapping a claw against my horn. "These are a new addition."

"That's it." He snaps a feather-covered finger. "You wear them well."

We make small talk over the next half-hour, which eventually turns to talk of our travels and the world outside of Goldspire. I tell him about the attack on Pruxford and the other kingdoms.

"I had no idea." He leans back against the wall, crossing his wing-like arms. They're covered with feathers, but strangely humanlike at the same time. "Though we're free to come and go as we please, Goldspire doesn't interact much with the outside world. Why would we?" He shrugs. "Life is good here. The loss of life is a travesty nonetheless, but I trust that Emperor Festa keeps us isolated for good reason."

That's easy for him to say when orcs and the undead aren't spilling into his backyard.

Even though I know it's not his fault, I finish off my glass of wine to keep from biting his head off. "I'm going to step outside for some fresh air."

Limery leans against the bar, softly snoring with his head on his hands.

Outside, a crowd has gathered around Caustic. The dragon preens himself, and I can tell he's putting on a show for the onlookers.

The beastkin admiring him are all leveled into their twenties. The strongest of the bunch is a small, cream-colored ratkin that's level twenty-nine.

Another reminder that there's so much power here. Most of Goldspire's civilians are on par with the other kingdoms' soldiers, and yet we can't convince them to lift a paw or a finger.

Caustic senses my frustration and nuzzles his head against my chest.

"A magnificent creature." The ratkin places a hand on its

chest. "It has been far too long since I've last seen a dragon. And a green one at that, magnificent."

"Thank you." I scratch Caustic underneath the chin. "He's still young, but he's growing fast."

They stand around for a few more minutes, ogling and asking questions before heading on their way. Once they're gone, I take a seat on the steps, stewing in silence. Caustic rests his head on my lap with a huff.

"Is that you, Big Blue?" I recognize Portia's vulpine voice before I see her.

The foxkin is a sight for sore eyes, and I forget about my frustrations for a moment as I take in her striking figure. Her orange fur is vibrant in the midday sun, and she wears a teal sash around her head, just below her pointy ears, that perfectly complements her coloring. Several small golden hoops dangle from her left ear. She wears a yellow tunic embroidered with a wilted red rose and silky pants that match her teal headband, almost mesmerizing the way they flow with her every movement. On her right hip rests an ornate dagger.

Portia stops next to me, fluttering her lashes and smiling. "You know, just the other day, I was wondering what you all had gotten yourselves into. Last we talked, you were heading to Frostmoor, was it?"

"We've been busy, alright."

"You'll have to tell me all about it." She reaches out a hand, hovering it a few inches from my horn. "May I?"

I nod, and she caresses her finger around the icy blue tip of the horn.

"A ram?" Portia laughs. "You did strike me as the stubborn type. I've heard of the Spirit of the Beast path, though not many beastkin have taken it. What brings you back to Goldspire?"

"I need to find Jegaar. Any chance you can point me in the right direction?"

She smiles. "Of course, but why don't we step inside first?"

I stand, crossing my arms. "I'll be honest with you, we're on a bit of a time-sensitive mission. I'd love to sit and talk about all we've been through since leaving Goldspire, but it's imperative that I meet with Jegaar as soon as possible."

Her brow furrows. "I see."

She steps past me and enters the inn. Limery is still passed out and has a giant snot bubble expanding with each breath.

"Falc, can you cover my shift tonight?" Portia gives him a pleading look. "I'll owe you one."

The falcon beastkin narrows his eyes at the foxkin and sighs. "I was supposed to go see Uncaged Minotaurs perform tonight. You owe me more than one."

"Deal." Portia smiles as she turns to me. "Find the dwarf, grab the imp, and let's get moving."

I can't help laughing at her enthusiasm. "It's actually just us this time. I guess you'll get to hear the whole story soon enough."

"Alright, big guy, try to keep up. The Scholars Guild is on the far side of the city."

"Of course it is." I scoop Limery off the bar and follow Portia out the door.

II. SCHOLARS GUILD

Portia takes our urgency to heart, moving swiftly through the streets. Caustic flies overhead, his shadow occasionally crossing our path. The foxkin is quick on her feet, like a breeze flowing through the city. In contrast, I lumber behind her carrying Limery, the imp's head bobbling in my arms as I hurry to keep up.

"Wake up, you little drunk." I jostle Limery enough to stir him awake.

He grumbles something unintelligible and buries his head against my chest.

"Wake up." I prod him again. "We're going to see Jegaar."

Limery lifts an arm, attempting to block the sun with his spindly fingers. "Okays, okays. Limmy will gets up."

He crawls from my arm, hovering in the air for a moment before fire flashes across his entire body and the effects of his day drinking vanish in an instant.

"That's betters." He grins as he darts upward to join Caustic.

Portia looks over her shoulder and laughs. "He's a funny little guy."

"He's something, alright." I smile at Limery and Caustic overhead as the duo perform a series of synchronized barrel-rolls. It must be amazing to see the city from that high up.

Portia leads us through a maze of streets and alleys as we journey across the city. I'm sure she's taking the most expedient route, but Goldspire is a sprawling city, and I don't recognize any of the structures from our last time here. At one point, we cut through a butterfly garden full of fragrant flowers. A pleasant aroma envelops me, and I stop, admiring the beauty of the butterflies as one lands upon my arm. I suddenly have the urge to lay down for a nap. The butterfly flaps its wings, and a prismatic dust sprinkles upon my blue skin.

"Oh no you don't." Portia wipes away the dust and grabs me by the arm, pulling me across the garden until the urge passes.

Soon after, we enter an imposing section of tall buildings and temples near the outer wall. Part of me wonders what threats wait beyond the borders of a city this powerful to warrant such defenses. Several guards patrol the parapet as the sun begins to set, and their shadows streak across the city like giants.

Portia stops in front of a building with colossal columns running along its facade. A multitude of stairs lead up to the building, and a statue of a lion beastkin stands out front, nearly as tall as the structure itself. The lion holds a book in one hand and a torch raised in the other. I stop for a moment to take in the beauty of the figure.

"Is this it?" I ask Portia.

"Close, but no." She grins. "This is the Goldspire Library. It pays for the Scholars Guild to be nearby in case they need reference materials. Follow me, though you'll probably want your dragon to wait outside."

Caustic lands at the foot of the statue, and I scratch him underneath the wing. "Wait here until we return."

He replies with a low growl and curls up in front of the lion's feet.

Portia leads us around the side of the library to a topiary garden filled with half a dozen fountains. Bushes are shaped into tigers, elephants, giraffes, and a host of other creatures, and calming water trickles all around. I could imagine losing hours to this place with a good book under the bright Goldspire sun.

Limery sits on my shoulder as I follow her further into the garden to a pergola covered in gorgeous pale-purple flowers. They dangle from the posts like curtains, rustling gently in the breeze. Inside the pergola, there's a raised pool on one end with four small tiger statues on each corner gazing into the water.

Portia rests her hand on one of the statues and pushes. The stone clicks as a mechanism activates, followed by the gurgle of water as it's displaced. The bottom of the pool lowers, forming stairs that lead underground.

I peer over the edge of the pool. "You guys really love your hidden entrances, huh?"

Portia smirks. "The surface of Goldspire may glitter, but the heart of this city is buried beneath."

I'm reminded of the underground fight club from our last visit, and how different it felt from the relaxed and peaceful atmosphere aboveground.

In one graceful movement, Portia leaps over the edge. "Watch your step. It can be a bit slippery."

I step into the pool and descend the stairwell into a surprisingly pristine corridor. The walls are polished marble, with elaborate sconces lighting the way.

Portia waits for us a short way into the tunnel.

"How do you know about the secret entrance?" I ask.

"Jegaar showed it to me many years ago when he was just a pup filing papers for the guild, long before he was a revered fighter and battle scholar. Sometimes he needed a break from the monotony. I would meet him by the pool, and we'd go for a little adventure around the city." Her green eyes sparkle at the memory. "There are a few more entrances I know of—one within the library, and the official entrance near the city offices, and probably a few more known only to the guild."

We follow Portia down the corridor, taking a sharp left and then a right before coming to a stop in front of a secure bronze door. Its massive hinges and sleek face remind me of a bunker entrance. There's no handle or knob, only a series of runes running along the outside.

"How are we supposed to get inside?" I ask.

Portia bursts out laughing. Then she raps her knuckles against the door.

The runes around the edge flash turquoise, and an orange circle forms in the center of the door at about eye level. The circle grows brighter, almost as if the metal is melting, and an eyehole forms through the thick slab.

A moment later, a bright blue eye peers through the peephole, and I swear someone laughs on the other side. As quickly as it appeared, the eyehole vanishes and the runes fade. Metal clicks, clanks, and grinds as hinges and latches unlock.

When the door opens, Jegaar wears a look of amusement. Gone are the gladiator skirt, buckler shield, and morning star he wielded at our first meeting at the underground fight club. Instead, he looks every bit the scholar in a neatly buttoned shirt and khaki pants. Some kind of magnifying contraption covers one eye, and he holds a massive bone nearly the size of a club. His fur is the arid tan of desert sand, so thick and shaggy that I'm still not sure how he's native to a climate as warm as Goldspire and not the frigid lands of Frostmoor. His bright blue eyes are piercing as he takes us in, his gaze lingering on my horns for a moment before moving to Limery and Portia. His husky tail swishes behind him, tipped black at the end to match his pointed ears and paws.

"You're not at all who I was expecting but a pleasant surprise nonetheless." He laughs as he removes the spectacled contraption and steps aside, gesturing with the bone for us to enter. "Come in. I'm in the process of cataloging some rare bones for the library."

Inside, the room is even more bunker-like. There are no windows, but plenty of lamps cast the room in a warm glow. All four walls, the ceiling, and floor are constructed from the same bronze metal as the door. There are two other exits, each one as impenetrable as the door we entered.

For all of its imperviousness, the room still resembles the haphazard office of a professor. Shelves line the perimeter, filled with books, scrolls, and manuscripts. There are locked boxes, precious stones, and artifacts scattered everywhere, along with a litany of notes and scribblings I can't decipher. In the center, one table is covered with the bones of partial skeletons. There's a skull of a ram with horns nearly as big as my own, and what I think to be the verte-brae of a snake mixed among the scatterings. The table next to it is littered with journals and textbooks, and a ring is clamped beneath a magnifying glass. It shimmers in the light of a white-flamed candle.

Item. Mysterious ring. ???

That's odd. The description reminds me of the Mysterious Green Egg I hatched Caustic from. The description didn't change to Green Dragon Egg until I discovered what it was. Whatever this ring is, it's either very rare or very powerful.

Jegaar steps beside me when he notices me staring at the ring. "This one has baffled the entire guild. It was recovered from the tomb of an infamous rogue. Supposedly, the ring grants the wearer invisibility when activated." He tilts the magnifying glass until it settles on cursive script barely readable within the metal.

"This inscription is a language I haven't been able to decipher. The ring was found in Ellynmylly, but the text doesn't match any of their native tongues. I've been sorting through dead languages but so far, no luck." He shakes his head. "But never mind that. To what do I owe the pleasure?"

"Chod is in need of your help..." Portia's attention falters, and she turns to the opposite table, examining the collection of bones. "Jegaar, is that one creature or three?" There's a reverence to her voice that I don't understand.

The wolfkin grins, revealing his sharp canines. "That is what I intend to find out. Either these are the remains of a chimera, or I have the useless bones of a lion, a goat, and a snake that happened to be buried in the same location."

Chimera? I remember the name from our days studying Greek mythology in school. As far as monsters go, they're pretty badass. I recall the creature having the body of a lion, with the head of a fire-breathing goat, and the tail of a venomous snake. This one seems different somehow, though I can't place what exactly is throwing me off.

Portia moves closer and runs her fingers over some of the bones. "How? I thought it was a myth."

"So did I, and yet..." He chuckles.

"What exactly is the chimera?" I ask.

Jegaar leans against the table. "There are some who believe that the chimera was the first beastkin. They believe that after the gods forged our lands and populated them with flora and fauna, they created the chimera as a guardian. The chimera was a mighty beastkin said to have two heads. One head was pure chaos—a goat capable of breathing fire that rivaled a dragon's. The other head was cunning and intelligent—the lion. Upon its rear, it had a tail tipped with the head of a venomous viper. Long before Goldspire had a name, it roamed the lands, guardian of everything within its domain."

That's what makes the bones look so different. It has the humanoid body of a beastkin and not the four-legged skeleton of a goat or lion.

He continues, "As time passed, the natures of the three beasts conjoined into one body began to darken. Its hunger grew, and it hunted the lands until no creatures remained. The gods looked down upon it with disdain, for they hadn't created a guardian but a creature with nothing more than an appetite for destruction. Even dragons take time to savor their kill and guard their hoard, but the chimera hunted day and night until the lands were barren. With the animals gone, chaos reigned, and the natural world fell out of balance. But still, the chimera's hunger grew, and with nothing to hunt, its powerful muscles shriveled away. When it was nothing more than skin and bones, the chimera turned to the gods. 'Save me,' it screamed. The gods were merciful, but they knew there was no place for this creature. They offered the chimera a choice. They could strike it down and end its suffering, or they could sate its hunger and allow it to make use of the time remaining.

"For the first time in its life, the chimera found peace. Its hunger abated, and it set about the task at hand. While it could not live on, it could leave a legacy. The gods granted the chimera the ability to infuse its remaining life force into the remains of whatever beings it chose. So, the chimera traveled through the graveyard of its destruction, giving life to bear and bird and all manner of animal it had once hunted. And that is the origin of the beastkin." Jegaar shrugs. "Or so they say."

"Do you believe it?" asks Portia.

"I'm a scholar. What I believe doesn't matter." He circles the table, eyes fixed on the scattered bones. "It's only what I can prove. Right now, I have someone searching the area where these were found for a split vertebrae. If it's located, then there may be some truth to the legends after all." He looks up, as if suddenly remembering we had a reason for being here. "You said Chod is in need of help?"

I nod. While the mythology of the beastkin is something I would love to dive into any other time, there are more pressing matters, so I elect to get straight to the point. "You told me to come find you when I reached level thirty. I'm ready to attempt the trials of the Warforged."

"So I did." He taps his chin with a dark claw. "I can sense a fire burning within you. I'm guessing this has something to do with the other kingdoms declaring war on Mosstar?"

"War?" Portia gasps, clearly unaware of the chaos happening beyond her borders.

"Yes, war." He shuffles a few papers and sets them aside. "There are few in Goldspire outside of the emperor's inner circle who are privy to the regional notices of other kingdoms. The Scholars Guild is an exception."

"Should I be concerned?" Portia's normally alluring tone is full of worry. Between learning of the chimera and Mosstar, her head must be spinning right now.

I look them both in the eye, answering before Jegaar has a chance to. "Kingdoms across Mythos have been attacked by creatures from the shadowlands. Pruxford suffered an attack from the sea orcs of Blacktide. And I've seen what waits for us in Mosstar. It's surrounded by an army of undead capable of razing cities to the ground. In a week, we plan to attack with everything we have. We'll gather with other heroes, adventurers, kings, and their armies in an attempt to end this threat once and for all. So, yes, you should be concerned. We know that Goldspire will not intervene, but know that if we fail, you will stand alone."

"As we always have." Jegaar's tone is gruff, but I can't tell if it's at me or the situation. He pauses for a moment, staring at his paws. "Though I may not agree with her decisions, our emperor has spoken, and our borders remain secure."

"Then I hope for your sake, we are successful." I take a breath to try and push the thought from my mind. For now, I need to focus on the present, on the reason I'm here. "So, can you guide me on the path to become Warforged?"

He looks me up and down. "We have a week?"

"Less. I will need time to return and prepare for the attack."

"I see." Jegaar strokes the fur on his chin. "I cannot promise you anything. I don't know what awaits within the trials, however, I do know the location for the trials' entrance. Once inside, there is no escape save death or victory. The challenge will be difficult, and more likely than not, you will fail, but if you have the mettle to endure, then you have the opportunity to reforge yourself into something greater."

"That's all I ask." My mouth curls into a devious snarl, and Limery's warm body matches my energy. "When can we start?"

Jegaar reaches for a notebook across the table. "I just need a minute to—" A knock at the door causes him to abandon the task. "Pardon me. As I said, I was expecting someone else when you arrived. This is probably them."

He traces a pattern on the door and runes blaze once again, mirroring the other side as a peephole forms. After Jegaar confirms the visitor, the latches and plates rearrange themselves, and the heavy door silently opens.

Armor clanks, and heavy boots thud against the floor as a tall figure steps inside covered in dark plate mail. Portia takes a step back at the stranger's appearance. A black aura seeps between the armored plates, and a dull buzz rattles within. A massive sword hangs from the visitor's waist.

"Chod." The stranger's voice is deep and distorted, like they're calling from the end of a cave. The warrior lifts his visor, revealing the blackness of death. "I like the new look."

"Thanks." As shocked as I am to see Pressley the death knight here, I'm even more surprised by his level.

Pressley Allen
Level 40
Death Knight
Human

Whatever he's been up to since we left, he's been busy.

12. A BAG OF BONES

Pressley's appearance is more sinister than ever as he stands in the doorframe. He's upgraded some of his gear since we last saw one another, and it has only added to his intimidating presence.

He's replaced the traditional knight's headgear with a black helm that has two horns jutting forward like a charging bull. The metal has red flecks that catch the lamplight, reminding me of Destroyer. Perhaps it too was forged in the heart of a volcano. A black iridescent cloak hangs from his shoulders, making him appear even larger, with a red skull that latches the cloak at the front. The dark metal of his breastplate is molded into a skull and crossbones, with a similar design on both kneecaps. The armor covering his boots curls up into a pointed spike at the ends.

"Presslies!" Limery flies over, grabbing hold of one of the horns and tapping the death knight's helm with his claws. A dull ring echoes from the opening, where his face is concealed behind a shroud of darkness.

Pressley grunts in response, and he hands a large satchel to

Jegaar as he steps into the room. The way the bag rattles when it changes hands, I can tell that it's filled with bones.

My gaze shifts from the death knight to the battle scholar and back again. "How the hell do you two know each other?"

Pressley went his own way once we entered the city, so it's a crazy coincidence that we're all here now.

"We're working together, in a manner of speaking." Jegaar sets the bag on the table. "You could say we each have something the other wants."

I look the death knight up and down. He must have been grinding nonstop since we parted. "How are you level forty? We weren't that far apart when I last saw you."

"I stay busy, and these lands are ripe with opportunity if you know where to look." He turns to face me, and I can feel his gaze even though his eyes are hidden behind darkness. "You seem to have done alright for yourself."

"I've been busy, too." I tap one of my horns and smile. "Though, it seems half my time is spent politicking lately. You're really leaning into the whole prince of darkness vibe, aren't you?"

"If people are going to fear me, I might as well act the part." He laughs, and the hollowness of it is a bit unsettling. "It's funny, though. The beastkin don't seem bothered by me nearly as much as the dwarves."

"We do not fear death." Jegaar peeks into the bag he's holding. "We welcome it with open arms when it arrives."

"Yeah, well, when it comes to those I care about, I want to fight it off for as long as possible." I turn back to Pressley. "What are you searching for, anyhow?"

"There's a creature called a manticore that resides in one of the dungeons outside of Goldspire. Apparently, only the Scholars Guild knows the exact location." He lets out a noise somewhere between a grunt and a sigh. "To save myself some time, I've been enlisted as an errand boy in exchange for the knowledge."

Jegaar scoffs. "I'd hardly call you an errand boy. You've gained a great deal of experience and levels in the name of academic research."

"Funny how this research consists of me fighting my way through a graveyard of dying beasts while you sit here playing with bones."

I can't help but laugh.

"What's so funny?" Pressley's armor clanks as he crosses his arms.

"It's not you. It's just that everything's a mystery here—hidden dungeons, hidden trials, hidden entrances to underground offices. The beastkin sure have a flare for the dramatic."

"What's life without a little mystery?" Jegaar turns to Pressley and gestures at the satchel. "May I?"

"Help yourself," Pressley's voice rumbles.

Jegaar empties the satchel onto an open section of the table, and bones spill from the bag. "To answer your question, Chod, Pressley is helping me with the chimera project. Being a death knight, he can sense bones in an area, locating them better than I could ever dream of. He can find corpses and remains, no matter how old or how deep they're buried. It would be a shame to waste an opportunity to use his skills. The chimera was long rumored to have been the first body to pass on in what is now known as the Valley of Death. So, I sent him there in search of the missing pieces."

The beastkin takes a bone and fits it in an open space along the lower spine of the chimera skeleton. His tail swishes as he searches the pile for another. I imagine fitting all of the pieces together is part of the joy of being a scholar.

"That's interesting. And in exchange, you show him how to find a manticore? Which is what, exactly?" I ask.

"It's a unique monster, and very powerful," Pressley answers. "They have the body of a lion, the wings of a dragon, and the tail of a scorpion. If I can defeat one, then I have an ability that allows me to enlist the reanimated corpse of a single unique monster to fight for me. I plan to use it as a mount."

The last time we fought together, his army of skeleton minions rivaled my horrors. At level forty, I can't even imagine what he's capable of summoning.

"Wouldn't the chimera be a better prize?" I ask.

"If it were a corpse, maybe, but the bones are so old that it could only be reanimated as a skeleton warrior. It would likely lose the perks of breathing fire and the venomous bite of its tail."

"Considering the chimera's history, that's probably for the best." Jegaar chuckles as he takes another bone and rearranges it several times in an attempt to fit it into place.

Pressley sighs, and it reminds me of a death rattle. "We'll be here all day waiting for you. Allow me to help."

Jegaar steps back, throwing his hands up. "By all means."

A deep purple aura swirls around Pressley's armored hand as he lifts his arm. The bones that were emptied from the bag all rise, glowing a vibrant white as they hover in the air. Limery's eyes bulge with anticipation when an outline forms over each bone, almost like a scientific diagram. I'm equally intrigued. With a flick of Pressley's wrist, the bones dart across the table, finding their proper position and forming the skeleton of the chimera in a matter of seconds. Midway up the spine, the vertebrae split into two separate columns, one for each head. Where a tailbone would be on a human skeleton, the end of the spinal column extends into a tail-like set of vertebrae ending with the head of a snake. It's both grotesque and strangely intriguing to look upon.

Portia covers her mouth as the pieces fall into place. Jegaar claps his hands and shakes his head in wonder.

"It's true," he whispers. "The legends were true."

"I can't believe it." Portia's eyes are as wide as saucers. "We've just witnessed history."

"You can write your histories later." Pressley flicks his hand, and the bones move from the air to the table, arranging themselves in perfect order. "I held up my end of the bargain, now it's your turn. Where can I find the manticore?"

"Heroes." Jegaar shakes his head. "Always in a hurry."

"My haste is none of your concern." There's an edge to his hollow voice that presses the issue. If there's anything I've learned about Pressley, it's that he doesn't stop when he's on a mission for something.

"No need to scuff your armor. I'm an honorable wolf, and you'll have your directions." Jegaar approaches the death knight and lifts a hand until it rests on the outside of Pressley's helm. There's a tiny spark just like when Chief Rizza gave me the knowledge of the ley lines on Isle of Mythos. "You're a powerful warrior, but the manticore will be a challenge even at your level."

Pressley grunts. "I will take my chances."

He turns to leave, but I call out after him.

"Wait." I rush across the room, blocking his exit. "You made a promise to me in the Glossop Forest. After we defeated the covey of hags you said, '*I will be there for you when the time comes for us to band together.*' Those were your words. And that time has come. In a week, all of the heroes and kingdoms I've been able to recruit will go to war with the dark wizard. We need you there."

The buzzing within his helm grows more intense and for a moment, I think he's going to push past me. But then he nods. "Then I will be there, but for now, I have business to attend to."

I press my hand against his breastplate as he tries to walk by.

"Just wait a moment. There might be a way for us to help one another." I turn to Jegaar. "These trials, will I be forced to enter alone?"

He looks at Limery and nods. "Unfortunately, yes."

Limery frowns. "Limmy can't goes?"

"Don't worry, buddy. It'll all work out." I pat him on the leg before returning my attention to Jegaar. "And what about a pet or a bonded creature? Can they enter?"

He shakes his head. "No. Your horrors will be available to you once inside, but no living creatures may pass into the trials or they will not begin."

"Not even a bonded dragon?" I ask, just to confirm.

"A dragon?" Jegaar's brow scrunches. "You have a dragon?" There's surprise in his voice, but he shakes his head. "Even still, no living creatures may accompany you."

I return my attention to Pressley. "It sounds like you're going to need help with this dungeon, and we're going to need everyone as strong as possible when the final battle comes. Take Limery and Caustic with you and they can help you with the manticore."

Limery flies across the room and perches on Pressley's shoulder. "Oh yes, Limmy and Caustics loves to fights."

There's a deep rumble within the death knight's armor. "Fine, but let's be on with it."

Jegaar looks pleadingly at the chimera skeleton. "One of the greatest mysteries of Goldspire's history unlocked, and I can't even savor the discovery before being whisked away." He sighs. "Come on, then. We're going to need a carriage."

He activates the runes on one of the interior doors and leads us down a pristine hallway. We pass at least a dozen other heavily armored bronze doors as we follow Jegaar through the maze of the Scholars Guild. Eventually, we come upon an opening where a wide stairwell leads to a massive arched doorway nearly two stories tall and embellished with elaborate knotwork.

"If you ever find yourself here again, those doors lead to the library." He points down another hallway. "This way leads to the stables, but we'll have to pass through Kolak's workroom to get there."

The second corridor has just as many closed doors as the first. I wonder how many scholars are a part of the guild. When we're almost at the end of the tunnel, Jegaar stops in front of a door and traces his fingers across the outside. Runes flash in a pattern different from the first, and then the mechanisms activate on the other side.

Inside, an elephant beastkin leans over a table examining a large shield covered with colorful gemstones. Dozens of golden earrings run along the edges of her massive ears, and she wears a magnifying contraption similar to Jegaar's over one eye. I take a moment to analyze the beastkin.

Kolak

Level ???

Scholar

Beastkin

She's not a battle scholar like Jegaar.

Kolak's trunk twitches as she makes eye contact with the wolfkin. "Do you ever knock?"

"We're just passing through." He holds up a hand in defense. "We'll only be a moment."

The room is similar to Jegaar's but with fewer bones, and two entrances instead of three. She has shelves filled with collections of precious stones and jewels. Many more sit on the table where she's working, and it appears she's trying to fill the empty sockets on the shield where some of the jewels have been removed.

Kolak lets out an agitated trumpet that reminds me of Stompy. "Just don't touch anything."

"I wouldn't dream of it." Jegaar smirks as we walk past. "I have something to show you when I return. It will blow even your giant mind, Kolak."

The elephant sits up, raising her magnifying contraption before her gaze pierces into the wolfkin. "Don't tease me, Jegaar. You know I hate being teased."

His lip curls from a smirk into a devious snarl. "I wouldn't dream of it." He runs his fingers across the outer door, and the runes flash. "See you later."

We exit into another marble corridor.

"She seems feisty." Portia laughs to herself. "There aren't many who will stand up to the mighty Jegaar."

"Oh, she is." Jegaar looks over his shoulder at the closed door. "And one of the best scholars in the guild. She has a knack for decoding, but she hates being disturbed."

"You all have access to one another's workspaces?" I ask.

"Not exactly. There are only two battle scholars in the guild, and we have the same access to guild workrooms and archives as the guild master. The scholars don't appreciate it when we barge in, but we're in a bit of a hurry at the moment."

Judging by Kolak's reaction, I get the feeling he's in a hurry more often than necessary.

As we near the end of the tunnel, the scent of hay and barn animals fills the narrow passage. The exit is less glamorous than the gardens by the library. There's no switch to activate, and instead, Jegaar pushes open a wooden door like one might find above an underground cellar. We step into an empty stall within the stables, and the neighs of horses and shouts of workers welcome us aboveground.

No one bats an eye as the four of us exit the stall into the main corridor.

"The manticore dungeon lies along the same route as the trials. We will travel together for part of the journey," Jegaar tells us before requesting a carriage from one of the stable-hands.

We wait out front as they prepare our ride, and I call to Caustic through our bond. A few minutes later, the flap of leathery wings announces his arrival. Jegaar watches him land with appreciation, and I'm not quite sure what Pressley is thinking.

"Is it friendly?" the death knight asks.

"Depends on who's asking." I grin as I call Caustic over and introduce the two. "This is Pressley. He's an old friend. While I'm completing the trials, you and Limery will be training with him, helping to clear a dungeon." I scratch him under the chin. "I need you to watch his back."

Caustic's chest rumbles, and he lowers his head until it's inches from Pressley's helm and sniffs. For a moment, I wonder if the aura around the death knight might be unsettling, but then Caustic extends his forked tongue and licks Pressley's helm, leaving a thick layer of slobber on the outside.

I laugh at the death knight as he tries to clean his helm. "I think you guys will be just fine."

13. COUNTRY ROADS

After a quick good-bye, Portia leaves us to return to the inn, and we find a carriage ready for us in front of the stables. It's pulled by two giant oxen, each one with a set of small wings just above the hooves on each leg. The two animals are both gray around the snout and not nearly as muscled as some of the others inside the stable. One of them has the milky eyes I've seen in older dogs.

Did we get the leftovers because of such short notice?

Pressley crosses his arms and huffs. "Do you expect me to reanimate them once we're on the road?"

Jegaar scratches one of the oxen behind the ears and smiles. "Winghoof oxen age like a fine wine, and these are two of the oldest in the kingdom. We use them for guild business whenever time is of the essence. I promise you, they are faster than they appear."

I take a moment to analyze the animals.

Winghoof Ox. *Level 28. Contrary to their appearance, winghoof oxen are not flying creatures. They are, however, fleet of hoof while still managing to pull heavy loads. Unlike most working cattle, elder oxen grow faster with age. They are most commonly used by farmers outside the city walls of Goldspire for transporting produce and grains to the market.*

Strange creatures, but if they get us to our objectives quicker, then I'm all for it.

We load up and leave the safety of Goldspire's high walls pulled by the two geriatric oxen. They move faster than I would have expected, leaving a trail of dust in our wake as we journey from the city, almost as if the animals are buffed by Strong Wind. My horrors quickly fall behind, but Jegaar assures me we have a ways to travel before I'll need them so I let them expire.

We pass by olive groves, golden meadows, and the occasional roadside tree ripe with oranges or figs. Farms speckle the land-scape and far ahead, there are low-lying dark mountains on the hazy horizon.

Every so often, I spot a marker made of blue stone on the side of the road.

"What are those?" I ask Jegaar after we pass the fifth one.

"Wards. They're designed to keep some of the more dangerous beasts from the main roads so that the farmers can transport crops to the city."

"Do they work?"

He nods. "They do, but they only extend for a dozen or so miles around the perimeter of the city. There aren't any farms beyond their range. If certain beasts get too close, the runes will activate, emitting an unpleasant energy to drive them back."

That's interesting. I haven't had many interactions with wards in Mythos, at least not that I'm aware of. The tower in Vanaria serves as a sort of ward against the undead. I wonder if it might be possible to construct smaller versions for the impending battle, using them to disorient the masses of undead at Valmar's disposal.

We pass the farms, and the land quickly becomes untamed, hilly terrain spotted with shrubs and bushes. The countryside is much dryer than Wandermere and Isle of Mythos, but underneath the desolate facade, it's teeming with life. A deer with glowing antlers grazes atop one of the hills, and giant birds circle overhead. Just like the beastkin themselves, the animals beyond Goldspire are large and intimidating. There's a scent to the air that's clean and crisp, almost calming in its simplicity.

Limery points at the birds, licking his lips. "Looks, Chods, big birdies."

"I'd be careful with those." Jegaar laughs. "My mother used to tell me stories of how the shadow vultures would snatch up the pups who didn't finish their meals and take them to their nests in the Black Mountains."

Limery's eyes widen slightly. "What do the birdses do with the pups?"

"To hear my mother tell it, they eat them in one bite." Jegaar chomps his teeth, and Limery lets out a squeak.

A herd of fiery-maned bison stampede through the hills, diverting our attention from the vultures overhead. Caustic's shadow stretches across the landscape as he soars above the herd. Maybe the bison sense the presence of the apex predator.

Not far ahead, a fluffle of bunnycorns lies on the road, bathing in the sun. Their pearlescent horns shimmer in the sunlight. When they notice the sound of our carriage, they dart into the underbrush in a blur.

I chuckle to myself that I actually remembered what a fluffle is, and I recall Taryn promising that he wasn't messing with me. He would love it here, far from the city and surrounded by nature. I wonder what he's up to right now, and how the preparation is going elsewhere.

Limery flies forward and perches on one of the oxen's horns, tapping it with his claws. "Look, Presslies, it's yous." He cackles as he points at the death knight's new helm.

"Humph," Pressley grunts.

"Get used to it." I laugh. "He's a real comedian."

Pressley leans forward, burying the front of his helm in the palm of his hand. "I'm going to regret this, aren't I?"

"Don't worry." I put a hand on his armored shoulder. "Once he's fighting beside you, you'll be thankful for the little guy. He's even stronger than last time, and the synergy between him and Caustic is pretty amazing."

"Speaking of Caustic..." Jegaar snaps the reins, but his eyes follow Caustic as he soars across the road. "I still can't believe you have a dragon. How'd that happen?"

I chuckle. "How much time do we have?"

As we travel through the countryside, I fill Pressley and Jegaar in on everything that has happened since leaving Goldspire. The beastkin is attentive, but it's impossible to read Pressley's emotions aside from the occasional grunt. The mountain range draws steadily closer as I tell them of the Mysterious Green Egg I found in Seascape, Stompy's death, the monsters from the shadowlands, our time in Wandermere, and the attack on Pruxford.

When I'm finished describing the council of leaders, there's silence aside from the crunch of earth beneath the wagon wheels and the breathing of the oxen. It's a lot to take in, I'm sure.

"I think you're right to mount an attack." Jegaar turns to me, his face stern. "If Valmar is testing the other kingdoms' defenses, then it means he's nearly ready himself. He wouldn't risk it otherwise."

"Have you noticed anything out of the ordinary in Goldspire?" I ask.

He shakes his head. "Valmar wouldn't be so foolish. Not again."

I hope he's right. The emperor turned Valmar back once, but if his goal is to spread his empire, then I can't imagine he would stop after conquering the rest of Mythos. If we fail, their paths will eventually cross again.

We come upon a fork in the road, and Jegaar pulls the wagon to a stop. "The path to the right leads to the Valley of Death and the Bleak Canyon beyond, the center will take us to the Narrow Pass within the Black Mountains, and the left leads to the abandoned city of Sungrove."

"Abandoned?" I raise a brow.

Jegaar turns to Pressley. "That's where you'll find the manticore. Her dungeon is located near the city. Long ago, Sungrove was the second-most populous city on the continent. Before we closed our borders, it was the trade hub of the region and populated by races from far and wide. When the manticore first laid claim to the dungeon, she began her stay by looting ships as they arrived at the port. After our borders closed and there were no more ships, she began abducting citizens under the cloak of darkness. Many ventured into the dungeon to try and stop her, but none returned. Eventually, more and more beastkin left the city for the safety of Goldspire, and Sungrove faded from relevance."

"What happened to the other races that were living in Sungrove when the borders closed?" I ask.

Jegaar furrows his brow. "They were banished from our lands, only allowed to return if they could defeat our gladiators in the arena."

I turn my gaze in the direction of Sungrove, wondering what awaits Limery and Caustic. "And the manticore has been living there ever since?"

"So the legends say."

I turn to Pressley. "You sure you want to go through with this?"

Darkness swirls beneath his helm as he nods. "I've made my choice."

Jegaar flicks the reins, and we veer to the left in the direction of Sungrove. "I'll leave you outside of the city gates, then Chod and I will make for the Narrow Pass so that he may complete the trials."

"This is kind of far from the city. How are they supposed to get back?"

Jegaar laughs. "On the back of the manticore, if they are lucky. And if they are not, the walk back should offer enough time to think about the foolishness of this endeavor."

My stomach tightens. For Pressley, failing the dungeon is merely a setback. He'll respawn wherever he last set his spawn point with the inconvenience of a lost level and his items. For Limery and Caustic, failure is death. They're strong, but I worry about what may happen when I'm not around to protect them.

Limery sits perched on one of the oxen's horns, bobbling along with each step, unaware of the apprehension brewing within me.

I gaze into the darkness of Pressley's helm in an attempt to see the man beneath. "Promise me that you'll play this smart. If it feels like you're out of your league, wait for me, and I'll help you once I'm done with the trials." I place a hand on his armor. "Please."

He takes a deep breath that sounds like the rattle of a hundred flies. "Fine."

"Thank you." I know it goes against everything he is to wait or ask for help. He's been going nonstop since he logged into Mythos on a quest to be the most powerful one here. We'll need that spirit for the battle ahead, but I need Caustic and Limery by my side when it happens. They're the reason I'm doing all of this.

True to Jegaar's words, Sungrove is nothing more than a

ruined city when we arrive outside the gates. I inhale the salty breeze as we come to a stop. The buildings are worn and eroded by time and the coastal weather. Several tall arches have crumbled at their peak, leaving slanting columns that frame the overgrown entry into the city. The walls that once protected it from the dangers outside are covered in moss and vines. Large black birds caw at us from the parapet, as if informing us that they're now the city's watchful protectors.

Pressley's armor clanks as he climbs down from the carriage.

Jegaar stands, stretching his arms overhead. "Say your goodbyes quickly. We still have a ways to go, and we don't want to be caught on the roads after nightfall if it can be avoided."

Judging by his ominous warning, there may be more than bison and bunnycorns lurking within the countryside.

Caustic lands beside me with a thunk as his massive frame touches down. Limery tries to take his usual spot on my shoulder, but I cradle the imp in my palm so I can look him in the eye.

"I need you to watch out for one another, and Pressley, too. But if you get the feeling that this dungeon is too strong, you leave. We'll tackle it again another day."

Caustic huffs and his meaning is clear. *A dragon does not run.*

I look into his golden eyes. "It's not running; it's living to fight another day. Beside me, together, when it really matters. I wish I could take you into the trials, but I can't. This is a way for us to help Pressley and grow stronger at the same time, but we have to remember that there is something bigger at stake. A lot of people are counting on us to make it back."

"Don't worries, Chods." Limery grins. "Limmy will take cares of Caustics."

"I know you will, buddy." I run a finger down his spine and then turn to Pressley. "Good luck. I'll see you back in Goldspire when this is all over."

He extends a hand, and when I grasp it, he pulls me close. "I may not understand the bond you have with the imp, but I know what it's like to care for someone. You have my word that we'll all make it out of here." Pressley releases his grip, nods to Jegaar, and turns toward the city. "Let's go."

Limery wraps his arms around my neck, giving me a final hug before perching on Pressley's helm. Caustic lowers his head, nuzzling against my chest and growling. Then he takes to the air, sending the birds along the wall flying.

I watch them go as they enter the open gates before joining Jegaar in the carriage.

He pats me on the knee. "Best to let the worry leave your mind. When you enter the trials, you must be focused."

Jegaar does his best to prepare me for what's to come as we travel back. According to him, the warforged trials are less about what I face and more about how I face them. For most races, and even most modern beastkin, completing the trials would be an impossible feat. Even in ancient times, the trials killed more than half of those who attempted them. If not for the combination of my race and barbarian class, I'd have no shot at completing them.

We reach the fork in the road once again and take the middle path toward the Black Mountains. As we journey closer, I realize that the mountains get their name because they appear to be made of solid black rock. There are no trees, just dark shards jutting from the earth.

By the time we arrive, the sun is setting behind their peaks. A gorge passes through the mountains, revealing a sliver of orange and purple sky on the far side that stands out in stark contrast to the obsidian stone. When we set out from Goldspire, the mountains were nothing more than dark shapes on the horizon, but the oxen are true to their description. Thanks to them, we made great time. There's no telling how long this trek might have taken on foot.

Jegaar tugs on the reins, and the carriage comes to a stop. "The Narrow Pass is barely wide enough to fit the carriage through. It's best if we go on foot. You may begin summoning your horrors now."

I do as he says, and three of the demonic creatures burst to life before me. "What's on the other side of the pass?"

"The Burning Desert that separates Goldspire from the rest of Mythos. In its center, the Lonely Volcano looms over its surroundings, scorching the earth for leagues in every direction. It makes the land so hot that wheels catch fire and hooves melt when they touch down. It's the reason our city is only accessible through the portals. With the monsters of the sea to three sides and the Burning Desert to our backs, there is no kingdom more defensible than Goldspire. The beasts capable of surviving in the desert are practically unkillable and too wild to be tamed. Those foolish enough to test them earn a quick death."

"There's always a bigger fish."

"True words, but I pray I never see them." Jegaar chuckles. "Now follow me."

The Narrow Pass is true to its name. The gorge is barely ten feet wide, and it keeps the same width from bottom to top, as if the gods had cleaved the mountain in two. The walls are jagged and dangerous, still sharp after who knows how long. The more I look at them, it appears like the two sides could fit perfectly if they were pressed together. I'm sure there's a history lesson Jegaar would love to share about this place, but right now, he's focused on finding the entrance.

My hands twitch with nervous energy. I continue summoning horrors and try not to think about failure and what that might mean.

I attempt to distract myself while Jegaar examines the rock face for some unseen sign. "Portia mentioned that there were trials you completed when you were children. Are they located here as well?"

He shakes his head. "No, those are beyond the other side of the city. Compared to what awaits you, they're quite literally child's play." He runs his claws along the walls, occasionally gripping rocky formations and pushing. "Just give me a moment. It's been a few years since I've ventured here."

He stops and presses an ear against the canyon wall while tapping his finger on its surface. Then he moves down and does the same thing several more times before stopping.

"Ah, there we go." He grabs a protruding shard of rock and pushes. The stone grinds as it moves, and a chasm forms along the left side of the wall.

He motions me forward. Heat radiates from within the cavern beyond, similar to when we found Limery's father trapped in the Greystone Mountains.

"This is where I leave you. When you enter, you'll receive a prompt from the trials. Please give me time to exit the pass before you accept." He places a hand on my shoulder and squeezes. "Good luck, Chod. I hope to see you later rather than sooner."

I take a deep breath and nod. If he sees me sooner, it's because I failed.

"Thank you." I extend a hand, and he shakes it. "For everything."

"Good luck."

I summon another round of horrors and step inside.

14. DUNGEONS & DEATH KNIGHTS

Creatures scurried in the maze of ruins as Pressley, Limery, and Caustic entered Sungrove. The coastal breeze rustled vines and overgrown foliage that had claimed the city, while the vultures perched atop the walls watched them with intrigue. The birds kept a safe distance from Caustic as he stalked behind Pressley, only occasionally squawking. With his wings tucked, the dragon was like a beast on the prowl, his tail dragging behind him on the ground.

Pressley's daughter had loved dragons. When Eva was young, she'd had a pink plushie of the one she watched on TV. Pressley couldn't remember the dragon's name, but he'd tucked it in bed alongside her at night, even going so far as to kiss it on the forehead. Eva took the toy everywhere she went, but that was years ago. Back before he'd gotten tangled up with the wrong people. He wondered if she still did.

The memories caused something within him to pulse at the emotion. Whatever energy powered his new form seemed to thrive whenever he thought about his daughter. He'd often used her as a catalyst when a fight was falling out of his favor. At level forty, that didn't happen often, but it gave him joy to know she could help him get through the tough times. He only wished he could do the same for her.

One day, he thought. *One day, I'll tell you all about my adventures in Mythos. About how Daddy rose to power and became a hero.*

He pushed the thoughts aside and returned to his new companions.

Pressley wasn't sure what to make of Caustic. Chod said the dragon was a juvenile, but he was already an intimidating presence, larger than any horse or oxen, and that wasn't accounting for his massive wingspan. The dragon had daggers for teeth, capable of ripping off Pressley's arm with ease, and his massive talons dug into the earth with each step. Pressley pitied whoever ended up on the business end of those monstrosities.

Once inside the gates, Pressley activated his Bone Detector ability. Glowing white outlines appeared across the city, but there wasn't much of note—dead rats, birds, the body of a long-dead beastkin buried beneath a stone building. That one had to be an interesting story.

Far off to his right, a white haze caught his attention. There were so many bones that their outlines merged together from so far away. Not as bad as the Valley of Death, but it was close for such a small area.

Pressley focused on the map Jegaar had given him, and it populated across his vision. The entrance to the dungeon was marked with an orange dot in the same location as the bones.

He chuckled to himself, the sound reminiscent of a hornet's nest. The manticore would be a worthy challenge, but Pressley had a dragon by his side. He glanced over his shoulder at the creature to analyze it again.

Green Dragon. *Unique Monster. Level 17. Green dragons rule* *with impunity over the forests they inhabit. They are the most territorial of all dragon species, and capable of spewing toxic gas in lieu of flames. Wherever a green dragon calls home, a dense fog is said to follow.*

The dragon's power was nice, but Pressley found himself in awe of the creature's beauty. The emerald scales that always seemed to shimmer. The antler-like horns that sprouted from his head. Not to mention the golden beard coming in around his chin. And when Caustic's golden eyes fell upon Pressley, there was an intelligence there that he hadn't seen in any other beast or monster. If this was what Caustic looked like as a juvenile, he could only imagine what the dragon would become.

Chod might have a target on his head more times than not, but he was a lucky son of a bitch. Stealing a mysterious item that ends up being a dragon egg? Pressley would kill for a dragon, but the manticore wouldn't be a bad consolation prize.

And then there was the imp. Limery hadn't been with Chod when he and Pressley fought side by side in the Glossop Forest, but he'd witnessed the imp's raw power when they faced the gladiators in the arena. He was fire made flesh, and he'd leveled up quite a bit since then as well.

Imp. *Level 27. Small, angsty creatures, imps often align themselves with beings on the more chaotic side of nature.*

Pressley laughed at the description. Chod seemed like a good dude, but chaotic was a fitting descriptor. Wherever the troll went, chaos followed.

They had that much in common.

"Where's the dungeonses?" Limery tapped Pressley's helm with a claw, and a hollow ring echoed from within.

The imp had taken to riding on the death knight's shoulder the same as he did with Chod. His natural body heat radiated through the metal of Pressley's armor, warming his core. The sensation was captivating. So much so that it took all his willpower to fight against lying down and basking in the warmth.

His appearance wasn't the only thing that changed when he'd become a death knight. When he first went through the transformation, there was a hollowness that pervaded his very being. His mental faculties hadn't changed, but anger and sadness had settled on his soul like an anvil. It had eased with time, but his body still felt like a cold echo of itself. The imp's heat was a reminder of what he'd lost.

And what he'd gained.

The power was worth the trade-off. He never would have accomplished some of his feats had he still been human. Technically, he was still human, just undead. Flesh and blood might be a more appropriate term. He still had the same bones, only now they weren't held together by ligaments and muscle but by some infernal energy.

"Presslies..." Limery tapped the helm again. "Helloes!"

"It's nearby." Pressley lifted an armored hand and pointed. "Over there."

"Limmy and Caustics loves to fights." The imp squeezed his small hands into fists. "We likes to make big booms."

"So I've heard. You'll need to show me what you're capable of before we enter."

"Okies." Limery flashed him a demonic grin.

They headed in the direction of the dungeon. The vultures followed at a distance, hopping from building to building and occasionally squawking at them. The same thing had happened to Pressley at the Valley of Death. He wondered if they could sense the death radiating from within him.

The entrance to the manticore's dungeon was barely more than a collapsing tunnel. It looked like the entrance to an old mining shaft. For a creature so feared and respected, Pressley had expected something more resplendent.

Manticore Dungeon. *Would you like to enter?*

He dismissed the notification and turned to face Limery and Caustic. "Chod was right when he told you this is a dangerous dungeon. I'm glad to have you by my side because this would be a challenge for me alone. He tells me you are both very powerful." At that, Caustic huffed. "Since we haven't fought as a team before, we should familiarize ourselves with one another's abilities. Limery, tell me what you can do."

"Oh, yes. Limmy can do lots." The imp took to the air, hovering a few feet in front of Pressley. "Limmy is very fasts."

He darted through the air, zigzagging several times before stopping to conjure a fireball in his palm. The flames licked at and distorted the air, but the imp remained unaffected. Pressley longed for the fire's warm embrace.

"Limmy can throws fireballs and make fire walls." With a flick of his wrist, the fireball soared toward a ruined building, hitting a vulture. Limery cackled as feathers exploded, and the bird took to the sky with an angry caw.

When the imp recovered from laughing, he conjured a flaming wall nearly six feet high and two feet wide.

"Very good." Pressley nodded his approval.

"Limmy can also dos mega-fireballs." He summoned a fireball and spread his hands wide. Each second, the flames grew until the fiery ball was larger than the imp itself.

The heat radiated like a furnace, and Pressley grinned beneath his helm.

Limery let the fireball dwindle into nothing before continuing. "Limmy can also turn to fires." In the blink of an eye, his entire body was engulfed in flame. He burned like a little impish torch, his eyes molten lava. "And now, Limmy can makes a shields."

Flame expanded from his body in a sphere, forming a fiery barrier around the imp. If Pressley had to guess, it would burn anything that tried to pass through.

The flames faded, and then Limery reached into a small satchel hanging from his waist. "Limmy also has somes of the fairies dust. It makes yous sleepies."

The imp had more abilities than Pressley had anticipated, and even though he was only level twenty-seven, he was raw power. A wrecking ball of fire. "Anything else?"

Limery tapped his chin as if considering before his eyes lit up. "Limmy has the necklace." He raised a silver necklace with a black teardrop pendant from his neck. Gray smoke swirled within. "It makes peoples confuseds. Limmy cans use it three times every days."

"Very good. I'm lucky you're on my side." Pressley turned to Caustic. "And what about the dragon?"

In answer, Caustic reared back and unleashed a stream of toxic gas that poured down the alley to their left. The gas was heavy, sinking to the ground and lingering like a dense fog. Being a death knight, Pressley was immune to most toxins and poisons, but the gas had the appearance of something especially potent.

"Chod says you two can use your abilities together. How does that work?"

Without responding, Limery tossed a fireball at the thick green gas. The gas ignited, and the world seemed to slow down for Pressley as chaos blossomed. There was a flash of green light, and then the alley exploded. Rubble flew across the city, and the force of the explosion knocked Pressley against the wall. The world sat in silence for a moment, and then a thunderous clap echoed, followed by another wave of energy. If he still had ears, he was certain they'd be bleeding.

"Damn." Pressley's voice was barely a whisper. Those two were dangerous.

The smoke cleared, and Limery grinned at the death knight. "What can Presslies do?"

"I'm similar to Chod in a way. I summon things to fight for me." He removed the satchel from his side and turned it upside-down. Bones and rusty weapons fell out, rattling against the dusty street. They poured out until the pile was waist-high, and then he stepped aside, shaking the bag again. Bones flowed from the satchel like a waterfall.

One thing he'd discovered since entering Goldspire was that he could store the bones of his minions in an expandable satchel when they weren't in use. It allowed him to keep a bigger army in reserve, and it accrued a lot less stares and panic in populated areas.

Limery grabbed a bone and tossed it to Caustic. The dragon snatched it out of the air with a crunch.

"Please, don't do that." Pressley sighed.

"Sorries." Limery gave him a sorrowful look.

Pressley activated his ability to summon skeleton warriors, and the bones rattled and clacked as they assembled themselves with dark energy holding them together at the joints. The warriors ranged in size from the thick, short bones of dwarfs to those with more human proportions. There were even a few beastkin and animal skeletons mixed in.

As the warriors animated, they grabbed weapons from the pile and formed into lines five wide. There were forty warriors holding swords, spears, and axes, and another twenty archers in the rear.

Pressley gestured at the group. "This is my skeleton army. They'll fight beside us until their bones shatter. As we make our way through the dungeon, I'll be able to reanimate some of the monsters we defeat to fight alongside us temporarily. All of my abilities are powered by my health, so the weaker I become, the more difficult it will be to use some of my abilities. I have ranged attacks that can replenish my health, as well as some area-of-effect abilities for tackling groups."

Limery flew over to one of the skeleton warriors and tapped it on the skull. The skeleton stood at attention, unflinching.

The imp frowned. "Theys is not very funs."

"No, but they are persistent." Pressley had witnessed his summons continue to fight after losing an arm or leg. Even without a skull, they would swing blindly. It wasn't until their HP depleted completely that they would turn to dust. They might not be semi-intelligent like Chod's horrors, but they could fight. And that was all he needed. Pressley turned to his two new companions. "Are we ready?"

Caustic growled and pawed against the earth with his massive talons.

Limery flashed a mischievous grin. "We readies."

The army of skeletons marched into the dungeon, their footsteps perfectly synchronized as they descended underground. At first, Pressley had been unnerved by his minions' lack of sound. There were no groaning or hellish grunts like in the movies, just silent motion as the bones moved, propelled by infernal energy. The corpses he reanimated were a different story. Much like the imp, those things never seemed to shut up.

Pressley followed with his sword at the ready and Limery perched upon his shoulder. Caustic brought up the rear, head raised as he sniffed at the surroundings.

The air changed as soon as they stepped out of the corridor

and into an enormous cavern. There was a heaviness about the place that he hadn't felt on the surface. Pressley felt it, and judging by the rumble in Caustic's chest, no doubt the dragon did too. Somewhere nearby, they could hear the sound of running water, and straight ahead, a platform barely wide enough for the skeletons to stand five abreast led across a nebulous chasm that seemed to descend forever.

On the other side of the platform, stairs led up to an expansive hall that stretched deeper into the earth, supported by colossal columns. Massive gargoyles of watchful lions loomed from above the stairs, water spouting from their roaring mouths into the chasm below. Mist hung in the air in a prism of colors, rainbows ignited by torches that lined the walls. Shadows danced from their flames, giving the gargoyles a lifelike appearance.

"Who dares enter my domain?" an amplified voice sounded all around them. It was feminine and somehow simultaneously alluring and threatening. "Who is foolish enough to challenge my might?" Laughter rang out. "It matters not, for I shall clean my teeth with your bones. Welcome to my dungeon."

A chill ran along Pressley's already frigid spine.

"Scaries." Limery's head swiveled as he inspected their surroundings.

Behind them, Caustic's chest rumbled as he surveyed the area.

"Are you familiar with the manticore?" Pressley asked.

The imp shook his head. "Limmy doesn't knows."

"I read of her exploits in the Goldspire Library, though I found no mention of what we should expect within the dungeon. But I know she will be a challenge. In most sources, she's described the same—the body of the lion with a woman's face and sprawling wings. She has the tail of a scorpion, though there were multiple accounts of its capabilities. Some say it has a single stinger. Others say it is barbed from base to tip and capable of shooting projectiles. She has an appetite for beastkin flesh and other humanoids, and she's said to have the ability to mimic their speech. Some reports say she can cast illusions, too, so be wary." The warmth radiating through Pressley's armor increased slightly, and he basked in the sensation. "Once we cross this bridge, be prepared for anything."

Limery's brow furrowed, and he nodded.

Pressley ordered his minions across the narrow platform. Their bony footsteps clacked along the smooth stone along with Caustic's talons and Pressley's boots. They wouldn't be winning any awards for stealth. Wind swirled underneath, and he wondered if the chasm led to a waterway that filtered into the sea. However deep it went, it was far enough to where the splash of water couldn't reach them.

They crossed the bridge and ascended the stairwell into the grand hall. It seemed to stretch for eternity with torches and columns as far as they could see. Up close, the gargoyles were made of white marble laced with red veins. It gave the lion's stone eyes an almost humanlike appearance.

Caustic's chest rumbled, and Pressley scanned the area for threats. With the columns, it would be easy for enemies to lurk out of sight.

"Do you see anything?" he asked Limery.

"Noes." The imp gulped.

The heat radiating through Pressley's armor intensified, making it harder for him to concentrate. "Let's move forward. Stay alert."

Pressley noticed the gargoyle's tail move a moment before a stone paw swiped for him. Limery flew from his shoulder, and Pressley raised his sword just in time for it to rain sparks through the eye-slit of his helm, briefly igniting the skull beneath.

A second paw knocked him to the ground from behind, and all

around, the lion gargoyles leapt from their pedestals, leaving a fountain of water gushing in their wake.

Fire crackled as Limery summoned fireballs and began pelting the lions. Skeleton warriors charged the beasts, and their weapons clanked against the creatures' stone hides.

Pressley barely had enough time to analyze the monsters as he crawled to his feet.

Gargoyle. *Level 34. Made of enchanted stone, gargoyles serve as excellent guardians with their ability to conceal their true nature until they move. While gargoyles have no magical abilities, they are extremely tough and can only be killed by shattering their core.*

A lion pounced on Pressley as he gained his footing, but the death knight was ready. He side-stepped the lunging beast and brought his sword down on its side. Sparks erupted from the hit, leaving a small crack in the stone.

Pressley grunted. The sword wasn't the weapon for this fight, and while Limery's fire was scorching the lions and coating them with soot, it didn't seem to be having much effect otherwise.

Stone paws padded against the floor behind him, and Pressley raised his sword just in time to block a set of claws from removing his head from his shoulders. He counted nine lions, their eyes now blazing with golden fury. Roars echoed down the hall, and Caustic answered the challenge.

The dragon's talons scraped against one of the beasts, leaving a deep gash in the stone, far more effective than Pressley's weapon. All around, the skeletons were scattered and shattered from the gargoyle's attacks. While his minions didn't expire, they could be disassembled. Once their HP depleted, the bones would turn to dust.

Pressley quickly summoned more warriors from the scattered bones and reached into his satchel for a weapon better suited to the challenge at hand.

An explosion rocked the cavern, and skeletons tumbled through the air like ragdolls along with giant chunks of stone that had been at least two gargoyles moments ago. A large lion head rolled to a stop at Pressley's feet.

"Sorries." Limery grimaced as a crack splintered up the column where the explosion had occurred.

That was two down, and a few lost skeletons was a small price to pay. If they defeated the manticore, it wouldn't matter if they destroyed the entrance.

Pressley gave the imp a thumbs-up. "Good job. Keep it up."

Limery grinned and returned to the fight.

Pressley cast Reanimate over the destroyed gargoyles but received a notification that it was unsuccessful. Cursing his luck, he pondered a new strategy for dealing with them. Nearly half of his abilities only worked on living creatures, and just as many only worked on the dead. The gargoyles existed somewhere else entirely.

He stored his sword and pulled a warhammer from his satchel. The silver head gleamed in the firelight. One end was a large hammer, and the other had a spike tipped with diamonds. He preferred the precision and weight of the sword, but he'd have better luck smashing the lions to bits with this.

His first victim sat in waiting, preparing to pounce from behind the nearby column.

"Here, kitty, kitty," Pressley's hollow voice called.

The stone cat leapt through the air, claws extended, and Pressley planted his foot. He swung upward with the spiked end and connected with the lion's jaw. Stone shattered against the diamond-tipped spike, and the gargoyle spun mid-air, somehow managing to land on its feet. It attempted to roar, but its lower jaw had been obliterated, so a pitiful groan was all that escaped.

Giant wings flapped like sails as Caustic flew by with a

gargoyle gripped in his talons. He soared over the chasm, dropping the lion into the depths below.

Pressley pushed the attack on his own opponent, but the gargoyle still had cat-like reflexes. It swatted away swing after swing.

Another explosion rocked the hall, giving Pressley an opening as one of the pillars collapsed. He caught the lion in the side of the head, turning it to rubble just as dust filled the area and obscured Pressley's vision. He stepped back, waiting for the dust to clear, when something knocked his chest like a sledgehammer and pinned him to the ground. Hot breath filled his helm as the lion roared, and his armor creaked beneath the weight of the stone monster as claws attempted to pull his chest plate away. Had he been human, they'd likely be ripping into his flesh.

But he wasn't human. He cast Lifesteal, and purple energy shot from his hands. At such close range, the effect was instantaneous. The damage he'd taken from the previous attacks healed instantly.

The lion gnawed at the horns protruding from Pressley's helm, wrenching the death knight under powerful thrusts as it attempted to pry the helm away. Pressley's health trickled down with every thrust as his bones creaked beneath the weight. Several skeletons had gathered around, hacking and slashing at the gargoyle to no avail.

Eva's face flashed across his vision, and power pulsed within his core. Energy built within him, just as a flaming outline blazed through the smoke. "Let go of Presslies!" Limery shouted as he landed on the lion's back, molten hands pressed against the gargoyle's head.

The lion yowled in pain, and Pressley activated Lifesteal again. Health surged into his body as the lion released the death knight, its jaws snapping over its shoulder at the imp.

"Gets it, Caustics!" Limery ordered, and the dragon descended, grasping the thrashing lion in his powerful claws.

The pressure released from Pressley's chest, and Caustic flew over the chasm to drop another victim into the depths below.

Pressley grabbed his warhammer, ready to fight, but the hall was quiet aside from the debris crunching beneath his boots. The skeletons that remained stood motionless with no threat left to fight.

Out of the nine gargoyles, he'd killed one. He was a higher level than both the dragon and imp by a wide margin, and yet they'd dispatched eight of the lions with ease.

Pressley needed to up his game going forward, or Chod was never going to let him hear the end of this.

15. TRIALS AND TRIBULATIONS

HORRORS GRUMBLE all around me as I wait for Jegaar to exit the Narrow Pass. We stand outside the entrance to the trials, and one of the Horrors of Finesse puts its long, spindly blue finger into a Horror of Power's ear. The stout warthog-like horror snaps its head around, snarling, and a scuffle breaks out. Dust flies as they tussle in the dirt before several of the furry, rotund Horrors of Vitality step in to separate them, grumbling something in their language my communication stone can't translate.

I've noticed recently that my horrors will sometimes mimic my emotions. When I'm more on edge, they seem to be as well.

"Calm down, everyone. We're all in this together." I equip Destroyer and let the comforting weight of the warhammer rest against my palm.

Jegaar looks over his shoulder a final time and then disappears from view. I summon Pharos, and my spirit guide appears. The frost goat blazes with white-orange ethereal energy that ignites the dark cavern. I follow Pharos inside, trailed by a platoon of horrors, and soon I'm greeted with a prompt.

Trials of the Warforged: *Would you like to enter?*

Once all of the horrors are crammed inside the cavern, I accept. The ground rumbles, and dust and debris fall from the walls and ceiling as the mountain outside shifts. The grind of a mountain moving reverberates in my chest and assaults my ears until both sides of the Narrow Pass fit seamlessly together. A solid wall of stone blocks the exit.

There's no going back. If I want to get out of here, I have two options: complete the trials or die trying.

The cavern empties into a room with enchanted pyres burning in the corners with a ghastly flames. In contrast to the rugged entrance that blends in with the outside pass, this room is polished obsidian that has been meticulously carved from the mountain. The white flames of the pyres reflect off the eyes of my horrors.

I step forward, and a molten orange outline forms in the center of the far wall. There's a hiss before a section of wall grates against the floor as it disappears, revealing the next room.

Please remove all items before entering the trials.

That's unfortunate, but I understand. If the goal is to forge me anew, then I can't complete the trials with outside help, even in the form of items. I'm not sure what would happen if I tried to sneak something in, but that's not a risk I'm willing to take.

I set my expandable satchel on the floor and place Destroyer beside it. With the pass closed, at least I don't have to worry about having my gear stolen. The first item I remove is the spaulder that has protected my shoulder on many occasions. With so many horrors active, I barely notice the loss of stat bonuses as I set the armor aside. Next, I untie the Tiger's Eye Pendant from around my neck. That little necklace has saved my hide more times than I can count with its ability to remove one debuff every ten minutes. It has been a constant reminder of how generous the forest trolls were when they had so little to give. After I remove the phoenix feather from my braid, I place the items inside the satchel. The last item to go in is Destroyer.

For as long as I've been in Mythos, I've had a weapon. From the gnarled branch I found on day one to Peacemaker and half-dozen others, I've always chosen to wield a weapon first and use my claws second. I guess I'm about to find out how big of a crutch that has been.

With nothing but a loincloth covering my trollberries, I follow Pharos into the first room of the trials.

The room is a long rectangle, crafted from the same gleaming obsidian, with an empty trough that runs around the edge of a raised platform. Numerous tunnels slightly wider than my head disappear into the walls. My heart races, and I try to find comfort in the mana that rushes to my fingertips, calling another round of horrors to replace the ones that expire.

I have zero doubts that something I'm going to hate is coming out of those tunnels sooner or later, so I position myself in the center of the platform, surrounded by horrors on all sides. The width of the platform is just big enough for them to surround me without falling into the trough.

A notification flashes across my vision.

Trials of the Warforged: *Commencing*

Stage One: *Heat*

There's a loud clank and steam shoots from the tunnels around the room. Horrors grumble at the disturbance. There's a sizzling sound and a faint glow comes from deep within the tunnels. Molten metal pours from within, slow and steady, filling the bottom of the trough that runs the perimeter of the room. With nowhere for the heat to disperse, the temperature surges immediately, and sweat erupts across my brow. The Horrors of

Vitality pant with their tongues drooping from their mouths, sweltering beneath their thick fur.

I stand on guard, pulse thundering in my ears, ready for whatever monster I'm about to face. Sweat drips from my nose, and my eyes burn from the heat, but nothing appears.

Molten metal continues to fill the trough, and the temperature steadily rises. My body shimmers from the perspiration beading down my chest and arms. One of my horrors groans, and I notice their health is depleting more rapidly than normal.

My vision blacks at the edge and for a moment, I think I'm going to pass out. I concentrate on my breathing and focus my gaze on the steady stream of liquid metal pouring from one of the tunnels. One breath at a time, I wait for my head to clear.

Once I regain my composure, I scan the room, searching for a way out—a crack in the wall, a hidden tile on the floor, anything that might make this end.

There's nothing.

I think back to Jegaar's words. *The trials are not about what you face but how you face them.* He told me I would need to endure. I thought he meant in battle, but it seems not. The heat dries the moisture from my eyes until every blink feels like a scrape of sandpaper. Sweat sizzles against my skin, and my health finally begins to drain.

The other horrors now have their tongues out, and their panting rivals the slosh of molten metal that surrounds us. There's nothing they can do to help me here, so I cast Sacrifice to save them from this misery. At least I can relish the influx of bonus stats for the next few minutes.

Pharos paces back and forth across the platform, his spirit hooves silent against the stone. I could sacrifice him for a boost to Wisdom, but then I wouldn't be able to call upon him again for twenty-four hours. Right now, his company is more valuable.

As tough as things seem right now, I try to think about all of the Warforged that came before me. They are legendary for a reason—because they completed the trials. If they can do it, so can I. I just need to take stock of the situation and see what my options are.

I have over seven thousand HP but at the rate it's draining, I don't know how long it will last. The floor grows hotter, and even my tough troll hide begins to blister, adding to my health decay. Every movement stings like the worst sunburn I've ever had. Eventually, I stand still.

Berserker Rage will boost my healing for a short time, but without anything to fight, I'll be unable to increase my rage meter. It's full now, but that means I'll only have one opportunity to use it unless lava monsters start climbing out of those holes.

On second thought, please don't let lava monsters crawl out of those holes.

Unable to move without pain, I'm left to my own thoughts as my body slowly roasts. I close my eyes and do my best to block out my discomfort. I'm not sure how much time passes, but eventually, my health drops to less than half.

I try to send Taryn a message, but the magic powering the trials must be blocking outside communication between him or any of the other heroes I have in my contact list. Valery is still an option, and for a moment, I consider messaging her to say just how fucked up all of this is. I think better of it. This was my choice to enter the trials, and the tone of her last message makes me think she has a lot going on outside the game, especially with the Dorothy situation.

I open my eyes, and fresh tears sizzle against my cheeks. Pharos stands before me, his head tilted up, and his fiery eyes gazing intensely at me. I lean into them, pushing away everything but the swirl of energy within his pupils.

I've never been one for meditation, but I lose myself in his spirit, blocking out the world around me as if nothing else matters. My health continues to trickle down like a leaky faucet. When it hits ten percent, I ready the only card up my sleeve—using Berserker Rage to amplify the increased regeneration that occurs when my health goes into the red.

Before I do so, something surprising happens. My health hovers at around ten percent. My HP drops, then the increased regeneration kicks in and brings it out of the red. Once above ten percent, the increased regeneration cancels, and my HP drops again. The cycle repeats over and over, with the increased regen enough to stay the damage as long as I remain below ten percent health. The relief is enough to make me laugh, sending a wave of pain through my searing flesh.

I take a breath of hot air and lock eyes with Pharos again. I can survive this. I just need to endure.

16. DISGUISES

Dorothy glanced at Valmar in the mirror's reflection as she adjusted her features. He stared ahead, the green light from the throne room's many torches reflecting off the necromancer's chiseled jawline. His deep red eyes burned intently, beacons upon his pallid gray skin, as he stared into oblivion. He wore his thick raven hair slicked back, and it fell just above his shoulders. For being nearly a thousand years old, he looked good. Not everyone could pull off the sexy Dracula vibe.

Valmar's fingernails tapped against the obsidian throne. "Are you nearly finished?" His tone was exasperated. "I have a council to attend."

Dorothy finished adjusting her eye color and met his gaze in the mirror. "With the warlock? That guy is such a tool."

Valmar nodded. "He has been a useful tool, and the reason you have been able to track your prey."

Dorothy smiled. She found it humorous when he took her words literally. "Yeah, well, he gives me the creeps. I'm sure he'd lick your boots if you let him."

Valmar's brow narrowed, and his glare pierced through Dorothy before he stood to join her by the mirror. He hovered behind her, resting a hand on her shoulder. The touch sent a chill down her spine, and she fought the urge to shiver. "You could learn from his devotion."

She met his gaze in the mirror as she changed her skin color from gray to ivory. "Have I not proved my worth?"

His mouth curled into a sinister smile. It reminded Dorothy of a predator, always a heartbeat away from attacking.

"You show great promise for an outworlder. It is the reason I have granted you so many boons. I would hate to see my investment wasted."

Dorothy scoffed. "I'll do what the warlock couldn't. The troll won't be a problem for you much longer." She altered her hair from silver to blonde and then dismissed the Disguise template from her vision. To anyone looking, she no longer appeared as an undead elf with the blazing eyes of a revenant, but a golden-haired, blue-eyed elf from the lands of Ellynmylly. "I'm ready."

Valmar's eyes took on the same eerie green as the flames, and a giant shadow appeared in the center of the room. A demonic finger the size of a man extended from the void, and its pointed nail ripped through reality, revealing a swirling white portal.

"You remind me a great deal of my sister." He removed his hands from Dorothy's shoulder and gestured toward the portal. "She had your spirit."

Dorothy wore a curious expression. "What happened to her?"

"It does not matter." For a flicker, his eyes lost focus as if Valmar was transported to some far-off memory. "She serves me now."

Dorothy glanced around the perimeter of the room, where several dozen armored skeletons stood sentry in deathly silence. Was his sister one of them, or was she elsewhere? Dorothy had seen the army of the dead beyond the city walls. Thousands of skeletons and undead. When they attacked, they would raze Mythos to the ground. She didn't care what happened to the rest of this world. She'd come here with one purpose—vengeance. If she had to ally with the villain to get it, then so be it.

Valmar squeezed her shoulder, and a revolting darkness seeped out from his touch. Thankfully, Dorothy's disguise concealed her grimace.

"Do not fail me." There was no room for argument in his words.

"Yes, master." She nodded, thankful to free herself from his grasp as she stepped into the portal.

At level thirty-three, Dorothy finally felt comfortable entering the broader world. She'd been in Mythos for two weeks—plotting, planning, and grinding—but when she'd learned from Ethan the warlock that Chod was only level twenty-eight during their fight in Pruxford, she made the decision to finally reach out to her old friend.

What she would have done to see the look on his face as he read that message.

Since then, she'd grinded a few more levels just to be safe. To hear the others tell it, Chod always had something up his sleeve. And if not, he seemed to have friends everywhere who would swoop in at the last minute to save the day.

That part bothered her the most. He'd seemed like a nice enough guy when they'd first met, but once they started gaming, he became a complete asshole. He snapped at her for every little thing, even though he was doing no better. Games were supposed to be fun. For her, they had been. Streaming had been fun.

Chod had taken that away from her.

Now, he was about to find out just how unfun games could be.

Dorothy exited the portal into Goldspire, and she felt the sun's warm embrace for the first time. In Mosstar, it was always cloudy. Perfect for Valmar's little act, but it was a real drag.

She grinned as she looked across the sweeping coliseum. It was an imposing presence, and the stands were filled with beastkin that cheered as gladiators clashed in the arena. No one talked about it, at least not openly, but this was the first place Valmar had ever been turned back. She'd been warned that mentioning Goldspire's emperor around her master would result in a fate worse than death.

Dorothy rolled her eyes. For all his villainous tendencies, and Valmar had plenty, he was just as sensitive as the next man.

He'd sent her to Goldspire for two reasons—to gather intel and to eliminate the troll problem. With her Disguise ability, even if she were apprehended, no one would know her true origins.

"Having second thoughts, girly?" A lion beastkin grinned in her direction from the sandy arena. Two massive gauntlets with spikes on the knuckles covered each hand. A matching set of spiked armor protected his knees and elbows. Aside from that, he wore nothing but a loincloth.

Easy pickings.

She returned his smile. "No, just monologuing."

He frowned in confusion. "If you wish to enter Goldspire, then you must defeat a gladiator in the arena."

She curled both hands into fists and placed them under her chin, speaking in a high-pitched voice. "Let me guess, I'm the lucky gal who gets to dance with you?"

The beastkin huffed. "You talk a lot."

She scoffed. "Yeah, and you breathe through your mouth."

He clinked his gauntlets together and growled. "Enough of this. Show me what you've got."

Her smile shifted from playful taunting to something more dangerous. "Oh, baby, I thought you'd never ask."

Dorothy activated One with the Shadows and darkness cloaked her, unyielding to the bright sun. She jumped from the platform, and two shadow copies sprang from her, surrounding the beastkin with a triangular formation. Until she attacked, she would remain cloaked, indistinguishable from the two clones. While her shadow copies couldn't fight, they offered something more valuable—she could switch places with them at will, almost like teleportation.

The beastkin held his gauntlets in front of him like a boxer, shifting his weight from one foot to the other. His head turned on a swivel, waiting for the attack.

Dorothy equipped one of her many daggers and waited until the beastkin's back was facing her. She activated True Strike and tossed the weapon. The poisoned blade lodged in his beefy neck just above the shoulder. The beastkin groaned as he spun around, and she ported to the shadow across from her, throwing another poisoned dagger at his backside. Without the aid of True Strike, it stuck in the beastkin's mid-back.

He growled, turning around and swinging wildly. An outline of an eagle covered his arm as he punched, and it ripped through the shadow, dissipating it as Dorothy ported away. She threw another dagger, sticking him in the ribs. With wild eyes, he attacked again. This time, a streak of orange energy blasted from the gauntlet and destroyed the second shadow.

The beastkin wobbled as the poison began to take effect. He reached for the tainted blade in his beefy neck, and Dorothy used the opportunity to push the attack. She activated Sleight of Hand, feigning an attack with her left hand. When the beastkin raised his gauntlets to block, she went low with a blade in her right, slicing him across the thigh.

Blood streaked his fur, and his health dropped rapidly as the poison stacked with each subsequent hit. His movements grew sluggish, and he no longer shifted from foot to foot.

Dorothy held up her middle finger. "How many do you see?"

He stumbled back and forth before falling face-first to the ground.

"Attaboy." She straddled his back and slid a dagger across his throat.

The crowd erupted, and Dorothy waved to them as they tossed flowers into the arena. She picked up a rose and sniffed it, surprised at how fragrant it smelled.

"I could get used to this." She tossed the rose aside and pulled up her map, locating Chod's position. "But first, I've got a troll to hunt."

17. MOONLIT FLIGHTS

Taryn's first day in Seascape was full of councils and strategy meetings. Now that war had been declared, there were a great deal of preparations to make, first among the individual kingdoms and then for the war effort as a whole.

A bevy of familiar faces sat around the council room—the two kings, Orso and Favian, Kurzol the cleric, Kassidy the teleportation mage, Chief Rizza and Jira of the forest trolls, Chief Laojin and Senzala of the arctic trolls, Lady Brollen the ice mage from Sandholde, and nearly a dozen other advisors. The most powerful and influential people on the Isle were in this room. They had days to gather their armies and prepare for an invasion that would determine all of their fates long after the heroes were gone.

They each took turns reporting on the current status of the guards, soldiers, and mages. Compared to the other kingdoms, the Isle of Mythos had fewer mages, but their heroes would more than make up for the deficiency. They did have something the others didn't, though—trolls. When it came to raw strength and power, only the beastkin of Goldspire rivaled the trolls.

Able-bodied men and dwarves would need to be recruited from across Seascape and Vanaria to serve as a last line of defense. While the two kingdoms both had a city watch, their militias had shrunk in the years after the portals closed, and neither kept a large standing army in waiting. Soldiers and guards would be part of the initial attack, but there was no room for failure. Farmers, miners, and everyday citizens would be forced to answer the call and fight if necessary.

Taryn prayed they never had to lift a weapon in battle.

He rubbed his eyes with both palms while King Favian continued his report on the state of Vanaria. The king had removed the stately armor he wore to Pruxford and now sported a simple blue tunic with a griffin crest. He looked tired. They all did. Taryn imagined Chod was having a much more exciting time in Goldspire. At least he wasn't cooped up in a castle every hour of the day.

But this was what Taryn had chosen, to aid his king in whatever manner His Highness deemed fit. He should be honored that King Orso valued his opinion so highly to allow him a seat on the council, and he was. He just wished he could be of more use.

With the portals opened, travel between Vanaria to Seascape was easier than ever. They could coordinate their efforts without delay, and messengers carried intel between the two kingdoms at all hours of the day.

If they were lucky, they might just be ready in time.

Taryn tried to send Chod a message, but it wouldn't deliver. The trials must have been blocking outside communication.

Flubs slinked out of the vial around Taryn's neck and poked the druid with a slimy appendage.

"Taryn..." King Favian raised a brow. "Do you think they will agree?"

"Come again?" Taryn sat up, completely oblivious to the question he'd just been asked.

"I said we should have the heroes lead the charge into battle. They'll be able to cause the most destruction. Do you think the others will agree to this?"

"I believe so." Taryn stroked his beard. "They're all training in Pruxford currently and making the most of the kingdom's many dungeons."

"Good." King Favian nodded. "I don't yet know what the other kingdoms will provide, but you will have air support from Chod's dragon and my griffin. The front lines will also have ground support from the forest trolls' three mana-infused wyrms." He gestured to Chief Rizza. "The troll tribes have requested to follow Chod into battle, assuming he doesn't have other plans once he returns. If so, then they will join our vanguard.

"Our plan, for now, is for King Orso to flank the heroes with both of our kingsguards. The city watches will follow, and I'll be able to offer tactical advice from above. We will continue to update our tactics as more information becomes available, as fluid as a slime." He winked at Taryn. "When we reconvene in Pruxford, we'll compare our plans with the others. Our citizens who take up arms will form a militia to serve as the last line of defense. We want to attack swiftly with the full force of a dwarven hammer." King Favian turned to Chief Rizza. "What news of the other tribes?"

Chief Rizza frowned. "The envoy has not yet returned, but I have confidence in Gord and the others. Lillith and Bazel have been sent to inform them of the Pruxford council and to return with an update as quickly as possible. We should have word soon."

"Keep us informed." King Favian leaned forward, resting his hands on the table. Dark circles underscored his bright blue eyes.

Like many here, he had slept little in the past two days. "We never thought we would be in this position again—the fate of our world hanging on the outcome of a battle between the living and the dead—but here we are. We have overcome this challenge before. Search your records and your histories, empty your troves. Any weapons that offer an advantage against the undead must be equipped. Our enchanters in Vanaria are hard at work as we speak." He nodded to the dwarven king.

King Orso stood. "I think that is enough for today. I must address my people, and there is still much to do. Shall we reconvene tomorrow evening?"

After several nods of agreement, he banged his gavel, and the table dispersed.

A large, charcoal-colored hand gripped Taryn on the shoulder as he was leaving, and Taryn turned to see Chief Laojin towering above him. The arctic troll's shaggy white fur looked out of place among the harsh lines of dwarven architecture. It covered the majority of his massive frame aside from his face, hands, and a patch on his stomach.

"I tire of these meetings." The troll chief smiled beneath his thick white beard. "Would you care to join me for a moonlit flight?"

Taryn laughed. "There is nothing in the world I would love more right now."

Moonlight cast the towers and spires of the castle in a silver glow. The gargoyles that sat upon the buildings looked as if they might spring to life and defend the city if necessary. Perhaps they would. Taryn still knew very little of Seascape's history.

He stood in the king's courtyard overlooking the turbulent

waters of the sea below. How different the world might be if sea travel had been possible when the portals closed.

"Heavy thoughts weigh on you, young druid." Chief Laojin's icy blue eyes offered sympathy.

Taryn watched the waves crash against the rocks below. He wondered if he was the rock or the wave. Was he set to try again and again only to be faced with the inevitable? Or was he the rock that endured the never-ending barrage? Images of his pets crossed his mind—Berry, Ruby, Jordy, Flubs. He rested his hand against his heart where Stompy's memory was tattooed on his chest. And then there was Breebis. He smiled at the memory of sitting with her in the hammock, dark green hair cloaking her shoulders as she looked at him with those warm red eyes. They'd rocked together underneath starry skies as she told him of her dreams and passions.

Bits of data or not, when he looked into the eyes of Breebis or his pets, he knew they were looking back at him. Taryn wouldn't be here forever, that much was certain. He needed to make sure they would be okay.

His fingertips pressed into the stone barrier, and he fought back tears. "We only get one shot at this, you know." He sighed. "One shot to save it all."

"You cannot dwell on the future, young druid. Be thankful for what you have accomplished already." Laojin squeezed Taryn's bicep. "When we last met, you and Chod were on a mission to unite Mythos against this threat. By my estimations, you've done a job to be proud of. If you can convince a tribe of trolls to fight alongside dwarves and men, then I believe you can do anything."

"It wasn't all me."

"You give yourself too little credit. Come, let's take to the air and ease your mind." Without waiting for a response, Laojin climbed on the wall and jumped.

Taryn leaned over the barrier, watching the chief fall as air fluttered through the thick fur covering the troll's body. Halfway down, there was an explosion of silver feathers as the chief transformed into his falcon form. The falcon dove deeper before extending his wings and catching the swirling air and soaring high. With a few flaps of his navy-tipped wings, he coasted high above the sea, a beacon under the light of the moon. It was like watching a shooting star as Laojin screeched and dove through the clouds.

A smile crept over Taryn's face. He hadn't flown for pleasure since that day high in the Frostmoor mountains when Laojin had tossed him from the cliffside. He still remembered Laojin's words from that day. *"This is how I take care of myself and clear my mind. Plummeting through the clouds has a way of putting things in perspective."*

If Taryn wanted to help those he cared about, he needed to clear his mind. He needed to be focused and determined, sure of his actions. Letting the heaviness of the future hang around his neck would only pull him into depths where he could help no one.

He tied the necklace containing Flubs around Ruby's neck, then hefted himself onto the wall and jumped. His cloak flapped like a sail and the clasps in his beard jingled as he fell. For a moment, he embraced the thrill of falling and the wind against his face. Then he used Transform. There was an eruption of red feathers as his body shifted, and his short red wings fluttered against the strong oceanic winds. He didn't have the same powerful wings as Laojin, but he soon found balance and flew upward.

Taryn embraced the cool air against his beak and soon Laojin joined him, the falcon's eyes alert with black slits that cut through their icy blue.

Together, they soared above the city. From a bird's-eye view,

Seascape was gorgeous. Its gothic architecture shimmered in the moonlight, more beautiful than anything he'd ever seen in New York. The mosaic of hammers and axes across Seascape Square glowed from the torches. Taryn recalled when they'd fought Glenn and Jude, and how Stompy had broken free from the stables to protect him.

Across the city, thousands of windows flickered with firelight, and forges burned as blacksmiths worked tirelessly into the night. He would fight to protect these people with everything he had.

But for now, he soared.

18. UNDER PRESSURE

I HAVE no idea how much time passes as I stare into Pharos's ethereal eyes. My vision blurs at the edges against the relentless heat, but I stand strong, my body statuesque even as my feet burn and sweat sizzles against my skin.

My health continues to rise and dip at ten percent, caught in a perfect equilibrium as my increased regeneration activates and cancels in perpetuity. At some point, I enter a trancelike state, mesmerized by the swirl of energy that makes up my spirit guide. Without him, I would have succumbed long ago.

A loud clank pulls me from the trance, and the last of the molten iron drips into the trough. The tunnels along the walls close, followed by a patter of clacking noises as new tunnels open above. It sounds like a pack of dogs with untrimmed nails running across a wooden floor.

Orange bulbs of freshly blown glass fill the openings over-head, and the chittering sound that follows sets my hair on end. I barely have a moment to process what's happening before the bulbs descend, legs protruding from them as glasslike threads lower arachnids into the room.

I'm much too weak to fight anything in my current state, leaving me with no other option than to activate Berserker Rage. As soon as I do, my health rises rapidly, and bonus stats flood my system. Wounds stitch themselves together, burns mend, and for the first time in who knows how long, I don't notice the pain of the scorching temperature.

I take a step back and analyze the creature.

Molten Spider. *Level 30. Forged in the fiery tunnels beneath the Burning Desert, molten spiders can withstand intense heat. While their bodies are fragile, their legs are covered in glass barbs capable of ravaging enemies, and their venom causes temporary paralysis. Their unfortunate victims often find themselves immobilized in glass cocoons where they slowly roast alive.*

Thanks for the offer, but I'm gonna have to pass. I've had enough roasting for one day.

I count a dozen spiders lowering themselves into the room. I summon three horrors, and they stand by my side. Not wanting to wait for the spiders to turn me into minced meat, I punch the closest one and my fist shatters its glassy abdomen. The hit deals double damage thanks to Horror of Power, and the passive from Ram Rage activates, unleashing a wave of splash damage that sends several spiders spinning as they descend. A lava-like substance pours from the spider's broken abdomen like hot jelly, and the jagged carapace rips into my arm as I pull my hand free. Blue blood trickles down my arm, steaming as it hits the floor.

The creature hangs limp from its webbing, and another carves into my shoulder from behind with its barbed legs. I grab the spider, smashing its abdomen against one of my horns before tossing it into the molten iron surrounding the platform.

Another spider lunges at me, jabbing its pincers into my arm.

Thanks to Berserker Rage, the venom has no effect as it's injected into my bloodstream. I rip the spider free and crush it against my horns like a frat-boy chugging beer on game day.

Two more spiders dangle in the air beside me, grasping for me with their barbed legs. I grab one with each hand and smash them together. They break like glass bottles, leaking orange fluid all around.

Even without my weapons, I'm a force of nature as I rage against the creatures. Every punch leaves me with dozens of cuts that my increased regeneration fights to heal. I'm a bloody mess as I stomp and smash.

Pharos charges around the platform with his horns lowered, but his ethereal form passes through them like a ghost. His presence only ever seems to effect shadowy beings.

I kill the last spider with a punch powered by Concussive Force, and it rockets into the far wall, shattering its fragile body just as my rage ends. The full force of the high temperature hits me like a hammer, and I wobble before gaining my bearings. Luckily for me, the fight was enough to build my rage meter back up, so I'll have at least one more opportunity to use it going forward.

As the last of the spiders sinks into the molten iron, I receive another notification.

Trials of the Warforged: *Stage one complete. Stage two commencing.*

Stage Two: *Pressure*

Awesome. Not even a chance to rest before I have to tackle the next phase. With the spiders gone, my horrors' health once again begins to deteriorate. Pharos stops his pacing and looks up at me.

I take a deep breath of hot air and sigh. "I'm gonna need you, boy."

The walls to my left and right shift, and the sound of grating stone echoes around me. Slowly, the walls close in, passing over the molten trough and then grinding across the platform.

I pace back and forth, searching for a way out, but once again, there's nothing. Scaling the wall crosses my mind, but the obsidian walls are slick, and the spider tunnels are much too small even if I were able to climb to them.

If I was Taryn, I could fly out of here. But I'm not. I'm not here to escape. I'm here to survive. To forge myself anew. Stage one was called heat, and I had to endure it. If stage two is pressure, then I think I know what I need to do.

I turn sideways, take a wide-legged stance, and extend my arms. I wait for the walls to come to me, knowing that if I'm wrong then I'm about to be a Chod patty, extra well-done.

The walls touch my fingertips, and the hot stone burns against my skin. A moment later, the pressure locks me in place as I set my frame and brace myself against the massive walls with both arms and feet. Tension builds against my muscles, and they burn with the effort as I attempt to become an immovable object. It only takes a few seconds for my joints to ache as the force pushing against me threatens to dislocate my bones.

Sweat beads down my face, this time from effort as much as heat. Pharos moves before me, and I once again lean into his gaze.

This is going to be a long night.

19. THE BONDS OF BATTLE

PRESSLEY AND COMPANY PRESSED ONWARD. Traps lay in wait down the grand hallway, but one of the best perks of having a skeleton army meant his minions could set them off without dying. They passed through tripwires, spiked pits, and poisonous darts with ease. As long as his minions had HP remaining, Pressley could reconfigure them even after disaster.

"Ouchies." Limery grimaced as a spear shot from the wall and impaled a skeleton between the ribs, pinning it to the wall.

Minions swarmed their compatriot, prying the spear loose in quick order, and they continued down the passage. Over the course of the day, they'd fought cobras with broad hoods that swirled with mesmerizing patterns, black ooze that seeped between tiles on the floor and ceiling, and giant hammerhorn beetles with metallic exoskeletons.

So far, nothing had given them as much trouble as the gargoyles. Throughout the dungeon, there were faces carved into the walls and columns depicting various forms of beastkin. Sometimes, Pressley swore that he saw blue eyes following him out of the corner of his vision. Whenever he focused on one, though, it was nothing more than stone. Probably just a trick of the light.

He'd managed to add several cobras and beetles to his undead army, but thanks to Limery and Caustic's explosive combination, all of the oozes had been obliterated into gelatinous mist. They decided it would be wise to use the dragon's toxic gas in planned situations going forward.

Caustic walked on all fours, munching on the remains of a cobra. Soon, they arrived at a narrow bridge crossing a pit of sapphire blue water. Shadows moved beneath the water's surface.

Pressley crossed his arms as he took stock of the situation. "You two fly across. I'll take the bridge."

"Is yous sure?" Limery asked.

Pressley grunted his affirmation at the imp. He was beginning to understand why Chod was so fond of him. For all his antics, Limery was caring and protective, always watching out for others despite his small stature and chaotic nature. Pressley hated to admit it, but the imp was growing on him.

Once Limery and Caustic were on the other side, Pressley ordered his skeleton warriors to cross the bridge. They made it halfway before the waters stirred, and winged crocodiles jumped from below, gliding through the air on tiny wings as they arced over the bridge and knocked many of his minions into the pit. The wings were more suited for a bird than a large reptile, making it impossible for the creatures to actually fly, but they were enough to keep the crocodiles airborne for a brief period of time.

Fire crackled in Limery's palms, and Caustic roared his challenge, but Pressley held up a hand.

"Leave it to me."

He counted at least eight of the monsters, but it was possible there were more in the water. He didn't want to risk losing his newly reanimated undead, especially the hammerhorn beetles, so he kept them on solid ground. Unlike the gargoyles, the crocodiles were living beings that allowed the death knight to use most of his abilities.

Pressley cast Pestilence in the pit, and darkness permeated the water. It would drain the health and lower the Constitution of whatever lurked beneath, giving his skeletons an advantage. From the tumultuous water, he assumed the pit couldn't be that deep, so he sent more skeletons into its depths. They fought as disease ravaged the winged crocodiles and blood swirled in dark tendrils.

He unsheathed his sword and marched onto the bridge. Midway across, a croc launched itself at the death knight. He activated Defile, and corrosive energy coated his blade as he sliced the monster along its side. The attack wasn't fatal, but it wasn't meant to be. The crocodile dove back into the water as the wound festered and after a few moments, the crocodile floated to the surface belly-up.

Caustic stood at the edge of the pit, chomping at the bit to join the action. His feet shuffled with excitement and his chest rumbled.

Pressley shook his head. "Don't worry. I've got this."

He cast Reanimate on the dead crocodile, and the death knight's health dropped as a tendril of purple energy slithered from his palm, encircling the dead monster. The beast twitched, and then its body thrashed as it came to life under Pressley's control. More crocodile bodies floated to the surface from a combination of Pestilence and skeletal fortitude. He cast Reanimate again and again, draining half of his health but adding five more undead minions to his cause.

The last few crocodiles were easy work after that.

Limery grinned devilishly when Pressley made it to the other side. "Presslies is strongs."

The death knight leaned over the edge, chugging a health

potion and watching as skeletons climbed atop one another, making a bony ladder against the wall for the rest to climb out. A few had missing arms or legs from the crocodiles' rampage, and one had a tooth lodged in its skull, but most had survived the encounter. His undead crocs swam above the surface, their hides punctured in dozens of places, and all but one had damaged wings. The biggest downside of casting Reanimate was that the undead were summoned in whatever condition they were killed in. With broken wings, his new pets weren't flying out of the pit.

Pressley turned to Caustic. "Any chance you can help me get them out of the water?"

The dragon huffed.

"Please," he added.

With a grunt, Caustic took to the air. The flap of his wings sent waves splashing as he hovered above the water. He lowered, clenching one of the monsters in his talons. One by one, he gathered the undead reptiles and placed them safely on land until six of them groaned and snarled as they roamed the expansive hallway.

The rest of Pressley's undead crossed the bridge unimpeded, and the skeletons once again led the way, disarming more traps until the wide corridor emptied into an even larger atrium. Colossal pillars ran the perimeter of the large concourse, and massive doors lined the room on each side. They probably led to more monsters and hidden treasure, but straight ahead was the prize—a wide set of stairs leading to a massive golden door that could only be a throne room.

"That's where we need to go. But I don't think we'll make it across without trouble." He pointed to the doors on opposite sides of the atrium. "You can never trust a room that has closed doors before the big boss."

Caustic growled his challenge. It was clear that the dragon

wasn't scared of anything. He'd managed to gain two levels over the course of the day, but they had to be in the late hours of the night at this point.

"We should go back and get a few hours of rest before we press on."

Limery yawned, stretching his thin arms overhead. "Oh, yes. Limmy is sleepies."

"Let's go, then." Pressley sent his minions ahead of them. "I'll keep the first watch."

He was sure that he didn't actually need sleep to survive as a death knight. Before his transformation, he'd received debuffs and notifications when he'd push too hard. But now, nothing. He wasn't sure how a lack of sleep in-game would affect his body in the real world, however, so he always made time to rest just to be safe. He had a daughter waiting for him outside, and there was nothing he would do to jeopardize that.

They returned to the pit where they'd fought the winged crocodiles, using it as a natural barrier while Pressley ordered his minions to guard the tunnel in the direction of the throne room. He positioned a handful of skeletons on the other side of the bridge to guard their rear just in case there were monsters they'd missed. During his grind to power, he'd spent a lot of time in dungeons and had become familiar with how most of them operated. They could only be entered by one party at a time, and the monsters within wouldn't respawn until the dungeon was cleared or the party was defeated. Compared to most dungeons, this one was enormous, and there was no telling if they'd bypassed hidden doors or passageways.

Pressley's armor clanked as he rested against the stone wall. Caustic curled at his feet like a giant cat, tucking his massive tail and burying his head beneath a wing.

Limery stood before the death knight, arms clasped behind his back as he gave Pressley a pleading expression.

Pressley recognized that look. "What is it now?"

Limery's bulbous yellow eyes fluttered. "Can Limmy sleeps with yous?"

Pressley grunted. The little guy was probably used to sleeping next to Chod during their travels. Limery was cute in his own way, so Pressley relented, holding out his hand. "Fine. Come on over."

The imp nestled within the crook of the death knight's arm, and his body heat radiated through the armor. The sensation was like being covered with a warm blanket on a cold day. Pressley let out a pleasant sight as he embraced the warmth.

The ground vibrated as Caustic snored, and Limery soon joined him, a giant snot bubble inflating from his nose with each breath. Beneath his helm, hidden by darkness, Pressley smiled. He recalled rocking Eva to sleep when she was a baby, his daughter's gentle snores, and the connection of her warm skin against his own.

He sat there in blissful peace for hours until Caustic woke. The dragon yawned, stretching his front legs while his tail swished from his raised hindquarters, knocking an unlucky skeleton into the wall. He huffed, then took a watchful position behind the undead army.

With a dragon watching over him, Pressley drifted off, experiencing the best sleep he'd had since entering Mythos.

***

A hollow ring woke Pressley from dreams of a life he'd lost. Bulbous yellow eyes blinked inches from his helm before a second gong reverberated through his skull.

"Wake ups." Limery tapped the helm again. "Limmy is hungries."

"I'm up." Pressley groaned, and another gong rang out. "Dammit, stop that. I'm awake." He gently swatted the imp's hand away as he came to his senses. The pervading cold cradled him in its frigid embrace, amplified by Limery's absence. An uncontrollable shiver passed through Pressley as he stood, but after a few moments, he grew accustomed to the chill within his armor once again.

Since becoming a death knight, Pressley no longer had a need to eat in-game and thanks to the nanites, his body was nourished within the pod. He still had rations of cheese, hard bread, and cured meats from before his transformation, so he shared them between Limery and Caustic.

He watched as the dragon ate, swearing that the creature had grown overnight. Caustic's paws seemed bigger and the bearded scales around his chin denser. After they finished the meager breakfast, the group set off toward the atrium.

"Stay close to me," Pressley ordered. "Things will only get more dangerous from here."

Limery perched on the death knight's shoulder, calm as ever, while Caustic scanned the room with the same intensity as Pressley.

The minion army passed the closest columns that ran the perimeter of the domed ceiling. Pressley gripped his sword, ready for whatever awaited. Once the last of their party exited the hallway, a giant slab of stone fell from the ceiling and blocked their exit.

He'd expected as much. With the boss room so close, they would be tested.

The towering doors to each side of the atrium groaned as they opened, and an unsettling clacking stirred within their depths. Ghastly shapes moved in the dim torchlight as nearly a dozen bone-white scorpions, each one the size of a small car, spilled into the room. Red eyes blazed as pincers snapped, and their dangerous stingers pulsed with venom.

Bonecrusher Scorpion. *Level 35. The aptly named bonecrusher scorpion is not only capable of breaking bone with its serrated pincers, but it can also grind bones to dust within the vortex of crystalline teeth located behind its chelicerae. Ingesting the bone dust replenishes weakened or damaged areas of the scorpion's exoskeleton. The venom secreted from the stinger has paralytic properties, making it even easier to separate its prey limb from limb.*

Pressley gulped. Bone-eating scorpions, and he'd just brought them a buffet.

While Caustic and Limery shifted the odds in their favor, his skeletal minions had a tendency to lose limbs during battle, and he couldn't afford to offer up free health potions to his enemies. He needed the skeletons off the playing field ASAP.

"Don't let the scorpions anywhere close until my skeletons are gone." He opened his satchel and tossed it on the ground. "Inside."

The closest skeleton jumped into the bag, disappearing as if it were the hatch to a submarine.

Caustic roared and unfurled his wings, ready to fight, while Limery took to the air. Fire crackled in the imp's palm as he summoned fire walls around the perimeter. Pressley spread out the rest of his undead in a defensive formation, protecting the skeleton warriors as they filed into the expandable satchel. One by one, they jumped inside, their entire bodies disappearing into the bag no bigger than their rib cages.

All the while, scorpions scattered, skittering around the room.

Some climbed columns and a few more scaled the walls as the sound of snapping pincers filled the area. One of the scorpions passed through Limery's flame wall, and Pressley's undead cobra rose in challenge. It spread its mesmerizing hood only for the scorpion to sever the snake's head with one quick snip of its pincers.

Caustic dove at the scorpion, smashing it against the marble floor with his full weight and sinking his teeth into the arachnid's tail. With a sickening crunch, the tail ripped free, leaving a trail of fluid and sinew as the dragon flew away with it in his mouth.

Maybe this would be easier than Pressley had thought.

A terrifying shriek drew his gaze back to the dying scorpion. Its mouth opened, revealing a swirling pattern of teeth that spun like a buzzsaw. Using its pincer, the scorpion stuffed the cobra's limp body into its vortex, and Pressley fought the urge to gag as churning teeth ripped the snake apart like a meat grinder.

Almost instantly, the scorpion stopped bleeding and a new, shimmering tail sprouted from the wound.

"Shit." Pressley unsheathed his sword, urging his skeletons to climb in the bag faster.

He grimaced as a hammerhorn beetle charged the scorpion, expecting the worst. The scorpion opened its pincer, clasping it around the metallic, hammer-shaped horn on the beetle's head. Pressley expected the horn to shatter but somehow, it held. The beetle thrashed until the pincer slid free. The scorpion countered with its giant stinger, but the barbed tip clacked against the beetle's hardened shell as it bounced off and lodged in the marble floor. The scorpion jerked its tail, but the barbed tip didn't budge. While its opponent was stuck, the beetle swung its horn, hitting the scorpion with enough force that it unfurled like a whip, falling belly-up with its stinger still trapped. Caustic seized the opening, descending on the arachnid and ripping through the monster's underbelly with his claws.

"The bellies are their weakest part," Pressley shouted as the last skeleton disappeared within his bag. Now, he could focus his attention on the fight.

Nearby, another cobra fell, severed in half, and a winged crocodile took a stinger to its undead brain. The death knight cursed under his breath. It had been a while since a dungeon challenged him this much. His minions were fodder, but at least the beetles were a formidable force.

Pressley joined the fight, and dark energy coated his sword as he activated Defile. A scorpion set its eyes on the death knight, its stinger striking with impressive speed. Pressley parried one attack, and then another, before a pincer clamped around his midsection. His armor groaned as pressure mounted and his health trickled down.

He cast Unhallowed Ground while he parried another barrage of strikes. The ground took on a deathly hue, and the scorpion's health began to drop alongside his own. Pressley hacked at the scorpion's backside, but its exoskeleton was too dense for his cursed blade to penetrate. The stinger lashed at him again and again. A few times, it pierced the crease in his armor, but the venom had no effect against the death knight. The two were in a stalemate, slowly draining one another while chaos reigned all around.

A second pincer grasped Pressley above the first, pinning his arms to his side. The scorpion's red eyes blazed, and the death knight's health dropped faster. If he could find a way to free his arms, then he could use Lifesteal, but he needed a plan. Brute force wasn't getting him out of this. He needed to be smarter.

Pressley quit fighting, and the claws pressed against him with their full force. Bones creaked within his armor as they threatened to pulverize.

He closed his eyes, embracing the pain until a high-pitched ringing filled his helm. His daughter's face appeared in the void, and Pressley let Eva fuel him as he cast Forlorn Wail.

An unholy scream tore from the death knight's visage, stunning enemies directly in front of him. The grip relented just enough for him to free his arms, and he removed the gauntlet from his left hand, dropping it to the ground. The stun faded, and the scorpion's chelicerae clicked at the sight of the death knight's bony arm inches from its face. Its mouth opened, ready to turn bone to dust. With his other hand, Pressley shoved his Defiled sword into the arachnid's mouth. Disease spread from the wound, turning the exoskeleton black as the monster rotted from the inside out.

The death knight pried himself free and re-equipped his gauntlet. Nearby, Limery zoomed through the air, dodging stingers and peppering fireballs on their enemies. The scorpions were quick for their size, but the imp was faster. He summoned a firewall beneath a scorpion trapped between two hammerhorn beetles, charring and weakening its exoskeleton. A hit from the beetle's horn shattered the scorpion's carapace, leaking a creamy fluid onto the floor.

Caustic roared above the carnage, plucking a scorpion from a pillar by its tail. He landed, shaking his head like a dog with a toy, and smashing the scorpion against the column.

Over half of the scorpions were now dead. Pressley had lost all of his cobras and all but one crocodile, but the beetles were holding their own. Their metallic shells were a formidable armor capable of withstanding pincer and stinger. Pressley wanted to add a scorpion to his army but using Reanimate now would put his health dangerously low. Instead, he sheathed his sword and prepared to cast Lifesteal. Purple energy swirled within his palms and spread up his forearms as the magic built. He held the attack as long as he could, charging its power, and then released.

Energy shot across the room in a long tendril, hitting a scorpion. The arachnid flashed purple and then a bulb of life force channeled back toward Pressley. The increased health hit him like a shot of adrenaline, raising his HP to forty percent and weakening the scorpion enough for Limery to finish it off.

Pressley burned through his newly replenished HP as he cast Reanimate on the monster. Its body twitched back to life, and he commanded it to fight. It charged into battle, severing the tail of a surprised scorpion with its pincer. Pressley downed a health potion and activated Blight of the Undead. The death knight's armor rattled as a swarm of insects poured from within, surrounding him with a dense shroud that functioned as a shield.

The buzz was deafening as Pressley followed on the heels of his new pet. He cast Defile and stabbed the open wound of the tailless scorpion. His swarming armor blocked a vicious stinger strike as he moved onto a second scorpion whose severed pincer lay harmlessly on the floor. The death knight slashed at the twitching nub, infecting it with disease.

The plague spread through the open wounds, and the creatures quickly fell to Caustic and the hammerhorn beetles. When the last one died, Pressley canceled Blight of the Undead, and the remaining bugs dissipated into the ether.

An eerie quiet lingered over the carnage. His cobras and winged crocodiles were gone. All that was left of his undead minions were a singular scorpion and three beetles. The latter had turned out to be stronger than he'd imagined.

Pressley chugged several more health potions. He offered some to Limery and Caustic, but the imp had taken no damage while fighting from the air and Caustic's tough scales seemed to have gone unscathed.

Once his health was replenished, Pressley reanimated three more scorpions that hadn't been ripped apart in the carnage. He emptied his satchel of bones and resummoned his skeleton warriors. Between the skeletons, scorpions, and beetles, his army was still looking pretty good.

He faced Limery and Caustic. "Good job today. One more baddie and we can get out of here. You two ready for the boss?"

Caustic growled, and Limery perched on Pressley's shoulder, clenching his fist in determination. "We's readies."

"Good." The death knight's gaze settled on the golden door, wondering what might wait inside. "Let's go over some tactics."

Pressley stood in front of the throne room with Limery and Caustic at his side. An army of skeletons lined the steps beneath them. There were precious few undead left, but they were as prepared as they could be in the current situation.

The enormous door was nearly twenty feet tall. Pressley ran an armored finger across the metal, and it scratched beneath his touch. Solid gold. From the far side of the room where they'd entered, he'd thought the door was engraved with an ornate pattern of flowers that resembled fleur-de-lis. He'd seen the golden lilies everywhere the few times he'd visited New Orleans.

Up close, he realized that each engraving was a unique face recessed into the gold, similar to those that were scattered throughout the dungeon. Hundreds of them covered the massive door from floor to ceiling, and the eyes seemed to follow Pressley no matter where he stood.

"Creepies." Limery tapped one of the eyes with a claw.

"You can say that again." Pressley pushed the door, and it slid open without any effort.

The way the hinges silently opened was unsettling. They'd fought tooth and nail to get here, and now it was as if they were being welcomed into the final battle.

Although the rest of the dungeon was grand with its marble floors and elaborate pillars, it did nothing to prepare Pressley for what awaited inside the throne room.

"Pretties." Limery's eyes were full of greed as he took in the scene.

There was so much opulence that it was almost overwhelming. White marble speckled with gold flakes coated the floor, and golden walls lined the room engraved with detailed landscapes of mountains and cliffs overlooking the sea. The arched ceiling was decorated with beautiful, jeweled mosaics separated by ornately carved gilded ribs. Sconces burned along the walls, setting the entire room ablaze in all its shimmering glory.

The door closed with a click as the last of the minions entered the room.

"You made it further than most," a voice called out. It was the same one from when they first entered, simultaneously alluring and threatening.

Pressley's gaze followed the voice's origin, up a set of golden stairs to a platform where the manticore sat perched like a cat. She was everything he'd imagined and more.

A lion with crimson fur loomed above all, her large leathery wings tucked at her sides. A black, scorpion-like tail curved upward from behind, hovering above the manticore's head like a hellish crown. The tail was tipped with a thick stinger surrounded by several long barbs that stuck out like spikes on a morning star.

She wore a golden mask surrounded by a mane of luscious black fur. If not for her icy blue eyes, she'd be indistinguishable from the many faces that lined the door. Pressley stared at the manticore, unable to decipher if it was an incredibly detailed mask or if her face was truly golden.

"A dragon, too." She looked down upon them with an unforgiving leer. "You'll all make wonderful additions to my collection."

A chill ran up Pressley's already frigid spine. He wasn't sure what she meant by collection, but it undoubtedly had something to do with all of the bones he'd seen earlier. He activated Bone Detector, and thousands of white outlines filled the perimeter of his vision. Directly beneath the throne room, bones were piled several stories high. The way they sat in a perfect rectangle, he assumed there was some sort of pit. As the ability cataloged and organized each bone, the list grew so long that Pressley had to scroll through it. There were bones from elves, dwarves, monsters, and beastkin. So many beastkin. How many had she plucked from Sungrove in its prime?

Pressley analyzed the monster before him.

Manticore. *Unique Monster. Level 42. Man-eater, Beast-killer, Winged Fright, The Golden Devourer—the manticore has earned many names during her time in Mythos. While her origins are murky at best, some say she was sent as the gods' judgment, and her reputation had been paid for with blood all across the continent. From EllynMylly to Goldspire, she has left terror in her wake, along with legends and stories used to frighten unruly children—tales of winged monsters with stolen faces and purloined voices who dine on the bones of their victims. Though she has many names, they all come with the same warning. Beware.*

Pressley had read many monster descriptions during his journeys, but none were this intense. The manticore was a higher level and a force to be reckoned with, but he didn't come here to be anyone's plaything.

The death knight stood straight, locking eyes with the manticore's withering gaze. "Actually, you'll make a nice addition to mine."

She leaned forward, arching her back as she stretched her forelegs. Caustic growled as her obsidian claws curled around the edge of the platform, digging into the gold. She stepped forward, descending the stairs like a lion on the prowl.

With each step, her gilded features shifted, as if her face was made of fluid gold. Her guise morphed into a wolf beastkin, and she spoke with Jegaar's voice. "Is that so?"

She transformed again, this time taking on the wrinkles and raspy voice of an elderly man. "You have courage. I like that."

She licked her lips, and her face rearranged into a golden troll with horns that curled around her mane.

"Chods?" Limery squeaked, his face radiating concern.

Caustic unleashed a roar that shook the cavern, and the manticore grinned. Pressley had never seen such malevolence on the real Chod's face.

"Fear has a way of contaminating everything it touches." Her voice matched the troll's in every aspect. "It infects the flesh, seeps into the marrow of bones. I welcome a worthy challenger, anyone who can oppose my dread. To taste the bones of the brave and fearless is a delicacy—" Her eyes narrowed. "—but they are always tainted in the end."

Her visage shifted into a dwarf with dreadlocks and a thick beard, then to an imp.

"Taryns... Mommies..." Limery turned to Pressley, his bulbous eyes glistening. "Limmy doesn't likes this."

Pressley touched the imp's feet, the only comfort he could offer.

The manticore laughed, the impish cackle reminiscent of Limery's. In rapid succession, the mask transformed into the faces of other heroes and people Pressley had interacted with during his travels. Some he didn't recognize, centaurs and gnomes, likely memories from Limery or Caustic. The face morphed again and again, like a slot machine cycling through images.

The manticore descended the final step onto the marble floor and the mask settled on the face of a young girl with curly hair.

"Daddy, come home," an innocent voice begged.

Eva's voice hit Pressley like a sledgehammer, and he dropped to his knees. "No," he whispered as the golden visage of his daughter stared at him with a pleading expression. "How..."

She had never been anywhere near this game. How was her face here now? And her voice, it was just as he'd remembered.

Pressley covered the eye-slit of his helm, blocking his vision. The AI was inside his mind, using his memories in the same way that made all of this seem like reality. Eva wasn't here. He repeated the phrase. *Eva isn't here.*

No, that was a lie. His armored hands dug into the floor. She'd been with him every day since he'd entered. She'd pushed him to go harder, to be stronger, to fight. He saw her face when he needed strength, when he needed to be better. Eva was his motivation, and he'd be damned if he let a monster use her against him.

Anger burned within the death knight, so pure that it pushed the cold at bay. "How dare you!" Pressley roared as he stood and pulled an enchanted spear from his satchel.

He stepped forward, activating Defile as he launched Shadowweaver with all of his might at the monstrosity before him. Tendrils of dark energy coated the weapon, and the torchlight dimmed as it whistled through the air directly at the manticore's head.

Her tail twitched at the last moment, hitting the spear with enough force that it lodged in the wall, humming as energy reverberated down the staff. The manticore's face returned to its original form. Golden brows narrowed above her blue eyes, and she pounced.

"Supernova!" Pressley shouted, activating Blight of the Undead as he turned his back to the manticore.

Toxic gas poured from Caustic like a fog machine as insects swarmed around Pressley. There was a risk with using his gas in enclosed spaces with Limery around, but they'd prepared a few contingency plans. Flames crackled in the imp's palm as he tossed a fireball over Pressley's shoulder. The death knight tucked the imp against his chest as the gas ignited with violent thunder and a fiery shockwave slammed him into the wall.

His insect shield disintegrated from the blast, and a ringing echoed inside Pressley's helm as he stood. His vision blurred at the edges from the impact. Ten percent of his health was gone even with the shield, which was better than he'd hoped for. Smoke drifted through the air, obscuring sight of the manticore.

"You okay?" He still held Limery cradled in his arms.

The imp shook dust from his head and then took to the air. "Limmy is okays."

There was a dragon-sized indentation in the wall behind Caustic. He'd lost a quarter of his health from the backdraft of the attack.

Bones lay scattered across the floor from unlucky skeletons that had taken the blast head-on, and the gilded walls were warped from the heat. Pressley repaired his minions as quickly as possible while he searched for the manticore. His scorpions and beetles were still alive, but they'd lost a chunk of health from the blast.

Leathery wings flapped in the dust, and a mixture of gold rubble and jewels clinked across the floor as the air cleared.

"You hurt me, Daddy." The manticore wore Eva's face once

again, mangling it into a sinister sneer. She'd lost nearly the same amount of health as Pressley from the direct attack, but her HP was already replenishing at a rapid rate.

Pressley growled as he equipped his sword and ordered his minions to attack.

The manticore took to the air as the undead swarmed her, black wings flapping like sails to keep her aloft. Her tail swung like a wrecking ball beneath her, tossing skeletons like bowling pins. Their bodies broke apart as they collided with the walls. Scorpions snapped their pincers and struck with their stingers, but the manticore evaded them with ease. Skeleton archers fired arrows that fell from her hide like they were nothing more than toothpicks.

They needed something stronger.

Pressley turned to Caustic and Limery. "I need a distraction. As much time as you can buy me."

Caustic took to the air, gathering the manticore's attention while Pressley readied Blood Strike. It was one of his most powerful abilities since it dealt damage equal to the amount of HP he channeled into it. If they wanted to win, then he needed to go big.

Limery darted through the air behind the dragon, peppering the monster with fireballs. Caustic chomped at the manticore, but she was quick to evade and left him snapping at air. He roared his disapproval, lunging at the beast with his talons outstretched.

The manticore spun mid-air, hitting the dragon in the side with her barbed stinger. Caustic cried out in pain as he launched into the wall. Blood trickled from between his armored scales where the spikes had pierced him.

Limery pressed the attack while Pressley continued to charge his ability. An orb of crimson energy pulsed in front of him, powered by nearly a quarter of his health. The imp zoomed through the air, dodging the mace-like stinger and dangerous claws.

The manticore shot spikes from her tail, narrowly missing Limery and turning the far wall into a dartboard as they buried in the metal.

Almost ready, Pressley thought as his health dipped below half.

"Yous can't hits Limmy!" the imp cackled as he dodged another set of spikes.

"Are you sure about that?" Chod's voice boomed as the manticore's face transformed into the forest troll.

Limery's eyes widened, and the momentary hesitation was all the manticore needed. A spike hit the imp in the wing, pinning him to the wall.

Pressley unleashed Blood Strike just as the manticore lunged toward Limery. The death knight's health plummeted as his life force imbued the attack. Crimson energy exploded across the room, blasting the manticore in the side and knocking her from the air inches from tearing the imp in two.

She landed on her feet, snarling as she steadied herself.

The death knight had channeled three-quarters of his health into the attack, but the manticore had only dropped to half. His minions charged, but she swiped them away with her tail. A gong-like sound reverberated as a hammerhorn beetle's shell was dented from a hit.

Pressley cast Pestilence and Unhallowed Ground on the area where the manticore stood, and her health once again started to dip.

Limery struggled against the spike pinning him to the wall, grimacing as he tried to pry himself free. He was too high for Pressley to reach, and the spikes were too thin for Caustic to remove. The golden walls around the imp shimmered as they softened against his warm skin.

"Limery, go molten," Pressley shouted.

Flames engulfed the imp, and gold trickled around him like hot wax as the wall melted. The spike fell, clinking against the floor.

"You okay?" he asked the imp as he returned to his side.

Limery nodded, his eyes focused on the manticore. There was a hole in his wing, but it didn't seem to be hindering him. Caustic wobbled to join them, and the death knight patted the dragon on the side.

"I've got a plan, but I'm going to need some time." He pulled two vials from his satchel. "Stay safe until I get back."

The first vial was filled with a deep purple liquid. He'd found it clearing the bogs in the Marshlands long ago.

Item. Infernal Darkness Potion. *Covers opponent in a veil of darkness, making them unable to see or smell their surroundings for one minute.*

Pressley tossed the Infernal Darkness Potion at the manticore, and the vial shattered against the floor. Dense black smoke spread from the bottle, surrounding the dungeon boss. She roared, and spikes shot out blindly from the darkness, clinking as they stuck in the walls around the throne. Pressley had one minute before the effects faded and they'd be facing one pissed-off manticore.

He cast Blight of the Undead, and a swarm of insects poured from his armor. It might be overkill with the potion, but while active, the ability not only functioned as a shield, but his location also couldn't be tracked.

He held the second vial in front of him. A cream-colored liquid sparkled within. It was one of the three legendary potions he'd attained.

Legendary Item. Sub-dimensional Serum. *User gains access to the sub-dimensional plane, allowing them to phase between objects for up to one minute.*

Pressley had envisioned big plans for this item, but right now it might be the only hope for all three of them to make it out alive. He downed the sweet, frothy serum, and the world shifted from color to black and gray. Everything became translucent, allowing the death knight to see the thickness of walls and what lay beyond. He could see through everything except for the veil currently surrounding the manticore.

A timer ticked down across his vision as he searched for the bone pit. At the foot of the throne, there was a trapdoor hidden within the floor. Pressley descended through the door, almost like he was flying, and lowered himself down onto the mountain of bones.

Using his Bone Detector ability, he started filling his satchel. He needed to be out before the potion ended or he'd be trapped, and Limery and Caustic would be consigned to death. Chod would never forgive him if something happened to either of them.

He floated back to the surface just as the Infernal Darkness Potion ended. With Blight of the Undead still active, Pressley hid behind the throne, undetected by the manticore.

He emptied his satchel, summoning the bones of beastkin, monsters, and the many warriors who had attempted the dungeon over the years. Their bones clattered to life, and they charged the manticore.

She swiped at them with her tail, but the minions kept coming as bones poured from the bag. Pressley's health drained rapidly from the effort as dozens and then hundreds of skeletons enclosed upon the manticore, pinning her beneath a mountain of bones.

"Gas her up," Pressley ordered Caustic.

He unleashed a stream of green gas that seeped between the bones of Pressley's minions.

"Behind the throne." He waved them over, and once they were shielded, he turned to Limery. "Boom time."

The fireball hit the gas and exploded like a skeleton grenade. The throne room shook, followed by an overwhelming heat as bone shrapnel bounced off the walls and ceiling. White dust filled the area, and notifications flashed across Pressley's vision.

As the dust settled, Pressley stepped out from the cover of the throne. Half of it had been melted by the blast, and chunks of bone were lodged in the gold. His entire minion army was destroyed, but he could repurpose many of the bones.

In the center of the room, the manticore lay on her side. Caustic sniffed at the body.

Limery frowned at the dead monster. "Limmy didn't likes this monsties."

"I hate to break it to you, but she's going to be sticking around for a while." Pressley removed two Hag's Eyes from his satchel, and the purple gemstones glittered in his palm. He'd taken them from the covey he'd fought in Glossop Forest and had been saving them for just the right moment.

*Item. **Hag's Eye.** The jewel from the eye of a hag. This enchanted jewel is created when a hag joins a covey. It replaces one of their eyeballs. The original eyeball is then worn by a minion, sealing the pact between them. The minion then functions as a summon, controllable by the hag.*

Pressley could reanimate lesser monsters to join his army without issue, but he couldn't reanimate unique monsters like the manticore. Thanks to the Hag's Eye, he could change that. While a hag used the eye to bring a living being under her control, two Hag's Eyes could be used to link the death knight with a unique monster that he could summon to fight for him.

"Look away if you're squeamish." Pressley took a dagger and

removed the manticore's left eye, replacing it with one of the jewels.

Limery picked the manticore's eye off the ground, scrunched his nose, and then fed it to Caustic.

"That's disgusting." Pressley placed the second jewel in his own eye socket.

The purple stone glowed within his helm, and he cast Reanimate on the manticore. Her eye flickered to life but she lay there, unmoving.

Pressley wondered if he'd made a mistake, then her paw twitched, and he felt the connection establish. As an undead, the manticore could no longer speak or use her magical abilities to shift faces and mimic voices. However, she kept her incredible stats and fighting prowess.

The manticore stood. Although she was shorter than a horse, her powerful muscles were capable of carrying the death knight without issue. He mounted the manticore and trotted her around the throne room. Once they returned to Goldspire, he could purchase a proper saddle but for now, he could hold onto her mane for stability.

Limery watched the manticore uncertainly. "Presslies can flies now?"

Pressley tested his mental connection with the undead mount, and she extended her wings, jostling the death knight as she took to the air and glided across the throne room. When they landed, he pulled several health potions from his satchel and shared them with his companions. They were all worse for wear after the boss fight.

While Pressley waited for the potion to work its magic, he looked through some of his notifications.

You have defeated Manticore Dungeon. *Claim dungeon prize.*
Congratulations! You have reached level 41. +1 stat point to

distribute. +1 Strength and Intelligence class bonus. +1 ability point to distribute.

He'd managed to gain the last bit of experience he needed to hit level forty-one, and he already knew what he wanted to unlock with the new ability point.

Frost Reaper. *A layer of frost coats your body, slowing the movement speed and dexterity of enemies within your immediate vicinity. Can be channeled into ranged physical attacks. Melee attacks double the debuff.*

Since he was already cold all the time, what would a little frost hurt? With his new mount, he could put his crossbow to use, firing bolts that would slow enemies on the ground for his minions to overtake.

Pressley dismounted. Caustic sat on the floor nearby, munching on a large femur that had once been a minion. Something seemed different about the dragon. He was bigger from the levels gained during the fight, that much was certain, but there was something else that Pressley couldn't quite put his finger on. Maybe Chod would be able to tell. Fighting such a high-level opponent had given Caustic two more levels, pushing him to level twenty-four. Limery was now level twenty-nine.

"Looks!" Limery dug through the rubble at the base of the throne, tugging on the handle of a large chest. "Limmy founds the treasures!"

Pressley joined the imp just as his little hands pried open the lid. Golden light emanated from inside.

"Golds!" Limery cupped a handful of gold coins and let them fall through his fingers.

Pressley dug through the coins searching for items, but there was nothing else there. Not that he was complaining. With this much gold, they could buy their own rewards.

He patted the imp on the back. "According to Jegaar, Chod is going to be in the trials for a while. What do you say we get back to the city and spend some of this hard-earned gold?"

Limery flashed a devilish grin.

Pressley activated the exit prompt, and they were portaled to the dungeon entrance, where the late afternoon sun beamed down. He mounted the manticore and took flight, her massive wings carrying the death knight above the clouds.

He'd never been a fan of heights, but the view was magical. One day, he'd tell Eva all about it.

20. A Test of Mettle

My joints throb and muscles ache from the constant pressure as I keep the two enclosing walls from crushing me into pulp. Sweat steams from my body amidst the unrelenting heat, and the smell of charred meat fills my nostrils with every breath of hot air. I'm pretty sure the skin of my palms has melted to the obsidian, but that's the least of my problems as my bones threaten to snap from their sockets.

All I can do is grimace and bear it as time loses all meaning aside from the debuffs I receive due to lack of sleep and nutrition. In my early days in Mythos, they would have incapacitated me, but sheer determination and troll fortitude keeps me going.

According to the debuff notifications, I've been at the first two phases for at least twenty-four hours, probably a lot longer. These have been the most grueling hours of my life but right now, enduring these trials is the best thing I can do to keep those that I care about safe. If I falter in the slightest, I'll be crushed to death and all of this suffering will have been in vain.

Pharos stares up at me, a calming presence amid the heat and pressure that promises to forge me into something stronger if I can just hold on. Whenever I feel myself giving in, I look into his swirling eyes.

As my spirit beast, he and I are connected in a way I can't fully explain. While he's a representation of the stubbornness and determination of my spirit, part of me resides in him as well. Maybe it's the heat or dehydration, but I can see myself in the depths of his eyes if I look hard enough. It's almost as if his spirit is composed of the memories that have made me who I am—the accomplishments but also the failures and struggles.

I lose myself in his eyes as visions of my past play out in shimmering hues of orange and white. I watch myself in some of my proudest moments as I win my first gaming tournament at school, when I gain my first followers on my stream, and then again when Taryn and I set a new record for active viewers during a dungeon raid. I see my struggles as well. Nights alone in an empty penthouse as I stare over a bustling city. Dad leaving a meeting and walking past me like I don't exist as I wait in reception.

And then there are my failures. The first time I was denied a spot on a pro team. The second. The third. Those failures shaped me, pushed me toward streaming as an alternative to still do what I loved. Taryn was right when he said I lost myself somewhere along the way. At some point, streaming became less about entertainment and having fun and more about proving everyone wrong. With so many people watching, I needed to be the best. I needed to show the world that those pro teams had made a mistake when they passed on me. To do that, I couldn't be the problem. If there was a mistake, I blamed it on my teammates. If things went south, then they were the reason.

The charity match—the one that got me here—appears in ethereal detail. I was at the Mythos Gaming headquarters with more eyes watching me than ever before. The event was supposed to be a fun time bringing streamers together from across the country to play before a live audience. For me, it was more than that. I wanted to show everyone once and for all that I deserved to be pro.

But I didn't. I was playing sloppy, and I knew it. It was my fault that Dorothy got ganked by the enemy. I'd pushed too far in my lane and then had to retreat to heal, leaving my opponent free to wander. I called out that they were MIA too late, and Dorothy paid for it. Our team started snowballing after that, and what did I do?

I raged.

I close my eyes when that portion plays out, but I still see it crystal clear in my mind. Ruthless, that's what I was. I was embarrassed, and I wanted to make someone else hurt the same way I did. Shame sinks into the pit of my stomach. Dorothy has every right to hate me for what I did. I deserved to be punished for my actions, and yet somehow, I got sent here.

I blink away the tears that burn my eyes and sting my skin. Dorothy will come for me. She deserves her vengeance for what I said and for everything that came after. This isn't a fight I can win, no matter the outcome. Still, I can't afford to let her kill me. Not when we're this close to the end.

The pressure against my palms relents, and I collapse to the floor. Heaving breaths wrack my body, and my muscles tremble uncontrollably.

The walls only retreat about a foot to each side, and I barely have time to savor the release before molten spiders descend from the ceiling again. With the limited entry points, fewer spiders enter at once, but I'm forced to fight them off in a narrow corridor.

I activate Berserker Rage, and all of my aches and pains alleviate as I smash through the crystalline arachnids. Their bodies and barbed legs tear into me with every punch, and shattered glass litters the floor. I leave smoldering blue footprints in my wake as I take out every frustration from the last few days on the fragile creatures until none remain.

Once my rage ends, the debuffs return in full force. I steady myself against the blistering wall and notice the vital fluids seeping from the broken legs and cracked abdomens that line the floor. I gather what I can salvage, tilting a leg until the hot, mucous-like liquid drips into my mouth. My passive Savage ability allows me to drink the fluids without getting sick. I fight the urge to gag as the unpleasant taste trails down my throat. While I can't do anything about the sleep debuffs, this should put the hunger debuff to rest for now.

The next phase of the trials will be starting soon, but I check the notification that I received from killing the spiders.

Congratulations! You have reached level 31. +1 stat point to distribute. +1 Strength and Constitution racial bonus. +1 ability point to distribute.

Hell yes! I saved the last ability point I received in case I needed it for the Warforged class after the trials, but now that I have two, I can finally unlock a summoner advancement.

Summoner Advancement.

Dreadbeasts. Unlock for further details.

Dual Subclass. Unlock for further details.

There's no point in unlocking a dual subclass when my horrors already synergize perfectly with my troll stats. I unlock Dreadbeasts, and a new set of abilities appear.

***Summon Dreadbeast. (Passive).** Ability to summon a dreadbeast (limit 10 per subspecies). Each dreadbeast grants a unique ability. For every dreadbeast active, gain 1% increased damage and health points. Unlike horrors, dreadbeasts do not decay outside of combat. While a dreadbeast is active, horror decay is reduced by 50%.*

***Dreadbeast of Torment.** Summon a dreadbeast with 20% of your Strength. Cost: 500 mana. Cooldown: 30 seconds. Bonus: While Dreadbeast of Torment is active, your attacks have a 20% chance to induce fear.*

***Dreadbeast of Despair.** Summon a dreadbeast with 20% of your health points. Cost: 500 mana. Cooldown: 30 seconds. Bonus: Opponents near Dreadbeast of Despair lose 1% health per second. (Maximum 10%)*

***Dreadbeast of Agony.** Summon a dreadbeast with 20% of your attack speed. Cost: 500 mana. Cooldown: 30 seconds. Bonus: Attacks from Dreadbeast of Agony reduce healing and health regeneration by 50%.*

Holy shit. I read over the descriptions several times, and my mind envisions numerous possibilities for each dreadbeast. I can only summon ten of each, and with my mana pool still at five thousand, that means I can only summon ten at a time before it needs to replenish. But since they don't decay over time, I can wait for my mana to refill and summon a full army. With only one dreadbeast active, my horrors will last twice as long. A grin plasters my face. These are going to be awesome!

Just like when I unlocked my horror summoning path, I still have the ability point to use on one of the dreadbeasts. As much as I would love to use both ability points and unlock two dreadbeasts, there's no way I'm risking not being able to unlock the Warforged class when I've come this far.

Each dreadbeast is similar to one of the horrors, basing their attributes off my Strength, Constitution, and Dexterity but their bonus abilities are completely different. Ten Dreadbeasts of Torment with a twenty percent chance each to cause fear could turn a battle. The Dreadbeasts of Despair can kill weak enemies just by being in their presence. And then the Dreadbeasts of Agony will make it difficult for opponents to heal during a fight.

While I'm thinking it over, I receive a new notification.

Trials of the Warforged: *Stage two complete. Stage three commencing.*

Stage Three: *Forge*

The walls start closing in again, and I unlock Dreadbeast of Torment while I get into position. If I can only summon one dreadbeast, then having the strongest seems like the best option.

I extend my hands and only have a few moments before the walls lock me into place once again. Heat swells in the narrow corridor, and I try to piece together what the third stage will entail in an effort to take my mind off the discomfort.

Stage one was Heat and to complete it, I had to endure the high temperatures. Stage two was Pressure, forcing me to keep the walls from crushing me. Stage three is Forge.

Pharos stands in front of me, and I look into his eyes.

"What do you think stage three will be, bo—"

A piece of the ceiling dislodges, and a hammer-shaped slab of obsidian swings on a pendulum, passing through Pharos's head and hitting me in the chest at the same time as an equal force smashes me in the back. The hit knocks the air from my lungs, and I gasp for breath while I try to hold my position between the walls.

An unseen force pulls the slab through the air until it rests against the ceiling, and then it drops again. I tense my muscles as the hammer falls, unable to protect myself from the impending blow. The two hammers crush me, and I scream as the pain radiates across my midsection. I'm thankful that I at least have air in my lungs.

Pharos paces in front of me as the hammers rise.

"It's okay, boy." I grimace as the agony from the blow fades. "There's nothing you can do."

He takes his customary position in front of me, and I brace for impact. The hammers fall again and again, each time threatening to unravel me. Even with my high Constitution, my health chips away with each hit, falling in slivers like in the first trial. Eventually, my increased regeneration will kick in. I just hope it will be enough.

The hits are rhythmic, like a metronome of abuse that I must endure. Unlike the first two trials, the pain isn't constant; it ebbs and flows, forcing me to acknowledge it each time.

I close my eyes and tense my muscles. All I can do is wait for it to end.

21. FATHER KNOWS BEST

Valery glared at her father as he hovered in the doorway to her office.

"Don't look at me like that. It reminds me of your mother." He scrunched his brow, squeezing the bridge of his nose between his fingers. "May I come in? We need to talk."

She ignored the jab, leaning back in her chair and crossing her arms. This was the first time she'd seen him since the inspector for the Federal Bureau of Prisons had announced he was recommending her program be shut down. "What do you want?"

"Come on, Val." Her father let out an exasperated sigh, as if she was the one inconveniencing him. "Can't you see I did this for you? You'll soon realize that this is for the best."

"Shutting down my program and causing trouble with the federal government is helping me?" Valery's lip curled in disgust. "If this is you helping, then please continue. Maybe I'll be an inmate for the next round of testing."

"Always so dramatic." He laughed, entering the room and sitting across from her. "Do I need to spell it out for you?"

Valery narrowed her eyes. She couldn't believe the gall of her father, not only showing up after wrecking the program she'd spent years working on but then acting like he was doing her a favor. "Please do."

"I owe you an apology."

Her frown faltered. An apology was unexpected. He was a man who never apologized to anyone. It was one of the many reasons her mother had left him.

When Valery didn't respond, he continued. "I'm sorry that I didn't believe in your program from the start. It seemed too unrealistic, too unachievable, and the practical applications never made the investment worth it from a business perspective." He leaned forward. "I was wrong. It has potential, real potential, but you're wasting it on a government program. I'm sorry I blew the whistle, but it's for the best. Once the program is shut down, it will allow us to develop the technology however we want."

"Us? This is not an 'us' program. This was my idea, my brainchild. I spent years in the research phase. Years failing. And when I finally start to see real progress, you decide to meddle around and fuck it all up." Valery stood, her finger striking like a viper as she pointed at the door. "Get out of my office."

Her father looked shocked. His expression was almost enough to make her smile. She'd never spoken to him like this before, but she was at her wit's end.

"Fine." He stood, pausing for a moment as if gathering his thoughts. "If you don't want me involved, then that's fine, but you'll still be better off doing things without government oversight."

"You still don't see it." She clenched her fist, and the nails dug into her skin. "That wasn't your decision to make. You could have talked to me. You could have told me what you were thinking.

Maybe I would have agreed, maybe not, but goddammit, Dad, you're not the only person with a brain in this family."

"I know that, Val." He looked at his feet, and for what might have been the first time in Valery's life, she saw the man beneath the mythos. "You're right. I should have talked with you. You've built something truly amazing, and I want to see you make the most of it."

"You sure have a funny way of showing it." She sighed and leaned against her desk. "We built this amazing world, but that was only part of the goal. Using the nanotech, I thought we could actually use it to help people in a way that had never been done before. We could heal trauma and provide therapy, all while the user becomes a hero in their own story. And believe it or not, it's actually working. I've witnessed some of these men changing right before my eyes." She met her father's gaze. "Now, I'm afraid we're going to lose it all."

"They aren't going to take what you built. You know that, right? They'll pull the prisoners, but the game will go on."

"That's what I'm worried about. The game is constantly evolving, reacting to the world as the users influence it. Right now, they are on the precipice of a war that could completely shift the nature of the world, and you may have shifted the odds just because you wanted to watch a little drama." Her hands shook as a fresh surge of anger coursed through her. She took a deep breath to steady herself. "You've seen the data. You've seen how many instances of the AI we tested before we got to this one. It doesn't matter how many opportunities there are if we can't recreate this again. Most of all, there's no guarantee we can recreate what happened to Chad Johnson." Valery turned to face the wall. Everything had been going so well, and now there was nothing left to do but let the chips fall and see if there were any pieces to pick up. "Now, please leave."

22. FORGED

I'm not going to make it. That's the only thing I can think as the obsidian hammers fall from the ceiling and slam into my stomach and back. Pain erupts from the hit, jolting through my nervous system all the way to my toes and fingers. Heat and pressure were one thing, but getting my ass beaten for hours on end is going to break me.

The blue skin around my midsection glows orange from the repeated hits I've taken. Luminous veins branch out from those spots, arcing down my thighs and across my chest. I'm not sure what's happening, but it feels like I'm about to combust. My head throbs with every beat of my racing heart.

Each time the hammers crash into me, my body grows hotter and my health drops into the red. Increased Regeneration takes effect as the hammers rise to the ceiling, and I replenish just enough HP to survive the cycle again.

The hammers fall, battering against my midsection. Every breath of hot air sends a wave of pain through my ribs and abdominals. I roar from the misery, my screams echoing through the narrow corridor. My eyes burn, my head throbs, and my muscles spasm as if they are about to give out. I've pushed myself to the brink, but I honestly don't know how much more I can endure.

Another blow, and my knee buckles for a moment. Cold sweat erupts across my body, quickly turning to steam as I force myself back into position.

My head tilts back, and I squeeze my eyes shut until stars dance in the blackness.

"I'm sorry," I whisper to no one.

As much as I want to succeed, my body is failing me. I should have been stronger before I attempted the trials. Now, I understand why the process killed most who attempted it.

"Do not give in," a husky and somewhat youthful voice calls to me.

"Who said that?" I look over my shoulder, but the corridor is empty. The tunnels above as well. "Pharos?" I scrunch my eyes at the spirit guide just as the hammer passes through his face, colliding with my body. A loud groan escapes as my chin falls to my chest.

"Do not give in," the voice says again.

This is it. My head bobbles as I force a laugh. I've finally lost my mind and now I'm hearing voices from a goat.

"I would be insulted that you confuse me with a goat were it not for your situation."

There's an edge of pride to the snarky voice. Is this some kind of bonus from my dreadbeast class? I haven't summoned one yet, so maybe it's talking to me from the shadowlands or wherever it is the creatures spawn from.

"Dreadbeast?" The hammers slam into me, and red veins spread from my chest to my shoulders.

"The dwarf is right. You can be very dense." The voice scoffs. *"Perhaps I should have bonded with him instead."*

Bonded? "Caustic? Is that you?"

"It is good to see the trials have not turned your brains to mush." Another wave of pain passes through me as the hammers collide. *"You have the heart of a dragon. I know because I chose you. You will not give in to this torment."*

I gasp for breath and hot air fills my lungs, igniting my throbbing ribs. "Where are you? How is this possible?"

"I have grown stronger during my time in the dungeon, and thus, our bond has strengthened. You are no longer alone."

This is crazy. Or maybe I've lost my mind to the trials. I wait for the next hit to pass and then speak. "I have so many questions."

"They will be answered in time. For now, you must endure."

"I don't know how much more I can take." My voice shakes along with my muscles.

"You will not give in." Caustic is still only a juvenile dragon, but there is no room for debate in his tone. *"You have been through much already. This is but another challenge to overcome."* His growl rumbles in my mind. *"You will not break."*

Against all odds, I believe him. *I will not break.* I repeat the mantra in my mind with every hit I take. *I will not break.* When the hammers crash into me, and molten veins branch down my arms and legs, I stand strong. *I will not break.* When my fingers and toes turn orange, like the blazing coals of a fire, I stay standing. *I. Will. Not. Break.*

When my vision blurs from the heat and all I can see is orange, I scream the words with primal ferocity. "I will not break!"

Something shifts within me, and Berserker Rage activates of its own accord. My muscles bulge, and stats flood my system. There's a gurgle overhead just before rushing water pours from the tunnels, hissing against the hot surface as a waterfall cascades over me. It does nothing to cool my molten body, and steam fills the corridor, thick and muggy as it obscures everything, even Pharos's glowing form.

When the obsidian slabs fall, they clank against me like a hammer striking the anvil. To my surprise, it doesn't hurt. Powered by unbridled rage, I extend my arms, and the walls grind against the floor, moving back several inches. The hammers fall again, and I push against the walls with everything I have. They grind several inches across the floor, allowing me to move as the stone slabs collide. I wrap my arms around one of the hammers, ripping it from the ceiling and turning it sideways to wedge between the collapsing walls as a brace. I wait for the second hammer to fall and catch it mid-swing, tearing it down.

Eventually, the steam fades, and I look down at the corded muscle of my troll body, no longer green or blue but the shimmering silver of fluid steel.

Metal as fuck. I did it!

A notification flashes across my vision.

Congratulations! You have unlocked the Warforged class. Through willpower and determination, your body has been honed and reforged into a weapon of war. This is a specialized barbarian sub-class.

New Abilities:

Warforged (*Passive*): *When entering a rage, your body transforms into fluid steel, increasing your Constitution tenfold. You cannot be stunned, slowed, poisoned, or otherwise affected.*

Cold Rage: *The Warforged are weapons, always prepared for a fight. Unlike Berserker Rage, which requires a full rage meter to acti-*

*vate, Cold Rage is always at your disposal, granting the same perks whenever they are needed. **Bonus:** Rage meter increased to 1000.*

This is too good to be true. I read over the ability descriptions several times to make sure I understand. If my interpretation is correct, I'm now able to activate my rage any time I want, and when I do, my Constitution is multiplied by ten. That would increase my already high Constitution from around fifty to almost five hundred. That's god-tier tanking ability. Not only that, my rage meter has grown from one hundred to a thousand, and I can use the rage I build up at any point without needing a full rage meter.

I just became a huge pain in the ass for someone.

As if to test my hypothesis, I hear the clatter of molten spiders just before they descend from the ceiling. My metal fist shatters the first, and shards of glass clink against my silver skin. A spider lands on my shoulder, and its barbed legs screech across my metallic body, leaving me unharmed. I crush its abdomen with my fist, grinding its glass body into dust.

What may prove to be the biggest advantage of Cold Rage is that my attacks still build my rage meter, even when I'm in my Warforged form. Berserker Rage has a time limit that counts down from activation, but I can use Cold Rage continuously as long as I'm building up my rage meter while I fight. This is a game-changer.

One by one, I destroy the spiders with ease. When there's nothing left but me and Pharos, I cancel Cold Rage. My body returns to its natural blue state, along with the sleep debuffs. I wobble under the stress of that before activating Cold Rage again. With a half-full rage meter, I can keep the debuffs at bay for a little while longer.

"You must rest," Caustic warns me. *"Even dragons need sleep."*

Before I have time to respond, another notification flashes across my vision.

Trials of the Warforged: *Complete*

Stone grinds as the walls retract across the platform, over the now empty trough and back to their original position. A glowing outline forms in the wall behind me, and I see a door leading back into the cavern I entered from.

As soon as I leave the trial room, I'm inundated with several notifications. My ability to send messages also returns and I reach out to Taryn, letting him know that I completed the trials.

I'm not sure what time it is, but Caustic is right. I need to rest. Once I check these notifications, I'll be out like a light.

The first one is no surprise.

Congratulations! Draconic Convergence has reached level 3.

This place must have blocked out any updates that weren't happening within the trials. I pull up the stats for our bond to see exactly what we unlocked.

Draconic Convergence: *The convergence fuses an unbreakable bond that grows stronger over time. No two convergences are the same. Each one evolves based on the relationship between the dragon and their chosen counterpart.*

Name: *Caustic*
Species: *Green Dragon*
Level: *24*

Convergence Level:

1. Draconic Bond- You have made an unbreakable bond with a dragon and forged a telepathic link that may expand in the future. In its current state, intense spikes in emotion may blend between psyches.

2. Spatial Bond- You are now able to mark the location of the dragon no matter how far apart you are.

3. Communication Bond- You are now able to speak to one another through your telepathic bond.

Damn, Caustic wasn't lying. He gained seven levels clearing the dungeon with Pressley. I can't wait to hear all about that.

The second notification is a message from Valery. My stomach sinks as I open it.

Incoming Message (Admin): *I don't have any updates for you on the state of the program, but I just wanted to say that I'm proud of you. You've come a long way from the kid I first met.*

I barely know the woman but for some reason, my eyes are misty. Valery is definitely not the person I envisioned that first day I walked into the lab. She's proud of me. How long have I waited to hear those words? I close the message and blink back the surge of emotion that those two sentences evoke. It's suddenly hard to swallow.

I don't know if she's watching me right now, but I look to the ceiling.

"Thank you," I whisper.

Pharos stands by the cavern that leads to the Narrow Pass. The exit is still closed, sandwiched between two sides of the mountain until I decide to leave.

I gather my weapons from the center of the room and reequip my satchel, eating some of the rations before finding a corner to sleep in. As I settle down, I realize that I didn't have to use an ability point to unlock the Warforged class. That means I can unlock another dreadbeast!

Sleep can wait. I pull up my stats to refresh my memory on the two remaining options.

Dreadbeast of Despair. *Summon a dreadbeast with 20% of your health points. Cost: 500 mana. Cooldown: 30 seconds. Bonus: Opponents near Dreadbeast of Despair lose 1% health per second. (Maximum 10%)*

Dreadbeast of Agony. *Summon a dreadbeast with 20% of your attack speed. Cost: 500 mana. Cooldown: 30 seconds. Bonus: Attacks from Dreadbeast of Agony reduce healing and health regeneration by 50%.*

The likelihood that I'll gain two more levels between now and the invasion is slim, so whichever one I pick will be joining the Dreadbeast of Torment in Mosstar. A monster that inflicts reduced healing seems great for battle, but then I recall the thousands of undead outside the city gates. We're going to be surrounded by enemies and having a constant health drain will likely be even more valuable.

I select Dreadbeasts of Despair, and then I put my new stat point into Dexterity.

"*Sleep,*" Caustic growls at me.

"Soon." He's the juvenile and yet it's me who feels like a kid being bossed around. "I just want to see one thing."

I summon a Dreadbeast of Torment, and the air in front of me cracks as reality tears and a demonic canine steps through the rift. Where my horrors only come up to my knees, this one is nearly waist high and the size of a massive wolf. The dreadbeast has black fur aside from a silver mane that runs the length of its spine. Its orange eyes stare at me, and two short horns jut upward from its head, arcing backward between its pointed ears. A set of dangerous fangs descend several inches past its snout.

The dreadbeast's massive paws pad against the floor as it approaches Pharos. Its hackles raise, and it snarls at the spirit guide. Pharos lowers his head, scraping his hooves against the floor.

"Easy now. We're all on the same side."

Shadow and light—the two animals are about as opposite as possible, but I'll need them both in the battle to come.

The dreadbeast continues to snarl even as it joins my side. Next, I summon a Dreadbeast of Despair. It appears in a similar fashion, stepping through a rift. The creature that emerges is both majestic and terrifying.

A giant black bison stands nearly chest high with thick, ebony fur so dark it's almost a void. Shadowy tendrils flicker and flare from its body, and two blood-red horns curve upward from its mighty head.

"Well, you guys are fucking scary." I pat the bison on its broad side, and it huffs, smoke shooting from its nostrils. "Now, that's badass. I need the three of you to keep an eye on me while I sleep."

The wolf-like dreadbeast settles at my feet, its gaze focused on the exit. Pharos stands by my shoulder, and the demonic bison doesn't move as tendrils of dark energy flicker along its body.

"Good night, Caustic." I reach out to the dragon through our bond. "I think I'm in good hands."

I cancel Cold Rage, and I'm asleep before my head hits the floor.

23. STONES

High in the clouds, Pressley watched the sun set beyond the Black Mountains. Streaks of pink and orange framed their dark silhouettes. The sight was beautiful, peaceful even.

This sure beat the dull monotony of a prison cell.

He held onto the manticore's dark mane as she shifted course, jostling the death knight with a flap of her black wings. Her normally curled tail lay flat like a rudder, helping to guide her path. They were almost back to Goldspire and had made the flight from the dungeon in a fraction of the time it had taken the wing-hoof oxen.

To his right, Caustic soared, his outstretched wings shimmering emerald in the fading daylight. The dragon's movement was smooth and graceful as his wings rode the current, as if he weighed nothing.

Limery darted through the air like a hummingbird, joining Pressley atop the manticore's back. He was an antsy little imp. The entire journey, he'd been zipping from the death knight to Caustic, or yapping about some adventure he and Chod had gotten into. Pressley had no idea how Chod put up with it, but he was stuck with the little guy until the troll returned. And probably after.

Pressley took one last look over his shoulder at the hazy mountains as they began their descent.

Chod had held up his end of the bargain. Pressley fully recognized he wouldn't have bonded the manticore without Caustic and Limery's help. Now, he had to fulfill his part. If war awaited, he could put the full extent of his abilities to use. For most of his time in Mythos, the death knight had sought gold and power. It had been the driving force behind his every action. Now, he felt his priorities shifting. Gold and power were nice, but he wanted to make his daughter proud. He wanted glory.

The manticore landed outside of the city gates as surreptitiously as a cat. For all of Caustic's grace in the air, the dragon thudded to the ground, stirring a cloud of dust.

"We's backs." Limery somersaulted in the air a few feet ahead.

Pressley dismounted the manticore. "Let me check her into the stables, and then what do you say we go grab a drink? We can spend some of this hard-earned gold."

"Oh, yes!" The imp clasped his hands together. "Limmy likes thats."

Pressley turned to Caustic. "Want me to book you a room, too?"

The dragon huffed before turning his back on the death knight and launching himself into the twilight sky. Pressley looked at Limery and shrugged. Maybe the dragon wanted to hunt something more challenging. Regardless, it wasn't as if Pressley could do anything about it.

The city guards were hesitant to let the manticore through the gates, but Pressley still had the parchment signed by the Scholars

Guild for his last venture. When he showed them Jegaar's signature, they reluctantly allowed them to enter.

Beastkin stared at the manticore as she strutted through the streets. There was a terror to her beauty, or more likely a beauty to her terror. In a place where Pressley had walked unmolested, she captivated every eye they passed. She held her head high, the gilded visage reflecting every face that looked upon her. The purple Hag's Eye glowed in one eye, matching Pressley's, and her barbed tail swayed with her movements. With wings tucked at her side, she followed the death knight to the stables, where a minotaur was sweeping the entrance as they arrived.

"I need a stable for the night. The best that you have." Pressley jingled his coin purse.

The minotaur's gaze shifted from the coins to the manticore, and his eyes widened. "Is that..." His words trailed off as he stared at the manticore.

"A manticore." Pressley patted her shoulder. "She's my mount."

"Is it safe?" The minotaur was still transfixed by the manticore, unable to look away.

Pressley cleared his throat, and the sinister sound was enough to draw the beastkin's attention. "*She* is under my control. That is all you need to know."

The minotaur gulped. "Very well. If you'll follow me right this way."

Pressley sighed. It was customary for the stable-hands to take the animals back themselves, but he couldn't blame the minotaur's reticence. Unlike a dragon, who claimed respect, the manticore was feared. She'd earned her reputation through her reign of terror. In that way, at least, she and the death knight were the perfect pairing.

After leading the manticore into a large stable, Pressley faced the wide-eyed, hulking minotaur. "See that she's fed and groomed. I'll return tomorrow."

Outside the stables, he searched for the nearest tavern and spotted a building with a sign depicting a silver falcon wearing an eye patch and holding a glass of wine. "That should work."

"Presslies." Limery stood in the street, his arms clasped behind his back.

"I know that look." He'd seen it from his daughter when she wanted ice cream before bed. "What do you want now?"

The imp fluttered his eyes. "You's saids that Limmy can spends some of the golds."

The death knight grunted. "I did."

"Limmy wants to buys something before we drinks."

"Of course you do." Pressley pushed thoughts of a relaxing ale aside. "What is it?"

Limery grinned, taking to the air. "Follow Limmy!"

He followed the imp down several streets, passing through alleys and over a bridge where gurgling water fed the bathhouses. Limery finally slowed down in front of a basilica, where the vendors of the open-air market were packing up for the day.

"This ways." Limery pointed, leading Pressley into a long, open hall. The interior was lined with ornately carved columns and a vaulted ceiling painted with colorful landscapes and floral designs.

Pressley grunted, not sure why this couldn't wait until the morning, but he followed nonetheless, reminding himself that Limery was a key piece of their success. There would be no gold without the imp.

The death knight had passed by the basilica on occasion during his time in Goldspire. It reminded him of a flea market with the variety of items for sale. Everything from spices to wool, clothing, and ancient books.

An owl beastkin leaned over a crate, packing away vials of pink perfume. Its gaze followed the death knight as he passed, its head twisting to the point that it looked like it would snap.

Pressley kept the owl's gaze as he walked by, and his helm twisted backward, his skeleton body no longer restricted by ligaments and muscle. The death knight's jeweled eye glowed menacingly, and the owl hooted in surprise, packing faster.

He found Limery talking to an elephant beastkin. The imp stood atop a table filled with dozens of flat, circular stones, each one with a hole in its center.

Pressley held one and examined it. They were communication stones, exactly like the one he'd been given in Vanaria. He couldn't recall the exact history of the items, but he knew they had something to do with the imps. They had been messengers once upon a time.

"What do you need a communication stone for?" Pressley set the stone back on the table. "Don't you already have one?"

Limery nods. "Yes, Limmy has ones. But these isn't for Limmy. If Presslies is sharing the golds with Limmy, then Limmy wants to takes thems homes."

"Don't you want to spend the gold on weapons and items for the battle? Things you can actually use."

Limery's eyes glistened, and he shook his head. The elephant behind the table wore a sad expression.

Pressley looked from the imp to her giant blue eyes. "There's something I'm missing here."

The beastkin nodded. "I've seen this imp before. Not long ago, he stopped by my table with a troll and a dwarf. I told them of the history of these items, and it seems they have become personal to him."

Pressley frowned, and then he scooped Limery off the table,

stepping a few feet away to talk in private. "Tell me what's going on."

The imp's lip trembled. He was on the verge of tears, but Pressley had no idea why.

Limery's voice shook as he spoke. "Limmy doesn't want to leaves thems."

"I can see that." Pressley patted him on the back. "Why are these so important to you?"

A tear ran down Limery's cheek and fell against the death knight's armor with a tink. "Because theys belonged to the impses. The impses that was tricksed by the bad wizard. He tricksed thems and nows theys is all dead." He glanced over his shoulder to the table. "These is alls that's left of thems."

The floodgates opened and tears streamed down Limery's cheeks. Pressley cradled him against his chest as he sobbed, warm tears spilling through his armor. It all finally made sense. Every communication stone on that table belonged to an imp who had been tricked into joining Valmar's army. For all the power flowing through Limery's tiny body, he was scared. Scared of suffering the same fate. Afraid of dying and having no one left to remember him, his legacy nothing more than an untraceable piece of stone.

Pressley placed a finger under the imp's chin and lifted until the imp looked him in the eye. "This is not your fate. Chod will tear this world to the ground before he lets anything happen to you. You understand?"

Limery whimpered and gave a slight nod.

"No one will forget you. I might be scary and ugly, but I carry you with me here." Pressley pointed to his own chest. "You will be remembered for all you've done. When my time here is finished and I return home, I'm going to tell my daughter all about you. How does that sound?"

Limery sniffled and then wiped away a string of snot running down his chin. "Limmy likes thats."

"Alright, good." Pressley sat Limery down and returned to the table. "We'll take them."

The elephant grabbed a small bag. "How many would you like?"

Pressley dropped his coin pouch on the table. "All of them."

***

A wide grin swept over Taryn's face as he dismissed the message, and the interface vanished from his vision. "He did it. He actually did it."

"Who did what now?" Jon tilted his head in confusion, shaggy brown hair falling across his forehead. He looked over his shoulder as if Taryn might be talking to someone else. "I was saying that my enchanter class has turned out to be a real blessing. I've gained over ten levels just from crafting and enchanting objects for King Favian."

Taryn and Jon sat alone in one of the castle's many meeting halls. King Favian had brought Jon from Vanaria to Seascape to showcase for King Orso some of the items he'd been working on. The meeting was scheduled to begin after the two kings spoke in private, so Taryn had invited Jon to catch up while they waited. The message from Chod had caught the druid off guard.

"Sorry. Not you." Taryn returned his attention to the enchanter. "I hadn't heard from Chod in three days and he finally checked in. He's unlocked the Warforged class."

"Warforged? Never heard of it." Jon adjusted his dual-colored glasses and brushed a strand of hair behind his ear. The red and blue lenses were supposedly helpful with carving runes for enchantments. "Sounds dangerous."

Taryn nodded. "Supposedly, the class will turn his skin into fluid metal when he rages."

"Yep, that sounds dangerous alright."

"He's been looking forward to it for a while now. Since our first visit to Goldspire. I was getting a little worried because I hadn't heard from him and none of my messages were delivering." He sat back against the chair, stroking his beard until the metal clasps clinked. "So, what was it you were saying about your levels?"

Jon removed a gold ring inlaid with rubies from his finger, turning it over as he talked. "I was doing it all wrong from the start. Not that I need to tell you. You and Chod saw the trouble I was in the first time we met."

Taryn chuckled at the memory. Jon had been under-leveled and alone. Things had gotten so bad that he'd taken to bribing kobolds with enchanted Charisma rings so they would rob local farmers. "You seem to be doing better now."

The enchanter wore a finely tailored blue robe embroidered with yellow stars and moons. Rings adorned every finger, and the chains of several necklaces disappeared beneath his collar. Somehow, the man had made it to level twenty-five since they'd last seen one another. No small achievement, considering where he'd started.

"Aside from you and Chod, and, well, I can't forget the graciousness of King Favian either, Sirina is the best thing to happen to me since I've been here. She's the head enchanter in Vanaria, and she's taught me how to expand my abilities better than I could have ever imagined. I've gained ten levels without having to kill a single thing. It's great!" He leaned in close, lowering his voice. "Don't tell anyone, but she's a fox. I think I've got a bit of a crush on her."

Taryn fought the urge to laugh. Not because it was funny but because of how secretive Jon was being. After spending time with Breebis, he couldn't fault anyone for growing attached to an NPC. From the outside looking in, it might seem weird, but anyone on the outside had no idea what it was like to talk to these people and live in this world.

"I'm happy for you. Truly." Taryn gave him a reassuring smile. Jon had been afraid of his own shadow when they'd first met, but now he was thriving. "What is it you've been working on?"

"To tell you the truth, I was a little worried about working in the castle. I'm not exactly the finest ilk back in the real world, you know. King Favian offered me this great opportunity, but it felt like a lot of pressure working among mages and royalty. But they treated me like I belonged, and I finally understood what Chod meant about finding his tribe. From day one, I had tutoring with Sirina and council meetings with King Favian and Lord Kassidy. They took heed of King Orso's warning with the belief that Valmar would return, and so I've been specializing in enchantments against the undead from the start. When they started spilling through the portal, I was glad that I did." Jon grimaced. "I went down there once just to see what it was all about. They vaporized as soon as they entered the city, but the smell..." Jon gagged at the memory. "God, it was so bad."

"I bet." Taryn grimaced. "We've seen our fair share of creatures from the Shadowlands. I wouldn't—"

There was a knock on the door, and Kurzol entered. The blood dwarf cleric motioned toward the hall. "The king is ready for you now."

Jon rubbed his hands together. "Showtime, baby."

Kurzol led them to King Orso's council room. Outside the entrance, the blood dwarves of King Orso's personal guard stood to one side, and the human guards of King Favian stood to the other. Inside, the two kings sat side by side at a round stone table in the center of the room. They couldn't be more different in appearance. Orso's thick black hair rested on his shoulders, neatly combed and contrasting against his dull-red skin. His beard was braided to perfection. Favian, on the other hand, sported three-day-old scruff he hadn't shaved since the council in Pruxford and tousled hair that looked like he'd just come in from a griffin flight. Dark circles rested beneath his eyes.

Next to King Favian, Kassidy waved his finger and a bowl of grapes teleported onto the table. He winked at Jon before tossing a grape into his mouth.

The massive table was carved from a single piece of stone and was big enough to seat at least twenty people. Similar pieces of furniture were located throughout the castle—all of them cumbersome items that weighed thousands of pounds. Taryn wondered if they'd been moved into the castle using teleportation magic or if someone actually had to carry them inside.

Compared to many of the meetings Taryn had attended the past few days, this one was small. Chief Rizza and Chief Laojin were training with the trolls that were already in the city, and more were scheduled to arrive any day now.

"Here's the man of the hour." King Favian winked at Jon as they entered. "I didn't want to steal your thunder, so please do the honors and show King Orso what you've been working on."

"Your Highness, er, Highnesses." Jon bowed slightly and then removed the satchel from his shoulder, setting it on the table.

Taryn took a seat next to Orso and waited for the big reveal.

Jon fumbled through his bag. "I, uh, thank you for allowing me to, uh. Shit." A white gemstone the size of a fist slipped from his fingers, clattering across the stone table. Jon scrambled after the object, cursing all the while. "Shit. Sorry. Shit."

"Take a breath." King Orso grinned beneath his beard. "You're among friends here."

"Right." Jon gulped, clenching the gemstone between both hands. He took a deep breath before continuing. "What I mean to say is thank you for the opportunity to showcase what I've been working on. Thanks to King Favian's support, and Sirina's training, I've been able to unlock a new specialty for my class." He held up the gemstone for everyone to see. It was transparent, and a silver substance swirled within. "Along with my normal enchanting abilities, I've also become a wardmaster. Due to your warning—" He nodded to King Orso. "—I chose to specialize in, uh, I wouldn't exactly call them holy wards, but they do affect the undead. While clerics and paladins have abilities that are extra powerful against the undead, I wanted to help the rest of us. These items aren't anywhere near as powerful as the protections in Vanaria, but they are portable and to hear King Favian tell it, we're going to need all the help we can get."

"Your king speaks the truth." King Orso leaned forward, examining the ward. "Tell me what they do."

"Yes, Your Highness." Jon pointed to the gem. "This one is capable of mimicking the effects of Divine Radiance. When it's activated—" Jon traced a pattern over the stone and a silver light erupted across the room. "—the ward weakens the Constitution of any undead or shadow creatures within thirty feet." He canceled the ward and light faded. "These take a while to enchant, but we hope to have a hundred ready. If you spread them across our forces, they should prove valuable, especially to those on foot."

Jon placed the ward on the table and removed a small pouch from his bag. "I've also been able to make these rings." He smiled at Taryn as he jingled the bag. "Each ring is capable of holding a single charge of Divine Blessing. We'll need clerics to bless the ring but once it is charged, whoever is wearing it can cast the ability once, either to bless someone nearby or to use it as an attack on the undead. They can be recharged, but I'm not sure how practical that will be on the battlefield. We'll have close to a thousand of these in a few days."

He reached into his bag, pulling out a silver chain that held an amulet set with an iridescent stone. "This one is a unique item. I'll leave its potential usage to brighter minds than myself, but I believe it's my greatest achievement as an enchanter. I call it the Amulet of Undetection. While wearing this, the wearer can pass undetected by undead unless they are physically engaged with them."

Taryn's mouth dropped. Jon had been busy, alright. Every item would prove valuable in the battle to come, but the amulet was a game-changer. Whoever wore it would be undetectable by Valmar's forces.

King Orso nodded approvingly. "You have done well. Thank you for your service, not only to Vanaria and Seascape but to the war effort as a whole."

Jon's cheeks flushed. "Thank you."

The door opened, and Kurzol stepped into the room.

"Kurzol, this is a closed-door meeting." King Orso narrowed his eyes. "I thought I told you we were not to be disturbed."

"Apologies, Your Highness, but you also instructed me to alert you once the imps returned."

"Ah, yes. I did. Bring them in." He turned his attention back to Jon. "Thank you again. Pardon my brevity, but there are many moving parts at play."

Jon bowed before gathering his items and moving against the wall.

Kurzol stepped aside, and Lillith and Bazel flew into the room.

The two imps had been flying around the Isle for the past three days, but they looked no worse for the wear. Both had the same bat-like wings and dull-red skin as Limery, only Lillith had a patch of dark hair in the shape of a heart on her chest. Bazel was nearly twice Limery's size, but there was no denying their relation. Taryn imagined that Limery would look almost the same when he was older.

"What news do you bring?" asked King Orso.

"Gord and Kronan shall return tomorrow," Lillith answered. "They are a half-day's journey from Vanaria."

King Favian rubbed his tired eyes. "And what news of the other troll tribes?"

Lillith smiled. "The seaside trolls march with them."

"That is excellent news, indeed." King Orso patted Favian on the back. "And the desert trolls?"

Bazel moved forward slightly. "Gord says that they are with the forest and mountain trolls in Tawdrybluff, though there are not many of them. According to Chief Rizza, they shall arrive tomorrow or the next day."

"The five troll tribes reunited at last." King Favian turned to King Orso. "This must be a good omen."

King Orso's brow furrowed, and his gaze seemed to look beyond the room. "I pray you are right and we are not sending an entire race to their doom." The room sat in an awkward silence before the king shook his head, as if clearing his mind. "Apologies. That is enough for today. Let's reconvene tomorrow and continue our preparations."

King Orso's momentary lapse sent chills up Taryn's spine. The king had been a pillar of strength in these tough times, but it was clear that even he had his doubts. They were preparing to attack Mosstar with everything they had, and there would only be one chance for success. Even though they weren't his people, King Orso felt a responsibility for the trolls' well-being. They had precious little and yet were risking it all for the fate of the realm.

Taryn shared his king's worry. There was still so much to do, and the days seemed to grow shorter. He said farewell to Jon and set off in search of Chief Laojin.

24. OUT OF THE PAN AND INTO THE FRYER

When I wake up, it's like a weight has been lifted from my shoulders. The sleep debuff is gone and I feel like myself again, even after sleeping on the hard surface all night. At my feet, the wolfish Dreadbeast of Torment sits on its haunches, standing guard. The Dreadbeast of Despair lurks by my shoulder, and shadowy tendrils flick and flare from the massive bison. Standing between the two, Pharos glows like a beacon.

His light reflects off the obsidian stone around the room, but it does nothing against the darkness of the two dreadbeasts. It's like their bodies pull the light into the void, never to release it. I bet they're hard as hell to see at night.

"Good morning," I say to my companions as I push myself up, and they all look in my direction. "Glad to see the three of you are tolerating each other."

Pharos turns around, lowering his head to me. The Dreadbeast of Torment snarls when the spirit guide moves too close to him, but the spirit guide ignores it.

"For the most part." I chuckle. "I think it's time for us to head back to the city."

"*I am glad to see you're well-rested,*" Caustic speaks to me telepathically.

"*You can tell when I'm awake?*" I ask him.

"*Our tether strengthens when you are conscious. I have guarded over the mountain while you've slept.*"

I smile to myself. With a dragon, two dreadbeasts, and a spirit guide watching over me, I really am in good hands. "*How long was I out?*"

"*It is nearly midday.*"

Wow, that sleep debuff was no joke. The last time I pressed too hard, I spent several days recovering. "*Where's Limery?*"

"*He is with the dead one. I trust him.*"

"*Good. Me too.*" I gather my satchel. "*I'll be out in a moment, and we can head back to the city. I've got some new friends for you to meet.*"

"*Be warned, there is an elf pacing in front of the mountain, and I do not trust their intentions. I believe you were tracked.*" There's an edge to his husky voice. "*Shall I eat them?*"

"*An elf?*" Odd, considering I haven't seen any elves in Goldspire. "*That's strange. And no, do not eat the elf,*" I add before Caustic decides to have a quick lunch. "*Let me handle it.*"

Caustic growls his disapproval, but I have a strong suspicion that I know who it is.

Three days in the trials gave me plenty of time for self-reflection. Maybe I can set things right before anyone gets hurt.

The prompt appears across my vision, and I confirm that I'm ready to exit the trials. The ground rumbles and the walls shake as the mountain splits, revealing the rugged pass that runs between the boundary of the Burning Desert and the lands of Goldspire.

The midday sun shines down the Narrow Pass, casting shadows along the jagged rocks. In the daylight, my dreadbeasts are just as intimidating as they were in the cave. Their dark fur blends in with the obsidian stone of the mountain. The Dread-beast of Torment and Pharos lead the way with the bison following on my heels.

"Stay where you are," I order Caustic.

If Dorothy is here, I want to appear as non-threatening as possible. Aside from the three summons I have with me, I'm not bringing anything else. No weapons. No horrors. No more dread-beasts. And definitely not a dragon.

"That is unwise," Caustic growls.

"Trust me, please. I have my respawn point set outside of the city gates. If anything happens to me, go there."

I'm sure he could have kept it to himself, but his huff of irrita-tion passes through our bond.

With each step, I'm aware of the crunch of earth beneath my feet. My pulse thunders in my ears as my heart races, not out of fear but apprehension. My fingers ache for the comforting grip of Destroyer, but I keep it stowed in my satchel.

I've made enough enemies in this world already. With Glenn and Jude, there's no coming back, but maybe I can make things right with Dorothy for what I did.

Either way, it's time for me to face the music. If I die, then the Revive Potion from the Quincentennial Tournament will keep me from losing the Warforged class I just worked so hard for. I pray that doesn't happen.

I take a deep breath to steady my shaking hands and exit the pass. A lone figure stands against the arid landscape, a tan shawl draped over her head and shoulders to protect her from the sun. She wears a form-fitting brown vest strapped with daggers and vials over a blue tunic and tan pants with calf-length brown boots. Several pouches hang from her belt and more daggers line her thighs. Aside from the pointy ears, she looks just like I remember her. Strands of golden hair whip in the breeze, and blue eyes stare at me with murderous intent.

Dorothy Jordan
Level 33
Marauder
Elf

Level thirty-three. How the fuck is that possible? Has she been in here for months just biding her time until she was strong enough to make a move?

And what the hell is a marauder? I hold up my hands in a gesture of peace. "Dorothy, I—"

The words barely leave my mouth before a dagger whistles in my direction. I activate Cold Rage, and my body turns to fluid metal as I jump out of the way. The dagger's path shifts midflight, tracking me like a homing missile. I throw up my arms to block the blade, and it darts between my forearms, clanking against my neck before falling to the ground.

That would have been fatal if not for my godlike Constitution from being Warforged. Shit. She's really going to try and kill me.

The Dreadbeast of Torment takes off after Dorothy, but I call it back before it has a chance to attack. Thankfully, it responds to my internal commands as easily as my horrors, but that doesn't hinder the menacing growl rumbling in its chest. Shadows flare from the bison, and smoke pours from its nostrils as it unleashes a deep bellow.

Her gaze flickers to the dreadbeasts, but her focus is on me. I've made some enemies, but I don't know if I've ever seen such a hateful glare.

I don't want to hurt Dorothy if I can help it, but she's making it hard as she slings another dagger toward me. Whatever ability she used on the first one must have a cooldown because I knock this one aside at the last second.

"Dorothy, please, listen. Just give me a chance to explain." I hold up my palms.

"Explain?" She scoffs. "What is there to explain? You ruined my life, you piece of shit, and now I'm going to make you pay for it."

Dorothy has the draw of a gunslinger as she pulls a vial of purple liquid from her vest and slings it in my direction. The vial smashes against the rocky terrain, and a cloud of black smoke spreads around me. I recognize the effects of the Infernal Darkness Potion from previous battles. The cloud blinds those within and follows them around while also obscuring their sense of smell.

Thanks to my rage, I can't be blinded by the potion, but I'm still unable to see through the dense smoke while I'm inside, like I'm stuck in a heavy fog. I step backward until my head breaks through and I see sunlight, just in time for an explosion to knock me into the mountain.

With my increased Constitution, I barely feel the impact of my body slamming into the mountainside. There's a loud crackling noise within the fog, and my Dreadbeast of Torment's presence vanishes. Soot covers my metallic skin as I crawl to my feet. Dorothy doesn't hesitate, unloading a half-dozen more vials in a matter of seconds. Lightning and fire flare within the darkness like the heart of a raging volcano and soon, the Dreadbeast of Despair and Pharos vanish as well. If she killed the bison, then she's not pulling her punches at all. Dorothy wants me dead by any means necessary.

A maelstrom of smells spread out from the fog, sulfuric and

sickly sweet, as my rage ticks down by the second. The meter sits at two hundred thanks to my battle with the molten spiders, but unless I start hitting back, I've only got a few minutes of continuous rage left before it hits zero.

"Can I eat her now?" asks Caustic.

"No!" I shout, but it only draws Dorothy's attention to me.

"I heard you were hard to kill." Her lip curls in a snarl. "Just like the cockroach you are."

"Please, just listen. I don't have a problem with you."

She laughs, but there's no mirth in it. "In that case, I guess I can pack my bags and go home."

Her movement blurs as she reaches down her side and pulls back with a set of knives clutched between her knuckles like claws. She slashes through the air, releasing the knives and pirouetting before unleashing a second barrage with her opposite hand. The six blades fly like a volley of arrows, clanking against me with enough force to knock me back a step. She might not be big, but damn if she isn't strong.

Dorothy uses Shadow Step and appears in front of me while leaving a shadow doppelgänger in her original position. She slashes with incredible speed. I manage to block the first attack, but the next screeches as the blade grates against my metallic skin. For every attack I block, she lands three more.

Caustic's frustration seethes through our bond, and I try to block it out as I stay on the defensive. With every scrape of metal on metal, Dorothy's anger builds, and orange rings form around the blue of her eyes. She refuses to let up, and my rage continues to dwindle.

I've never seen this side of her. From what I remember, she was witty and a bit crass but never angry. She was known as a tactician, someone who planned several moves ahead. Right now, she's a rabid dog.

"Die already!" Dorothy screams as her blade grates across my chest in a burst of sparks. The orange outlines completely consume her eyes, and they burn with a molten ferocity.

A wave of energy surrounds her. Her moves quicken, so fast that I can't block anything as she picks me apart. Sparks fly with every hit as metal clashes.

"Enough!" I roar as I extend my arms and hit Dorothy square in the chest. Her health dips by a fraction from the blow, and she flips over backward. Just before she hits the ground, she activates Shadow Step and switches places with the doppelgänger. The shadow copy bursts into dark mist upon hitting the ground, and whatever rage is powering Dorothy heals her damage almost instantly. Her eyes smolder like embers as she charges again.

I block the first stab with my forearm, but the next scrapes against my ribs, and the lack of damage only fuels her anger. I can't fight her off forever, and soon, I'll be forced to either fight back or die. The look in her eyes tells me she won't be happy killing me once.

"Do you really think hurting me is going to make you feel better?" I ask as I stay on the defensive, backpedaling as she carves me up.

"Only one way to find out." Dorothy goes for my neck, but I swat her hand away with enough force that the dagger flies from her grip.

She reaches behind her back, cursing when she comes up empty. At least a dozen of her weapons litter the mountainside, so the one she's holding must be her last. I have maybe thirty seconds before her attacks start spilling blood.

I take another step back, keeping her at a distance. She circles me like a predator, spinning the dagger across her palm without taking her eyes off me.

"I'm sorry." My shoulders slump forward, and I stop retreating.

Dorothy's eyes flare, and her jaw stiffens.

"I know it doesn't do much good now, but I'm so fucking sorry, Dorothy. I was an asshole, and you didn't deserve what happened to you."

Her lip twitches and her grip tightens around the dagger. "You're damn right, I didn't."

She activates Shadow Step again, appearing behind me and plunging the blade between my shoulder blades. Metal screeches, and I turn to face a shadow with Dorothy already returned to her previous location.

I cancel Cold Rage before it completely runs out, leaving me with a few seconds of protection if I need it. Whatever rage is empowering her fades as well, and her eyes return from orange to deep blue.

"I wish I could change what happened, but I can't. I was a stupid kid, and you were the unfortunate victim of my anger. Believe it or not, this place has changed me. I found something I never had in the real world—a sense of purpose." I spread my arms wide and take a step forward. "So if you need to kill me, if that is what will make you feel better, then go ahead. You deserve it."

She buries the dagger in my chest, just beneath the shoulder, and white-hot pain flares from the impact. My jaw clenches, and it takes everything I have not to fight back.

Dorothy looks me in the eye as blue blood trickles down my chest, and her lips curl into a smile. She twists the blade, and pain surges across my chest.

"*I'm coming,*" Caustic growls.

"*Do not move.*" My order is firm, and I pray that he listens. "*I can handle this.*"

Dorothy kicks at the dirt, and a dagger flies into her free hand. She stabs it into my ribs. Warm blood runs down my midsection.

"Tell me," she leans in and whispers, setting my hair on edge. "What purpose could be so important that anyone would believe you're not an asshole?"

I grimace at the burning sensation spreading from both wounds. "They know I'm an asshole." My health goes down with every word, and I'm certain the blades are coated in poison. "I'm just *their* asshole."

She pulls the blade from my ribs and slices it across my stomach.

"You're really not going to fight back, are you?" She watches me with a curious expression.

"You deserve your vengeance." My breaths grow labored as the knife in my chest twists under her pressure. "If you want to kill me, go ahead. Make it quick or bleed me out. It doesn't matter to me." I wrap my hand around hers, and her eyes widen as I pull the blade deeper into my chest. "The first one's free, but this is it. This is your chance to kill me, to torture me, to do whatever you need to make me pay for my actions. Right here, right now—I deserve it. But if you come for me again, I won't hesitate to kill you. Our beef can wait, but I can't let your actions hurt those that I care about. There are a lot of people counting on me right now."

Dorothy pulls the dagger from my chest and steps back, her brow furrowed. "Shit. You really believe that, don't you?"

I nod. Blood pours from my open wounds, and the poison burns as it spreads through my shoulder and down my thigh. I never re-equipped any of my items in the cave, so I can't use the Tiger's Eye Pendant to clear the effect.

Dorothy wipes the blood from the dagger on her pant leg and sheathes it. "So the rehabilitation, it really works?"

"That depends on who you ask." I shrug. "Maybe I'm just growing as a person."

She scoffs. "Playing the hero in a game doesn't make you a hero."

"It doesn't make me a villain, either."

"No, I suppose not. You look like one, though, especially with those monsters you had." Dorothy crosses her arms. "What were those things?"

"Dreadbeasts. I'm a barbarian summoner."

"Dreadbeasts? That definitely doesn't sound villainous." She arches a brow. "So, Chod, you pick that name out yourself?"

I'm not sure what's going through her mind right now, but something has shifted between us. I elect to run with it. "No, I think it was the game's way of trolling me when I first logged in. Everyone else got to use their real name."

She chuckles, and for the first time, there's no hatred in it. "This place is something else, isn't it? When John told me what it was that you were up to here, I was pissed. And then once I logged in, I was even more pissed." She looks around as if she can't believe the world we're in. "This is the future of gaming, and you got sent here as a punishment." She shakes her head. "Such a lucky son of a bitch."

"It hasn't all been roses." I wince as a fresh wave of pain passes through my chest. "Trolls were attacked on sight when I first logged in. I put in a lot of work to earn respect from the other kingdoms."

"So I hear." Dorothy reaches into one of the pouches on her waist and pulls out a vial of yellow liquid. "Here, take this." She tosses the potion to me. "It's the antidote for the poison."

As soon as I down the antidote, my health stops depleting. I let out a sigh of relief. We may be on shaky ground, but she's offered me an olive branch, so I press onward. "How long have you been here? You're a higher level than some of the heroes who've been here since day one."

"Heroes. That still gets me." She laughs, taking a seat on one of the boulders and brushing a strand of golden hair behind her pointed ear. "I've been here a while. I chose to spawn in Ellynmylly so that I wouldn't accidentally run into you before I was ready. I didn't have any world-spanning quests, so I was able to grind through the dungeons and loot. It would have been a lot more fun if I weren't so pissed at you."

"That's fair." I sit on the ground and try to keep the conversation going. "It says your class is marauder. This is the first time I've seen one of those."

"It's pretty nice." She leans back, letting the afternoon sun warm her pale cheeks. "I get bonus loot and can sense where the most valuable items are in a dungeon."

"Is that how you got all of those potions you nearly killed me with?"

"Something like that." She grins. "Though you're not exactly easy to kill."

I return her smile. "I just spent the past three days going through hell to unlock that ability."

"I guess it was worth it, then." Dorothy leans forward, looking at me with a serious expression. "You said there are people counting on you. What did you mean by that?"

Her gaze is intense, so I look away, focusing on a flock of vultures circling in the distance. "There's a battle coming, one I'm not sure we can win."

I go on to tell Dorothy about Valmar, and most of what has happened in the past few weeks. She hangs on to every word, genuinely interested in what I have to say. Just another reminder of how fucked up my actions were. When I finish my story, she stares at me incredulously.

"That's crazy. And this Valmar guy, he has no idea you're about to attack him?"

"How could he?" I pick up a pebble and toss it. "He's the only one with the power to open the Mosstar portal. After the attack in Pruxford, he must assume we'll be preparing for war. He has to think the odds are in his favor, though, that we can't all unify because we need to be prepared for him to invade any of the portals. My guess is that he's gathering his forces as we speak, and he thinks he'll attack us before we're ready. But there's no way he could know that we're going to open our own portal outside of the city."

Dorothy walks over to me and offers me her hand. "I want to help."

"Why?" I'm unable to conceal the surprise in my voice.

Thirty minutes ago, she wanted to kill me, and now she wants to help. Putting our beef aside so that she can enjoy her time in Mythos is one thing, trusting her to watch my back and protect the ones I care about is quite another.

Dorothy keeps her arm extended. "You say you're not the same asshole that made me cry on a televised stream. I hope that's true, but I want to see it. I might have come here for the wrong reasons, but I've grown attached to this world. It'd be a shame to see it crumble."

I meet her eyes, and the friendliness in them is so far removed from the murderous rage I saw not long ago.

She has a point, though. Saying that I've changed is not the same as showing it. It was my actions that proved to the trolls I was one of them. My actions convinced King Favian and King Orso to put their faith in me. My entire time here, it's been my actions that have gained trust and helped me to unite Mythos. Why should it be any different with Dorothy?

Letting her in might be what she needs to put this mess behind us, but is that a risk I'm willing to take?

Can I trust her to have my back when the lives of Limery and the trolls are on the line? When the fate of Mythos hangs in the balance?

In my heart, I know the answer. As uncomfortable as it might be, trust is a two-way street.

"Alright." I take her hand, and she helps me to my feet. "If I'm being honest, we can use all the help we can get. Best to get moving, though. It's a long way back to the city."

I reach out to Caustic through our bond, and a moment later, he soars down from the mountain. His shadow stretches across the landscape. He's grown a considerable amount over the past three days. His beard is a deep gold, and his wings are as wide as a small plane.

Dorothy equips her daggers, ready for a fight.

I hold up a hand to stop her. "Don't worry. He's with me."

Her mouth drops open. "You had a dragon this whole time, and you still let me stab you?"

"I do not trust her." Caustic's throat rumbles. *"She reeks of ill intent."*

"She thought the same thing about me not too long ago. Be nice." I pet Caustic on the belly once he lands, and then turn back to Dorothy. "Like I said, I'm trying to be better."

"I will not fly her." Caustic may not eat her, but there's no room for argument in his tone.

"Wait, you can bear a rider now?" Now, I'm the one who's shocked as I look into his golden eyes.

He huffs and raises his head to its full height, striking an imposing figure. After gaining so many levels, he must be at least twenty feet tall. *"I can bear you."*

Caustic takes some convincing, but he eventually agrees to carry Dorothy in his talons. Against his protests, I made him promise that he wouldn't drop her once we're hundreds of feet in the air. Dorothy isn't too happy with the situation, but she understands that time is of the essence.

I understand Caustic's hesitance to trust her. Dragons are not ones to easily forget, and he just watched her try to kill me. If not for my newly Warforged body, she might have succeeded. He'll come around in time.

My braid whips in the wind as we soar above the countryside. I welcome the cool air and bask in the moment since this might be the last bit of peace I have for a while. Caustic's scales are smooth and cool against my thighs, his muscles powerful as he flaps his massive wings occasionally.

After the past few days, it's nice to sit here and appreciate the beauty of this world and everything I have accomplished. I mean, I'm riding on a fucking dragon!

Still, I can't believe Dorothy found me. She's still angry, of that much I'm certain, but I have hope that I may be able to mend that fence with time. There's nothing better to forge a bond than fighting side by side. As strong as she is, she'll be a valuable asset in the battle to come.

As we approach the city, the golden spire gleams in the fading sun. From this high up, it's magnificent. Once we're back, I'll track down Limery and Pressley, and we can head to Seascape first thing in the morning.

25. A Troll and an Elf Walk into a Bar

CAUSTIC IS OFFICIALLY so big that booking him a stable has become an effort in futility. The first stable doesn't have an enclosure large enough for a dragon his size, and when we finally find one that can house him for the night, he holds his head high and refuses to look at me.

"A dragon should not be caged."

I roll my eyes at the stubborn ass. *"You didn't have a problem with it before."*

"Before, I was a hatchling." His head tilts and his golden eye meets mine. *"Do I look like I need protection?"*

"Fine." I let out a sigh. Caustic may still be young, but he has a point. He's not a pet that I have to look after. We're bonded, so more than anything, we're partners. "Come find us in the morning, then."

"Trouble in paradise?" Dorothy arches her brow.

Caustic growls, and she takes a step back.

"Something like that." I narrow my eyes at the unruly dragon. "He's in his rebellious phase."

"I wonder where he learned that." A smile tugs at the edge of her mouth.

I laugh, but Caustic lowers his head, blowing hot air that unravels the shawl covering Dorothy's head and shoulders. Her smile twists into a frown.

"I still do not trust her."

"I'm well aware." I pat him on the chest. *"Go have some fun doing whatever it is that dragons do."*

His body rocks back and forth before he launches himself skyward.

Dorothy is transfixed as she watches Caustic fly away. "I've always loved dragons. In books, games, films, you name it, they're always so majestic, you know? Beauty and power all rolled into one." She turns back to me once he disappears into the night. "None of it compares to actually seeing one."

"Yeah, it's pretty amazing." I smile at the thought of Dorothy finally experiencing this world as it should be, without the burden of revenge weighing her down. "If you think Caustic is cool, just wait until you meet Limery."

Using my map, I track Limery's location until we come to a tavern called South of the Spire. It's a bustling business near the city's center, and beastkin of all shapes and sizes drink wine as they chat and listen to music. A couple of ratkin weasel through the crowd, delivering drinks and food. At the far wall, a goat-like beastkin with the long horns of an antelope plays a lute. She's tall and wiry, with a wispy goatee, and her hoof taps against the floor like a woodblock, keeping time with the music.

I spot Pressley sitting at a table in the corner, his dark and sinister appearance out of place in such a lively establishment. Limery stands in his chair across from the death knight, holding a wine glass as he sways to the music. A wide grin spreads across my face. Pressley raises an armored hand at me, and Limery turns around.

"Chods!" His bulbous eyes nearly pop from his head when he notices me, and he darts across the room, jostling a ratkin who miraculously avoids spilling the bottle of wine he's pouring. Limery wraps his arms around my neck and squeezes. "Limmy missed yous!"

I hug him back. "I missed you too, buddy. You having fun?"

"Oh, yes! Limmy loves the musics and the drinks."

"Why don't we have a seat, then." I turn to Dorothy and nod toward the corner table. "There's someone I want you to meet."

We follow Limery to the table, where Pressley sips on a glass of rosé. A purple gemstone pulses within the death knight's dark visage. Looks like he finally put the Hag's Eye to use. He lifts the glass to his visor, and the pinkish wine disappears into the void beneath his helm. Considering he's nothing more than bones and energy, I'm not exactly sure where it all ends up. I glance beneath the table just to check if there's a puddle underneath, but it's as clean as the rest of the tavern.

"You didn't strike me as the rosé type." I give him a friendly smirk as I take a seat.

His breath rattles within his helm. "Wasn't it you who said not to judge people based on their appearances?"

"Fair enough." I laugh and gesture to Dorothy. "This is Dorothy. She wants to join the fight. Dorothy, this is Limery, my partner in crime, and Pressley. He might be the strongest hero we've got."

Limery climbs on the table to shake Dorothy's hand. "Nice to meets yous." He burps and then cackles. "Excuse Limmy."

Dorothy smiles as she holds his tiny hand. "Nice to meet you, Limmy."

Pressley offers her his armored hand and nods. "How'd he convince you to join us?"

She looks from Pressley to me and shakes her head. "Despite my best intentions, somehow, I managed not to kill him."

Pressley laughs, and it sounds like bugs flying into a wood chipper. "He certainly has a way with people." He waves the ratkin over and asks for two more glasses. Once we have them, he pours Dorothy and me a generous amount of rosé, finishing off the bottle. "We might as well celebrate our last night in the city."

"Cheers to that." I raise my glass in a toast. "How long have you all been here?"

"Not too long." He swirls the wine and then takes a sip. "We spent most of the day running errands. I had to restock potions and supplies after the dungeon, and then Limery wanted to watch the performers in the square. I figured we deserved a little downtime after the past few days."

Limery grabs my arm excitedly. "We's saws the fire-breathers, and the dancers, and the buffaloes that plays musics with they's horns."

"Sounds like a blast." I'm not quite as elegant with my wine, taking a healthy gulp. It's crisp and refreshing and goes down way too easily. "I hear the dungeon was a success. Tell me all about it."

We go through two more bottles of wine as Pressley recounts their time in the dungeon, explaining the various monsters and the strategies they used to defeat them. A drunken Limery offers his input when he feels the death knight isn't doing the story justice, acting out several fights and giving his best imitation of the various monsters.

After detailing the boss fight with the manticore, Pressley's jeweled eye lingers on me. "Fighting alongside Caustic and Limery, I took to heart what you've been saying all along. There are some things that can't be done alone. I wouldn't have been able to bond the manticore without your help."

"I'm glad it worked out for you." I smile at the fact that even he has managed to open himself up a little, a far cry from the surly knight I met in Lynchton. "To be honest, I don't think I could have completed the trials if Caustic and Limery hadn't joined you."

"What do you mean?" asks Pressley.

Limery grumbles as he leans back against his chair, eyes heavy now that the story is over. I give him two minutes before he's snoring like a freight train.

I take another sip of the refreshing, tart rosé, letting the flavors linger on my tongue before swallowing. "I almost didn't make it. There was a moment when I felt like giving in, but then I heard Caustic's voice in my head, encouraging me to keep going. He'd gained enough levels during the dungeon that our bond strengthened and now we can communicate telepathically. So I think we can call it even on who owes who for our adventures outside of Goldspire."

"One less debt for me to repay." Pressley flags down the ratkin for another bottle of wine then returns his attention to me. "I've done enough talking for one night. What were the trials like?"

My story doesn't take nearly as long as I describe my experiences in the trials. It's hard to really do justice to just how grueling the first two phases were. Saying that I stood in a hot box and held some walls apart doesn't sound as cool as fighting bone-crushing scorpions and flying crocodiles but when I get to the third trial, where my body was pulverized like raw meat, Dorothy grimaces as I describe the searing pain and constant torment. Pressley makes a noise that I'm pretty sure is a groan.

"That sounds like torture." Dorothy shivers as if she's imagining what the experience was like.

I shrug. "It was rough, but I was warned that it would be challenging plenty of times. It had a level cap just to be able to enter."

"And yet you still did it." The look she gives me is, I'm not sure, respect, maybe.

My gaze drops to Limery, who snores softly in the seat next to me. "I didn't really have a choice."

"There's always a choice." Pressley sets his glass on the table, and it clinks against his armored hand. "We make them every day. Some choose the easy road or the road without conflict. Others choose to wander through life without ever finding a sense of purpose. And then there are those who choose to take their lumps in the name of what they believe is right or noble. I wish I'd chosen differently at times."

"We all make mistakes." I reach across the table and tap his armored hand. "The real choice is in how we respond to them."

He nods silently, and the swell of music fills the void before he takes a deep breath and stands. "I've had enough socializing for one evening. I'll see you in the morning for Seascape. Limery and I have a room booked at The Merry Minotaur a block over."

"See you in the morning." I wave to him as he leaves.

Dorothy shifts her chair so that she's sitting across from me. "He looks scary, but he seems like a nice guy."

"He is." I laugh. "He was actually a human knight when I first met him, but then there was this whole thing with a cleric and the god of chaos. He's definitely a force to be reckoned with."

"You both are." She pours the last of the bottle between our glasses. "With a death knight riding a manticore and a troll on a dragon, you two are gonna be pretty damn fearsome on the battlefield."

"And what about you?" I tilt my glass in her direction. "You're pretty formidable yourself."

"Not my style." She smirks. "I prefer to go unnoticed and strike when they least expect it."

As we finish the last of the wine, I do my best to prepare Dorothy for what's coming tomorrow. I'm sure it'll be pandemonium in Seascape, so I try to give her a rundown of all the major players.

The past few days may have felt like an eternity, but I have a feeling that once we're back, time will be the one thing there's not enough of.

26. GOOD-BYE GOLDSPIRE

"Ungh." Limery stirs next to me, his miserable grunts pulling me from sleep.

I open my eyes just as he turns over and his hand swats me on the side of the head. He sits up, groggy-eyed as he looks around the room uncertain of where he is or how he got here.

"You really need to learn some moderation, you know that?" I fold the pillow over my ears to drown out his groaning.

He grumbles something unintelligible and then hovers in the air. There's a sizzling sound, and the room's temperature rises by several degrees as he burns through the toxins of the previous night.

"That's betters." He grins as he lands beside me on the bed. "Time to goes sees Taryns!"

I prop myself on my elbows. Compared to some of our rowdier nights, I didn't drink that much. For my part, I'm feeling fine, and I'm sure Dorothy is, too. Pressley, on the other hand... I wonder if death knights can even get hangovers.

After gathering our things, we find him downstairs a short

while later, but his demeanor gives nothing away. He's as dour-looking as ever as the morning sun spills through the open window. Dorothy sits across from him, sipping on a mug of steaming tea.

The bottom floor of the inn has a cozy feel to it, with warm light shining on the pristine tile. The entire room is decorated in shades of yellow and green, reminding me of spring flowers. The smell of fresh bread wafts in from the kitchen, mixing with the smoky aroma from the platter of bacon a wolfkin picks at while reading her scroll.

My stomach growls, and I wipe away a bit of drool forming on my lip. For the past three days, all I've had to eat was the blood from the molten spiders and the rations I had stored in my satchel. They satiated my hunger, but it was hardly a meal.

"Good mornings!" Limery beams as he joins Pressley and Dorothy at the table.

"Good morning to you." Dorothy smiles in response, pulling out a seat for the imp.

I order some food for Limery and myself from the barkeep and then take the chair next to Pressley. A few minutes later, a platter of assorted meats and wheat pancakes drizzled with honey arrives along with a carafe of juice. I don't waste a moment before digging in. Limery's appetite matches my own, and we devour the deliciously fluffy pancakes and savory strips of bacon like we may never eat again.

My mouth is stuffed when I notice Pressley and Dorothy watching us.

"What?" The words come out muffled, but the meaning is clear enough.

Dorothy's lip curls in disgust. "It's like watching pigs eat from a trough."

"Hey, I didn't eat for three days, and then all I had was days-old bread and cheese." I stuff another sausage into my already-full mouth. "Forgive me for enjoying myself."

"There's a fine line between enjoyment and gluttony." She scrunches her nose. "I have a cat that used to do that. He'd eat his food like I was going to steal it, and then five minutes later, I'd have to clean it off the floor." She shakes her head in disappointment. "That's the bar you're failing to meet, Chod."

Pressley lets out a raspy laugh, and I narrow my eyes at him.

"She's not wrong." He scoots back from the table and stands. "I need to go pick up the manticore from the stables and make sure she hasn't seriously injured anyone. She's on the other side of the city. Want to meet at the portal in an hour?"

I wash down the food with a giant swig of juice. "Sounds good. I was planning to see Jegaar before we left anyway."

After I settle the tab, we leave The Merry Minotaur. Outside, a large, green tail dangles from above the porch. I step out into the street and look up to find Caustic sprawled out on the roof of the inn. Many of the clay tiles are cracked and disheveled, and the edge of the roof is clearly sagging from his weight. Tiles crunch as he sits up, and broken pieces fall onto the street.

"Did you sleep there all night?" I ask.

Caustic hops down from the roof, landing on the cobblestone with a thud. He breathes hot air at Dorothy, tousling her hair, before turning his gaze to me.

"I did many things during the night." He lowers his head until it's level with my own.

"Of course you did." I scratch him on the chin.

Dorothy takes a few steps back. "I don't think he likes me."

I shrug. "Well, you did try to kill me."

"Fair enough, I suppose."

Limery flies to Caustic's head and wraps his fingers around

the golden antlers like they're handlebars. "Limmy wants to flies with Caustics."

"Alright then, meet us at the library." I pet Caustic on the chest. "Dorothy and I will go on foot."

The dragon launches himself into the air, and Limery laughs maniacally as the duo takes flight. Every beastkin on the block stops what they're doing to watch them soar across the sky.

Dorothy and I enjoy a peaceful stroll on the way to the library. Long fronds rustle in the gentle breeze, and the aqueducts gurgle as they carry water across the city. Judging by the calm streets, you'd never know the majority of Mythos was on the brink of war. Several beastkin walk by at a leisurely pace as if they don't have a care in the world.

"You're really attached to him, aren't you?" Dorothy finally breaks the silence.

"Who do you mean?" I ask.

"Limery." She glances at me, then fixes her gaze straight ahead. "I could tell by the way you carried him to bed last night. You cradled him like he was made of glass. I do the same thing with my cats."

"As powerful as he is, he's still childlike in so many ways. I worry about him, probably more than I should, but he's been by my side pretty much since the beginning. I don't know how deeply you've interacted with the NPCs, but it's like he's real. He has his own personality. His own dreams and fears."

"A weird little accent." She chuckles.

"That, too." I laugh. "I'd do anything for him."

Caustic and Limery sit by the fountain outside of the library when we arrive, both of them basking in the sun. I have Caustic wait outside while we head through the front of the library this time, using the special entrance to the Scholars Guild that Jegaar showed us. We catch a couple of skeptical looks, but no one stops us as we make our way to the wolfkin's office in his underground bunker.

I knock on the blank metal door and a moment later, the runes flash bright orange before a peephole appears. A bright blue eye peers through and then the door opens. Jegaar welcomes us inside.

He places a hand on my shoulder and gives me a wolfish grin. "Good news, I assume?"

I activate Cold Rage for a few seconds, and my skin turns to metal. "Good news," I echo. "We're in a hurry, but I wanted to stop by to say thanks for all of your help."

The battle scholar leans in close, looking at his reflection on my chest. "May I?" He gestures toward my arm.

I lift my hand, and he wraps his paws around my wrist and forearm, examining my skin and testing the metal with his claw.

He nods approvingly. "Well done, Chod. I knew you had it in you."

"We'll be heading to Seascape shortly." I cancel Cold Rage to save the precious few moments I have left. "Pressley is gathering his manticore from the stables."

"Sounds like a productive outing all around. Too bad you're in a hurry or I would love to study the Golden Devourer." He turns to Dorothy. "And who do we have here?"

"I'm Dorothy." She extends her hand. "Here to lend my talents in the upcoming battle."

He grasps both hands around hers. "Dark tidings, but you'll be in good company. I wish you all the best."

I pace across the room, wishing I had the magic words to bring Goldspire into the fray. "Is there nothing we can do to convince you to join us? There has to be some of you willing to fight."

"There are many of us who would welcome the glory of a

battlefield." He clenches his fist, and his eyes burn with passion as he stares into mine. "But the emperor's word is law. We will not be joining this fight, as much as I may wish otherwise."

I nod solemnly. "This is it, then."

"No." He places a paw on each of my shoulders and shakes his head. "This is not the end. This is just the beginning."

I force a smile. "Take care of yourself, Jegaar."

Pressley waits for us by the portal next to one of the most badass monsters I've ever seen. Limery flies over and perches on the death knight's shoulder, laughing as he taps his claw on Pressley's helm. A hollow gong reverberates within the void but to Pressley's credit, he joins in the laughter. A couple of days together in the dungeon has brought out a side of the death knight I've never seen.

Looking at the monster before me, I understand why he was so keen on finding the manticore. She's a massive beast, not nearly as big as Caustic, but her frame rivals a draft horse. Plenty large enough to make Pressley an even more imposing figure when mounted.

Her golden face is strangely human as she watches us approach. Beneath the gilded mask, her one blue eye tracks each of us in turn, while the Hag's Eye glows eerily in the other socket, matching the death knight's. Her luscious black hair gives way to the crimson fur of a lion's body, and large, leathery wings are tucked at her sides. A dangerous scorpion tail curls up from behind, the end tipped with a thick stinger and several barbs.

The manticore approaches Dorothy, scrunching her nose when she sniffs at the elf's hair. Dorothy wears a nervous expression as the manticore breathes in her scent. The undead monster attempts to speak, but the words are an incomprehensible mess.

"She lost her ability to speak when I reanimated her." Pressley pets the manticore on the shoulder, and she loses interest in Dorothy. "She can still fight, though."

"She's badass." I examine the manticore from several angles, and when I step too close, she hisses at me, earning a reproachful growl from Caustic.

"Be careful." Pressley tugs on the reins. "She's not the friendliest."

Dorothy scoffs as she looks at Caustic. "Seems to be a lot of that going around."

The dragon curls his lip and unleashes a menacing rumble, making Dorothy take a few steps back.

Pressley laughs. "When we're on the battlefield, friendly won't matter." He tugs on the manticore's reins, repositioning her toward the portal. "We ready?"

I take one last look at the beautiful city and try not to think about how many of its citizens would fight by our side if given the opportunity. Wondering about the what-ifs will get me nowhere. What matters are the ones we have, and they're waiting on the other side of the portal.

"Let's go."

27. HOMECOMING

WE EXIT the portal into Seascape Square, where tall buildings and gothic architecture surround us. The dwarven capital might not be made of crystal but its craftsmanship is a work of art, and unlike most kingdoms who have their portals set at the edge of the city, Seascape's is at its heart.

Behind us, King Orso's castle looms from the city's highest point. I take a moment to admire the beauty of fine lines and details on the behemoth of a structure. Somehow, it manages to appear both fragile and imposing. Dozens of towers, spires, and flying buttresses claw at the heavens, and hundreds of stained-glass windows reflect the midday sun, depicting scenes and imagery from Seascape's long history.

Proud and menacing gargoyles watch over the city below, which is equally magnificent. Every building is built from brick or stone and so tightly packed that it reminds me of New York.

Living there day to day, it was easy to lose sight of the magnificence of the city when it became a background to the chaos of life. But whenever I'd return from a trip and see the towering skyline, I was always reminded that it was like no place on earth.

This is no different. So much has happened since I was last here, but it still feels like a homecoming. I've traveled from Goldspire to Frostmoor and then to Wandermere and Pruxford, but Isle of Mythos is where it all began. From the troll forest to Vanaria and Seascape, this is my home. These are the lands that made me, and this is what I'm fighting for.

Ivory, ebony, and even a few blood dwarves bustle about as the kingdom prepares for the upcoming battle. Carts of weapons and armor line the edge of the square as soldiers pass out gear to citizens. More dwarves carry crates filled with vials of colorful liquids down from the castle, where a lava-skinned blood dwarf marks inventory as each box is loaded into a wagon.

There's a shout as someone notices us exiting the portal, and the square goes silent. In the lower city, the rhythmic clank of the blacksmith carries on as every eye falls on the dragon and manticore. The legendary monsters are so enthralling that no one seems bothered by Pressley's presence.

Caustic raises his head high, and several of the commoners drop to one knee.

"Don't let this go to your head," I tease.

Caustic huffs. *"A dragon commands respect by simply existing."*

If this is his attitude now, I can only imagine what it's going to be like when he's fully grown.

"Chod!" a deep voice calls to me from the crowd.

I do a double-take when I see a massive forest troll making his way through the crowded dwarves that are half his height. Malak grins, and I return his smile. He's one of the guardians that protects the borders of the village, a beast of a troll but innocent and friendly in a way Gord could never be. The last time I saw him, he was nearly swindled by a human trader selling a knife for ten times its value.

Beyond him, a large group of forest, mountain, and arctic trolls stand together. Brutus is a head taller than the rest, a mountain of lean muscle with a hawk nose, braided mohawk, and an unmistakable scar that runs across his lilac chest. He and I nearly came to blows when I first encountered the mountain tribe.

"Damn, that's a lot of trolls," Dorothy mutters under her breath.

Limery is unusually quiet as he takes in the scene. Pressley sits stoically atop the manticore, and his mount's one good eye scans the crowd as if she's deciding which one she wants to devour.

Malak extends his arm, and I clasp it in mine as we embrace.

"Good to see you." I grin, patting him on the back.

He looks at me with wonder in his green eyes as he takes in my appearance. "You have horns."

"That I do." I laugh. "There's a lot to catch you up on."

The other trolls follow Malak's lead, Brutus leading the throng of green, purple, and white bodies through the sea of dwarves. More trolls than I imagined spill into the square from the side street, all of them eager to see the two mighty beasts. The dwarves that aren't focused on Caustic and the manticore ogle at the massive trolls nearly double their height. For those traveling from the countryside, I'm sure this is their first time seeing a troll in person.

"Chod." Brutus nods, which is a friendlier greeting than many of our encounters have been. We stare at one another for a moment before his mouth twists into a grin and he extends his hand. "It has been too long since I've cracked heads. I look forward to fighting by your side for the fate of Mythos."

I chuckle as I grip him around the forearm. "Likewise. It is good to see you. Where's Chief Rizza and the others?"

Brutus gestures toward the castle. "Chief Rizza and Laojin are meeting with the king. The forest and mountain trolls only just arrived this morning. A messenger from Vanaria has sent word that Gord and Kronan should arrive with the others by nightfall."

"Chod!" I recognize her feminine voice, but I can't find Yashi among the crowd. The trolls part until the diminutive troll steps into view. She's a good two feet shorter than the others and wears her hair in two long braids that reach her waist. What she lacks in size, she more than makes up for in skill and knowledge. I doubt there's a better archer or potion-maker among all of the trolls. Plus she has a mana-infused wyrm now. "You big oaf. I was worried I'd never see you again." She wraps her arms around my midsection.

"It's good to see you too." I return her embrace and glance through the crowd, searching for the other two members of our original party. "Where's Ismora and Tormara?"

"Ismora is meeting with the blacksmith about weapons more suited for trolls. Tormara is still in Vanaria. She'll be arriving with Gord and the others."

I lose focus of what Yashi is saying when I see Senzala watching me from across the square, her blue eyes locked on mine. The shaman is just as tall as the other arctic trolls, but about half their width. She has the same white fur across most of her body, except where the males have an exposed patch of black skin on their chest, hers is covered in fur. Her white hair is pulled into a bun that rests atop her head. She raises a hand in acknowledgment and smiles, and I can't fight the grin that consumes me. Her tusks are much smaller than most trolls, barely rising above her lips. They only add to her beauty, which is both reserved and ferocious at the same time.

Our time together in Frostmoor was too short, and things have gotten so crazy that I haven't even thought about what I might say if I saw her again. All I know is that I enjoyed being in her presence.

Yashi and Brutus both follow my gaze and then share a mischievous look.

Brutus claps me on the back. "I hope your luck is better than mine."

"I don't think your luck was the problem." Yashi laughs. "You're about as smooth as a splinter. Judging by the way she's looking at Chod, he's clear blue water, and she's ready for a drink."

My cheeks burn at her comments, which only makes Yashi laugh harder. Dorothy snickers behind me, and Limery questions what's so funny.

In an attempt to change the subject before the imp starts singing "Chods has a girlfriends," I introduce my new companions to those still watching us. Both the trolls and dwarves are mesmerized by Caustic and the manticore. Eventually, the fascination dies down, and the dwarves return to their business of handing out armor and weapons.

Pressley dismounts from the manticore and joins my side. "Sounds like we're still waiting for some of the major players to arrive, so I'm going to check into the stables and find a room for the evening. Send me a message if you need anything."

"Will do." I shake his hand. "Thanks again for everything."

"Mind if I join you?" Dorothy places a hand on Pressley's shoulder and smirks at me. "I don't want to get in the way of Chod and the lady trolls."

"It's not like that." I try to sound cool, but my cheeks flush uncontrollably.

She blows me a kiss as she walks away. "See you later, lover boy."

Limery waves to Pressley and Dorothy from between Caustic's horns as they leave. "See you laters, lover boys!"

I bury my head in my palm and hope he forgets that phrase as quickly as he learned it.

With the manticore gone, Caustic basks in all of the attention, preening himself as the trolls gather around. The dwarves carry on with their duties, but they're constantly glancing in the dragon's direction.

Senzala makes her way over, and Yashi wraps her arms around Malak and Brutus's backsides, ushering them away.

"What was that all about?" Senzala smirks.

"Beats me." I shrug and attempt to regulate my breathing so that my cheeks don't burst into flames. "How have you been?"

"Good." She nods. "It has been good for all of us to be around our kin."

"I understand that feeling. I thought the desert trolls were here as well?" I frown as I search the crowd. They're the biggest of all the troll races, and I don't see one anywhere.

"They are with the chiefs. There are so few of them left, and King Orso wanted to meet them personally." She looks toward the castle. "He is a good king. I see why you support him."

"He's a good dwarf. That has made him a good king."

Caustic yawns, and Limery dangles from the dragon's horns like a monkey in a tree. There's an audible gasp from those around us as Caustic's deadly teeth show in all their glory.

"Taryn told us some of the story, but I really want to hear all about how you hatched a dragon." Senzala shifts her gaze from Caustic to me. "I'm sure Oyana would like to record the tale for our histories when there is time."

"I'd love to tell you about it sometime. Where are you all headed now?"

"Nowhere at the moment. We've been training since dawn,

and preparations are being made to acquire more weapons but for now, we're waiting for the rest of our people to arrive from Vanaria." Her blue eyes lock onto mine. "Until then, I'm all yours, if you'll have me."

I choke on my saliva at her words and cough as I try to regain my composure. Senzala pats me on the back, laughing softly.

Once I'm back to normal, she and I find a less crowded area in front of an apothecary. A sign on the door reads, *'Closed to help with the war effort.'*

All hands are on deck.

As I look over the crowded square, I realize it's true for the trolls as well. There are so many faces I recognize. Jojin and Watu, both guardians of the forest. Ahso, the leatherworker, and Kina, the council member with some of the most gorgeous hair I've ever seen. She's one of the few forest trolls that doesn't wear her hair in a braid. There are a dozen others that I've interacted with during my time in the forest, and many more I never had the chance to. Aside from those still in Vanaria, the only forest trolls who aren't here are the elderly and the children. This is true of the mountain and arctic trolls as well.

Many trolls are gathered around Limery as he sits on top of Caustic's head with his legs crossed, recounting their adventures in the Goldspire dungeon. For now, at least, they can enjoy a distraction. Soon, every troll hand will hold a weapon as we march.

"You sure you don't want to hear his story?" I gesture at Limery as he summons a fireball in his palms. "He has a way with words and he's quite the performer."

Senzala laughs and places her hand on my arm. "I'm more interested in what you have to say."

"Okay, then." I gulp. "When we left Frostmoor, we went straight to Wandermere. It was unlike any of the other kingdoms

I'd traveled to. The portal emptied into a sprawling forest with trees so tall that they blotted out the sun. There was fog everywhere, and all we had was the egg and no sense of direction."

She hangs on my every word as I recount our adventure through the forest, meeting the centaurs, and our agreement to clear the forest of wisps in exchange for help with the egg.

"There's a green dragon that sleeps underneath the lake?" She wears a shocked expression when I tell her about Verdaria sleeping within the Hidden Lake.

"Yep." I grin. "That's where all of the fog comes from that protects the village. She's been there for over a hundred years, I think. Speaking of dragons, will Nesira be joining us?"

Senzala places a hand over her chest. "Her place is in Frostmoor, but our bond is still strong."

I still remember the dragon's power from the first time I saw her. A blizzard followed the white dragon everywhere she went. It makes me wonder what other abilities Caustic might unlock as he continues to grow. Nesira and Senzala aren't bonded in the same way as he and I are, but as a totem, Nesira grants the shaman powerful abilities just as the phoenix does Jira.

"So then what happened?" She nudges me in the side. "After you put the regeneration items on the raft?"

"We waited as the life force gathered. Taryn, Limery, and I went to fight the shadow wisps, and when we returned to the village, it was almost time. The entire herd had gathered around the lake, and it was like I could see the life aura flowing through the forest." I close my eyes, remembering the scene in vivid detail. "And then I took the egg into the forest to hatch."

"To witness a dragon hatch..." She squeezes my arm, and goosebumps sprout along my body. "It must have been amazing."

"It was." I tell her about our first moments together, our training in Pruxford, and the final fight of the tournament, when

Caustic chose me as his bond. I'm in the middle of explaining our bond when the portal flares and a mass of bodies enter into the square.

Gord stands at the front, the broad-shouldered troll as fearsome as ever. He wears the bone armor that we looted in Paltras Ruins, and the massive battle axe—Peacemaker—is strapped across his back. One of his yellowed tusks is snapped in half, and a large metal ring dangles from his nose. His black eyes scan the crowd.

To his side stands Kronan, who rivals him in size. The chief of the mountain trolls has skin the deep purple of a plum, and one of his tusks is splintered at the tip. He wears his hair in a braided mohawk that hangs over one shoulder, and the shaft of a silver warhammer rests on the other. Two giant scars cross his chest in an X, and several more cover his arms and shoulders. He's a fighter first and foremost.

Kronan lifts the warhammer in the air. "The trolls are united at last."

A booming roar sweeps over the square, startling many of the dwarves going about their duties. Kronan steps aside, revealing a short blue troll no bigger than Yashi.

Chief Lida raises a staff tipped with a white shell into the air, and the roar intensifies. The seaside trolls are the smallest race of trolls, their small stature and webbed fingers and toes making them perfect for semi-aquatic life. She wears loose fabrics adorned with shells that sway with her movement and a shell necklace. Her eyes are as blue as the sea as she looks out at the trolls before her, and the water mage's navy dreadlocks stand out against her baby-blue skin. Despite her fragile appearance, she commands powerful magic.

The crowd parts as the group exits the portal, followed by more seaside trolls. Each one is the same light blue as the chief.

Behind them, Tormara rides her wyrm. Her braids are as fiery as her personality, and they sway from the movement. I nearly burst out laughing when I see the goblin Cheevus following her on his mangy wolf. Several dozen of his kin trail close behind him. The goblins all have the same dull-green skin, lanky arms, and pointed ears. Their eyes are a dark shade of orange, and tiny noses hook over wide mouths full of sharp, triangular teeth.

Altogether, the four tribes take up the majority of the square. We might not be an army, but we're a force to be reckoned with.

Caustic moves to greet the newcomers, Limery still sitting on his head. The seaside trolls take a defensive stance at his approach, raising their spears at the dragon's sudden appearance. Both Gord and Kronan have their weapons at the ready.

The dragon huffs, and his breath rattles the many seashells adorning their clothing and hair. There's no malice in his temperament, but I rush over in case the trolls do something stupid.

"I hope you're a better judge of friend or foe on the battle-field," I shout as I arrive at Caustic's side.

"Chod?" Gord lowers his weapon when he finds me among the crowd, and his eyes go wide. "Just when I thought you couldn't get any uglier." He booms with laughter as he strolls over and wraps his arms around me, his bone armor rattling as he lifts me off the ground. "Good to see you brother!"

I laugh when he lets me go. The two of us have come so far from wanting to kill one another. "Good to see you too." I nod toward the seaside trolls. "Looks like you finally did something I couldn't."

"A dragon?" Kronan steps up behind him, extending his arm as his gaze shifts from Caustic to me. "You're always full of surprises."

"What can I say?" I grip Kronan around the forearm with one

hand and pat Caustic on the chest with the other. "This is Caustic. He'll be watching your backs."

Chief Lida makes her way between the two massive trolls and kneels before the dragon. "I was wrong to have ever doubted you."

Caustic lowers his head, sniffing her head. *"She smells of fish."*

I try not to laugh as I extend a hand and help Chief Lida to her feet. "You're here now. That's all that matters."

"You have done the impossible." She shakes her head in disbelief as she takes in the mob of trolls. "I didn't believe it could be done, but you've united the trolls."

"I didn't do it alone. Gord, Chief Rizza, Kronan—none of this would be possible without them." I turn to the many trolls watching our greeting unfold and raise my voice so it carries across the square. "We may be from different tribes but when the time comes to raise our weapons, we'll fight as one horde."

I reach out to Caustic through our bond, and he unleashes a powerful roar. It echoes off the buildings, and I feel an energy building among the tribes. Several trolls beat their chests in response, and Caustic roars again. This time, I join in, beating my chest and roaring as power pulses through my veins. These are my people. Every troll present answers the call, and their roars echo in my bones.

The dwarves within earshot stand frozen, mesmerized by the display of unity.

Cheevus weasels his way through the trolls, followed by the goblins until they are at Caustic's feet. He looks from the dragon to me and then grins. "Dragon strong. We follow."

28. UNITED WE STAND

Limery stands on Caustic's head, using the dragon's horns as a podium. He's been entertaining the trolls and goblins with stories while we wait for Chief Rizza and the others to finish their meeting. He's a natural storyteller, acting out many of the scenes in detail. At one point, he slides down the dragon's snout with fireballs blazing in each hand as he recounts one of their battles in the dungeon with Pressley. When that story ends, he jumps into the next, narrating our experiences in the Pruxford tournament.

To Caustic's credit, he's been exceptionally patient with Limery. I'm pretty sure he's basking in the attention just as much as the imp.

"Your kin approach," Caustic speaks to me through our bond, and his head shifts slightly as he looks toward the top of the enormous set of steps that lead to the castle.

I follow Caustic's gaze and find Chief Rizza standing on the terrace overlooking the square. She looks mighty in her leather vest that showcases her lithe and defined arms. Her dark hair is braided perfectly and rests on her shoulder. She's the personification of what it means to be a strong leader. She's made the tough decisions, and the unpopular ones, all in the name of preserving the tribe. I can only imagine what she must be feeling seeing so many trolls gathered together.

She's brought them so far. When I first came to Mythos, the ley lines were blocked, cutting off the mana that kept the trolls hidden within the forest. The tribe was hunted and faced death just for existing. Now, here they are, about to go to war for the fate of not just the trolls but for all of Mythos.

Chief Laojin steps by her side, his thick white beard blowing in the breeze, followed by Jira. The forest troll shaman has a bird perched on his shoulder with fiery feathers in shades of reds and oranges. The phoenix picks at the white tips of his dreadlocks with her beak. After the fight with Ethan and his goons outside of Lynchton, the powerful bird was reborn as a chick. She's a far cry from the magnificent creature we found chained in a cave, but she's about the size of a parrot now.

A moment later, five massive desert trolls join them, each one at least a foot taller than the arctic chief. I recognize the center-most troll from our run-in in the desert outside of Sandholde. Back then, he wanted nothing to do with me but somehow, they convinced him to come. His skin is a dull tan with patches of toffee-colored skin on his shoulders and neck from the harsh desert sun. His hair is the deep burgundy of dried blood, pulled into a ponytail, and his thick, short tusks frame his stumpy, bulbous nose. The desert trolls carry a thick layer of fat over their muscles, much like a camel, but I have no doubt he's a formidable force. He wears armor made from bone and pieces of a scorpion carapace lashed together with strips of leather.

Two female desert trolls stand to his right. Their bodies are not that different from his own except for their wider hips. One has hair that's a deep brown, pulled into a bun. The other sports an orange, braided mohawk. Two males stand to the left, only a fraction smaller than the one I met in the desert. One leans against the stone balustrade, his brown hair braided to drape across his left shoulder. He's missing his right ear, and a nasty scar runs from the crown of his head to his jaw. He's definitely seen better days. The last troll has a bald head, and though he's still stout, his body is marked by age. Dense wrinkles frame his eyes, and sunspots speckle his skin. He reminds me of an old wrestler, where the muscles are still there but the skin hangs just a tad too loose.

Five desert trolls. Is that all that remains of their race?

There's movement at the bottom of the steps as a green figure maneuvers against the tide of dwarves bringing supplies from the castle. I recognize Ismora's striped skin marked with the hard-earned lessons of combat as she takes the steps three at a time. Lines of faded green and white run along her powerful arms like a tiger. The weaponsmaster is the only troll capable of rivaling Kronan for sheer number of battle scars.

She climbs the steps that wind up the landing until she finds the chief. The two have a brief conversation, and then Chief Rizza returns her attention to the square and raises her arm. The square goes quiet aside from the distant sounds of the city. Even the dwarves pause to hear what she has to say. Outside the square, carts clatter along the streets carrying supplies, hammers beat in rhythm as the smiths prepare weapons of war, and coastal birds caw from their perches upon the buildings.

The chief's golden eyes fall upon Caustic, and then me. She nods, and I return the gesture. Anticipation builds as the silence lingers, and she scans the crowd, taking in the many faces that have chosen to join her in battle.

"I wish this were a time to celebrate." A sad smile forms across her narrow face. "For the first time since the mother birthed five troll sisters and sent them out into the world, all five tribes have gathered together under one banner. Despite our differences, we share a common ancestry. We are bonded by the blood of the earth. For too long, our numbers have dwindled, and we've hidden away in fear and isolation while the world passed us by.

"And now we face an enemy that threatens to destroy not only the great kingdoms of Mythos but what little we have—" She pauses, and her fists clench. "—what little we've gained. We face an enemy with an army that doesn't tire, and soldiers that do not feel pain. They will attack, never slowing, until their bones turn to dust. I have witnessed its scope with my own eyes, and I assure you, they will not show us mercy until we vow to give up everything that makes us who we are."

She shakes her head, and her hands grip the stone railing. "But we are trolls, and we do not yield. We do not bend. We do not break. Our young ones are safe in the castle at Tawdrybluff, cared for by the elders. It is our job to ensure that they grow up in a world where trolls are free, where the legends of our might upon the battlefield are sung in every tavern and told by every campfire across Mythos." She takes a deep breath and leans over the balustrade. "We come from the earth, and when the time comes, we will return to it again. For we are the bedrock of Mythos, and we will not fade silently into the night. Together, we will fight because even if we fall, this will not be our end!"

A fire burns in my bones, and goosebumps cover my body by the time she finishes. There's an energy among the trolls that tells me every one of them feels the same way.

The largest of the desert trolls beats his chest and unleashes a deep roar. His cheeks flap and spittle spews from his mouth as the baritone cry echoes off the walls of the square. His fellow trolls join in, amplifying the thunderous howl like a crashing wave.

Caustic answers with a roar that rumbles in my chest and an

intensity that rages through our bond. For the second time today, the square thunders with the raucous clamor of the trolls as we all unite. The cries of the desert trolls fade, and their bodies heave with deep breaths, but the storm of the tribe swells. For several minutes, we unleash our frustrations in the most primal way we know how.

There's no doubt about it. The trolls are ready for war.

Chief Rizza looks over her shoulder, and a moment later, King Orso joins her side followed by several members of his council and Taryn. The kingsguard stands sentry at the rear.

The crown atop King Orso's bushy black, hair glows red like hot lava, its tines shaped into alternating battle-axes and warhammers. He wears a black cloak and tunic, each one embroidered with silver thread, and a red breastplate engraved with a warhammer that matches the dull-red tint of his skin. Even though Orso is tall for a dwarf, he only comes up to the chief's elbow.

He waits for the commotion to die down before speaking. "It is an honor to have the trolls gathered in Seascape, and it will be an honor to fight by your side. For my kingdom's part, I am sorry that it took such circumstances for the trolls to be treated with the respect they deserve. Know that from this day forward, you will always be welcome within our borders, and the castle in Tawdrybluff will be given all the privileges of a sovereign nation."

King Orso looks to Chief Rizza before continuing. "This is a momentous occasion for your tribes, and I do not want to detract from that. Once you've had the opportunity to acquaint yourself with one another, I will be opening the troves of Seascape to the trolls. When we march into battle, I do not want a single piece of armor or weaponry left in the castle that can be used."

Wow. My jaw drops. Opening the treasures of Seascape to me and Taryn was one thing, but offering its contents to all of the trolls is something else. There are treasures and items beyond measure within the vault, and the gesture will not be forgotten.

Chief Rizza and King Orso embrace one another around the forearm. As the king turns to leave, Limery shouts over the crowd.

"Waits!" He hovers in the air above Caustic's head. "Waits! Limmy has somethings to say!"

King Orso turns around, a smile forming beneath his twitching beard. "Yes?"

Limery flies up to the terrace, settling on the stone railing in front of Chief Rizza. "Limmy has somethings for the trollses."

Chief Rizza finds me among the crowd and raises her brows. I shrug. For once, I have no idea what the little guy is up to.

"What is it you have for us?" Her voice is full of kindness.

Limery reaches into the tiny pouch tied to his waist and pulls out a small object. Chief Rizza's eyes soften when he hands it to her.

"A long times agos, there's was many impses. The bad wizard tricks thems to fight for hims, and theys all dies. Limmy wants to gives these to the trollses so that theys can talk with the others. And so that theys can remembers the impses. Theys wasn't bad. Theys was just tricked."

Limery reaches into the pouch and pulls out another, handing it to Chief Laojin. Then one by one, he gives a communication stone to each of the desert trolls. "Limmy has hundreds of thems. Enough for all the trollses."

So, that's what he spent his gold from the dungeon on. He could have used that gold for anything and yet he chose to honor those that history had forgotten. A lump forms in my throat, and I blink back the tears forming at the edge of my eyes. I don't know if I'll ever know how truly lucky I am that he came into my life.

While King Orso and the other leaders have been able to communicate with the trolls through their own communication stones, this will be a monumental advantage on the battlefield. Most of the other kingdoms speak the common tongue, but now the trolls will be able to converse with them without the need for a translator.

"Thank you." Chief Rizza bows slightly to Limery. "You are a truly special imp. Would you be so kind as to hand them out?"

"Limmy can doos its!" He smiles devilishly as he flies down over the crowd, tossing out communication stones like they're candy at a parade.

King Orso and his council return to the castle while Chief Rizza and the other trolls descend the steps. Taryn follows, trailed by Ruby and Flubs. The slime is in its natural form and springs down the steps like a gelatinous Slinky. Jordy and Berry are nowhere to be seen, so they must be in the royal stables.

The chief heads for the newly arrived seaside trolls, and I take a moment to catch up with Taryn, though there's not nearly enough time to fill him in on everything that's happened the past few days.

He grins when we're face to face. "That was some speech."

"Yeah. It gave me goosebumps." I lift my arm to see if the hairs are still raised.

Taryn steps back, taking in Caustic's appearance. "How is it you were gone for a handful of days and he's nearly doubled in size again?"

I pat the dragon on the leg. "He and Limery cleared a dungeon with Pressley while I was doing the trials. He gained seven levels, and now we can communicate telepathically."

"You're kidding me?" He shakes his head and the clasps in his beard jingle. "I want to be able to talk to my pets telepathically."

"*I am no pet.*" Caustic huffs, and Taryn's dreadlocks fall across his face.

"Don't call him a pet. He's a little sensitive about that." I smirk at the irritation I feel seeping through our bond. "How are things coming along here?"

"We're almost ready. Or as ready as we can be on such short notice. The imps have been invaluable. Lillith had the idea to station those who wanted to help in Pruxford since that's where we'll be launching the attack from. They've been delivering messages between all of the other kingdoms faster than we could have ever hoped. There's a lot to catch you up on, and I didn't want to send it all through message."

"You have no idea. There's so much I need to tell you." I chuckle. "You're never going to guess who I ran into in Goldspire."

Taryn raises his brow. "Who?"

"Dorothy."

"Shit. How the hell did she find you?" His eyes are wide as he looks me over for signs of injury. "I'm guessing you survived the encounter."

"It's a long story, but the short version is that I was going to let her kill me to try to make things right. She didn't, and instead, she wants to fight alongside us. I think I convinced her that I'm not the same asshole I was a few months ago."

"And she believed you? Just like that?" Taryn gives me a questioning look.

I shrug. "I'm not dead. And she's here in Seascape."

"Wait, what?" Taryn's head swivels like a sprinkler as he searches the crowd. "She's here?"

"Relax." I laugh as I clasp him on the shoulder. "She's with Pressley at the moment. I'll give you the full story when we have time to talk. Right now, I need to talk to Chief Rizza, and then I need to find King Orso."

Taryn grips me on the arm, his brown eyes locking with my own. "I'm glad you're back."

"Me, too, buddy." I wrap my arm around his shoulder and squeeze.

We search for Chief Rizza among the crowd. Ruby and Flubs are both naturally evasive, weaseling through the throng of bodies like water, somehow evading danger at the last second. Caustic waits by the portal, surrounded by plenty of admirers.

Many of the trolls are examining their communication stones. Malak, bold as ever, has already put his to use and is engaged in conversation with the dwarves handing out weaponry.

I find Chief Rizza standing in a circle with the desert and seaside trolls. Gord, Kronan, Jira, Chief Laojin, Senzala, Yashi, and Ismora are there as well.

Jira's phoenix chirps when it sees us, and Taryn hurries over excitedly to scratch its head.

Chief Rizza gives me a warm smile when I arrive. "For those of you who have yet to meet him, this is Chod. He's the hero of the forest trolls, and we would not be where we are without his aid."

"He's also the hero of the mountain trolls," adds Kronan.

"The arctic trolls stake claim as well." Chief Laojin smirks.

"How about we just say 'Hero of the Trolls'?" I laugh.

Chief Lida nods. "I have heard tales of your bravery since you left our beaches. Long have the days been since the trolls have left such a mark on the world. It will be an honor to fight by such a hero."

The biggest of the desert trolls steps in front of me. His heavy breaths rattle the bone armor on his chest as he looks down at me. "I am called Abo. You tried to help me once," his voice booms a deep baritone, "but I was too blind to see it." He extends his arm. "If you fight for the trolls, then we will fight for you."

"No." I shake my head, and a deep frown sets on Abo's face. "You will not fight for me. If you fight, then you fight *with* me, because we're in this together."

I clasp his forearm and squeeze.

His scowl shifts into something resembling a smile, and he clamps a vice-like grip around my arm. "It has been spoken."

"It has been spoken," the four desert trolls echo, and Abo returns to his position among them.

Gord crosses his arms and leans closer to Kronan. "If they blow any more smoke up his loincloth, he may get lost in the clouds." His attempt at a whisper is loud enough that everyone in the circle hears it.

Taryn and Kronan snicker.

Chief Rizza narrows her eyes at Gord and clears her throat. "There is still much to do as we prepare for the impending battle. The dwarven blacksmiths will be forging as many weapons fit for a troll as they can in the time we have, and we now have access to the items stored within Seascape's vaults. I suggest we send a small party from each tribe to sort through the items and decide what will be most fitting. We must not be swayed by the glamour of wondrous artifacts but choose the items that will aid our cause. Once you've decided on who will go, meet me atop the terrace."

The trolls split up into their respective tribes, and Chief Rizza finally has a moment to talk to me in private. "It is good to have you back among your people."

"It's good to be back." I place a hand on her shoulder. "Good call about the vaults. There are way too many trolls to fit inside."

She smiles. "I trust your time in Goldspire was fruitful?"

I give her a mischievous grin. "It was. I've got a few new tricks up my sleeve."

"I look forward to seeing them." She lets her arm fall to her side. "King Orso has permitted us to use the royal training grounds this evening. I'm sure there's much for a hero to do, but we would be honored to have your company."

"I wouldn't miss it."

"Good. I will see you then."

Chief Rizza rejoins the forest trolls, where Taryn is still playing with the young phoenix, feeding her something from his pocket. Rizza gathers Gord and Ismora and heads for the steps. Kronan and Brutus follow, representing the mountain trolls. For the arctic trolls, Chief Laojin and Senzala go. The seaside trolls send Chief Lida and Imoko, the little turd who captured me at spearpoint when I was swimming outside their tribal grounds. Abo is the sole representative of his small tribe.

After giving the phoenix a final pet, Taryn returns. "Bro, I can't wait to see the trolls decked out in magical gear."

"We'll take every advantage we can get." I gaze up at the castle where the midday sun is starting its descent. The closer we get the faster time seems to move. "Let's go find King Orso."

29. SHADOWS

I FILL Taryn in on as much as I can while we go in search of King Orso. Limery and Caustic stay in the square with the trolls, which is probably a lot more fun for both of them. I tell Taryn about Pressley and the manticore first, and then move to my own adventure. When I get to the trials, I gloss over the challenges and focus on my new abilities instead.

"Bro." He looks at me with disbelief. "So, you're telling me that you can rage indefinitely as long as you're hitting shit and that you basically have an unkillable Constitution while you're doing it? That's so OP. And now you've got dreadbeasts and a dragon to go along with it. Why don't we just send you in alone to bash your way to the gates and then join you after?"

"If it were only that easy." I rub my forehead.

"You are the main character, after all." He grins. "Just think of the stories they'd tell about you."

"Oh, shut up." I shove him in the shoulder. "I never would have gotten this far without you. Without everyone who has helped me along this path."

"I'm just messing with you." He pushes me playfully. "I have a feeling we're going to need every trick you've got when the time comes. It's a shame that we couldn't convince the beastkin to join us."

"Yeah, none of them were willing to go against the emperor's will. It speaks a lot to how much they respect her, but it's a fucking shame." I kick a loose pebble from the courtyard, and it hits a dwarf carrying a crate of potions.

"Hey, I'm walking here!" The potions rattle as he adjusts his grip.

"Sorry!" I throw my hands up in apology and try not to laugh at how much he reminds me of a New Yorker before I return my attention to Taryn. "Still, if you would've told me a month ago that we'd have seven kingdoms and all of the trolls on our side when it finally came time to fight, I never would have believed you."

Taryn laughs. "What if I told you that Richard was the one responsible for getting us there?"

"Ugh." I let out a long sigh. "I still don't trust him, but it is what it is at this point."

We arrive at the castle entrance, and the guards step aside for us to pass.

"Follow me." Taryn motions toward one of the stairwells. "He should be in his chambers drafting letters to send abroad."

"We've been talking a lot about me. What have you been up to this whole time? More than just sitting in meetings, I hope."

"So many meetings." Taryn rubs his eyes and then pinches the bridge of his nose. "But there have been some benefits to being here. Analyzing plants in the royal gardens gained me enough experience for another level. Check this out." He stops in front of a dark corridor and waggles his brows. "Hey, what's that?" He points over my shoulder.

I follow the direction of his finger, searching the ancient stone of the circular stairwell for anything out of the ordinary, but there's nothing there. "Very funny, Tar—" I turn back around but he's gone, and Ruby and Flubs are standing at my feet.

The slime gurgles as it clings to my feet, its cool body tickling the space between my toes. I fight the urge to kick it away.

I turn back toward the dark corridor we just passed. "I'm sure you're real sneaky, but you know I have nightvision." I look down the empty hall, and my nightvision cuts through the shadows. It's just a storage alcove, and there's not even a door at the end.

"Where the hell did he go?" I ask Ruby, but she just stares at me.

Did he just sneak off and leave me with his pets? He has the Cloak of Silence that allows him to move silently but if this is his idea of a joke, he's definitely been sitting in too many meetings.

I kneel and stroke Ruby behind the ears. "Not his best work."

Something grabs me around the midsection, followed by a shrill scream that echoes through the stairwell. A shiver runs up my spine as I turn to see two arms reaching out from the darkness. Taryn pounces from the corridor, screaming like a banshee, and I roar in alarm, falling on my back and tumbling down several stairs. Taryn watches me fall, cackling like it's the funniest thing he's ever seen.

"What the hell was that?" I rub my backside as I climb to my feet.

"Shadow Cloak." He grins. "That's what I used my ability point on. I figured it would be pretty useful in the shadowlands."

"And they say I'm the asshole." I chuckle. "How's it work exactly? I have nightvision and couldn't see you at all."

He gives me a mischievous grin. "It's a shadow druid ability that gives us increased stealth at night or in the shadows. As long as I don't attack, I'm pretty damn sneaky. Not even nightvision can see me when I'm hidden. It doesn't even need to be full darkness; I can blend in with twilight."

"No shit? That's badass. Kind of like the trolls' Camouflage ability, except you can actually move around." My brow furrows when I realize what using his ability point on Shadow Cloak means. He was supposed to be saving it for something else. "Why didn't you use your ability point on Scry? Don't get me wrong, I think you made a great decision, but I thought you wanted to track down Jude and Glenn."

"I did. I mean, I do." He sighs. "This is bigger than me now and having Shadow Cloak is going to make me a lot more useful than being able to track down those two assholes. Besides, if they're in Mosstar, I have zero doubt that they'll make their presence known."

I wrap an arm around his shoulder. The fuckers do always show up when we least expect it. "If they do, we'll make them pay."

He nods solemnly. "That's enough of that, though. You want to hear something cool? King Orso told me there's an active dungeon located in the volcano underneath Seascape. I knew the city was built on a dormant volcano, but I had no idea that there was a dungeon down there. I wish we had more time to explore it."

"After the trials, the thought of a volcanic dungeon makes my stomach turn." I grimace. "How about we add it to our bucket list for when all of the fighting is done."

"Deal."

The kingsguard allows us entry into King Orso's office, and we find him leaning over a sheet of parchment with a black feather quill in his hand. The king's lips move silently as he formulates his thoughts, the quill hovering an inch off the parchment.

Limery's parents flutter in the air to each side of the king. Bazel holds a letter sealed with wax clenched in his spindly fingers. Lillith smiles as we enter, pressing a finger to her lips for us to remain quiet.

King Orso's desk is a thick slab of black stone flecked with red. It reminds me of Destroyer the way the red catches the light of the sconces. Large jewels serve as paperweights, pinning down a plethora of letters and scrolls. Shelves line the walls behind him, each one filled with leather-bound books, ancient tomes, scrolls, and stacks of parchment.

The king's face is set in deep contemplation as he writes the letter. He pauses, mumbling something to himself, and then scribbles another line before finally setting down the quill. After blowing the ink dry, he folds the letter and stamps the wax seal with his royal crest, never once acknowledging our presence.

"Please deliver this one to the Pruxford Council." He hands the letter to Lillith and then turns to Bazel. "Yours will be going to the Mistville Court."

"It will be done, Your Majesty." Bazel bows, and both imps head for the exit.

They stop for a moment in front of Taryn and I.

"I trust Limery is well." Lillith gives me a motherly look that says he better be.

"Never better." I grin. "He's down in the square with Caustic. You should see him on your way out."

"Good. We'll see you soon, Chod." She winks, and they disappear out the door.

Traveling by portal, I'm sure she'll be back within the hour. For Bazel, though, I have no idea what the journey to Mistville entails.

"Chod, I'm glad to see you return. Forgive me for not greeting you upon arrival, but there is so much to do." King Orso stands from his desk. "Who would have thought a day would come where the trolls are the second-most populous race in Seascape?"

"It was kind of you to offer your vaults to arm them."

"It was the least I could do. What good is it to sit on our treasures when we are fighting for our right to live?" He gestures for us to sit. "We'll need to keep this brief, but tell me, how was your travel abroad?"

"Eventful," I say as I take a seat in the plush leather chair. Somehow, it manages to comfortably fit my large troll body. Taryn takes the chair to the right, and Ruby curls between his legs. Flubs gurgles as he crawls into the vial around Taryn's neck. "I attained the Warforged class, Caustic is now strong enough for me to ride him, Pressley the death knight acquired a manticore as his mount, and I found another hero who wants to help us fight."

"Good news all around. A manticore, you say?" He strokes his beard. "A fearsome beast of legend from what I recall."

"She'll be dangerous on the battlefield, and we now have two more options for aerial support."

He nods. "Good, good. Have you learned any more details regarding when you and the other heroes may be forced to return?"

I shake my head. I haven't heard anything else from Valery since the trials, and judging by her tone, she has her own problems to deal with. "Unfortunately, no. When are we planning to attack?"

King Orso sighs. "You said that we may have as little as a week. If that's our timeline, then we need to be ready in two days' time. That means we need to gather our forces in Pruxford tomorrow. It will give us a day to finalize our plans with the other kingdoms before we attack. Our soldiers and mages have all gathered in the city. They will be the frontlines of the assault, and citizens are still traipsing in from across the kingdom. Those that are unable to reach the city in time will stay behind to guard the portal in the event of an attack." He massages his temple. "There is very little room for error."

"I understand." It's honestly amazing how they've been able to rally so much in such a short amount of time. Then again, Seascape has been on high alert since the behemoth came through the portal. "Do we have a plan of attack yet?"

"Not as firm as I would like. The imps have been instrumental in transporting information between kingdoms in record time. I have an idea of each kingdom's forces, and the heroes, but it will be hard to know for sure until we are all gathered."

"You want me on the frontlines?" I ask.

He leans forward, and his forehead scrunches. "I want you to do what you think is best. You know the heroes and what they are capable of better than I, and I know the trolls would follow you to the ends of Mythos if you asked. Our objective is to end Valmar once and for all. The undead outside the city and the elves within are merely obstacles in our way."

"Your Highness, if I may." Taryn, who has been unusually quiet, raises his hand.

"Go on." King Orso sits back in his chair.

"I think I might have a solution for defeating Valmar, or at least how to get to him."

King Orso and I both perk up. Taryn has always been a great tactician, so I'm intrigued by what he's come up with.

"I want to use the Amulet of Undetection that Jon crafted." When he sees the look of confusion on my face, he elaborates. "It's an item that allows the wearer to pass by undead without detection unless they are actively engaged with them. I already have my Cloak of Silence and the Smuggler's Boots that allow me to walk without making noise or leaving tracks. And now that I've unlocked Shadow Cloak, I can hide among the shadows. With the amulet, I could walk right into the city without being spotted."

"And then what?" I raise my hands, palms up. "What's your plan to kill Valmar when you find him? It's not a bad idea, but you're not exactly an offensive juggernaut. We don't even know how strong Valmar actually is. What are you going to do if it's just you and him all alone?"

"That's the part I'm still working out. I was hoping that between seven kingdoms, someone might have a weapon capable of killing him. And if not..." He reaches into his cloak and pulls out the Shadow Daggers. The twin daggers have broken blades but when he holds them, shadowy blades form that can bypass armor and drain an enemy's health directly. "I was thinking a surprise attack with these." He looks to King Orso expectantly.

King Orso strokes his beard as he ponders the situation. "I fear Chod is right. It's an intriguing prospect, but Valmar will most certainly have his castle warded for intruders. Bypassing the undead might get you into the city ahead of us, but it does not guarantee you entry into the castle. As far as weapons go, it's not so simple. Valmar walks hand-in-hand with death. Save the death knight, necromancy is not practiced within our kingdoms, and we don't know the true breadth of his power. While we have strategies to deal with the undead, Valmar is a different matter, and I fear a single strike will not slay him, no matter the weapon. However, I will present the idea to the council and perhaps they will have a better idea of how to utilize your skillset."

Taryn nods, sitting back in his chair. I can tell he's disappointed, but I agree with King Orso. The likelihood that this war could be won so easily is almost zero.

I tap Taryn on the hand. "Don't worry. We're going to figure this out."

Before he can respond, there's a knock on the door, and an imp I don't recognize enters the room.

She dips her head slightly. "I have word from Wandermere, Your Majesty."

"Give me a moment." King Orso says to the imp as he stands, his gaze shifting from me to Taryn. "We leave for Pruxford tomorrow. Make the most of what time you have."

Taryn and I take our leave, and the door closes behind us.

I squeeze him on the shoulder. "Ready to meet Dorothy?"

30. TROLLBREAKER

Taryn and I stop by the portal to find Limery before we go in search of Dorothy. She and Pressley were headed to find a tavern, and the little guy would never forgive me if I went without him. The trolls are disappointed to see their entertainment go, but it's the goblins who are inconsolable after Caustic flies off to hunt.

A tear runs down Cheevus's cheek as he watches Caustic disappear among the clouds.

The goblin leader looks up at me with determination in his orange eyes. "Cheevus serve many masters in his life. He never dreams to serve a dragon."

"Don't worry, Cheevus." I kneel beside him and pat the wiry fellow on his bony back. "He'll be back."

The mangy wolf nuzzles against Cheevus, and he climbs on its back. The goblin leader turns to his kin who still stare longingly after Caustic. "We go. Find food."

The troupe of goblins disappears into one of the side streets amidst a patter of bare feet.

"Strange little dudes." Taryn chuckles as we head further into the city.

"See yous laters!" Limery shouts from my shoulder, waving to the trolls. He turns back around and sighs contentedly. "Limmy likes the trollses. They's fun."

I pull up my map as we move against the flow of dwarven citizens retrieving weapons and armor from the square.

Since Pressley agreed to join our party after he acquired the manticore, I can finally track his location on my map. I find his marker located at The Gargoyle Inn, an elaborate stone building with intimidating gargoyles perched on every corner of the roof. The stonework is so detailed that it includes indentations around the gargoyle's feet as if their claws are actually digging into the stone.

Inside, the tavern on the ground floor is rowdy with flowing ale and chatter. Ebony and ivory dwarves from across the kingdom intermingle, and their newly acquired weapons and armor are spread about the tables among even more empty mugs.

"Me grandpappy was a great warrior." A drunken ivory dwarf wearing a helm sways like a flower in the breeze. The helm is well-made, with a warhammer-shaped noseguard that comes down to his salt-and-pepper mustache. "This helm belonged to him." He knocks the helm with his fist and nearly falls from his chair before I catch him.

"Easy there." I lift him beneath the armpits and position him back on the chair.

Taryn covers his mouth and leans in. "These guys are sloshed."

"Can you blame them?" Tomorrow, they'll be going to war. These precious moments of camaraderie could be their last.

I search the room for Pressley, but his massive frame is nowhere to be seen. After scouring the room, I finally spot

Dorothy in the corner, hiding in the shadows. Her brow is knitted, and she wears a murderous frown as she stares into a half-empty mug of ale. I wonder what has her so sour.

"There she is." I point. "I'll introduce you, and then we can order a drink." When we arrive at the table, I rest my hands on the chair across from Dorothy. "Having second thoughts?"

She looks at me with a scowl for a fraction of a second before it shifts into a bright smile.

"No, just thinking." She laughs. "You get the trolls all settled in?"

"Something like that. They're gearing up right now." I step aside and usher Taryn in. "This is Taryn. I don't think you two have ever formally met."

Dorothy extends a hand, and they shake. "Not officially, but I saw you on a few streams together. It's easy to see who the brains of the operation is."

"Game recognizes game." Taryn grins, elbowing me in the side. "I caught a few of yours as well. You're a hell of a jungler."

"Depends on who you ask, I guess." She gives me a knowing look that tells me even though we're cool, I'll never be able to live that moment down. "Well, are you going to stand there all day or are you going to have a seat?"

Limery hops from my shoulder to the closest chair and leans against the table. "Limmy wants a drinks."

"I'll grab a round for everyone." Judging by how crowded the place is, I'll have better luck at the bar than flagging someone down, but even the bar is packed three to four dwarves deep.

I tower over everyone around me, making it hard to ignore all the staring. Most of these dwarves come from the smaller towns and villages outside the capital, where troll appearances are all but unheard of. At least they're staring out of curiosity and not malice.

While I'm waiting in line, I glance over my shoulder and notice Limery has stolen Dorothy's mug. He tilts it back, and amber liquid trickles down his chin.

Taryn and Dorothy are both laughing as they chat it up. For being so skeptical of her, he seems to be getting very chummy. Or maybe it's just the effect of being around someone from our world with similar interests.

"Oy!" The bartender shouts, and I turn to see he's looking at me. "Friends of the king don't wait. What'll it be?"

"A pitcher of your best ale, please." I hold up three fingers. "And some mugs."

He nods and fills the pitcher to the brim, placing three mugs on the bar beside it. I reach over the dwarves in front of me, pay for the ale, and grab the pitcher.

When I return to the table, Limery lets out a loud belch and smacks his lips. "Yummies."

I narrow my eyes at the imp. "What did I tell you about stealing?"

"Limmy didn't steals." He shakes his head rapidly.

"I gave it to him." Dorothy meets my eye. "I'm not much of a drinker."

"More for us, then." Taryn takes the pitcher from me and fills our mugs, pouring a splash into Dorothy's. He raises his tankard. "To fighting the good fight."

We clink our mugs, and I let the cool amber ale wash away my troubles if only for a moment.

"Where's Pressley?" I set my drink on the table. "I figured he'd be with you."

"He's in his room. He said something about wanting some alone time." She arches her brow. "Not sure how to take that."

Taryn laughs. "He's a bit of a loner. Probably wants a chance to gather his thoughts before the shit hits the fan."

"It's still crazy to me that this program was developed to help prisoners." She sits back, gesturing at the tavern. "I mean, look at this. There's not a gamer in the world who wouldn't do anything to experience this, and Mythos isn't even talking about it."

The dwarves at one of the nearby tables bust out a chorus of some drinking song about axes stuck in the wall, and Limery flies over to join them.

"It's something else, that's for sure." Taryn takes another swig of his ale. "Chod tells me you want to join the fight. If your streams are anything to go by, we'll be lucky to have you."

"You flatter him this much, too?" Dorothy smirks. "If so, I see why he keeps you around."

Taryn rolls his eyes. "I'm just a nice guy."

"Sure you are." Dorothy laughs. "So, what's the plan? I'm itching for a fight."

"You won't be waiting long. We leave for Pruxford tomorrow." I take a swig of my ale. "Once all of the forces are gathered, the leaders will finalize battle plans and then we attack the next morning. I expect the heroes will lead the charge, so you'll have plenty of opportunity to scratch that itch." When I finish my ale, I stretch my arms overhead. "We're gonna head back up to the castle soon. King Orso opened his vault to the trolls, and they're going to be training with their new weapons. You want to come?"

"Do I want to watch some trolls smash about with their shiny new weapons?" She shrugs. "Sure. Not like I have much better to do."

***

We climb the steps to the royal courtyards just as the sun dips beneath the flying buttresses of the magnificent castle. The setting sun paints the sky with shades of vermillion and coral, igniting the clouds with a purple sheen and casting the castle's many spires as silhouettes. From our vantage point, it's like we're walking into a work of art.

Dorothy stops at the top of the steps, taking in the view. "This never gets old."

"I'm gonna miss it. That's for sure." Taryn kneels to scratch Ruby behind the ears, and the jackal grunts in pleasure. "Back home, you'd be lucky to catch a sliver of sunset passing through the buildings."

For the past few days, I've tried to keep my mind on the task at hand—saving everyone I care about. Taryn's comment is a reminder of what comes after. My days in Mythos are numbered, and this time when I log out, there's no coming back.

I give Limery's leg a gentle squeeze as he sits on my shoulder. Everything I do over the next few days is so that he can live a happy life long after I'm gone. For now, though, I push those thoughts to the back of my mind. Right now, I need to focus on preparation.

In the rear of the castle, there's a sprawling courtyard that ends at a rocky cliffside overlooking the turbulent waters of the sea. The center of the courtyard has stone tiles depicting the warhammer of the Brightgaze crest. To one side, there's a fountain with a statue of a dragon that shoots water from its open maw. To the other, a dwarf holds a warhammer overhead, and water spouts from each face of the weapon. Topiaries shaped like animals are speckled throughout.

Aside from the handful of blood dwarves that guard the entrance to the castle, the courtyard is occupied by nothing but trolls. They're split into five groups, with each tribe gathered around its leaders as they pull a seemingly endless supply of items from satchels no bigger than a backpack. A few trolls have already equipped armor, and the polished metal gleams in the fading sun.

Fortunately for them, enchanted armor resizes itself to fit the wearer.

Limery zooms across the courtyard to see the action up close, but Taryn, Dorothy, and I stand back to watch. Among the forest trolls, Gord holds a bag while Chief Rizza removes its contents. By the looks of it, each item was selected based on the individual skillsets of each troll. She hands Yashi a pearlescent bow that's intricately carved. It has an obsidian grip and a golden string that gives off an aura as she holds it. Ismora is gifted a set of daggers as well as a sword unlike any other that I've seen in Mythos. It has a curved blade that is only sharpened on one side, and a red ribbon wraps the grip. Tormara still has her enchanted daggers from our venture into Paltras Ruins, but she's given a pair of vambraces with hooked spikes, turning her forearms into deadly weapons.

For the guardian trolls, the chief hands out an assortment of maces, axes, and warhammers. One thing that trolls and dwarves have in common is our desire to smash things. A few of the guardians select shields, but the troll way is to dish out pain. With only a few days to prepare for this battle, I doubt any of them were comfortable learning a completely new fighting style. For herself, the chief takes a shortsword that has a red hue to the blade. While the majority of trolls prefer the freedom of movement over wearing armor, I see many wearing spaulders and vambraces, and a few who have donned helmets.

I'm reminded of when Taryn and I were lucky enough to search through the vault. It's where I found Destroyer, thanks to Kurzol's guidance, as well as my expandable satchel and the Mysterious Green Egg that would one day become Caustic.

King Orso's generosity has been the difference between life and death on countless occasions, and it still proves so. He could have had armor or weapons forged, but instead, he's given away the treasures of the Brightgaze lineage. The weapons and armor the trolls wear are priceless, many of them gifts from foreign king-doms given long before the portals closed.

As I look around the courtyard, I recognize a few of the weapons Kurzol showed me before I settled on Destroyer. A seaside troll wields the long pike capable of dealing air damage, and a female mountain troll has the slightly smaller twin warhammers that are meant for speed bludgeoning. Brutus holds a massive axe forged from the same metal as Destroyer. Both weapons were forged in the heart of a volcano, and I had wavered between the axe and the warhammer, but Destroyer seemed more practical at the time. Seeing Brutus's corded muscles flex as the axe cuts through the air, it's undeniably badass, and it'slarge enough to rival Peacemaker in size.

I leave Dorothy and Taryn to join Brutus, equipping Destroyer for him to see. "You have good taste. That weapon will serve you well."

He raises the axe and nods. "For the tribe."

I raise my warhammer, in a kind of cheers of weapons. "For the tribe."

Maybe he's not such an asshole after all.

Nearby, Chief Lida is nearly finished outfitting the seaside trolls. She had her people's best interest in mind as she chose her weapons, bringing enough spears and pikes for the tribe to replace their wooden weapons with metal.

The desert trolls all wield massive morning stars, and the spiked maces look terrifying in their hands. Abo pulls a silvery-green helm etched with leaf patterns from his bag, handing it to the troll missing an ear. The disfigured troll shoves Abo in the chest and then lets out a deep laugh that carries over the court-yard. When other tribes turn to look at the disturbance, laughter rings out. The one-eared troll slides the helm over his head and then equips the full set of armor. It's some of the most beautiful plate mail I've ever seen, almost like a layer of metallic vines have covered the troll's sun-worn skin.

Once all of the items have been doled out, the trolls show off their new weapons and armor to the other tribes. It's like watching kids show their new outfits on the first day of school. Malak is particularly proud of his golden warhammer as he swings it through the air.

While trolls are natural warriors, these weapons will raise their destructive capabilities to new heights. Unfortunately for the trolls, most of them have no mana, so they can't activate any special abilities. Any passive abilities will still work as intended, though. These are powerful weapons, each one buffed with stats and more deadly than anything the blacksmiths could craft on such short notice.

I clap Gord on the shoulder when I see him. He already has Peacemaker and the bone armor, so he was the only troll not to receive anything. "Was someone a bad troll this year? I hope you're not feeling left out."

He lifts Peacemaker, and his mouth curls upward around his broken tusk. "I have all I need right here."

Chief Rizza stands off to the side, admiring her new weapon. Up close, I notice a flame pattern etched into the metal.

"That's a nice sword," I say.

"Its name was Trollbreaker. A gift from Vanaria to Seascape during a time when the trolls were feared for their might, not just as monsters." She holds it up, and the metal seems to flicker under the last rays of sunlight. "If I had mana, every strike would deal burn damage. I'm sure you can see why it was named."

"I do." A weight settles in my chest as I imagine how it earned its name. "Why would you take it?"

"Who am I to let the past define my future?" The flames of the sword reflect in her golden eyes. "You're the one who opened my eyes. We're here to blaze a new future. How fitting would it be for a weapon meant to break trolls to be their savior?"

She grins as she places it in the scabbard.

"How fitting, indeed." I return her smile. "I spoke to King Orso earlier. Tomorrow, we leave for Pruxford."

She nods. "So I heard. Are you ready?"

I look over the hundreds of trolls gathered in the courtyard, each one armed with some of the best weapons in the kingdom. Am I ready to go to battle knowing that it'll be the last time I'll ever see some of them? Because no matter how strong we are or what weapons we have, I don't see a future where every troll makes it back. The true cost of war is paid in lives lost, and there's nothing I can do to change that.

"No, I'm not ready, but *we* will be."

31. ANCIENT PROTECTIONS

Thanks to Taryn's connections, Limery and I have a room in the castle for the evening. With how crowded the city is, I'm not sure how Pressley and Dorothy were able to find a room at the Gargoyle Inn. I imagine the death knight's intimidating presence was enough to convince some of the villagers that they'd be better off sharing a room for one evening.

If the amount of ale they drank was any indication, they wouldn't be remembering most of their stay anyway.

The guest quarters in the castle are remarkable, not that I expected anything less. The only other time I've stayed somewhere this opulent was when I visited Vanaria. If I had to compare, I think Seascape takes the cake. Our room has a four-poster bed resting against the far wall, its frame carved from dark gray marble with veins of gold. The four posts are more like columns of elaborate dwarven knotwork. Lace curtains adorned with seafoam-green pearls drape from the frame. As beautiful as it is, the mattress is even more comfortable and covered with the finest silk sheets and soft pillows. Not that I need it with my troll body, but it's still nice.

Limery sighs as he falls onto his back, sinking into the lush fabrics. He digs his fingers into the blankets. "Oh, yes. Limmy likes."

The rest of the room has an air of sophistication. There's a desk, shelves filled with books, and figurines carved from precious stones placed all around the room. A long leather couch and reading chair make up the lounge area in front of the hearth. The fire within radiates a gentle warmth. There's a tapestry of an erupting volcano on one wall and a large painting of a female blood dwarf on the other. Her vibrant red sideburns are braided and hang across her shoulders. *Queen Lumona Brightgaze* is inscribed on the metal plaque at the bottom.

I crawl into bed and sink into the mattress. After a long day of socializing, I welcome the gentle embrace. Tomorrow will be a busy day.

The next morning, there's a regional notification waiting for us when we wake up.

Regional Alert! *The time has come to join King Orso as he fights against the darkness. All able-bodied dwarves are to report to Seascape Square this morning to travel to Pruxford. Those who have not yet gathered weapons and armor must report to one of the mobile armories located throughout the city. Stay alert for further updates from your king.*

I send a message to Pressley telling him we'll meet him in the square after breakfast. Then, I find Taryn and we head to the great hall, where royal banners hang from the rafters and jeweled chandeliers paint a kaleidoscope of colors on the ceiling. Before us, several rows of long tables are filled with platters of food.

We're some of the last to arrive, and for the first time, I see the scope of King Orso's inner circle. The king sits at the royal table with Kurzol and Lady Brollen, the ice mage from Sandholde, as well as two generals who will be in charge of the infantry. Their table is located at the far end of the hall, sitting perpendicular to two rows of tables that stretch the length of the hall.

Taryn informs me of who the rest of the dwarves are as we find a place to sit.

The various tables are filled with kingsguard, clerics, and mages, along with some of the nobility and higher-ranking officials in the city. Together, these are the king's most trusted advisors and most powerful magic wielders—the dwarves he trusts with his life and the fate of his people. It's an honor to be counted among them.

Everyone talks in hushed voices as if speaking at full volume might erupt the dormant volcano slumbering beneath the city. I can't even imagine how much there is to coordinate, not just from Seascape but across all of the kingdoms. Imps come and go by the minute, delivering scrolls, letters, and sometimes verbal messages.

Once we take our seats, Limery dives into his food like he hasn't eaten in days, but I can't seem to focus on the plate before me. My mind is elsewhere, consumed by my own obligations. I need to get to Pruxford and reconvene with the heroes. As much as I want to be in the know about the war plan as a whole, I know it's not my place. I have to trust that King Orso, King Favian, Chief Rizza, and the other leaders can handle their own forces. Not only that but that they can coordinate together. I may be a strong fighter, but I know next to nothing about controlling an army, let alone multiple. Even with my horrors, we're more like a stampede than a tactically trained unit. My job is to take the most powerful fighters in Mythos and wreak havoc on the battlefield. We're the hammer of Mythos, and the leaders are the hands that guide us.

I pull up my message interface so that I can send Michael the paladin a message. Thanks to the Oath of Protection, I'm able to contact him even though we're not in a party.

Message (Chod): *We'll be returning to Pruxford in a few hours. Can you gather all of the heroes together by then?*

I expect to wait a while for him to respond, but he answers almost immediately.

Incoming Message (Michael): *Already done. This place is pure chaos right now, but we've been keeping close and training together. We've all gained at least a couple of levels since you left. I hope your travels were as beneficial.*

"You good over there?" Taryn looks at me with concern, the honey from the biscuit he's holding dripping onto the plate. "You've barely said anything since we sat down."

"Sorry, I was just thinking." I massage my eyes with my palms. "I sent Michael a message. He says the heroes are all together and that Pruxford is chaos."

"I bet." He takes a bite of the biscuit, and crumbs fall into his beard. "I'm sure some of the kingdoms are already arriving."

Limery burps and covers his mouth with spindly fingers. "Oopsies."

I can't help but laugh at how nothing fazes him. We're in a room surrounded by royalty, mages, and nobility, and he acts the same as he does around the trolls.

When I finally take a moment to focus on my food, to no surprise, it's delicious. I indulge in crisp bacon, savory sausages stuffed with spices, and a purple egg that's so spicy it leaves my tongue tingling. The food takes my mind off everything if only for a moment.

When we finally leave the castle, there's already a crowd formed in the square. We wait atop the terrace, looking down upon hundreds of soldiers in plate armor that await King Orso's command to enter the portal. A train of wagons loaded with supplies spills down the streets and deeper into the city.

From our vantage point, there's not a section of street that isn't occupied. Though I can't see them, I'm sure the trolls are down there somewhere.

The only place where there's any breathing room is the circle of space about three feet wide surrounding Pressley and the manticore. Dorothy is the only one brave enough to stand beside the death knight. I wave to them, and Pressley lifts his gauntlet in acknowledgment.

"This is crazy." Taryn leans on the balustrade. "Reminds me of the city on New Year's Eve."

A shadow moves across the crowd, eliciting gasps as Caustic's billowing wings announce his arrival. He lands next to us with a thud, his green scales shimmering in the morning sun.

I reach out to him through our bond. *"How was your night?"*

"The sheep in the countryside are more flavorful than those in Goldspire."

"I hope you weren't a glutton." Looking at the crowd below us, a few missing sheep are the least of their worries.

Caustic blows warm air against my shoulder. *"They should be honored that I desired their flock."*

Before I have the chance to explain property ownership to him, I hear the clank of plate mail as the guards escort King Orso from the castle. We step to the side, joining the rest of his entourage as the king takes his place overlooking his people.

He wears his battle armor, all black except for the red breastplate engraved with a silver warhammer. An obsidian horn covered in gilded runes hangs by his side. In his hand, he grips the shaft of a mighty warhammer. The head of the weapon is black and flecked with red, the same as Destroyer and the axe that Brutus now carries. The sides of the hammer are engraved with gilded knotwork, each pattern centered with a rune. Three sockets run along the upper half of the shaft, each one fitted with an enchanted stone. I watched the king wield it only once when the behemoth attacked Seascape, but I saw enough of its power in that moment.

King Orso clears his throat. When he speaks, his voice is magically amplified and carries across the city. "Seascape, I address you today not only as your king but as a citizen of Mythos. Generations past, before any of us had taken our first breaths, the portals far and wide were locked, and Seascape was cut off from the world at large. In these times, our ancestors did what we as dwarves always do. They persevered. Our kingdom flourished in isolation even as a great darkness lurked beyond the portal languishing in our city's heart. We thrived, and in doing so, many forgot about the atrocities that our forebears faced in the greatest war Mythos has ever known."

King Orso lets the heavy words settle on the crowd. "I was not afforded that luxury. As a prince, I was raised to remember the battles my ancestors fought, the lives that were lost, and the darkness that would one day return. I prayed that I would not be the one forced to answer that call, for I wanted what all leaders should want for their people. Peace and prosperity. Unfortunately, the gods have other plans—for me and for you. We've been preparing for this moment since the portal first stirred back to life. When the shackles broke and fast-travel once again became possible, we compounded our efforts even more."

He takes the obsidian horn from his side. "Not many know that there are ancient protections built into our city. Defenses that a king may call upon if his lands are ever under siege. I will not sit idly by and wait for war to come to us. In order to protect our home, we must take the offensive. Therefore today, I call forth a garrison to aid us on the battlefield as we defend our way of life."

King Orso lifts the horn to his lips and blows, his red cheeks puffing as a cavernous note echoes all around. The buildings shake as the reverberations wrack the city. I feel the thrum through my bones, and a piece of stone crashes against the courtyard.

There are shouts of surprise from below, and I look up to see the gargoyles sculpted upon the castle moving. Red fissures sprout upon their stone bodies like molten lava as all across the city, the stone guardians spring to life.

My hair stands on end, and even the kingsguard are awestruck as the gargoyles pry themselves from their posts. The sound of flapping wings fills the air as hundreds of guardians find a place to perch around the square. Heads twist on a swivel, and so many whispers pass through the crowd that even this high up it sounds like a den of snakes.

King Orso lets the horn fall to his side once again. "There is a darkness out there that wishes to subjugate us all, to grind us to dust beneath a boot of disorder and chaos. I do not intend to let that happen. When we march on Mosstar, your king will not sit in a tower watching the battle unfold. I will be by your side, ready to bleed and die for you and yours. So I ask you this, who will fight side-by-side with your king?"

The words boom through the city as King Orso lifts his hammer overhead. His entire body takes on a golden aura, and when the resounding call of the dwarves thunders in response, a shimmer sweeps across the city, buffing every dwarf with some unknown power.

King Orso lowers the warhammer, and his face is carved from stone as he passes by. Passion burns in the depths of his eyes like a volcano ready to erupt. If I were one of his subjects, I'd follow him into the depths of hell and back again.

That time may come but first, we go to Pruxford.

32. ALL QUIET ON THE PRUXFORD FRONT

I STAND behind Caustic as he steps into the whirl of white energy. While his body is still capable of fitting through the portal, his wings protrude beyond the arch, even when tucked. Lucky for us, the magic powering fast-travel doesn't seem to mind, and he vanishes in the ethereal swirl.

Our group exits into the square, which is just as crowded as Seascape's, if not more so. The first time I visited, this area was full of merchants, peddlers, tourists, and travelers all coming and going. Now, it's a one-way route as guards and city officials direct traffic from the platform toward the outer gate.

Even though Pruxford is a gnomish kingdom, a large percentage of their city guard is composed of different races. Though they come in many shapes and sizes, the pearlescent armor is their defining characteristic. The city officials are mostly gnomes, easily recognizable in their matching robes and biretta hats topped with fuzzy little balls.

"Wow, that's beautiful." Dorothy stops and grabs my arm, pointing toward the Crystal Palace on the far side of the city.

The building is like something out of a fairy tale with its translucent crystal in hues of green, pink, and violet. Emerald and amethyst spires catch the light of the morning sun and glow like beacons. I remember the first time I set eyes on the shimmering palace. At night, the view was awe-inspiring as the moonlight reflected off the palace's exterior like the Northern Lights.

"Keep it moving!" a guard yells, waving his arms like a traffic cop. He's taller than most, so definitely not a gnome. His pearlescent armor shifts through a rainbow of colors as we pass him. "All foreign kingdoms are assembling outside of the city gates. Keep it moving, people!"

"Alright, alright." Dorothy rolls her eyes. "We're moving."

Our small group looks like a circus of misfits surrounded by dwarves on all sides as we follow the never-ending line toward the outer gate. Taryn leads the way, riding Berry, with Ruby curled in his lap and Flubs peeking from the vial around Taryn's neck. Jordy flanks their right side, the frost goat lowering his horns whenever someone gets too close.

I walk next to Dorothy, sandwiched between Pressley and his manticore on one side and Caustic on the other. Limery stands on the dragon's head, holding onto Caustic's horns like he's a captain at sea. I'm almost certain Caustic has grown a bit more since his feast throughout the Seascape countryside. He's a towering presence, and if his growth continues at this rate, I'm not sure how much longer the portal will make an exception for his size.

Dorothy gawks at the Crystal Palace as the foot traffic slows before we're ushered along again. Even though the guards give Caustic and the manticore a wide berth, they keep us moving.

"This is too many people," Pressley's hollow voice rumbles. "I'll find you once you're settled in."

He grips the reins of his manticore, and she extends her wings, nearly knocking a dwarf over as they take to the air. Caustic has no such qualms as he lumbers beside me, basking in the reverent looks of everyone he passes.

"Not much of a people person, is he?" Dorothy grins as the death knight soars away.

"He's a nice guy." My gaze follows Pressley until he disappears beyond the wall. "Probably just tired of all the sour looks."

She shrugs. "What do you expect? He's a walking bag of bones."

Taryn looks over his shoulder, a few paces in front of us, and smirks. "A can of bones would be a more fitting term."

Dorothy scrunches her brow. "You really have a way with words, you know that?"

"What can I say, I'm a—" Taryn's eyes go wide as saucers as he passes through the gate. He gestures for us to hurry up. "Damn. Bro, you've got to see this."

Caustic's chest rumbles, buying us some space as we push our way through the gate. I don't know what I expect to find on the other side, but this isn't it.

Tents, pavilions, and caravans stretch for as far as I can see around the city's perimeter. It's like we've arrived at an outdoor festival. I spot the blue-and-silver banner of Vanaria, followed by the white and gold of Antadale's catfolk. Further down, there are even more banners that blend together in a multi-colored mosaic.

Chills run up my arm. "This is unbelievable." I can't fight the sense of amazement at seeing so many people banded together under a common cause. When we were traveling from kingdom to kingdom, it always felt like the odds were stacked against us. Even in the council room, surrounded by the leaders of Mythos, it felt like we were outnumbered as we gazed through the portal into Mosstar.

Spending most of my time on the Isle of Mythos, it's easy to forget that Seascape and Vanaria are relatively small kingdoms compared to the vastness of greater Mythos. There are thousands gathered here, maybe tens of thousands, and this isn't even everyone.

"Keep it moving!" a guard shouts from behind, and I realize I'm holding up the procession once again.

"I'll catch up with you all shortly. I want to get a look at our forces." I pat Caustic on the chest, and he lowers his body. "Let's fly."

"First Pressley, now you." Taryn lifts his arm and sniffs under his pit. "Do I smell or something?"

"That's a conversation for another time." I use Caustic's wing to pull myself up, straddling just below the base of his neck. "Hold on, Limery, we're going for a ride."

Caustic shuffles back and forth, and dwarves scatter just before he extends his wings and launches skyward. It's impressive how something his size is able to fly, but the boisterous sound of his wings flapping is proof that it's no easy task.

People rush out from their tents to catch a glimpse of the dragon as we pass over the Vanarian camp. We fly higher until their bodies are like ants as they scurry around. From this height, I can see the far side of the city past the Crystal Palace and the gemstone arena where we fought the sea orcs. To my other side, beyond the camps, there are rolling hills filled with dungeons and the occasional farm or village strewn across the countryside.

Limery laughs like a madman as Caustic dives. My braid whips behind me, and cool wind assaults my face as we plummet toward the earth. I clench my thighs and wedge my claws between Caustic's thick scales to keep from sliding.

At the last moment, Caustic pulls back, sending ripples through the white-and-gold circular tents and pavilions of Antadale. Armored elephants trumpet as we pass, jostling the catfolk sitting in the covered saddles on their backs.

We soar over the colorful array of tents that make up the Ellynmylly camp, and their rainbow banners blow in the breeze of Caustic's wake. At the back of their camp, the eclectic nation has a row of catapults and wagons filled with boulders. Several dozen giants roam through their campgrounds, nearly twice as large as the other races that make up Mythos's Melting Pot.

We reach the final camp, where banners of green and purple make up the Mistville forces. They have the largest caravan of wagons. Some of them are massive, as big as a bus, and resemble giant casks on wheels. Something slithers across the ground near one, and a merfolk activates a massive spigot at the back of the cask-like wagon. Water flows out, and a giant sea snake nearly as long as the mana-infused wyrms rises, basking in the water. Several more slither out from beneath the nearby wagons to enjoy a drink. I'm sure it's a challenge being away from the waters of Mistville, but they came prepared, which is good considering I doubt there will be much water where we're going.

Caustic ascends, flying over the city walls, where guards are stationed around the battlements, before turning to soar over the camp once again. This time, the camps are full of people eager to catch a glimpse of the dragon. Caustic is more than just a powerful weapon to everyone below, he's a symbol, something for them to believe in.

Looking at the kingdoms gathered, we're still waiting for Wandermere to arrive. All of Pruxford's forces are within the city. Even so, we have a more formidable force than I could have ever hoped for.

As we near the Seascape camp, I search for Taryn and Dorothy and find them outside of the largest pavilion, which I assume belongs to King Orso. With its red and silver stripes, it looks almost like a circus tent.

Caustic hovers above the campsite, making it increasingly

difficult for the dwarves attempting to stake the tents, and I slide down his backside before he takes off into the hills to go hunting.

"Where's King Orso?" I ask. There are plenty of mages and nobles in the area, but the king and his guards are nowhere to be seen.

"He went straight to the palace." Taryn scratches Berry behind the ears, and the umber bear groans. He looks past me into the endless sea of tents. "I can't believe how many of us there are."

I laugh at Limery as he plays a game with Flubs where the two toss a pebble back and forth. Every time the slime shoots the pebble from his gelatinous body, there's a loud slurping sound that sends Limery cackling.

"Yeah, it's crazy. You're not gonna believe some of the things I saw. The catfolk have elephants, and Mistville have an army of sea snakes nearly as big as wyrms." I turn to Dorothy and gesture over my shoulder. "Ellynmylly is just past the catfolk, if you wanted to say hi to anyone."

"I'm gonna pass." Dorothy shakes her head. "I'm not quite as beloved as you are. I kept a pretty low profile because I had other priorities than being a hero."

Right. Making me pay was all she thought about for the longest time. Even if things are better now, she missed out on a lot because of me. An awkward silence lingers in our little bubble as tents go up all around us. The billowing flap of wings saves me from crawling into a hole as Pressley finally rejoins us.

"You weren't lying. Mythos is going to war." He dismounts from the manticore and removes a handful of bones from his satchel, tossing them on the ground along with some folded canvas. While he's pulling out rods and rope, the bones assemble themselves into skeletons and immediately get to work erecting a tent. "I haven't needed a tent since my transformation, but we should stake our claim to an area before we lose it."

"That's generous of you. And to think, someone called you a bag of bones." Taryn nods in the direction of Dorothy and then settles his gaze on the skeletons as they work. "How many of these guys do you have?"

"Lots and lots." Limery abandons his game with Flubs and perches on Pressley's shoulder. "Limmy seens thems."

Pressley grunts, but there's no telling what it means or who it's intended for.

Eventually, the trolls make their way through the gate. Chief Rizza, Yashi, and Tormara lead the way on the backs of the three mana-infused wyrms. Behind them, Chief Laojin rides a mammoth that made the trip from Frostmoor. He's flanked by Cheevus and the goblins. The rest of the trolls follow, the tribes intermingled. It turns out Ellynmylly isn't the only melting pot. Ours is just a blend of Mythos's so-called monsters.

The trolls lay claim to a field with a copse of trees not far away. While I may have managed to get some of them into a castle, I doubt I'll ever see a troll use a tent.

More dwarves pull up the rear, followed by the troop of gargoyles. The stone guardians position themselves around the perimeter of Seascape's camp before settling into sculpturesque sentries. Each one must weigh a ton, because they leave craters for footprints.

Pressley's skeletons finish setting up the tent, and it's much bigger than I expected. More like a canvas room than a camping tent, and it manages to fit all four of us comfortably with room for Taryn's pets. He and I are used to sleeping under the stars when we're on the road, but it's nice to know we have this as an option since I'm sure there won't be an empty room in the city tonight.

"So, what now?" Taryn plops against Berry, who has staked his claim to a corner. The bear lifts his head, huffs, and then lays back down.

"We should go find Michael and the other heroes while we have time. I doubt there's much else for us to do until the leaders finish meeting."

Taryn groans. "Man, I just got comfortable."

I reach out to Michael, and he responds with their location a few minutes later. The Puzzling Peacock has become home base to the heroes and a few of the challengers who decided to hang around.

"Yo, Pressley." Taryn guides Berry over to the death knight once we're about to leave. "As long as your manticore doesn't eat other people's pets, I've got the hookup for a nice stable in the city. Breebis is the best around." He looks at the manticore with a worried expression. The undead mount sits like a statue at the back of the tent. "She won't eat them, will she?"

A sigh rattles inside the death knight's helm. "For the third time, she does not attack unless ordered. But if you ask me that again, we might test her fondness for bear meat."

I fake a cough to keep from laughing. Dorothy isn't as considerate, and her laughter rings out.

"Come on, don't be like that. I was just making sure." Taryn crosses his arms. "I thought you might want someone to clean her up so she doesn't smell like death before the big battle. But I guess I was wrong."

"She smells like death because she's dead," I mutter under my breath loud enough for Dorothy to hear.

Dorothy leans in, whispering in my ear. "Shh, let him keep digging."

As if it was a premonition, Taryn keeps going. "I trust you. It's just, well..." He puts a hand to his mouth and speaks in a hushed voice. "She's scary looking, and I've heard the stories."

"You know what?" Pressley grabs the manticore's reins. "She

could use a bath. It's not like she earned the name Beast Killer or anything. What's the worst that could happen?"

Taryn's eyes go wide. "Wait, maybe this was a—"

I squeeze Taryn's shoulder and usher him along. "Don't worry, bro. They'll be fine."

When we arrive at the gate, several guards stand sentry, barring our entry. There are still the occasional stragglers leaving for the camps, and a few imps zip by carrying messages, but no one seems to be going back into the city.

"What's your business?" a gruff-sounding lizardfolk calls to us as we approach. His purple-scaled hand grips the spear by his side.

I offer him a smile. "We have a meeting at the Puzzling Peacock."

The guard taps the butt of his spear against the stone street. "Unfortunately, entry is barred unless you have permission from the council."

Pressley steps forward like he's about to say something, but Taryn extends an arm and blocks his way.

"Allow me." He clears his throat. "I know you're just doing your job, but we really need to get inside the city. You remember the attack on the arena? The one where a big, ugly, blue troll fought tooth and nail to send those sea orc scum back to where they came from. You remember him?" Taryn uses both hands to gesture at me like I'm a showpiece at the jewelry store. "He might stink a little, but he's the troll that's going to be on the front lines of this invasion along with all of the heroes he's been able to rally to the cause. And yeah, he might have a temper, but he's the same troll who managed to unite all five troll tribes, and who has spent every waking moment trying to bring the kingdoms together so that you and yours have a home to come back to. If you want us to have the best chance possible at winning this thing, then you should probably let us inside. Oh, and don't forget that he brought a godsdamned dragon to fight by your side."

"Er, yes, uh, well." The guard looks to the others for help, but they've already stepped aside. "Um, I guess, well, shit." He sighs and steps aside. "Just go."

I don't know if I've ever been so insulted and flattered at the same time. I keep my face straight until we pass and then give Taryn the biggest grin I can make. "Damn, T, you didn't have to do the poor guy like that."

<hr>

We make a quick visit by the stables, which I'm certain is more of an excuse for Taryn to see Breebis than anything his pets might need. To my surprise, the gnomish stable master isn't fazed by the manticore's appearance.

After bowing to the creature, Breebis approaches cautiously and strokes the manticore's fur along her neck. "She's majestic. What's her name?"

Pressley's breath rattles in his helm before he answers. "She doesn't have one."

"Well, we'll just have to fix that, won't we?" Breebis scratches the manticore's chest. "A creature this renowned must have a name, undead or not."

Taryn raises a finger in the air. "I might have a suggest—"

"No." Pressley's voice booms before Taryn can finish the sentence. He turns to Breebis. "Name her what you wish."

Breebis beams as she leads the manticore into the stables, followed by Taryn's pets.

After we leave, Taryn sulks as we make our way to the Puzzling Peacock. When Limery perches on Pressley's shoulder, the death knight doesn't object. Whatever happened in the dungeon forged a true bond between the two.

Taryn increases his pace until he's beside Pressley. He huffs and finally speaks what's on his mind. "So you're just going to let her name your mount without issue, but you won't even let me make a suggestion?"

"I trust her. She has a calming presence."

Taryn rolls his eyes. "Oh, and I don't?"

"Do we really need to go over the names of your pets again?" Dorothy laughs. "I mean, come on. Berry. Jordy. Flubs. Ruby is okay, I guess. There's a ninety percent chance you were going to suggest calling the manticore 'Manty.'"

"I'm offended you would even think that." Taryn tries to defend himself, but his reddening cheeks tell another story.

In the outer boroughs, the atmosphere is much different from the first time we visited. Despite how many people currently reside outside the city walls, the streets are sparsely populated. There are no tourists, no cleanup crew keeping the city in pristine order, just the occasional, hurrying gnome or an imp zipping over the top of the buildings.

Pruxford has been preparing in earnest, and their citizens were already being armed before I left for Goldspire. I expect there is not much for them to do now but wait.

When we arrive at the Puzzling Peacock, there are only a handful of heroes downstairs. An old gnome bartender polishes mugs behind the counter. Despite the rooms being booked, this is the first time I've seen the place this empty. Light from some unseen source shines on Michael the paladin in the far corner. He sits at a table with two of the heroes I know the least about. Sam the monk leans back in his chair with his hood pulled over his eyes, his dirty feet resting on the table. Next to him, Scotty the sniper has an assortment of arrows with various tips and colored fletching laid out before him as he organizes his quiver. He nods to me before returning his attention to his arrows. Sam and Scotty were both in the Challenger's Tournament but I've never had a moment alone with either of them. They fought beside us against the sea orcs, and they are here now. That's all that matters.

Still, I can't fight the knot forming in my stomach as I wonder where everyone else is. I expected more.

"Where is everyone?" I ask, unable to hide the disappointment in my voice.

Michael walks over, extending his arm. As we clasp one another around the forearm, a shimmer of light passes over my body.

"Don't worry. Onera has her watchful eye on us." He smiles, and I swear his teeth sparkle for a moment. "Many of those from the Challenger's Tournament have chosen to join their kingdoms now that they've arrived, but they will still be fighting. They felt it would be best to empower their people. As for the others, Arty stopped by after I received your message and asked if anyone wanted to clear one more dungeon. The council has barred reentry into the city without permits for now, but the Adventurers Guild still has its portal stones. They should return within a few hours."

I let out a sigh of relief. "Thank goodness, I was beginning to think they'd all backed out."

If they're still trying to scrape up a little more experience this close to the battle, then they're truly committed.

Michael pats me on the back. "We are ready for a fight."

"Good. Judging by what I've seen outside the city, it's going to be a big one." I step aside so he can see Dorothy and Pressley. "I brought two more for the cause."

"May Onera's light shine on you." Michael's gaze lingers on Pressley before he looks at me and laughs. "You really are something if you managed to convince this one to fight with you. He had his pick of any alliance he wanted when we first arrived, and he turned down every one."

Pressley acknowledges the comment with a grunt before taking a seat at a nearby table.

"I guess he was just waiting for the right one." I chuckle. "Should we have a drink while we wait for the others? We can catch each other up in the meantime."

"Oh yes!" Limery is suddenly hovering next to us. "Limmy would like a drinks."

The bartender has dull-blue skin and streaks of gray in what used to be vibrant sapphire hair. He lingers for a moment after placing a pitcher and several mugs on the table. "Tonight, your drinks are on the house." His brow furrows, and he clenches his fists. "We lost good gnomes during the attack. I lost friends. Make the bastards pay for what they did."

Michael grabs the gnome's fist in his own. "We'll give them hell just for you, old-timer."

While we wait for the others to return, Taryn and I tell Michael, Sam, and Scotty about the forces outside the city and King Orso's plans of attack. The battle plan is certain to change once he convenes with the other leaders, but it beats twiddling our thumbs and gives us something to talk about.

Michael has been keeping tabs on everyone, so he's able to fill us in on their new abilities. One of the most interesting is Don's Nullification Zone. It allows the void mage to create an area around him where other abilities don't work, not only preventing any magic user who stands within the zone from casting but also blocking any magical projectiles once they reach him. Sam has unlocked a new dual ability called The Tortoise and the Hare, where he can either gain increased movement speed or form a protective shell that blocks a certain amount of damage. Scotty unlocked Barrage, which allows him to form up to twelve copies of whatever projectile he's firing, even mimicking their effects, though they do slightly less damage than the original.

We're deep in conversation, and Limery is deeper into his mug, when the door opens and heavy footsteps fall against the aged timber.

A familiar voice calls from behind, "Leave it to a troll to stop for a drink while we're all hard at work." Arty is covered in mud and blood, but the cyclops grins from ear to ear.

I stand to greet him, and he wraps his arms around me in a massive bear hug. "Good to see you again, Chod."

Behind him, the rest of our remaining crew filters into the room. Randy the rogue and Don the void mage. Arty's two brothers, Roddick and Reddick, as well as a half-dozen of their adventuring companions. Drizz'rt the golden-scaled assassin and Kazzandra the giant both chose to fight with us instead of their countryfolk.

While we lost a good number of challengers, this is more of the crowd I was expecting. Every one of them is at least a level or two higher than the last time I was here.

We all stand in silence for a moment before Taryn nudges me in the ribs. "This is your show. You better say something."

I clear my throat, and every eye falls on me. "I appreciate all of the work you've put in over the past week. It might be that a hard-earned level is the difference between life and death for some of us. Tomorrow, we face a threat unlike anything else we've experienced. Look around the room at those standing among you. We'll be the ones leading the charge, and it will be us that the rest of Mythos looks upon when they need the courage to press onward. So pour yourself a drink, and let's get to work."

33. BLESSED BE THE SLEEP

Twilight creeps across the Pruxford countryside by the time we return to camp. King Orso's tent is still empty, but I spot King Favian on the back of his griffin, talking to Chief Rizza across the road. Since the trolls volunteered to follow me into battle, I'll need to speak to her once I have a better idea of the roles the heroes will play in all of this.

All around, fires flicker among the campsites like hundreds of fireflies. By this time tomorrow, we'll already be in Mosstar. For many, this is the last night they'll see.

A thunderous sound rumbles from the direction of the gate. I sense Caustic's alertness and pull mana to my fingertips just before a stampede of centaurs appears down the road, a trail of dust following in their wake. I let the tingle of mana fade as Swift Thundercrest leads a herd of hundreds down the dirt road toward us. The herd's leader is built like a draft horse from the waist down, and his majestic silver beard and hair whips in the wind. Thannis, Daimun, and Sylvie follow close behind him, the ground quaking as they pass. A cloud of pink and purple celestial fairies surrounds the centaurs, their iridescent bodies shimmering in the fading light. Behind the trail of dust, some of the elder centaurs pull wagons loaded with supplies. They might not be as fast or as nimble as they once were, but they're still doing their part.

Swift leads the herd to a prairie just past the trolls on the opposite side of the road, where they run in a circle, trampling the overgrown grass. The centaurs shout and thrust their weapons overhead until Swift unleashes a deep yodel that cuts them off. They disperse and fall into perfect formation, their hooves thudding against the earth in unison several times before quiet settles over the camp.

I'll give it to Swift, he knows how to make an entrance. Aside from Pruxford's army, this is everyone.

The centaurs and fairies begin setting up camp when a notification flashes in the corner of my vision.

Regional Alert! *On behalf of Pruxford, Mistville, Antadale, Ellynmylly, Wandermere, and the Isle of Mythos, we commend those who have chosen to fight back against the encroaching darkness. Our combined forces have gathered, and battle plans have been drawn. Orders will be delivered by your leaders. Until then, make your peace and rest well. At dawn, Mythos goes to war.*

I swallow hard after reading the message. We're on the brink of a war that could destroy everything these people have ever known. How in the hell is anyone going to sleep tonight?

There's movement in my peripheral as the gate opens again and a convoy of emerald carriages exits the city. One stops by the Vanarian camp, where Kassidy the teleportation mage, and Warwick, captain of King Favian's kingsguard, emerge. I'm sure Warwick isn't happy that King Favian left on the back of his griffin without him.

More carriages pass by, carrying the leaders of Antadale, Ellynmylly, and Mistville. At the end of the convoy, two carriages stop outside of Seascape's camp. King Orso, Kurzol, and a few members of the kingsguard exit the carriages. King Orso waves to his people as he makes his way to the royal tent. There's no mirth or excitement to his features, only unreadable stone. Knowing what awaits, this can't be easy for a king who cares so much for his people.

He turns around at the entrance to the tent as if he's about to say something. A cavernous roar from the direction of the troll camp cuts him off. I turn to see every troll standing along the roadside, divided into their respective tribes. At the far end, Abo's head is tilted back as he bellows at the heavens. Birds flock from the trees, and the jowls of the desert troll stretch to their limit as his powerful lungs continue their sonorous barrage. His deep clamor echoes off the hills, seemingly never-ending.

Abo's roar finally relents, but Kronan steps forward before it completely fades, unleashing a roar of his own. Where the desert troll's was deep and resonant, the mountain troll's is violent, terrifying in its fury. It cleaves through the night like the snarl of a lion in the darkness just before it attacks.

All around me, canvas hisses like a den of snakes as dwarves and humans emerge from their tents to see what's happening.

Kronan's boisterous roar fades, immediately replaced by Gord's. The forest troll booms with guttural passion, and my hair stands on end as I feel my connection to the tribe through his intensity. Chief Laojin answers for the arctic trolls, his roar icy and raw, like the cutting bite of an unexpected cold snap. The next roar is softer, resembling the swell of the tide just before it crashes against the rocky coastline, as Imoko does his part for the seaside trolls.

As he finishes, a familiar sensation stirs within me, and my body tingles with electricity. The first time it kindled, I was only beginning to understand my place among the forest trolls. This time, a fervor passes through me and sparks along my bond with Caustic.

I answer the call of my brethren, startling the dwarves around me as my roar thunders with anger and desperation, a prayer that the trolls may survive what's coming, that Limery and everyone I care about will see better days. Somewhere in the darkness, Caustic cries out, his primal ferocity enough to quake the heavens.

When all five tribes join in together, it's like a volcano erupting. None of this was planned and yet it's like I know my part, like I always have.

The roars of hundreds of trolls fade, leaving behind a deafening silence. All across the camp, we sit in a soundless vacuum, no one uttering a word.

Gord steps forward and beats his chest, the hollow pounding like a cannon. A heartbeat later, Malak and the other guardian trolls do the same. The male mountain trolls mirror the action, followed by the arctic trolls, then the desert, and finally the seaside trolls. I make my way through the dwarven camp until I'm standing in the road. I'm with them, yet on my own. All at once, we slowly lower into half-squats, the muscles of our massive thighs rippling with the movement.

In perfect unison, we smack a palm against our leg, and it echoes through the night. I bring my second hand down on the opposite leg, followed by a thunderous stomp and a deafening roar.

There's a pause just before the higher-pitched roars of the female trolls join in. They step forward, taking their places beside the males and mirroring our sequence, their dance every bit as raw and powerful as our own. When it's finished, Chief Rizza lets out a yodel that echoes off the hills.

We pound our chests in unison, our drums of war, and something inside of me takes over as I become one with the trolls across from me. The sequence of stomps, slaps, and roars change but somehow, I don't miss a beat as the rhythm continues, a musical madness composed of flesh and bone as we do our tribal dance. Braids whip through the night like striking vipers, and the music of our bodies clears the wildlife for miles. I close my eyes, letting the vibrations wash over me, and then they end.

The silence that follows is all-consuming, and I feel the void creeping in. Across from me, a song erupts from Chief Rizza, and her golden eyes lock with my own. She sings a wordless hymn, a guttural cry that wails against the darkness with a melody of power and melancholy. A song of farewell to the world we know and the ones who may not see what comes after.

My body tingles as electricity sparks within, and the shouts of surprise all around tell me that I'm not alone. Shockwaves course through my veins, threatening to explode like lightning, and I clench my fists to hold onto the feeling for as long as I can. As quickly as the sensation came, it fades away, and several notifications flash across my vision.

Alert! You have been blessed by the forest trolls.

Alert! You have been blessed by the mountain trolls.

Alert! You have been blessed by the desert trolls.

Alert! You have been blessed by the arctic trolls.

Alert! You have been blessed by the seaside trolls.

For the longest time, no one moves, no one even speaks, basking in the moment of what we all witnessed. What I was a part of. I have no idea what the troll blessings will do, but one saved my life once. Maybe they will offer us some protection in a land of shadows.

"That was beautiful," Dorothy whispers from behind.

I'm not sure when she found me but when I turn around, she, Taryn, and Pressley are all there.

Limery comes flying out of nowhere like a meteor and wraps his tiny arms around my neck. "Chods made Limmy feels the lightnings."

"I didn't know you could do that." Taryn looks at me with a reverence I'm not sure I deserve. Dorothy does as well, maybe even Pressley too, but his jeweled eye gives nothing away.

"Me neither. It just kind of happened." I chuckle, patting Limery on the back. "Like I'd been waiting for this moment my entire life."

"Chod, Taryn." King Orso appears from behind a tent, his kingsguard trailing a few feet away. "May I have a word? There was a great deal of deliberation, but the Mythos Council has a plan for the heroes. I'd like to discuss it with you."

"Of course." Taryn bows.

I nod in agreement and then turn to Pressley and Dorothy. "We'll meet up with you after."

King Orso's molten eyes burn with intensity as he leads us into his royal pavilion. He ushers everyone else out before revealing the council's plan. It's bold, and the trolls will be putting themselves in danger if they choose to follow, but if we can pull this off, then there's a chance to save Mythos before too many people are hurt.

Taryn and I exchange glances once we leave the tent. Before we have a chance to talk about the plan, a soothing hum comes from the direction of the Antadale camp. I close my eyes and listen to the catfolk chant. There's a disconnect between what they're saying and what I'm hearing, so I remove my communication stone and store it away.

The chant builds, settling over the campsite like a warm embrace as hundreds of voices meld together. It reminds me of the Gregorian chants I listened to once for history class, both ominous and comforting at the same time. I don't need to understand the words to appreciate the effect as the tension in my shoulders lessens and even my anxiety seems to ebb. The chanting continues for about ten minutes, and when it ends, my eyes are heavy, and a new notification flashes in my vision.

Alert! *You have been soothed by an Antadalian Chant. Rest without worry.*

"Limmy is sleepies." The imp rests his head on my shoulder.

"Me too, buddy."

Taryn yawns. "We can talk in the morning." He pats me on the back.

Limery is fast asleep by the time we reach Pressley's tent. Even though the death knight might not need sleep, his helm rattles as he sits in the corner.

I curl up next to Limery and welcome the sweet oblivion.

34. MYTHOS GOES TO WAR

I wake up to the sound of wagons crunching along the dirt road. Even though it's still dark out, the camp bustles with activity. I stretch my arms overhead, feeling as refreshed as I ever have. There's no telling how many sleepless nights the catfolk saved with their chant.

Around the tent, the others stir awake as the effects of the sleep buff come to an end. Pressley is missing, but several of his minions stand sentry in the corner.

"Today's the day," I say to myself more than anyone as I pull back the flaps of the tent. Although torches burn across the camp, I don't need them to see with my nightvision. "Holy shit."

My mouth drops open once my gaze falls upon the massive contraptions being rolled out of the city. The gnomes are well-regarded as great tinkerers, but I had no idea they made such impressive weapons of war. They seem centuries ahead of what most other kingdoms have. A convoy of catapults, siege towers, ballistae, trebuchets, and battering rams flows from the city, interspersed with battalions of soldiers wearing armor that has a purple hue to it. I can't help but wonder how many of the soldiers are everyday citizens thrust into the conflict.

Limery lands on my shoulder, his body warmer than normal. The catfolk may have helped us sleep, but the nerves have returned in full force this morning.

All around, dwarves and humans bark out orders as camps are dismantled and soldiers head to their locations.

I let the tent flap fall close. "You all ready?"

Dorothy looks up from the dagger she's using to clean her fingernails and grins. "This is going to be fun."

I wish I shared her disposition. For her, she's about to experience an epic battle in the most realistic game she's ever played. For me, the stakes are real. Everything I've grown to care about is on the line.

Taryn pats Berry on the side and then climbs on the umber bear's back. He nods solemnly. "Let's end this."

I send a quick message to Michael, telling him where to meet us, and we head for the trolls. Kassidy is supposed to join us as well. The crux of the plan revolves around the teleportation mage.

At the edge of camp, we find Pressley standing by a pile of bones. Hundreds of bones in various shapes and sizes litter the area, and more fall from his satchel each time he shakes it. There must be enough pieces for over a hundred minions. Even though the dwarves know he's on our side, they give him a wide berth as they work.

"Question." Taryn raises a finger. "How exactly are we supposed to tell your minions apart from the ones we're about to fight?"

I hadn't even thought about that, but he makes a good point.

Pressley waves his hand, and the bones begin assembling themselves. "They'll be the ones not trying to kill you."

Dorothy laughs, but I'm not sure if he's joking or not. Taryn blinks a few times, seemingly unsure himself.

Pressley grunts and stops what he's doing, motioning for one of his minions to join him. The death knight points an armored finger at the skeleton's elbow joint, where a dark purple energy holds the bones together. "Look at their joints. It's not easily noticeable, but the infernal energy that powers their bodies is the same as mine. Though some may look similar, every necromancer has a unique energy source. Once we see Valmar's, it will be easier to tell them apart."

Dorothy grins as she unravels the shawl from around her neck and dangles it in the air. "You could always tie ribbons around them."

Pruxford's forces continue to file down the road, setting up position across from Antadale and next to the centaurs.

A streak of silver passes overhead as King Favian flies by on his griffin. There are so many moving pieces right now. I just need to focus on the task at hand.

"Meet me by the trolls." I reach out to Caustic through our bond.

"You meet me by the trolls. I am already here."

I roll my eyes and continue onward. Is this what I was like as a teenager? Who am I kidding? I was probably worse.

The trolls are up and about, equipping armor and testing their new weapons. Caustic casts an imposing figure at the back of the camp, where he stands on his hind legs with his wings spread wide. He's surrounded by the three wyrms and a host of goblins. The wyrms lower their heads to the ground like snakes in deference to the mighty dragon. Not that long ago, they were nearly the same size. Now, he's much bigger. Caustic lowers himself to all fours, dipping his head and sniffing each one in turn before allowing them to rise. He moves in our direction, the wyrms and goblins following.

The chiefs and many of the councilmembers are gathered together just outside the copse of trees. They wear a gamut of emotions as we approach. Chief Rizza's face is stoic, the picture of leadership that has united the trolls for a chance at a better life, even though it may cost them dearly. Then there are Gord and Brutus, who grin with the thirst for battle. Chief Laojin gazes contemplatively toward the other camps while Chief Lida of the seaside trolls keeps adjusting her grip on her staff. Kronan looks like he's ready to fight the first person who breathes wrong. And then there's Abo, one of the last of his kind, whose welcoming smile is at odds with his fearsome appearance.

Abo extends his arm. "We are ready for war."

I grip his massive forearm and squeeze. "Good, because there's been a change of plans."

Once the other heroes arrive, I gather the trolls to inform them of the council's strategy. For better or worse, we're together in this. Kassidy hasn't arrived yet, but I'd wager he's fitting in a final meal before the battle.

There's a mixed reaction from some, but Gord, Brutus, and Kronan are giddy with excitement. Their thirst for battle is matched only by the rogues, Randy and Drizz'rt. They ache for somewhere to unleash their fury, no matter how it comes.

After we all know our roles, I summon horrors as we get into formation, starting with the dreadbeasts since they won't decay outside of combat. As long as I have at least one of them active, it'll prevent the horrors from deteriorating as rapidly, so I'll be able to summon fifty percent more than I normally would.

There's a crack as a rift tears through the air and the Dreadbeast of Torment steps from the void. Murmurs of excitement and awe surround the appearance of the demonic canine the size of a giant wolf. Its thick, black fur blends into the darkness except for a trail of silver that runs down its spine and orange eyes that burn like embers just beneath a set of dangerous horns. Saliva drips from the dreadbeast's fangs as it takes its position by my side like a feral guard dog.

"Scaries." Limery's body warms against my shoulder.

I pat him on the leg. "Don't worry, bud. They're on our side."

Cheevus traipses over on the back of his mangy wolf. "This one likes." The goblin's eyes are full of greed, and he smiles devilishly.

The dreadbeast snarls when the wolf gets too close, and Cheevus lets out a surprised yelp. His wolf tucks its tail and whimpers.

"You might want to give him some space." I chuckle as the wolf slowly backs away.

Next, I summon a Dreadbeast of Despair. There's another crack, and the mighty black bison steps through a rift, majestic and terrifying in its appearance. Shadowy tendrils flare from its ebony fur, and two crimson horns curve upward from the side of its head. It's the biggest of my summons, large enough that I could ride it as a mount if I didn't have Caustic.

"Damn!" Taryn guides Berry to the opposite side of me, away from the dreadbeast. "You didn't tell me they were this badass."

I shrug. "What'd you expect with a name like that?"

The demonic bison blows a thick stream of smoke when Michael the paladin moves closer.

Don the void mage nods approvingly. "Nice."

Gord approaches the Dreadbeast of Torment without fear, Peacemaker slung across his broad shoulders. He kneels and extends his hand. "You will dine on the bones of our enemies tonight."

The dreadbeast lets out a low growl as it sniffs Gord's hand, but the brutish troll doesn't flinch. After a tense moment, the dreadbeast licks his knuckles. A smile tugs at my mouth. No matter what Gord faces, he does it without fear. I'm lucky to have him accompany me into battle.

I slap him on the shoulder, rattling his bone armor. "I can summon ten of these at a time. This one is yours."

He grins. "It would be my honor."

While everyone ogles the new dreadbeasts, I summon a round of horrors and wait for the short cooldown on the dreadbeasts to reset. Compared to their brethren, the horrors look like Chihuahuas standing next to Rottweilers. They have just as much fight and fervor, but for the first time, they look small. The Horror of Finesse circles the dreadbeasts with its spindly limbs, sniffing at the air. Even the Horror of Power, which was once my most terrifying summon with its stocky frame and dangerous tusks, only comes up to the dreadbeasts's knees. The rotund, furry Horror of Vitality is enamored with the Dreadbeast of Despair, grasping at the smoking tendrils that flare from its body.

The horrors might not be as big or as powerful on a one-to-one basis, but with every new summon, I grow stronger, gaining one percent damage and HP for each one active. Combined with my Warforged ability, I'm the perfect choice to lead the charge.

I continue summoning until my mana runs out. I've never run out of mana before, but the dreadbeast take a lot more to summon than the horrors. Luckily, I came prepared and have a nice supply of mana potions I picked up in Goldspire. I down one and continue summoning until I have ten of each dreadbeast and twenty of each horror, increasing my health and damage by eighty percent. The horrors scatter amongst the trolls and goblins, and I send one of each dreadbeast to accompany each of the chiefs.

Behind the trolls, Pressley holds the rear, mounted on the

manticore with several hundred skeleton minions to each side of him.

Between the two of us, we have enough minions to form our own battalion.

A final carriage exits the city, and the gate closes. My heart rate quickens and I force myself to breathe. Even though we're an army that's tens of thousands strong, we're going into a hellscape where the dead will outnumber us. Not to mention whatever else lurks in the shadows.

I take another deep breath as the carriage passes by with Richard the cleric and several of the gnomish councilmembers inside. My gaze follows them until their carriage stops across from the Antadale camp where the rest of the Pruxford forces are stationed.

The air crackles like a staticky radio just before the voice of Dezmin Dreamwader, head of the gnomish council, booms all around us.

"Soon, the sun will rise across the countryside, bringing a new day to Pruxford. For all of you gathered here today, this is a new dawn for all of Mythos. There comes a time when we must make difficult decisions, when we must choose between what is right and what is easy. In Pruxford, we have taken the easy road for far too long, choosing to ignore a mounting threat even as it tested our borders. You know why this fight is necessary. At first light, portals will open, and our idle hands will take on the weapons of war. Fight without mercy. Fight for your lives. Fight for Mythos."

Cheers erupt across the countryside as weapons are thrust into the air, and the trumpeting elephants of Antadale bellow their challenge. The cheers fade, and a cacophony of voices blend together as each leader gives a speech of their own. The words of King Orso, King Favian, and Swift's all muffle together, but the trolls stand silent. Chief Rizza motions for me to join her.

I call for Caustic to join me through our bond and take my place next to the chief.

She looks at me expectantly. "You should be the one to send us off."

"No." I shake my head. "They might believe in me, but they followed you to this moment. *I* follow you." I take her hand in mine. "Because you put your faith in me when I didn't deserve it. You helped me see that there are things in this world worth fighting for besides myself. Let me fight for you now."

She nods, and her golden eyes sparkle with emotion as she squeezes my hand.

Caustic lands behind us with a thud and raises his head proudly as he looks over the trolls.

"I'll be back shortly." I give Chief Rizza's hand another squeeze before climbing onto the dragon's back. He pushes off and soon we're soaring over the biggest army I've ever seen.

Seven kingdoms stand side by side in formation. King Favian soars above his people on his griffin, an inspiring sight if I've ever seen one. The Vanarian forces are led by the royal soldiers and city guards, their blue capes draping over silver armor. Beside them, the dwarven army stands ready with hundreds of statuesque gargoyles in the rear.

The giant elephants take point for the catfolk, their white-and-gold banners waving proudly from the giant saddles atop the magnificent beasts. They trumpet as we fly by, and catfolk thrust their spears in the air. Further down, the giants of Ellynmylly push their catapults into position behind soldiers holding shields of a dozen hues. At the far end, the merfolk form several columns on each side of their wagons, and massive sea snakes slither through their ranks.

Caustic roars as he turns around, where the forces of Pruxford, Wandermere, and the trolls wait on the other side of the road.

Pruxford's siege weapons are ready for war, and I spot a familiar caravan among their ranks. Three wagons emblazoned with a large red lion across the canvas.

I guess the Underground Circus is going to Mosstar.

Next to them, the Wandermere herd stands at attention, hooves shifting at the prospect of battle. Among the trolls, Chief Rizza sits on the back of her wyrm and pumps her fist into the air. There's a flurry of movement as the trolls answer in kind.

The first rays of sunlight begin to creep over the hills, and a cloaked figure joins Dezmin Dreamwader in front of the Pruxford forces.

Richard pulls back his hood and drops to his knees. The air suddenly grows thick and humid, and static sets my hair on end. I watch the cleric with fascination as a red aura surrounds his body. The air crackles with energy, and red lightning strikes all around us. Caustic roars as he dives to rejoin our kin.

Lightning crashes as we descend, and thunder rumbles as the night sky burns crimson. Along the road, jagged fissures tear through reality as rifts appear. They splinter and fracture, growing larger as a swirl of silver and black forms within. Unlike the viewing portal we witnessed at the council, we're unable to see what waits on the other side.

Smoke rises from Richard's prone form, and the black chain that hangs from his neck glows molten red. Thunder crashes again, reverberating through my chest as the portals stabilize.

Silence settles across Pruxford, and I dismount Caustic to take my position next to Taryn and Dorothy.

"Where's Kassidy?" I look around for the teleportation mage but still don't see him. None of this works without him.

Taryn points over his shoulder. Kassidy sits on the back of the manticore behind Pressley with a pastry in one hand and the other wrapped around the death knight. He waves the pastry in my direction.

"That's as good a place as any, I suppose. Everyone ready?"

Taryn nods, and Dorothy smirks as she spins a blade in her palm. Limery perches on my shoulder, his claws digging into my skin, and all around me trolls march toward the portal as drums beat in the distance.

"I'll find you when it is time." Caustic's anticipation vibrates through me as his voice growls in my head.

A powerful gust sweeps across us as the dragon flies off. He's the first one to disappear through the portal, followed by a stampede of horrors and dreadbeasts. All around me, trolls, humans, dwarves, gnomes, and a myriad of races from across Mythos march through the portals.

I equip Destroyer and lift it in the air. *"Let's give them hell."*

35. EVERYONE HAS A PLAN UNTIL THEY GET PUNCHED IN THE MOUTH

THE PORTAL EMPTIES us into Mosstar, where dark clouds blot out the sky, leaving the kingdom in a state of perpetual twilight. A sulfuric stench permeates the air as I look across the wasteland. We're positioned to the far left of Mythos's forces, maybe half a mile from the outer wall. There's a sea of fog where the terrain dips slightly that stands between us and the horde of undead protecting the city.

Limery scrunches his nose. "This place is stinkies."

The smell is going to be the least of our problems, but I keep that thought to myself.

My gaze falls upon the city, and I swallow hard. It's bigger than I expected, easily the size of Vanaria. An eerie glow comes from within, drawing my eye toward the green flames that burn atop four colossal towers surrounding the keep. An obsidian spire rises from its center, shimmering like a beacon as it reflects the fiery towers.

I force my eyes away from the keep to take in the rest of the city. Only a smattering of windows glow across the elven stronghold.

They have no idea we're coming. Maybe we can end this before they know what's happening.

Our forces continue to exit the chaos portals, and I feel Caustic's presence as a shadow moves through the clouds overhead.

"Do you see anything?" I ask him.

"The city is quiet for now. We must hurry." The uneasiness in his voice sets my nerves on edge.

Steadfast, we march toward the city walls. I summon new horrors as the older ones expire. Unlike the dreadbeasts, they'll continue to decay until I engage in combat. I glance at the rage bar in the corner of my vision. It's dangerously low, but I haven't had a chance to replenish it since my fight with Dorothy. That leaves me about thirty seconds of Cold Rage before it runs out. Once I start smashing heads, that won't be a problem.

Something snaps behind us. When I turn around, the portals have vanished. There's nothing but a barren landscape covered in fog to one side and a forest of dark trees to the other. Despite my nightvision, there's a shroud hanging over the forest that I can't penetrate.

We're trapped here now. Our only way out is if we take the city and open the Mosstar portal.

"We have been spotted!" Caustic roars in my mind.

No sooner do I hear the words before the spire in the heart of the city flares a toxic green. Limery grows warm against my shoulder as the fiery towers surrounding the keep burn higher, and pyres erupt around the battlements. Figures move atop the city wall, and outside, a wave of chartreuse energy passes through the undead as they stir awake. If that's the color of their joints, then it'll be easy enough to tell them apart from Pressley's minions.

Michael the paladin drops to one knee, a golden aura surrounding him. It pulses, and a wave of energy passes over everyone in his immediate vicinity.

Alert! *You have been blessed by Onera. Deal increased damage against undead and take reduced damage from undead attacks for the next thirty minutes.*

Not bad. I'm even more glad he's on our side now.

We continue our steady march—a battalion of trolls, horrors, heroes, and undead. Even if Valmar knows we're here, it will take time for him to mobilize the rest of his forces. If we can push through the undead, we have a shot to overtake him before he can call in reinforcements.

"What's that?" Taryn points to the far right, where a blur of purple and yellow darts across the fog in front of the merfolk army.

Tozzet, the tidal mage from the tournament, propels himself on a low-hanging wave until he's nearly a hundred yards ahead of everyone else. He glides like a surfer until the wave suddenly dissipates, and he vanishes beneath the fog.

This wasn't part of the plan. *What the hell is he up to?*

A blue aura swells beneath the fog, and the mist constricts like it's being sucked into a vacuum. A glowing blue vortex circles the area where Tozzet disappeared as the particles merge into raging water, swirling like a miniature hurricane. The vortex grows higher, its spout swaying to the point that it might topple as the mage tries to contain it. Suddenly, it whips forward as the merfolk channels the fog into a crashing wave.

Chief Lida runs ahead, gathering fog around her as she mimics the merfolk. Down the line, two water mages from Seascape and another from Antadale do the same.

Tozzet's wave gathers momentum as it tears through the fog and collides with the undead. They scatter like flotsam as the wave passes through the horde and crashes into the outer wall. Water and bones splash a hundred feet in the air before settling into puddles across the battlefield.

Four more waves follow, less powerful, but enough to clear our visibility between here and the outer wall, knocking down more of the undead in the process.

Scattered bodies and detached bones lay motionless, the first casualties of the battle. I wonder if having so many undead means that each one is less powerful, but then all at once, they stir, rising from the muddy earth in haunting unison. They charge toward us silently, their battle-cry composed of thousands of bones that clack together like the chattering teeth of gods.

An avalanche of white descends from the city as more bodies pour from the far side.

"We make for the wall!" I roar above the chaos. "That is our only objective!"

We have our mission, and that's all that matters. If we don't succeed, then the whole plan is doomed.

Caustic descends from the clouds, his emerald scales reflecting the eldritch light of the city as he dives low, breathing out a stream of toxic gas. Dense green fog settles among the undead, a splash of color among a field of white, but it does little to damage their fleshless bodies.

Out of the corner of my eye, the fiery tips of the Ellynmylly archers sparkle against the darkness like fireflies as they raise their bows skyward. The arrows loose, streaming against the night, and my heart stutters as I wait for them to land.

The flaming arrows hit Caustic's gas with a thunderous explosion, and hundreds of skeletons are blown apart. Shards of white rain down upon the battlefield, and Caustic dives again, unleashing another stream of gas. Moments later, arrows fall like shooting stars into another bombastic blast.

Relief floods through me for a moment, but it's quickly squelched by the blood-curdling screams coming from behind us.

"Oh, noes." Limery's body flares with heat, so intense that I grimace.

The pain radiating through my shoulder is the least of my concerns once I notice the source of his distress. The shrouded trees of the forest are nothing more than skeletal branches, and above them, a swarm of darkness moves across the twilight sky. What I thought were leaves are actually giant bats, and they're flying toward us, their wings flapping like erratic sails.

Nearby, Scotty the sniper readies his bow. The weapon is slender and nearly as tall as he is. He nocks an arrow and as he pulls back, tendrils of white energy coil up and down the arrow's shaft. His face strains from the effort as the energy builds until it glows blinding white. He releases the arrow, and it splits into twelve copies as he activates Barrage. The arrows connect with a dozen massive bats, and chains of arcane energy wrap around their bodies. They plummet to the ground, but hundreds more flitter out from the forest.

I ready Destroyer for their attack, but the bats fly straight over us. Their eyes are set on Caustic as he continues to breathe gas upon the battlefield.

King Orso is quick to react, and the gargoyles take flight, but the bats reach Caustic first, tearing at his scales with claws and fangs. The dragon is undeterred by their attacks. He snaps a bat in half with his massive jaws, and entrails rain upon the undead. He rips the wing off another with his claws.

He's only swarmed for a moment before the gargoyles join him and chunks of flesh and stone start falling from the sky.

"Are you okay?" I reach out to Caustic through our bond.

"Do not worry about me." He rips another bat in half and tosses it aside. *"Make for the wall."*

Behind us, Pressley's minions swarm the fallen bats, with the trolls helping to finish them off. Malak crushes skulls with his golden hammer, and Abo wreaks havoc with a morning star that looks more like a baton in his large hand.

Nearby, Yashi shoots arrows from the back of her wyrm. Even though her aim is true, she's having little effect against the massive creatures. The bats fly past, arrows protruding from their wings and bodies. She manages to hit one in the eye, and the critical hit drops it like a brick.

Giant icicles soar skyward, ripping massive holes in the bat wings as Senzala calls upon the power of her totem.

Scotty continues to launch arrows into the sky with unnatural speed, dropping bats in droves with his magical arrows. He hits one with a combustible arrow, and it ignites the sky like a fiery meteor. Another stuck with an ice arrow plummets to the ground, its body smashing into thousands of shards upon impact.

Horrors and minions swarm the creatures as they fall. Several bats besiege a lone gargoyle, breaking a wing from its body, and it falls like an anchor straight toward Chief Lida.

I scream her name, but she doesn't hear me as she shoots darts of ice from a water pouch around her waist. There's nothing I can do but watch as the gargoyle plummets toward her.

Seconds before she meets her fate, a brilliant blue portal forms just above her head, swallowing the gargoyle and spitting it out of a second portal onto the approaching undead.

Thank god for Kassidy.

The sky is pure chaos as bats, gargoyles, and a dragon fight among the clouds. Below, imps and fairies dart across the battlefield, their synergy of fairy dust and fire evident in the pink and purple explosions that thunder around us.

A Dreadbeast of Torment growls by my side, eager to attack as its paws dance up and down. *Not yet.* The dreadbeasts have strict orders to defend those they're stationed with, and the undead army is almost upon us.

I set my gaze on the approaching enemies and squeeze Limery's foot. "Stay safe. If you need to fly away, you do it."

"Yous stay safes toos, Chods." Flames crackle in his palms.

I activate Cold Rage as I rush toward the horde of undead, side by side with Gord and Chief Rizza. My metallic skin shimmers, and I catch Gord grinning out of the corner of my eye. Michael buffs us with another blessing as the Dreadbeasts of Despair charge ahead, and the demonic bison bulldoze through the first line of skeletons like bowling pins. I swing Destroyer in an upward arc and bones go flying. The passive from Ram Rage sends a wave of energy that knocks back more skeletons as all hell breaks loose. The Dreadbeasts of Torment attack like feral wolves, crushing bones in their powerful jaws, and my rage meter rises as I hammer my way through the undead. Their rusted weapons and bony hands screech against my hardened skin as fireballs blaze around me from Limery and Jira. Up close, I notice the green tint to their joints but in the chaos, it'll be easy to confuse them with Pressley's. I summon horrors between hits, exploiting the buff from Horror of Power to deal double damage, and the Horrors of Vitality slow the surrounding undead enough to give us an edge.

Gord shatters bones as he cleaves through three undead with a single swipe. To my right, Chief Rizza's wyrm rips the head off another. Explosions rumble in the distance, and thunder roars in several directions. Everything happens so fast that I can only keep track of what's going on in my immediate vicinity.

I smash like a troll possessed and feel a gravitational pull as a ball of black energy sails past my shoulder into the horde of undead. It expands like a dying star before collapsing in on itself and pulling several dozen enemies into the void as it snuffs out of existence. Lightning crashes nearby, followed by a stream of sizzling moonlight as Taryn wreaks his own brand of havoc, his powers amplified against the undead. I hear Berry's roar as I smash through skeletons and turn to see Taryn in the midst of battle, the bear Imbued to twice its normal size. Lightning strikes, stunning a handful of undead in place just before Jordy rams into them and sends bones clattering.

With full stacks of Inferno, my warhammer glows a vibrant red, charring bone with each hit. Noxious odors linger on the battlefield from magic and the undead.

I activate Sweeping Slash and Concussive Force, stacking their effects to clear a path forward. The blow knocks a host of bodies backward, and two shadowy forms pass by as Randy and Drizz'rt dart into the fray. The two rogues fight back to back, surrounded by undead, and their bodies move in a blur as they slice through bone like it's butter.

An arrow hits my shoulder with a clink, followed by a host of cries as arrows pepper our location. Archers line the battlements, their silhouettes outlined by the green glow of the city as they fire without worry of injuring their own forces.

A seaside troll takes an arrow to the neck and collapses. Tormara snarls as she rips one from her arm.

"Archers!" I reach out to Caustic and a moment later, his body soars above the castle walls. "Limery, help him!" I point toward the diving dragon, and Limery dashes away.

The imp moves across the battlefield like a speeding bullet, and there's a thunderous explosion as his fireball ignites Caustic's gas. Bodies tumble from the high walls, but the structure withstands the blast. The attack will buy us some time but it won't be long before reinforcements take their places. We need to keep pushing.

A lone wail echoes from behind us, drawing my attention. Before I turn around, hundreds more join in. Their cries carry like the sirens that blare before a dangerous storm. The amplified howls drown out the clamor of weapons and the roars of beasts and monsters, and my eyes follow the sound to the top of the barren hillside where a new enemy awaits. Hundreds of large, fur-covered humanoids tilt their heads back and howl, setting my hair on end.

Fuck. Nobody said anything about werewolves.

Our battalion is the closest to the hillside, and it looks like we're about to be fighting on two fronts.

A rusty sword slams against my shoulder from behind, shrieking as it grates against my Warforged body. I turn just in time to see a black-and-red axe whistle through the air as Brutus decapitates the skeleton attacker.

"Watch your back," he growls, the joy of battle radiating in his eyes as they fall upon our new challengers.

The werewolves drop to all fours and storm down the hillside. Hundreds descend like a landslide, and even from here, I can see the blazing red eyes and matching aura that surrounds their deadly claws. I saw this once before when we fought the gnolls. They're in some kind of rage or pack frenzy.

Brutus grabs Kronan by the arm, turning the mountain troll to face the werewolves. Kronan's eyes widen, and then he looks over his shoulder toward the city wall.

"Rizza!" he bellows and somehow his voice carries across the carnage.

Chief Rizza looks at him from the back of her wyrm, and Kronan points toward the werewolves. A fierce frown spreads across her features, and I see the understanding in her eyes as she turns the wyrm to face the hill.

Michael pushes past me, his spotless silver armor pulsing

with golden energy. I grab his arm. "Can you buy us a minute against the undead?"

He takes in the charging werewolves, glances at the undead, and nods. "By Onera's might." He raises his shield into the air, and it blazes with holy light. "Heroes, on me!"

The paladin slams his shield into the ground and a wave of brilliant energy shoots out in front of him, knocking the undead back a good twenty feet. Sam the monk appears at his side and lowers into a fighting stance. His arms move in a practiced motion, and colorful energy trails each movement like the strokes of a paintbrush. A brown aura rises from the earth, morphing into a herd of ethereal buffalo.

I turn my attention back to the werewolves and hear the stampede of hooves before bones clatter behind us.

Chief Rizza extends her sword, Trollbreaker blocking me from joining the fight against the werewolves. She meets my gaze, shaking her head. "The trolls will guard the rear. Lead the heroes to the wall."

Dammit! I want to argue, to stay and fight beside my kin, but I know she's right. This isn't how it was supposed to go. We were supposed to have the element of surprise but somehow, we're the ones caught off guard and forced to adapt.

"Trolls!" Her voice rings with authority. "We have a new challenge!"

Gord steps up beside me, his shoulders covered in a layer of bone dust. He wears a maniacal grin as he takes in the new challengers. When he beats his chest, something pulses within his eyes.

"Guardians! Rage with me against the darkness!" His skin sizzles, and steam radiates from his body as he unleashes a battle-cry that rivals Caustic in its ferocity.

All around us, the other male trolls answer his call. Abo joins his side. The massive desert troll is covered with cuts and missing a few fingers, but he stands tall. Steam emanates from his shoulders, and when he roars, his wounds begin to stitch themselves together.

Gord taps Peacemaker against my chest with a metallic clink. "Take care of yourself, brother. I'll see you on the other side."

His muscles bulge, and the guardian trolls rage in unison.

"Give 'em hell." I raise Destroyer in the air. "Heroes, with me! We've got a castle to storm."

We fight our way forward, a battalion of horrors and heroes. Behind us, trolls clash against werewolves amidst a maelstrom of roars, snarls, yelps, and battle-cries as they give us a fighting chance at reaching our target.

Ahead of me, three Dreadbeasts of Despair charge in an arrowhead formation, bulldozing through the skeleton army. The demonic bison have lost nearly half of their HP but with my high Constitution, it's far from worrisome.

Above us, Caustic and the gargoyles continue to battle the frenzy of bats among the clouds. Portals dot the skyline as Kassidy keeps the falling gargoyles from crushing our forces.

I fall back, letting Michael lead the attack as I search for the teleportation mage. I find him on the back of the manticore, his gaze focused on the skies as he searches for stone to redirect. Pressley swings his sword from the back of his mount while the manticore tears through the undead with her dangerous claws.

"How close do we need to be to the wall?" I shout at Kassidy as I smash a skeleton and its bones explode into dust.

The teleportation mage glances past me. "To move all of you, we need to close half the distance."

"Get ready, then. I've got a plan."

I search for Limery and find him hovering between Taryn and Dorothy. Taryn's Moonbeam sizzles against the undead, disintegrating their bones, and Dorothy wields a dagger in each hand, rivaling Randy and Drizz'rt with her fighting prowess as she cuts through our enemies.

"Taryn, cast Strong Wind on my horrors." I pull my last vial of Boom Dust from my inventory and throw it into the horde. "Limery, fireball!"

The imp tracks the vial as it arcs through the air, throwing a fireball that ignites the explosive mixture of fairy dust at just the right moment. It explodes like a bomb, dismembering undead and leaving a crater about twenty feet wide. I send my horrors forward, their smaller bodies worming between the legs of the undead directly in front of us.

Once they're in position, I cast Kamikaze, and the horrors detonate, dropping my bonus HP and damage by a sharp margin but clearing a path toward the wall.

"Push forward!" I shout.

A swirling blue portal hovers a few feet off the ground where the crater is. My dreadbeasts lead the way, with Michael the paladin and Don the void mage right behind them.

I stop in front of the portal, fighting back the horde from closing off our path. Pressley's minions join me, holding back the undead so the others can pass. Sam and Scotty leap into the swirl of blue energy, followed by Randy and Drizz'rt. I summon more horrors every chance I get to replace the ones I lost. Arty, his brothers, Kazzandra, and several adventurers rush past. The cyclops has a gash on his shoulder, painting his chiseled bicep a vibrant red, and several broken arrows protrude from the giant's back.

A massive stone wall forms across from me, crushing undead and creating a barrier as Taryn and Dorothy come bounding my way. Some of the skeletons spill around the wall and into the crater, falling through the portal.

"Hurry!" I yell as I activate Sweeping Slash, knocking back a host of skeletons.

Taryn and Berry pass through the portal, followed by Jordy, Ruby, and Dorothy.

"I'll be right behind you," I tell Limery, and he disappears.

Everyone is through but Kassidy and Pressley. The manticore hovers above the battlefield, allowing Kassidy to maintain his focus while the death knight shoots dark energy into the undead.

An arrow lodges in Kassidy's stomach, and the portal falters, shrinking in size as blood pools around the wound to his abdomen. The teleportation mage grimaces, holding a hand to his midsection and redoubling his focus until the portal returns to its original size.

"Pressley, let's go!" I shout.

Blood seeps through Kassidy's fingers. I don't know how much longer he'll be able to hold on. The manticore lands beside me, and Pressley's minions fight against the horde as he dismounts.

"You go. They need me out here."

"We need you!" I argue, but then I take in the rest of the battle for the first time. None of the other kingdoms have pushed close to the wall. Dead elephants litter the landscape like giant boulders, and many of the gnomish siege weapons are swarmed by undead like ants on a piece of candy. The merfolks' wagons are cracked, broken, and emptied. All the while, the undead continue to funnel from the far side of the city. There's no telling how the trolls are faring against the werewolves.

Our only hope is ending Valmar so that all of this stops.

"What can you do against this? You're one man."

Pressley pulls a vial that glows bright pink from his satchel. The Potion of Reincarnation that we looted in the Glossop Forest. "Go save Mythos. Let me do my part."

Kassidy coughs, blood pouring down his chin. "You have to go now."

Pressley downs the vial of pink liquid, and his body begins to morph. The last thing I see as I jump through the portal is a two-story-tall death knight drawing his sword.

36. BLAZE OF GLORY

Pressley's bones thickened and elongated as the Potion of Reincarnation coursed through him, transforming his body by epic proportions. Increased stats jolted his system, and his bones vibrated with the power. A shiver passed through the death knight, his entire being tingling with unspent energy so intense that it pushed back the cold that always lingered. Enchanted armor and weapons adapted to his changing body until the death knight stood so tall he could see the boots of the elves stationed on the outer wall. Arrows clinked off his helm, about as bothersome as gnats. He was a titan, a goliath, a mountain of death.

Pressley stared at the empty vial in his hand. It had morphed alongside him and was now the size of a boulder. He read the potion's description a final time.

Legendary Item. Potion of Reincarnation. *(Only usable by heroes.) User gains increased size and doubles all stats for the duration of the potion. Health drains with each step. When user's health reaches zero, their character is randomly re-rolled to level 1.*

A new health bar appeared across Pressley's vision next to a timer that ticked down from ten minutes. Every step the death knight took would deplete his health, and when his HP reached zero, he'd be rerolled into a new level-one character. A new race, a new class, and he'd have no choice in either. The timer was there to prevent him from hunkering down in one place in an attempt to hold onto such god-like power.

He laughed to himself. When he'd first read over the potion's effects, they had sounded awesome. Doubling his stats would double his power. But he'd been wrong. Doubling his stats amplified his power exponentially. This was as close to being a god in this world as he could come.

For the majority of his time in Mythos, Pressley had cared about one thing—acquiring power. Through hard work and devotion, he'd achieved his goal, and now he was throwing it all away. When the potion ended, everything he'd worked toward would fade away with his current body. Every choice he'd made and every bit of power he'd accrued would soon be for nothing.

No, that wasn't true. He was making it count for something right now. He'd be able to tell Eva that when the fate of Mythos was on the line, he'd stood for something. She'd learn what kind of man her father had always wanted to be. Strong. Powerful. A man of honor. And though he'd been selfish too many times in his life, this was proof that he could be selfless.

He was going to lose everything he'd worked toward, but he'd gained something that would endure. As much as he hated to admit it, he'd made a few friends in this world. Sacrifice was a part of friendship.

Now was his chance to go out in a blaze of glory so that the name of Pressley Allen would be revered across Mythos forever.

The timer ticked down, and he surveyed the battlefield. Below, his minions pushed back Mosstar's undead, hacking against bone with new fervor empowered by the death knight's increased stats. When he looked at his minions, they carried an aura of undeath that only he could see. It would have been much easier for his allies if they could tell the distinction as easily. In the dim light of the shadowlands, they'd be hard pressed to notice much of a difference between the two undead. He wouldn't hold it against anyone if a few fell to friendly fire.

Further away, the forces of Mythos were being overwhelmed. The merfolk's convoy of wagons was nothing more than kindling, and the siege engines of the gnomes had been overrun by skeletons, making them useless obstacles that prevented advancement. Bodies littered the battlefield, mixed among the broken bones of the undead. Magic flared across the landscape as waves crashed, fires blazed, and earth shifted at the whim of powerful mages. Fairies and imps darted through the chaos, leaving pastel explosions in their wake. King Orso fought side by side with his kingsguard and clerics, a myriad of auras flashing with each attack. They held back wave after wave of undead, but their positioning in the center of the battle meant there was no respite. King Favian rode his griffin above the battlefield, offering aid where he could among the maelstrom of bats and gargoyles that remained. He stooped low to pull a blood-covered giant fighting for her life from a swarm of undead. Skeletons clung to the giant's legs as she rose into the air, falling away like insects in a stiff breeze.

Despite all the powerful magic Mythos had brought, there was no escape from the wave of death that flowed from around the city. Thousands upon thousands of skeletons fought without tiring and marched fearlessly even as their forces crumbled around them. They had no desires of their own, no self-preservation, only the unceasing determination to fight.

Unlike the dead, the werewolves attacked with the coordinated tactics of a pack, tearing through the ranks of Mythos's less-skilled fighters. Giant spiders and hobgoblins had joined the fray, descending from the forest along with monstrous creatures cloaked in shadow. Everywhere Pressley looked, the situation was dire. Only the trolls held their own, but he could see the bodies of many among the dead. They fought with a fury of those who had nothing to lose. Pressley knew better, though. Chod had made sure of that. The trolls had everything to lose, and still, they raged.

He'd make sure their efforts weren't in vain. He raised his arm, aiming Bloodstrike at a pack of werewolves. After charging a fraction of his HP into the attack, he released, and a bolt of red energy shot across the battlefield like liquid lightning. It exploded upon impact, tearing through werewolf bodies and giving the trolls an edge to push their attack.

Pressley threw the giant potion bottle into the horde of undead, angling his throw as he let go. Earth sprayed from the impact as the massive bottle skipped like a rock on water, crushing hundreds of enemies as it bounced across the battlefield.

With all of his stats doubled, he might be the most powerful person in Mythos for the next few minutes. He needed to cause as much destruction as possible with what time remained.

Pressley's health depleted by a sliver as he took a step, crushing undead beneath his boot with a satisfying crunch. He cast Unhallowed Ground to his right, and the earth sizzled like acid beneath his newfound power, rotting away the bodies of skeletons that passed into the area of effect. Their bodies melted like chocolate on a hot day, leaving behind a cream-colored gelatinous puddle.

While Pressley focused on the enemies on the ground, his manticore terrorized the skies alongside Caustic, showing why she'd earned the name Winged Fright. She ripped through bats with a vengeance, empowered by the death knight's increased stats. The bats' numbers had dwindled, but there were still hundreds of them, and they were powerful enough to break the stone bodies of the gargoyles when attacking together.

Caustic descended from the clouds, crushing a bat with his powerful jaws and spitting the mangled corpse onto the horde below. The dragon hovered in front of Pressley for a moment, roaring at the death knight.

"Don't worry. I'm on it." Pressley crushed more undead beneath his boots, and the dragon turned, soaring above the clouds to surprise his next victim.

Pressley cast Pestilence over the area directly in front of him. Dozens of undead decayed rapidly, crumpling to the ground as their bones were ravaged by disease.

The timer continued to tick down, along with Pressley's health as he took another step. One way or another, he was running out of time. He activated Frost Reaper, the new ability he'd unlocked in the manticore's dungeon, and a thick layer of frost coated his armor and trailed down his blade. As he moved across the battlefield, frost spread out from beneath his boots, slowing the undead in the death knight's immediate vicinity. He slashed his sword with enough force that it left a frozen trench in the earth. Skeletons sailed through the air with the arc of his blade, and Lifesteal replenished some of the HP he'd lost. If not for the timer, he might have one of the few classes that could counter the potion's adverse effect.

But nothing was ever that easy.

Pressley hacked through undead as he moved across the battlefield, leaving frozen channels and gaping holes of destruction from Pestilence and Unhallowed Ground in his wake.

The invasion had gone on long enough for forces inside the city to rally to its defense. Boulders and burning pitch launched at the death knight from catapults behind the walls. Pressley canceled Frost Reaper and cast Blight of the Undead, summoning a deafening buzz of insects that swarmed his colossal body, shielding him from the projectiles as he moved across the battlefield.

More undead focused their attack upon the towering menace, and skeletons piled around his feet, climbing over one another like a mound of ants. They fell from his legs with each thunderous step as he made his way toward Seascape's forces. Pressley slashed his sword through the air, swatting bats like they were flies, and fired Bloodstrike into the enemies attacking at the rear. His HP was at fifty percent by the time he found King Orso.

The king wielded his warhammer with unforgiving authority, shattering bones and tearing undead limb from limb. Pressley cast Unhallowed Ground, forming a barrier in front of the king and giving him a moment of respite.

The death knight canceled Blight of the Undead as he knelt, crushing enemies beneath the weight of his giant knee. "Chod has breached the wall. I don't have long in this form, but I should be able to offer you a fighting chance if you can rally your troops."

King Orso nodded, raising his warhammer into the air. "We will not fail."

The death knight stood, his gaze settling on the city. A green aura pulsed from the keep like a toxic heartbeat. Somewhere inside the walls, Chod was fighting his way to stop its beating.

Pressley activated Bone Detector, and his vision flooded with white. He grinned beneath his helm. *I can't believe I'm about to do this.*

His helm rumbled like thunder as he laughed. "This one's for you, you son of a bitch."

He sheathed his sword and cast Lifesteal with both hands. Purple energy shot into the horde of undead, the massive damage output refilling his HP completely. It was a good thing, because he'd need every last bit for what came next.

The earth shuddered as Pressley cast Summon Undead, and his health plummeted into the red as thousands of bones reassembled themselves under his control. The timer ticked down to less than a minute, and he ordered his minions into position while he waited on the cooldown to cast Lifesteal again.

Though his body blazed with energy, he took a deep breath, finding that sense of cold he'd grown accustomed to. Closing his eyes, he embraced the chill as he waited for his daughter's face to appear in the void. In the emptiness, he found comfort as her outline began to take shape, and deep within his core, he felt a spark of warmth.

Pressley opened his eyes, using Lifesteal to replenish his health a final time before he poured everything he had into Corpse Explosion.

Eva smiled at him, and then the world went black.

37. ANGEL OF DEATH

Kassidy's portal releases me inside the city walls, where dead elves lie across the cobbled streets. Randy and Drizz'rt wipe blood from their daggers, and Arty grimaces as he downs a health potion. The cyclops sighs as the wound on his shoulder starts to close.

We've cleared our first obstacle by making it past the wall, but the mission is far from over. Mosstar is a city of shadows, but I get the feeling that it always wasn't that way. The green flames from the keep give life to the gloom, where the dark streets are at odds with the beautiful architecture. Each building flows into the next with curves and ornamentation, and skeletal trees grow from within them. I can only imagine how beautiful this city was before darkness overtook it.

"This area is clear for now, but we need to get moving." Michael shines like a beacon in the center of the group. The effect adds to his paladin aesthetic, but it's terrible for sneaking through a city. That's the precise reason why I haven't summoned Pharos yet.

"Any way you can tone that down a bit?" I wave my hands up and down, gesturing at his entire being.

Dorothy scoffs. "Believe me, we already tried. He's a permanent glowstick."

Michael narrows his eyes at Dorothy. "Onera prefers I walk in the light, even among the shadows."

I suppress a laugh and focus on our situation. Kassidy portaled us into the left corner of the city, far from the action around the gate. After taking an arrow to the stomach, I hope he's okay, but I push the thought from my mind, along with my concern for everyone still fighting outside the city walls. There will be a time for that but for now, I need to be focused.

I peek around the corner and see elves rushing through the streets. They move chaotically. Some head toward the gate and others climb the battlements. Despite how dire the situation may seem outside the walls, we managed to catch the city off guard. Things could be a lot worse.

Feet patter down a nearby alley as an elf emerges from a side street, almost running past us before sliding to a halt. His eyes go wide as he takes us in, and he opens his mouth to scream.

An arrow lodges in the elf's throat before he has a chance, leaving him croaking as he gasps for air. Blood trickles through his fingers as he clutches his neck, panic in his eyes. Scotty approaches and jerks the arrow free in a swift motion. Blood spurts from the wound as the elf falls to the street.

I doubt that will be the last elf we run into, so I summon more horrors and feel the comforting grip of Destroyer against my palm. "You guys ready?"

What's left of our party of heroes focuses on me. Taryn, Dorothy, Randy, Don, Michael, Drizz'rt, Sam, Scotty, Kazzandra, Arty and his two brothers, Roddick and Reddick, and two more adventurers. For the life of me, I can't recall their names. One of them is Orin or Dorin, and I think the other one was something stupid like Matt. Regardless, I'm glad they're here.

"We've made it past the undead, but there's still a city of elves between us and our objective." I raise my warhammer and point it toward the keep. "Taryn, you have the amulet?"

Taryn reaches into his cloak, lifting a silver chain that holds an amulet set with an iridescent stone. It glimmers in the twilight. He scratches Berry behind the ears and then slides off the umber bear's back, where Jordy gently rams his head into Taryn's side.

My best friend looks up at me with eyes full of worry. "Keep them safe."

I squeeze his shoulder, and we both know that's a promise I can't make. "I'll do my best."

Taryn buffs us with Strong Wind, and then there's a burst of feathers as he transforms into a small red bird. He's almost invisible underneath the twilight sky, and if King Orso's theory holds true, the Amulet of Undetection will protect him from Valmar's gaze as well.

Half of my dreadbeasts are still outside the wall fighting alongside the trolls. I take the fact that they're still alive as a good sign. The ones still with me lead the way as we hurry about the perimeter, doing our best to cling to the shadows. With the attack concentrated around the gate, the streets are strangely empty. As we move further away from the sounds of battle, the chatter of the undead creep over the wall.

More than once I see a head disappear behind twitching curtains, and I can't help but wonder which side these people would fall on were they given a choice.

I reach out to Caustic for an update on the battle. *"How are the forces holding up?"*

There's a moment before he responds. *"I have taken many lives but the advance has stalled. Reinforcements have attacked from the forest, and elves fire upon us from the walls. The dead one fights with the strength of a dragon, but I do not know if it will be enough."*

A knot forms in my stomach. This is exactly what we didn't want to happen.

Incoming Message (Taryn): *Two streets ahead on your left. Group of six.*

I relay Taryn's message to the others, and we approach with caution. The soldiers turn the corner with swords and spears raised, and unlike the last elf, they don't seem surprised to see us. Randy, Drizz'rt, and Dorothy use Shadow Step in almost perfect synchronicity, appearing behind the elves and slitting the throats of the three at the back. Michael raises his sword. It beams with golden light, blinding the three remaining elves, while Don casts a void spear that extends outward and skewers two of them.

The lone elf turns to run, but Dorothy is waiting with a vicious snarl and plunges her blade into his neck.

I give them a look of surprise. "Have you guys been practicing behind my back?"

She looks from Randy to Drizz'rt and grins. "Great minds, I guess."

Incoming Message (Taryn): *Someone knows you're here. Three units moving from the north. Two more on your rear. Do you need me to come down?*

Message (Chod): *Stay where you are. We need your eyes in the sky.*

"Get ready for a fight. They know we're here." I summon another horror and turn my attention in the direction we came from.

My Dreadbeasts of Torment sniff at the air, and a low growl rumbles in their chests. Their bison brethren paw their hooves against the cobblestone, smoke pouring from their nostrils.

We split our forces in half and position ourselves back to back as we wait for our assailants. Taryn calls out enemy positions and intel, and since the non-heroes aren't capable of party chat, I relay it to the others. With aerial advantage, we pick off the enemies before they know what's happening.

"How the hell do they know we're here?" Randy pulls a dagger from a dead elf and flicks the blood into the street.

Dorothy nods in Michael's direction. "Could be the walking nightlight we have with us?"

I don't know if it's the stress of the situation or what, but Michael's gallant facade finally cracks.

He slams his shield into the ground and stares daggers at Dorothy. "I'm getting really tired of your little quips."

"Oh, is that so?" She spins her daggers in her palms. "You want to go, big guy?"

I step between them with my arms raised, and dreadbeasts flank me on both sides. "Guys, we're on the same side here. It doesn't matter how they know we're here. What matters is we get to the keep. Now, let's—"

The air distorts behind Michael as the fabric of reality tears, a sight I've become all too familiar with recently. Before I have a chance to call out, a blade pierces from the darkness, stabbing the paladin in the back of the neck. The sword rips through his throat, and his knees buckle as the divine light fades. A moment later, his body vanishes, leaving a pile of armor on the ground.

Someone cackles from within the portal, and heat radiates from Limery as his claws dig into my shoulder. The void stretches, and three figures step from the darkness. Ethan French, the warlock, is the first to emerge, his tattooed body held aloft by phantom wings. His dreadlocks float in the air like he's weightless, and a dark aura surrounds his body. He wears a sleeveless black robe that reveals the silver tattoos glowing against his dark skin. He's flanked by his two companions, Otis Wiggins the barbarian and Kevin Harris the sorcerer.

Otis grins as he rests his massive double-edged axe on his shoulder. He wears a black vest trimmed in white fur, and with his bald head and bushy beard, he's a prototypical movie villain. It's assholes like him that give barbarians a bad name. He's a mindless tool—the kind where if I gave him a penny for his thoughts, I'd get change back.

Opposite Otis, Kevin wears a wicked grin as he surveys our group. Ethan has power and Otis has brawn, but the sorcerer is a tactician. I know from experience how dangerous his Arcane Chains can be, and his robe is strapped with vials in a myriad of hues. I'm sure there are some powerful potions within his arsenal.

We'll need to end this before he has a chance to use them. Taryn sends a message, but I dismiss it. My complete attention is focused on the situation in front of us.

Don steps toward our assailants. "What are you idiots playing at?"

"Us?" Otis laughs. "We're not the ones pretending to be heroes."

"That's probably because you lost your imagination the tenth time your mother dropped you on your head." Randy joins the void mage's side. "I've seen zombies with more brains than you."

Otis lifts his axe from his shoulder and sneers. "I'll show you brains when I spill yours in the street."

He takes a step, but a shadowy hand reaches from the portal and pulls him back.

Ethan lowers himself until he's hovering a foot above the street. "Give us the troll and you can all go home safe and sound. No one else needs to get hurt."

Don takes another step forward. "That's not going to happen."

Ethan chuckles, but there's no mirth in it. "You're willing to die for him?"

"I'm willing to fight beside him because he's a lot more likable than you three assholes." Don doesn't wait to make the first move, clapping his hands together and sending a wave of energy pulsing from his body. His Nullification Zone expands, closing the portal and severing the shadowy hand in the process. It dissipates into a fine mist, and the warlock's wings vanish. Ethan falls to the ground. Behind him, Otis tumbles over backward from the weight of his axe as Don's spell disables everyone's abilities in the immediate vicinity of the void mage. I don't know if it's because I'm too far away or if Cold Rage is protecting me, but my Warforged body doesn't falter.

"Get out of here!" Don yells. "We'll handle these fucks."

Randy moves slower than I'm used to seeing, but he's still quick enough to get the job done as he stabs Ethan in the shoulder. Drizz'rt doesn't need his speed, choosing to stick a dagger in Kevin's chest from ten feet away.

"Come on, let's go!" Dorothy pulls me by the forearm before I have a chance to join the fight.

Limery and I follow her down the side alley trailed by horrors, dreadbeasts, and Taryn's pets. There's a moment of panic as I search for Flubs, but then I notice a gelatinous green layer covering Berry's saddle. Good. They're all here.

We pass several streets and then an explosion rumbles outside the walls.

Limery looks over his shoulder. "What was thats?"

I reach out to Caustic with the same question. *"What the hell was that?"*

He doesn't answer, and three elves appear in front of us. My Dreadbeasts of Despair trample them to the ground at full speed, and the Dreadbeasts of Torment finish the job. They may be wearing armor, but these are definitely not soldiers.

"This way." Dorothy points down a street that runs perpendicular to the keep.

I shake my head, gesturing toward the towering structure ahead of us. "The keep is that way."

"Trust me. The keep will be heavily guarded, and my marauder class helps navigate ruins. There's a hidden tunnel a few streets over that leads straight under the castle."

"Okay, let's hurry." My mind drifts back to the explosion. The longer we take, the more danger everyone is in. *"Caustic?"* I reach out to him again as we follow Dorothy.

"The dead one sacrificed himself. The tide turns in our favor. I will join you shortly."

Before I have a chance to respond, Taryn sends a message.

Incoming Message (Taryn): *What's going on down there? The castle is the other way.*

My mind is pulling me in a dozen directions when I need to stay on the task at hand. As much as I want to ask about Don and the others, it can wait.

Message (Chod): *Dorothy says there's a hidden tunnel a few streets over.*

Incoming Message (Taryn): *Watch out. There's a group at the end of the street.*

I catch up with Dorothy and extend an arm, signaling for us to slow down as we approach the corner.

She nods, letting me and my summons take the lead.

When I turn the corner, my blood boils at the sight of Jude and Glenn surrounded by an escort of elves. Jude has cleaned up a bit since our run-in outside of Boneholde. The shaggy-haired fighter has new leather armor accented with green thread and a host of glittering daggers strapped to his chest and thighs.

"I knew we'd meet again." He licks his lips as he takes in my appearance. "As much as I dislike you, I've got to admit that bringing an army this big into the shadowlands just to die takes some troll-sized balls."

Glenn laughs, but it doesn't reach his soulless eyes. For the first time, he wears a set of pristine armor that isn't composed of mismatched pieces. His plate mail is solid black, fitting for the kind of sadistic asshole he is, and he holds an obsidian sword with a shimmering golden hilt.

His expressionless eyes meet mine. "I'm glad to see you again. I should thank you for making my job easier. Once we finish you, the rest of the trolls will be child's play."

My grip tightens around Destroyer, and mana blazes at my fingertips. I've killed them both before, and I can do it again.

"I wouldn't do that if I were you." Dorothy's frigid tone sets the hair at the back of my neck on end.

"Chods." There's a desperation in Limery's voice that freezes every cell in my body, and my heart sinks into the pit of my stomach.

I turn around, and Dorothy has Limery held against her chest, a dagger pressed to his throat.

"Please…" I search for words as Destroyer falls from my grip, but I can only repeat the same word again. "Please. Dorothy, please."

Her blue eyes flare orange, the same as the day we fought outside the trials, and her visage shifts as her mouth twists into a sinister smile. Cracks form along her face as her pallid white skin flakes away, revealing a deathly charcoal complexion. Her golden locks fade to a dull silver and when I analyze her, her class description has changed.

Dorothy Jordan
  Level 33
  Revenant
  Elf

Icy dread settles inside of me. She played me. All this time, I thought I had made amends, but she was just waiting for me to let my guard down. She knows I care about Limery more than anything in the world and she's going to use him to hurt me.

"Ethan was right. You are way too trusting." She presses the blade into Limery's throat until he whimpers, and beads of red sprout along the blade's edge.

"Please." I repeat again as panic flares in my chest. I try to fight against the soul-crushing dread so that I can find a way out of this, but it presses in on me from every angle, like I'm in the trials all over again. "I'll do anything, just please, don't hurt him."

"*What is happening!*" Caustic's voice rumbles in my mind. He must sense my distress through our bond.

"I bet you would. Anything to save your precious little Limmy." She laughs. "Too bad, Chad. You're not talking your way out of this one. I told you that I came here to make you pay. Turns out you pissed off a lot more people than just me. They were right, though. You do have a hero complex. I knew that if I was patient, if I played along, then my opportunity would come." She laughs again. "You should see the look on your face. Priceless." Her smile fades. "It'd make a great meme."

"You don't have to do this." I hold my hands up. "Let him go. You can take me instead. I won't fight it."

"You don't get it, do you?" She lets out an exasperated sigh. "You have no say here. There's no out. The only way this ends is in immeasurable pain for you. Then maybe you'll understand what it's like to be helpless while your world crumbles around you."

"Dorothy..." I step toward her, and her grip on the dagger tightens. Red trickles down Limery's neck, freezing me in place. "Why are you doing this?"

"Why? Don't be stupid. You know why." Her voice is strangely calm as she holds Limery's life in her hands. "You think I would just forgive and forget, Chad? That isn't how this works. It's cute that you care for him so much. Maybe I'd be sympathetic if you weren't such an asshole, but you ruined my life, and now I'm going to cause you as much pain as you caused me."

She pulls the dagger across Limery's throat, and his bulbous yellow eyes widen in shock just before my world comes crashing down around me. His head hangs limp, and a loud ringing fills my ears, blocking out everything. It can't end like this. It just can't. I pray to whatever god will listen as I shove the Angel of Death Brandy into the mouth of my closest dreadbeast and cast Sacrifice.

The demonic wolf explodes in a shower of shadows and gore. Then nothing. The ringing in my ears amplifies as I realize I failed.

I promised to walk through hell for Limery and in the end, it was me who got him killed.

If not for me, Dorothy wouldn't be here.

She lets Limery's lifeless body fall from her grip like he means nothing, and anger flares in my core, a volcano ready to erupt. His body is inches from the street when time stops. For a brief moment, nothing moves, and then the world moves in reverse as the Angel of Death Brandy takes effect. Time rewinds for two seconds.

Limery's corpse floats back into Dorothy's arms, and blood surges into his small frame, allowing the dagger to seal it back inside.

"What the—" Dorothy blinks, unsure of what just happened.

"Go molten!" I shout.

Dorothy is too slow to react as Limery's body transforms into molten lava, melting the blade pressed against his neck. His eyes blaze white, and the flames surrounding his body turn blue as he burns hotter than ever, so hot that he incinerates Dorothy's arm up to the elbow and scorches her chest and face.

She recoils, her vest smoldering as her screams of anguish cut through the ringing in my ears. Limery darts past me, his face pure hatred as he collides with Jude in mid-air. The imp's small arms clench around Jude's throat, and Limery ignites his fire shield. A circle of heat surrounds him, and Jude's face blisters before turning to saggy mush that melts off the bone.

Glenn turns to run, but I throw Destroyer at him with all my might. It clanks against his armor, knocking him to the ground. Red feathers explode in front of him as Taryn appears, pinning the psychopath's arms by his side with the vines from his Sapling Staff.

Taryn kneels beside Glenn. "This one's for Stompy," he whispers before plunging his shadow blade into the man's skull.

I turn my attention back to Dorothy, who stands there in shock, looking at her stump of an arm.

"How?" she mumbles, and there's a far-off look in her eyes as a shadow descends upon her.

Caustic's jaws wrap around the revenant, severing her body in half with a powerful bite. He lands in front of me, a deep rumble emanating from his chest.

"I told you I do not trust her."

"I know." I should never have doubted a dragon's instincts.

Limery extinguishes his flames as he wraps his arms around my neck. He trembles against my body, and I fight back tears as I hold him tight.

"I'm sorry, buddy." I came so close to truly losing him.

"Limmy was scareds." He sniffles. "But Chods saves Limmy."

Taryn kicks a piece of Glenn's armor across the street. "I wonder where they're respawning."

"If I had to guess, it can't be too far."

"Dorothy, man..." Taryn shakes his head. "What a piece of work."

I try not to think about it. Unpacking what just happened is a rabbit hole for another time.

"We need to end this while we have a chance." Our plan has gone to shit, but my gaze falls on the obsidian tower in the center of the keep, sparking an idea. "You mind if I borrow the amulet? Maybe your cloak, too?"

Taryn follows my gaze. "What's the plan?"

"The others still need help. Take Limery and my horrors with you." I pick up Destroyer and sling it over my shoulder as I climb upon Caustic. "It's time for me to smash some shit."

38. THE KING OF EVIL

Caustic and I fly above the twilight city. I summon a Horror of Finesse from atop the dragon's back, and the gangly blue creature watches me with a look of betrayal as it plummets toward the earth. I cast Sacrifice, buffing my stats, before summoning the next horror in the rotation.

Far below, the outer gate has fallen. Mythos's forces push through the undead and into the city, clashing with the elves waiting on the other side. The keep will be surrounded within the hour, and Valmar will be forced to make his last stand. There's no telling how many will die trying to take down the wizard.

Unless I do something about it.

"Do you think this will work?" I ask Caustic.

"There is a chance." The dragon's muscles flex as he climbs higher, taking us above the clouds. *"It is foolish to fight without me by your side."*

Gotta love his unfiltered honesty. If I had only listened to him when it came to Dorothy.

"For this to work, I need the element of surprise."

"If you survive, that will be the surprise." He huffs.

Dragons aren't exactly known for their comforting pep talks, but he's not wrong. There's a good chance that this goes sideways. Relying on a castle map that hasn't been updated in over four hundred years isn't the most intelligent decision. And then there's the assumption that Valmar would be—

"This should suffice." Caustic interrupts my thoughts, and as much as he may try to conceal it, I can sense the worry in his tone.

I lean to the side and gulp as I look at the city below. From this high, even the elephants seem like ants. Of all the stupid things I've done during my time in Mythos, this might be the dumbest. I take a deep breath and fill my lungs with confidence.

"I'll be fine. No matter what happens, remember that I'll respawn. Focus on helping the others take the city." I pat Caustic on the back. *"He's never going to see this coming."*

I release my grip and slide from the dragon's back, summoning a surprised horror that flails wildly before Sacrifice snuffs it out of existence. For a moment, I enjoy the cool wind against my body, then I equip the three items that make up the Regeneration Triad as my body plummets toward the earth like a falling meteor.

I read over their stats one final time to ensure that this is just dumb and not suicide.

*Item. **Renewal Spear.** Capable of holding life aura equivalent to 500 HP. The Renewal Spear gathers aura passively while equipped and can steal health from enemies during battle. Life aura may be absorbed by the wielder at any time. **Bonus:** When paired with Regeneration Stone and Shield of Vigor, user will be granted a ten-foot aura that provides 20% increased regeneration for companions within its radius.*

*Item. **Shield of Vigor.** Increases HP by 30%. **Bonus:** When paired with Regeneration Stone and Renewal Spear, user will be* *granted a ten-foot aura that provides 20% increased regeneration for companions within its radius.*

__Item. Regeneration Stone.__ Increases health regeneration by 20%. __Bonus:__ When paired with Shield of Vigor and Renewal Spear, user will be granted a ten-foot aura that provides 20% increased regeneration for companions within its radius.

__Notice! Complete Set: Regeneration Triad.__ While wearing all three pieces of the Regeneration Triad, user will be granted a ten-foot aura that provides 20% increased regeneration for companions within its radius.

Good. The thirty percent HP buff will help with the impact, and the health regeneration should keep me clinging to life if I've severely underestimated how strong my Warforged body is.

The Amulet of Undetection whips in the air as I fall, clinking against the side of my metallic head. I shift the angle of the shield to adjust my trajectory, using the four blazing green flames as my personal runway lights. The keep comes into detail far quicker than I expect, and the terror of what's about to happen finally settles in.

Is tenfold Constitution enough to save an idiot who essentially just went skydiving without a parachute? *Just breathe.* I'm Warforged. I could bellyflop in the middle of the street and still survive.

I hope.

I pull the shield against my chest and tighten my grip on the spear, squinting for the last few seconds as I fall toward what should be the throne room. Unlike in the movies, there's no slow-motion impact as I crash through the ceiling. No heroic moment where the walls explode, and me and Valmar rise from the rubble, lone survivors, as dust settles all around us.

Instead, I pierce through the roof of the keep like a speeding bullet, leaving a hole barely bigger than my body as I smash into the floor like a wrecking ball. My health drops by half from the impact, even with the thirty percent buff, and a deep metallic thrum echoes through my bones.

The room spins as I crawl to my feet among the cracked marble that surrounds a troll-shaped indentation. I can sense Caustic speaking to me, but the words swirl within the maelstrom of my addled brain.

A modicum of dust flits across the room, not nearly as heroic as I imagined, and I'm uncertain whether I'm seeing stars or if the tiny particles are sparkling in the torchlight. The hole in the ceiling casts a stream of green light from the fiery towers that reflects upon my metallic skin, reminding me of my first days in Mythos.

I chuckle to myself at the irony.

My vision finally settles, and I take in the rest of the room. Torches line the walls, burning with the same eerie green as the towers, and dozens of armored undead stand sentry around the room. Unlike the skeletons outside the city, these haven't been ravaged by the elements. Dried skin still covers their bones, and wispy hair hangs about their shoulders. They wear fine, polished armor and seem unfazed by my presence. Either the amulet is doing its job or Valmar is unthreatened by my sudden appearance.

He sits upon an obsidian throne at least twenty feet away, watching me with a curious expression. I missed by a long shot.

The infamous dark wizard is nothing like I expected. He has a menacing look about him, but for a necromancer, he's kind of handsome, with his chiseled jawline and his thick hair slicked back to fall over his shoulders. His skin is the dull gray of the undead, but he reminds me more of a vampire than some decrepit-looking lich. There's a suppleness to his flesh that other undead don't have, and his intense eyes burn similarly to Dorothy's.

"I'll give you credit, troll. You have been a constant thorn in my side." His mouth curls at the edge. "I admire your resolve."

I step out of the crater, stone crushing beneath my feet. "Yeah, well, I thought you'd be taller."

He laughs as he stands from his throne. His boots clack against the marble as he approaches nonchalantly. "Of all the outworlders, you show a surprising amount of promise. Join me and the world can be yours, for you and your trolls. You can make a new name for trollkind in your image."

He stops about three paces in front of me.

"Is that what you did?" I shift my gaze to the undead standing on each side of me. "We're in a city of elves and yet you're surrounded by the dead."

His eye twitches. "I'm surrounded by loyal soldiers. Every one of them swore an oath to protect me in their first life and the next."

I think I've found a sore spot, so I press onward. "And what about your citizens? For a city this big, it's awfully sparse. How many of your people are you marching to their deaths?"

"What would an outworlder know of our struggles?" He scoffs, and his eyes narrow. "You may call me a villain but tell me, where were the heroes when Mosstar's luscious lands slowly fell to the darkness? Where were the kingdoms that prospered when our soil turned to ash? When we begged for aid, who answered?" He shakes his head in disgust. "No one. Left alone, it was our fate to be consumed, but we refused. When the light offered no aid, we embraced the darkness. We allied ourselves with it, and I made it our power. Funny how they noticed us then, fearing what they did not understand, even though it was their inaction that forced us down this path." He tilts back his head and laughs. "If that makes me a villain, then crown me the king of evil."

Judging by the throne, someone already has.

"You killed innocent people," I argue.

"I did what was necessary to save *my* people. You of all people should understand this." His eyes blaze like embers. "You've seen what lurks beyond our city walls. This is no place for the elves. Not anymore. Once we were branded enemies, our only refuge was to take it by force. For four hundred years, I've watched my people waste away in the darkness. For four hundred years, I've added them to my ranks so that one day, we could start anew."

"That's not going to happen." I feel the cold metal of the spear against my fingers and wonder which of us has the faster reflexes. "We've breached the wall. Soon, the city will be overrun."

"The walls may fall, the city may surrender, but this is not the end for Valmar Worren or Mosstar. You may have caught me unprepared, but my forces are spread far and wide. Darkness can never be truly extinguished because it is merely the absence of light. It's always there, even when you can't see it."

I take a step forward, pointing my spear at him. "You're not leaving this city."

"Have it your way." He sighs like a teacher who's heard one too many excuses. "If you won't fight by my side, then you will fight for me. And after I raise your body, I'll use it to kill those you've sworn to protect. How many do you think will die at your hands?"

"That will never happen." I summon Pharos. The spirit guide bursts to life in front of me and charges at Valmar. The necromancer recoils from the ethereal light, and I plant the spear in his chest. Armor rattles as the undead charge from around the room. I summon a Dreadbeast of Torment, and the wolf lunges at the closest guard, tackling it to the ground.

Valmar snarls with a ferocity that could have come from Caustic as he pushes the spear deeper into his chest until the pressure releases and it juts through his back. He lunges, climbing up the spear's shaft and burying it deeper until his cold hands wrap around my arms and squeeze like vice grips. My increased Constitution does nothing to stop the ice-cold dread that courses through my body as frost forms along the necromancer's hands. His eyes rage with fury as ice spreads along my metallic skin and my health drops with each passing moment.

I let go of the spear and bring my arms up and outward, forcing Valmar to release his grip. Metal screams as swords and spears spark against my body. My dreadbeast yelps, and I summon its bison kin along with horrors to provide a distraction for the undead.

The spear skewering Valmar is an afterthought as the necromancer unleashes his rage. A black aura surrounds his hands as he fires a bolt of black energy. The first goes over my shoulder, blasting a hole in the far wall big enough to drive a bus through. The second bolt catches me in the chest, knocking me into the wall. My Warforged body absorbs the impact, and I crawl to my feet. My health is down to twenty percent as I equip Destroyer and charge Valmar.

He cracks his neck, stalking toward me like the predator he is. An explosion thunders from outside the keep as he casts a spell, and a wave of energy flares through the necromancer's body. His undead guard rushes toward me, and I imbue my next attack with Concussive Force, punching the closest minion with enough power that its breastplate warps around my fist as it goes flying into the others like a bowling ball. I fight my way through his minions, smashing the ancient bodies until their armor clamors against the floor.

I swing Destroyer at Valmar, and he raises a fist to meet the head of my warhammer. His knuckles take the blow like an anvil, refusing to give under the force of my full power. Energy recoils down the weapon and through my body as I go flying backward.

What the hell was that? He must have an ability similar to Sacrifice that siphons power from his undead. And he has a lot of undead.

Valmar pounces across the room with superhuman speed, landing on top of me before I even hit the ground. His fists thrum as he punches my Warforged body. Marble cracks beneath my backside with each hit.

I summon a Horror of Power and swing blindly, hoping to connect with any part of the terror I'm facing. Valmar swats my fist away and clamps his hand around my throat, his icy grip crystallizing upon my metallic skin. I expected him to be more powerful than me, but I never thought he'd be stronger.

I never should have come alone.

Bright light flares behind the necromancer as Pharos rams into his backside. Valmar hisses at the spirit guide's presence. He rolls to the side and tosses me across the room like I weigh nothing.

I slam into a column, which cracks under the force of the impact. Valmar sets his gaze on Pharos, and his hands hum with dark power followed by an explosion that rocks the throne room as shards of darkness erupt from inside the frost goat. Void spikes protrude from Pharos's spirit, and his body dims before he vanishes into mist.

Valmar growls as his attention returns to me. There are no quips, no monologues, just unbridled anger that burns within his eyes.

A black bolt of energy crashes inches in front of me, sending exploding marble clinking against my chest. I scurry back and hear the familiar whir of a portal as something clasps around my midsection. Giant demonic fingers cinch around me, sending chills through my body as they hold me in place. Whatever being this is, it's far stronger than I am. I might not be susceptible to stuns or slows while I'm raging, but it does nothing to prevent me from being physically restrained by something stronger.

Valmar's face is expressionless as he kneels before me, the spear skewering his upper body scraping against the floor. He takes my chin in his long, slender fingers and looks into my eyes as if searching for something.

"You could have had everything." He cradles my chin, shaking his head in disappointment.

I hear the frost crackling along his fingers before the frigid cold settles in my jaw. Unable to move, I sit there helplessly as my health drops. When my HP dips below ten percent, my increased regeneration kicks in and holds the drain at bay.

Valmar smiles. "Tricky little troll."

His free hand blasts me in the chest, and my vision darkens at the edges as pain surges through my metal body. He blasts me again, and it's like my nerves are on fire. The third time, my body screams, and everything goes black.

39. SURVIVORS

ALERT! Revive Potion activated.

The blackness fades, and I respawn in the crater I created when I crashed through the ceiling. I always assumed I would miss smashing Valmar like a pancake, but it made for a nice distraction while I set my spawn point.

I have full health and all my items, thanks to the Revive Potion.

Across the room, a black aura shrouds Valmar as the necromancer leans over a doppelgänger of my body. The Renewal Spear still protrudes from his chest and back, nothing more than a hindrance as he works.

With the Amulet of Undetection, neither Valmar nor his minions have any idea that I'm here. On top of that, I had the wherewithal to borrow Taryn's Cloak of Silence. I equip the cloak, muting my footsteps as I sneak across the throne room.

If this plan doesn't work, I'm going to be immensely fucked once Valmar discovers my trickery. He'll be able to spawn camp me back to level one, and there'll be nothing I can do about it.

The necromancer's body hums with energy as dark tendrils flow from his hands toward my lifeless corpse. They hover around the doppelgänger, unable to permeate the illusion.

Valmar grunts, and the tendrils fade as he shakes out his hands. "This isn't right."

Because it's not real, dumbass.

When I'm a few feet behind him, I activate Return to Sender and the enchanted stone triggers, ripping the Renewal Spear from Valmar's body and returning it to my hand. I plunge the weapon into the back of Valmar's skull and activate the life aura stored inside the spear, the anathema to his undead being. His head explodes like a grenade of dark matter. The torches extinguish, leaving me in darkness as a gust of cool air escapes through the ceiling. All around the room, armor clatters against the floor as his minions collapse, robbed of their energy source. The eerie glow surrounding the keep is gone. Whatever magic powered the fiery towers left with Valmar.

Caustic's voice is once again clear in my mind. *"The dead have fallen, and the elves have surrendered. I'm coming to find you."*

Emotion swells within me, and I drop to my knees. The Renewal Spear falls from my grasp, clanging against the marble floor, and a hollow ring echoes through the empty throne room.

Valmar's gone. Mosstar has surrendered. The war is over.

We survived. Not only that, but against all odds, we managed to win.

I'm sitting on the steps to the keep, deep in thought, when Caustic arrives.

For some reason, I can't stop thinking about what Valmar said. Did his rise to power happen because the elves were left to fend for themselves? And what happens to the elves, and Mosstar for that matter, now that Valmar is gone? I was so intent on ending the threat he presented that I never took a minute to think about what would come after. We saved the trolls. We saved Mythos. Valmar is no more. But what about the elves who will face the consequences of his actions?

We may have won the battle, but the work is just beginning.

The dragon huffs, and his golden eyes bore into me. *"You saved many lives today."*

I stroke his golden beard. *"We did."*

Caustic preens at the compliment, flexing his wings.

I let out a long sigh and cancel Cold Rage. The metallic sheen fades from my body, leaving me as a light blue troll, a ghost in the twilight.

Taryn and the other heroes arrive soon after. Limery darts toward me, nearly knocking me over as he wraps his arms around me.

"We dids its, Chods!" He grins. "We beats the bad mans."

I hug him back, grateful for the little guy more than ever. I came so close to losing him, and I still can't shake the image of his body tumbling toward the ground. With Dorothy and the others out there, will they try again to get their revenge? None of them know about the program's status, so I hope that they bide their time and we're all pulled from the game before they can hurt anyone else.

Even though they look a little worse for the wear, there are plenty of smiles to go around as the others catch up.

Scotty takes a seat on the steps, closing his eyes as he leans back and rests his elbows. I don't blame him. After today, we all need a long rest and a strong drink. The physical taxation of battle is nothing compared to the mental toll. Drizz'rt's golden scales are covered in crimson. Whether the blood belongs to him or someone else, there's no telling. Probably a little of both. Arty carries one of his brothers on his shoulder, and Don, Sam, Randy, Kazzandra, and one of the adventurers are nowhere to be seen.

"What happened?" I ask.

Taryn climbs down from Berry, inspecting me for injuries. "We got there just as Ethan summoned some kind of demon through his portal. Randy got the worst of it, and then Kazzandra put an axe in Ethan's head. He died, but the demon didn't fade away. In the chaos, we all forgot that he still had a Revive Potion from the tournament. Ethan showed back up and took out Don, and then Sam took one of Kevin's potions to the face. We got them in the end, though. No idea where their spawn point is, but I'm sure they'll find us." When he's satisfied that I'm not hurt, Taryn takes a seat beside me. "We lost Borin and Kazzandra, but Arty says we shouldn't mourn them, that there's no greater honor for an adventurer than to die with a weapon in their hand. He wants us to drink to their names. Roddick is still unconscious but he should come around soon."

Borin. The man died fighting beside us, and I never knew his name. Kazzandra could have fought alongside her kin, and yet she chose to stay with us.

Taryn glances past me in the direction of the keep. "Looks like your stupid plan worked."

I chuckle. "Looks like it."

Taryn raises a brow. "Then why don't you seem happy?"

"I am. At least part of me is." I stand up when I see the rest of our forces making their way up the main avenue, King Favian leading the way on his griffin. "We did what we came for. We saved Mythos. If you told me this would be the outcome a week ago, I'd have been ecstatic. But I don't know, man. Even though this is a victory, I don't know that we won."

Arty sets his brother gently on the steps before placing a

massive hand on my shoulder. He gives me a sad smile, his lone eye blinking a few times. "That's the thing. There are no winners in war, only survivors."

After recounting my fight with Valmar, the clerics cleanse the necromancer's body to ensure that he's truly dead. I stay out of the way while the leaders deal with the aftermath. Deciding what's next for the elves and Mosstar will be no easy task.

My days here are numbered, so I leave the discussions to those who will be here to see it through. Many leaders wear the scars of battle. From the shredded fins and mangled scales of the merfolk to the blood-soaked fur of the Antadalians, they've paid for this victory in blood. Some more than others. Swift leaves bloody hoofmarks with each step, the centaur's legs a mess of cuts and gashes. Despite the noticeable limp, he smiles at me as he passes.

I wait for the trolls to arrive, but they never come, so I set off in search of my people. Limery stays with Caustic and Taryn. They'd all follow me, but I need a few moments to myself to process everything that has happened.

Hundreds of despondent elves line the city streets, forced to sit and wait while the fate of everything they know rests in the hands of leaders they've never met. In the aftermath of battle, I notice their gaunt faces and pale skin for the first time. They may wear armor, but these are no warriors.

With the dead no longer a threat, it won't take a large force to police the city. But there's still the worry of what lurks beyond its borders. Bats and werewolves were only some of the terrors residing in the shadowlands, and there's no telling what they'll do when they learn Valmar is gone.

I pass the Mosstar portal, where some of our forces have

begun their journey home. For the average citizen who took up arms to defend their way of life, their duty has been fulfilled.

When the broken gate comes into view, I stop in my tracks. Beyond the city's border, a sea of white spreads across the landscape. Hundreds of thousands of bones cover the land like a blanket of snow.

Outside, I find the trolls among those gathering the bodies of the dead. My heart sinks when I see a line of green, blue, and purple corpses.

I find Chief Rizza leaning over the body of a fallen forest troll. Malak. He was a gentle guardian with a curious soul, always the first to laugh and the last to anger. Next to him, Yashi and Ismora lie hand in hand, the body of Yashi's wyrm stretched above them. I kneel next to Rizza and place a hand on her shoulder.

"I'm sorry," I whisper.

"They made their choice." Her golden eyes glisten. "We all did. Their names will not be forgotten."

I spot Chief Laojin, Senzala, and several more arctic trolls breaking apart some of the siege weapons to create a pyre.

A loud wail draws my attention to a group of goblins gathered around the body of a mountain troll. Cheevus has his hands wrapped around Kronan's feet, tears cutting streaks through the bone dust that covers his cheeks.

Kronan looks more peaceful than he ever did in life. His jaw is relaxed, and a warhammer rests across his chest, hiding the grievous wound that took him from the world. A handful of goblins lay beside him.

Cheevus howls as he buries his face against Kronan's feet.

"How did he fall?" I ask.

Cheevus sniffles as he looks at me. "Kronan protects Cheevus, protects goblins with his life." Fresh tears pour from his eyes.

"He was a good troll." We may have gotten off on the wrong foot, but I counted him as a friend in the end.

I walk among the dead, some I knew well, others I only ever saw in passing. I find Gord loading bodies into a wagon. I recognize one of the seaside trolls lying between the corpses of two dwarves. Gord's bone armor hangs in tatters, and cuts run across his legs and arms. His good tusk is broken at the tip, the bright white enamel contrasting against his forest-green skin.

"If you wanted them to match, you could have just asked me." I offer him a half-smile in my lame attempt to lighten the mood. "I would have done it for free."

Gord chuckles, but there's a sadness in his eyes, one I feel all too well. "Many say that young trolls are born with a thirst for battle. They say that violence is in our blood." He grabs the handle of the wagon, lifts it, and then lets it rest. His lip trembles before he speaks. "I used to believe it but standing here today, I would consider myself a lucky troll if I never fought again."

His body heaves, and I rush forward to embrace him. He squeezes me hard as a grief-wracked roar pours from the depths of his soul. I hold him tight, feeling the waves of emotion pass through the body of this so-called monster.

He swallows hard and lets out a shaky breath. "Enough of that. There is much to do."

"Mind if I give you a hand?"

He nods, grabbing the wagon and pulling it forward. Bones crunch beneath the wheels until Gord stops again, and I help him load more bodies into the wagon. An arctic troll. A human. Two dwarves. On and on we work until I lose track of time. He could do it alone, but there's a comfort in the company.

We work in silence, honoring the dead in the simplest way we know how, by being useful.

40. CURTAIN CALL

THREE DAYS LATER.

Taryn and I sit at the edge of a crystal-blue lake, basking in the afternoon sun. Ducks quack as a gentle breeze blows across the water, disturbing the reflection of the lush forest on the opposite side. Ruby snores softly at Taryn's feet, and the sounds of birds chirping and insects trilling play her the perfect lullaby. To our left, Tormara leans against her outstretched wyrm as she watches the young trolls play in the shallow water.

"This is heaven." Taryn crosses his arms behind his head and closes his eyes.

After everything that's happened, it's pretty damn close.

There's movement to our right as Limery swings on a rope hanging from a tall tree at the lake's edge. "Cannonballs!" he yells as he lets go and his tiny frame curls into a ball. He sinks into the lake, sending a splash of water that wakes Berry from a pleasant nap.

"I can't believe you taught him that." I grin at Taryn. "He's going to be insufferable."

"Who are you kidding?" Taryn sits up, pulling his knees to his chest. "He's always been insufferable."

"Cannonball!" Leo zooms through the air, barely touching the rope as he launches himself at his brother, sending a wave crashing into Limery's face.

They both cackle as they splash water at one another.

I lean back, propping myself on my elbows, and my gaze drifts up the hillside to the left, where Tawdrybluff Castle looms over the surrounding valley. My castle, and yet I'll only ever spend two nights in it.

Limery laughs maniacally as he flies over to the rope and flings himself into the lake again. I smile at the fun-loving imp as he swims across the water like a spindly-legged frog. It's high time he has the chance to enjoy himself and just be a kid with his brother.

He's not the only one whose life is changing. Yesterday, I sat down with Chief Rizza and the council, explaining that I'd be leaving soon, most likely never to return. I gave the trolls my items, my gold, and the deed to the castle. Caustic will be around to watch over them, after he attends to a personal matter in Wandermere. The dwarven countryside will be perfect for a green dragon.

I think the days of the tribes living in isolation are over. At the very least, they've agreed to yearly councils. While they all have their ancestral homelands, Tawdrybluff is home to a massive forest. I hope that one day it's filled with trolls from all over.

Valery says we'll all be pulled from the game tonight. While I wish we had longer, I'm grateful to have had a couple of days to just enjoy my time here. No monsters. No fighting. No quests. Just peace and quiet. I can't think of a better ending than that.

There's been no sign of Jude, Glenn, Dorothy, or the others since the battle. I imagine they're together licking their wounds and preparing their next plot. Joke's on them, though. They lost, and Mythos is destined for brighter days.

I wonder if they'll wish they'd done things differently once we're all back in the real world.

"I'm going to miss this place." Taryn plays with Flubs, and the slime oozes from one hand to the other. "Any idea what you're going to do once we're back?"

"Honestly, it's been about the last thing on my mind." I guess I'll have to catch up with my parents at some point. When I first came here, they were on my mind a lot. I was pissed at them for their absence in my life, and I let that resentment fester until it reared its ugly head in ways I'm not proud of. Sitting here now, I can't recall the last time they crossed my mind. Whether it's because of the rehabilitative effects of the program or I've finally learned to take responsibility for my actions, a giant weight has been lifted from my shoulders. I roll over on my side to face Taryn. "I just want to enjoy tonight."

He raises an imaginary mug. "Cheers to that."

A twig snaps behind us as footsteps approach, and I look over my shoulder to see Senzala walking down the path.

The arctic troll shaman waggles her brows and flashes me a mischievous smile. "It's time."

Senzala and I walk side-by-side as we arrive at the courtyard, where a bonfire roars and embers swirl through the twilight sky like fireflies. Tawdrybluff Castle is more rustic than Seascape, its exterior composed of thick blocks of rough granite. It's an imposing fortress with a courtyard that marries spartan architecture with natural landscaping. Vines crawl along thick wooden trellises, and several towering trees grow between the rows of stone tiles, tall enough to view from the castle's highest windows.

If the trolls were to ever build a castle, I imagine it would look something like this.

The celebrations are underway, and many dwarves from the surrounding areas have come to enjoy the festivities with their new troll neighbors. Casks of ale and wine flow like a river as dwarves and trolls share laughs and drinks like old friends. After what they've endured, this generation will be bonded for life. Perhaps the next will grow up in a world where a friendship between the two is no longer an anomaly.

A smoky aroma lingers in the air from giant slabs of meat roasting on spits around the courtyard. A dwarven celebration might not be complete without ale, but a troll revelry requires something to sink your tusks into. Drums mirror the heartbeat of the tribe as one of the young trolls takes a dwarf by the hand and leads her into the drum circle. Elder trolls and dwarves laugh as the younglings dance, stomping and flailing their arms with abandon.

This is my last evening in Mythos, and I have no idea how I can say a proper good-bye to everyone here. So many of those before me have played an integral role in the troll I've become. For a moment, I just stand there and take them all in.

On the far side of the courtyard, Gord and Chief Rizza lean against a balustrade overlooking the lake below.

Limery flies straight to the ale, grabbing mugs for himself and Leo. Their mother and father are perched atop one of the trellises with several of their kin. Lillith shakes her head as Limery downs the first mug like an impish frat boy. Bazel just shrugs. Limery is going to be a handful now that he's not following me into dangerous situations. Once the heroes are gone, he might be one of the strongest beings on the Isle. I wouldn't be surprised if he's the most famous imp to ever live, when all is said and done.

Senzala squeezes my hand, bringing me back to the moment. "Go on, say your good-byes. Just promise to save me a dance before the night is over."

I grin, feeling the warmth of her hand against mine. "As long as you show me the steps."

As I'm making my way through the crowded courtyard, I come across a gnome sitting by himself beneath one of the large oaks. His rose-colored hair and dusty-pink skin stick out like a sore thumb among the trolls and dwarves. He leans against the trunk with a book in one hand and a mug of wine in the other.

"You're a long way from Pruxford," I joke.

Pressley looks up from his book and rolls his eyes. "You should leave the jokes to the dwarf." His voice is high-pitched and nasally, the complete opposite end of the spectrum from when he was a death knight.

"Hey now, no need to be hostile." I grin as I crouch down beside him. "I'm glad you're here. What's it like being level one again?"

"It's weird." He takes a sip of his wine. "I feel weak."

"You're anything but weak. Look around you." I gesture at the full courtyard. "None of us would be here if it weren't for you."

"Oh, I'm not mad about it. This is the first time I've rested since I've been here. It's been nice to take a load off." He lifts the book he's reading. "I know I shouldn't be surprised, but did you know that every book in the library has an actual story in it? I've read three already, and I'm hoping to finish this one before the night's over. It's about a blood mage who retires and opens a tavern. Kind of nice to read about something where the fate of the world isn't on the line."

"I can't argue with that." I extend my arm, and he bumps his fist against mine. "Enjoy your book."

If Pressley can find some solace in the mundane, I'm confident anyone can.

I take a moment to say good-bye to as many trolls as I can. Jira and his tiny phoenix. Tormara. Guilda, the village elder. Jojin and Watu, who seem a bit lost without Malak around to lighten the mood.

Near the bonfire, I find Brutus surrounded by a group of goblins. He holds a massive rack of ribs in his hands, and Kronan's warhammer rests by his side. Cheevus sits next to the massive troll, and his mangy wolf stares at the ribs with ravenous desire.

I guess the goblins have found a new leader to follow. Of all their options, they picked the troll most likely to punt them into the lake for staring at him the wrong way. Then again, they've never seemed too concerned with their treatment as long as it's by someone or something stronger than they are.

To my surprise, Brutus breaks off a rib and hands it to Cheevus. Then one by one, he offers a piece to the wolf and the rest of the goblins.

"What's going on here?" I ask.

"Sharing a meal with some mighty warriors." Brutus grins as he offers me his last rib. I take it, sinking my teeth into the smoky meat. "I believe I finally understand what Kronan learned that day on the mountain. Power alone does not make one strong and following another is not a sign of weakness. To be a leader, one must know when to show strength and when to rely on the wisdom of others." He looks at the goblins as they devour their bones. "But above all, the tribe is at its greatest when we have a community."

I nearly choke on the rib when he says the last part. "How much have you had to drink?"

"So far?" He laughs. "Not nearly enough."

My brain is still reeling at Brutus's evolution when I finally make my way over to Gord and Chief Rizza. They stare out at the lake as the last rays of sunlight vanish beyond the trees.

"Aren't you two a couple of wallflowers."

Gord turns around. "I was wondering when you'd make your way up here." He lifts his mug in my direction. "To finally getting rid of you."

Good to know our moment outside of Mosstar hasn't changed his sense of humor.

"Gord." Chief Rizza gives him the same reproachful look she might offer to a mischievous child.

"He knows I don't mean it." Gord takes a swig from his mug and then slaps me on the shoulder. "In truth, the tribe will not be the same without you."

"I will hear none of that." There's an edge to Rizza's voice when she speaks. Her golden eyes meet mine, and her face softens along with her tone. "Whether in Mythos or elsewhere, Chod will always be a member of the tribe. Nothing will ever change that."

I gaze up at the stars, blinking back tears. There will be a time for that dam to break but not now, because once I start, I'm not sure I'll be able to stop. For now, I want to celebrate one last night with my friends, with my brothers and sisters, with my tribe.

Even though my sentence may be ending, the story of the trolls is just beginning.

EPILOGUE

FOUR MONTHS LATER.

Taryn and I sit on a bench in Central Park, eating hotdogs from a street vendor. There's a chill in the air as squirrels scurry through the bushes, stashing away acorns beneath trees tinged with orange. Soon, fall will stake its claim to the city, followed by the cold discontent of a New York winter.

I pull my jacket a little tighter, remembering the time I walked barefoot up a snow-covered mountain wearing nothing but a loincloth.

Taryn shoves the hotdog into his mouth, devouring half of it with one bite. He moans as mustard drips into his scruffy beard. "This is good," he says with a full mouth.

He's been growing the beard for a couple of months now, but it's nothing like the one he had in Mythos. Whenever he sends me a text or we talk on the phone, I still picture the short, stocky dwarf on the other side, not this mountain of a man sitting beside me.

I give him a mock grimace. "At least no one can say you don't feed the creature latched to your face."

Taryn rolls his eyes. "Come on. It's not that bad."

"Trust me, T." I laugh. "It's worse. I mean, it looks like you walked into a barber shop, swept the floor, and decided you'd rather glue someone else's hair to your face than actually grow a beard."

Taryn's mouth hangs open, and he places a hand over his chest. "Chod, I am wounded."

He still calls me that sometimes. Every time he does, it takes me back to Mythos, and I can't help wondering what all of my friends are up to.

Are Limery and Leo going on adventures together? Are the trolls sleeping in the castle, or are they more comfortable in the forest behind it? And Caustic, what does a young dragon do with all of his free time when he's not saving the world?

Taryn shoves the rest of the hotdog in his mouth and pulls up the sleeve of his sweatshirt. "Bro, I can't believe I didn't show you yet. Check this out." He grins as he lifts his wrist, revealing a fresh tattoo of a cat skeleton covered in slime. "Pretty sick, right?"

"Nice!" I lean in for a closer look. "What is that, four now?"

"Yep, Jordy is the only one left, but I can't decide where I want to put it. This one is cool, though. The green ink glows in the dark."

"No shit?" I raise my brows incredulously. "That's pretty cool."

We were out of the game a couple of weeks when Taryn decided he wanted to honor Stompy with a carrot tattoo over his heart. Not long after that, he got a bear head on the opposite side of his chest, followed by a ruby on his left wrist. It warms my heart to know I'm not the only one who still thinks about them.

Since we've been back, Taryn has re-enrolled in community

college. With all of the money he made testing the rehab project, he'll be able to transfer to a university in the spring.

I can't say I've been quite as productive. I've felt a bit lost, to be honest, so I took some time to... I don't really know. There's been an emptiness in my life that I haven't been able to fill. Dad offered me a job working with him, but I turned it down. That's the last place I want to be.

While I figure things out, I try to keep myself busy. I read a lot. I've started running. I go to the gym, something I never thought I'd say, but without the nanites keeping me in shape, I've got to do something to keep this amazing body I've been given. It's been three months since we logged out, and the one thing I haven't thought about is gaming.

My phone vibrates, and I pull it from my jacket pocket, frowning at the unknown number flashing on the screen.

"Who is it?" Taryn raises a brow.

I shrug, showing him the phone.

He reaches for the phone, but I pull it back. "You're not gonna answer it?"

"Do you answer unknown numbers? It's probably a scam. I'm not exactly Mr. Popular, you know?" I place the phone back in my pocket and wait for it to quit vibrating.

"Eva, get back here!" a deep voice calls just as a young girl with curly black hair comes running down the path. She stops in front of us, where two squirrels are fighting over a piece of dirt-covered pizza crust beneath a tree.

"Daddy, look!" She grins, pointing at the critters. "They're hungry."

Her father smiles as he catches up, resting a hand on her shoulder. "How about we let them eat in peace? Your mother will kill me if we're late to the museum."

I watch them as they leave hand-in-hand. There's something vaguely familiar about the man, but I can't put my finger on it.

Taryn leans forward, his attention focused on the two squirrels. "My money's on the one with the fluffy tail."

My pocket vibrates again. Another unknown number.

"Come on, bro. It's either important, or they're very dedicated. Just see who it is."

What the hell? It's not like I have much else going on. I tap the screen. "Hello?"

"Chad?"

I almost drop the phone at the familiar sound of the woman's voice on the other end. "Yeah, uh, yeah, it's me."

I can hear the smile in Valery's voice when she speaks. "It's been a while. How would you like to take a vacation to Mythos?"

The End

ACKNOWLEDGMENTS

Congratulations! *You have finished* Sentenced to Troll.

+1 stat point to distribute.

+1 review to leave.

6 of 6 completed. Reward: Isn't making it to the end a reward in itself?

No? In that case, I'd like to officially welcome you as a member of the troll tribe.

There was a time when I didn't think I would finish this series. The same week I released the audiobook for *Sentenced to Troll 4*, I found out that two of my family members were going to prison for a very long time. They are still incarcerated as I write this.

Even though I wanted a break, I pushed through and wrote book five. Once it was finished, I needed to take a step away from the series. So, I took a year and a half to write two cozy fantasies. Those books offered me an escape. It was the breath of air I needed to take a step back and reflect. In doing so, I realized that this was the time to bring *Sentenced to Troll* to an end. I'd been planning the ending since book one, and I had plenty of notes for how I wanted the story to conclude. The only question was, how many books would it take to get there?

I was driving down to Hot Springs, Arkansas, when the ending for the series came to me. It felt natural and allowed me to give this series closure in a fitting way that didn't feel rushed or like a copout. I hope that it delivered.

***

This is the part where I tell you about all of the wonderful people who helped make this book possible.

Thank you to Caroline for your continued support and understanding. You've seen what happens behind the curtain, the good and the bad, especially the moodiness, the worry, and the struggle of bringing this series to a close.

Thank you to my beta readers for the constructive feedback. To Sean Flint, Paul Tuson, Janet Beane, Rick Lemann, Aaron Eichler, Gregg Trotti, and Loren Foster, this book wouldn't be the same without you.

So much credit goes to Cindy Koepp for being an integral part of this series. She was a beta reader for book one, and then became my alpha reader for the remaining five books. She's seen versions of this story that would give you nightmares and somehow decided to stick with it. Thanks for all of your help!

To Eric Jason Martin, the man who brought Chod to life in audio form. I knew from the moment I heard your audition that you were the man for the job. It has been a pleasure to work with you for so many books.

To my editor, Mia, your watchful eye and attention to detail are felt on every page.

Finally, thank you to my amazing Patreon supporters. Your support between releases is a constant reminder that there are readers waiting for the next adventure.

Silver Tier: Nicholas Kelly, Rickie Brookes, Sami Taylor

Gold Tier: Amanda Blackburn, Angie F, Elise Raposa, Jessica Worgo, Justin Lane, Laura Lee Davidson, Robert Schaefer

Diamond Tier: Joel Southard, Willa Elliot

Until next time, thanks for reading!

If you're looking for more books similar to my own, check out LitRPG Books.

ABOUT THE AUTHOR

S.L. Rowland is a wanderer. Whether that's getting lost in the woods or road-tripping coast to coast with his Shiba Inu, Lawson, he goes where the wind blows. When not writing, he enjoys hiking, reading, weightlifting, playing video games, and having his heart broken by various Atlanta sports teams.

SLRowland.com

Patreon-For signed paperbacks, advanced chapters, exclusive short stories, art, merch, and more.

Newsletter: For updates on new releases, sales, and behind the scenes content!

Email: slrowlandauthor@gmail.com

Find out more at https://linktr.ee/SLRowland

ALSO BY S.L. ROWLAND

Tales of Aedrea

Cursed Cocktails

Sword & Thistle

The Halfling's Harvest

Pangea Online

Pangea Online: Death and Axes

Pangea Online 2: Magic and Mayhem

Pangea Online 3: Vials and Tribulations

Sentenced to Troll

Sentenced to Troll

Sentenced to Troll 2

Sentenced to Troll 3

Sentenced to Troll 4

Sentenced to Troll 5

Sentenced to Troll 6

Path to Villainy: An NPC Kobold's Tale

Collected Editions

Pangea Online: The Complete Trilogy

Sentenced to Troll Compendium: Books 1-3